07/24

THE FOURTH PROPHECY

A SEAN WYATT ADVENTURE

ERNEST DEMPSEY

ENCLAVE PUBLISHING

PROLOGUE

YUCATAN, AD 1523

General Alvarado looked out over the battlefield—if one could call it that. He was more accustomed to a proper war, not the extermination of an indigenous people. Not that it mattered to him. He didn't feel the slightest hint of regret other than the fact that the natives hadn't been able to put up a fight.

They certainly did their best with what they had. Their primitive weapons and lack of modern strategies, however, made the outcome inevitable. Alvarado gazed out across the bodies of the fallen strewn over the ground under the rain forest canopy. Some of his men had already finished digging the first of the mass graves where the dead would be buried.

He'd only lost a few of his own men in the fight, poor souls unlucky enough to catch an arrow or a spear in the wrong place. Several more had been wounded.

The overwhelming sense Alvarado felt wasn't accomplishment. This wasn't a victory he'd celebrate. He doubted it would even be mentioned in the annals of Spanish history. He'd beaten a severely outmatched, outnumbered, and outgunned primitive people. There was no glory in that. There would be no honors for him upon his return to Spain. He might—might—get a medal, but even that was doubtful. This battle was more the squashing of annoying insects than a fight between equals.

He heard footsteps from behind but didn't turn. Whoever it was could wait. It was something General Alvarado had learned from his superior. General Cortes always made his subordinates wait until he asked them to speak.

It was a power play and Alvarado knew it, but he didn't mind. The men beneath him needed to know their place and understand that to speak to someone as esteemed as a general of the empire was a privilege.

Alvarado heard the man breathing behind him. He knew who it was. The general had been expecting him. It was one of his officers— Carlos. He recognized the labored breathing. Carlos, for all his abilities as a leader, had a penchant for eating large quantities of food, even when food was scarce for everyone else.

"Yes, Carlos?" Alvarado said after another moment of quiet contemplation.

"What are your orders, General?"

The general turned around and stood with his hands folded behind his back. "Are they all dead?"

"Yes, sir. We hunted down the last ones who tried to flee. They're with the rest of the heathens now."

"Excellent."

"Would you like us to bring the bodies back and throw them in the pits with the others?"

Alvarado pulled in a long sniff of air. When he shook his head, the shiny metal helmet reflected bright sunlight across his second in command's face.

"No, Carlos. Leave them for the animals to eat. They won't last long out here with all the beasts lurking about."

Carlos stood at attention, staring his commander in the eyes as if waiting for something.

Alvarado's forehead wrinkled as he frowned. "Is there something else you'd like to tell me?"

Carlos took a deep breath and sighed. "It's...well...."

"Spit it out, Colonel. If you made a mistake, I'm sure it's nothing major."

"The men, sir, they found something."

Alvarado didn't look impressed. Since arriving in the jungles of the Yucatan Peninsula, they'd seen all manner of strange things. Massive step pyramids, along with abandoned ancient cities, dotted the landscape. During the evenings in his tent, he'd spent hours wondering who put the enormous stone structures there and why. The indigenous people didn't live there. From the looks of things, no one had for hundreds of years. The jungle had taken over most of the buildings, covering them with vines, leaves, and moss.

"What did they find, Carlos?"

"We...we don't know, sir."

Alvarado's scowl deepened. "What do you mean you don't know? If you found it, then you must know what it is."

"It wasn't me who found it, sir. It was the men. They're too frightened to investigate further."

Alvarado couldn't have been more befuddled. He cocked his head to the side and looked over Carlos's shoulders at four men standing twenty feet behind him.

"Are these the men who found this...thing you're talking about?"

"Yes, sir," Carlos said with a nod.

"Come forward!" Alvarado shouted, motioning with his fingers.

Carlos took a step to the side. He kept his head low, a sign of humility and deference. *More like weakness*, thought Alvarado.

"Which one of you found this...whatever it is my colonel here can't seem to tell me about?" Alvarado asked the question to the men as they came to attention a few feet away.

One guy in the middle raised his hand. "Rafael, sir," the man said. "I found it."

"Go on, Rafael. Don't be afraid. What was it you found?"

Rafael's voice trembled as he spoke. The fear in his eyes seeped out of his sockets. "I...I don't know, sir. It looks like it might be an ancient temple, but it isn't like any of the others."

"What do you mean not like the others?"

"It was buried, sir."

"Buried?" Alvarado still didn't understand.

"Yes, sir. As if they'd cut the tunnels right out of the hillside."

Finally, they were getting somewhere. "So, there were tunnels?"

"Yes. An entrance into the structure."

"And did you go inside?" Alvarado's irritation was turning to curiosity.

Rafael shook his head vigorously. "No, sir. We...we were afraid."

The general's annoyance returned. "Afraid? Why?"

"Because," Rafael stammered, "there were strange sounds coming from the darkness inside."

"And there was a wind," one of the other men said.

Alvarado turned his attention to the man on the left end who'd spoken. "A wind?"

"A hot wind—like the devil himself was breathing out of the passage."

Alvarado sighed. His men were being ridiculous. Their paranoia was no better than the superstitions of the people they'd just slaughtered.

"Is it possible you were imagining these things?" the general asked.

Rafael defended his comrade. "No, sir. It was real. Our whole unit heard the noises and felt the heat coming from the entrance. Ask any of them."

Perhaps his men had been in the jungle too long. They weren't accustomed to a climate like this because there really wasn't anything of its kind in Spain. The sweltering heat and humidity—along with the constant nagging of insects—was enough to drive even the most hardened soldier mad.

Still, it would be uncommon for several of them to experience the same sorts of hallucinations—unless they'd been drinking too much wine.

"Where is this...temple?" he asked. "Is it far?"

"No," Rafael said, shaking his head. "It won't take long to get there."

Alvarado never dropped his stern expression. "Show me."

The hike through the jungle was a short journey, but it wasn't easy. Heavy rains that day and an almost constant, lingering humidity made sure things never really dried out. Several times, the general's boots stuck in the thick mud, and he had to wiggle them free, nearly losing his footwear in the process.

Luckily, the men had hacked their way through the forest on their previous trip, so at least the path was somewhat clear of limbs, brush, and huge leaves that had the annoying habit of smacking people in the face as they walked.

"How did you find this place?" Alvarado asked. He and the rest of the men paused for a moment to catch their breath at the top of a ridge.

They couldn't see far across the valley due to the vast forest in their way. Somewhere in the distance, they heard a waterfall churning, its faint roar giving away its location.

"One of our patrols, sir," Carlos answered. "They were sweeping the area to make sure any stragglers were eliminated."

"That's a wider swath than ordered."

"Yes, sir. Our men...they got lost in the jungle."

"Easy to do in this dense rain forest," Alvarado said with a hint of sympathy in his voice.

While Cortes had the propensity to be harsh most of the time, Alvarado let his human side show more often. He'd be stern when it was appropriate, but he also realized that men also appreciated a little leeway every now and then.

"Yes, sir. Fortunately, after finding the temple—or whatever it is— they were able to make their way back."

Alvarado nodded. The sun had come out overhead, parting the blanket of dark clouds looming in the sky. While the sunshine meant no rain for the time being, it also caused the moisture on the ground to turn to mist in a matter of minutes. The fog soon enveloped the small group, and sweat poured down their necks and into their armor.

"How much farther?" Alvarado asked, eager to get moving again.

"Not far, sir. Another ten minutes, and we'll be there."

"Good," Alvarado said. "Let's get moving. The sooner we get out of this heat, the better."

Carlos wondered what the general meant by that. Surely, the man didn't intend to enter the temple, not after the story he and the other men relayed. He wasn't about to question Alvarado's comment, though, and instead led the troop deeper into the jungle and down the slope.

When they reached the bottom of the shallow valley, the group turned right and followed a creek upstream until they came to a place where the water parted and an outcropping of rocks provided a natural bridge across to the other side.

"Just over there," Carlos said, pointing over the water to a place in the jungle covered in vines, brush, and trees.

Alvarado gave a nod, ordering the men forward.

They made their way across the rocks, careful not to slip and fall in the water since the liquid would potentially ruin their armor. Even with a liberal amount of oil applied, the heavy metal components of their gear easily turned to rust after a short exposure to moisture.

With every man safely on the other side, Carlos continued down a path—probably worn down by natives or animals—until they arrived at a pair of giant boulders. The huge rocks were set ten feet apart, facing the creek. They each stood around eight feet tall, towering over even the largest man in the group.

"Where did these come from?" Alvarado asked in a hushed tone.

"We're not sure, sir," Carlos answered. "We haven't seen stone like this in the area. We assume they were brought here by someone."

Alvarado scanned the area, paying close attention to the ground. If the boulders were dragged there, it was done so long ago. There were no signs of the earth being disturbed anywhere around the creek or the rocks.

Carlos interrupted the general's thoughts. "It's just through here, sir," he said, pointing between the boulders.

Alvarado and his men followed Carlos between the twin stones. The trees and vegetation seemed denser as they continued on. The fog even felt thicker than it had been on the path by the creek. The birds in the trees no longer sang their exotic songs. Squirrels and other animals were also eerily and inexplicably silent.

After another minute of slowly moving through the foggy jungle, Carlos stopped and put his hand back to signal everyone else to halt, too.

"What?" Alvarado whispered. "What is it?"

"We're here," Carlos said without looking back.

"Here? I don't...." Before Alvarado could finish his sentence, the fog parted before him as if a strange breeze blew it away. Less than twenty feet away appeared a massive, bulging face carved out of limestone.

A few of his men took an involuntary step backward at the sudden sight. Alvarado had seen strange things before. This wasn't much different. In fact, it reminded him of one of the pyramids they'd seen upon arriving in this new world. The ancient people who lived there before had a habit of carving dramatic images out of rock and covering their temples and palaces with them. He'd seen faces similar to the one staring at him right now, though not as large or intimidating. Then again, that was probably the point. Wrapping something so frightening around the entrance to a sacred place was a good way to keep out intruders—at least the more superstitious ones.

Alvarado had never been a man given to superstition. He'd lived long enough to know what was real and what was imaginary. His faith was the one thing he allowed in his life that stood without room for explanation. While he'd never personally experienced anything miraculous, he still believed in miracles and the supernatural. That being said, it would take more than an oversize stone face with bulging eyes and a menacing grin to keep him from investigating this bizarre place.

The rest of the structure was designed much like the other pyramids in the area, with a few minor differences. One was that it had three places where the steps flattened out on their way to the top— platforms that wrapped around the entire thing. At each plateau, there were two statues carved in limestone, staring out into the jungle as if standing guard against some airborne invader. Most of the pyramid—standing at around sixty feet—was covered in vines, moss, small plants, leaves, and debris. It was no wonder the thing had remained hidden for so long, even with the two giant boulders acting as its gate near the creek.

"Have you gone inside?" Alvarado asked, staring into the pitch-black entrance within the beast's mouth.

"No," Carlos said. "Like I reported earlier, the men were scared away when we approached the darkness. We returned without investigating any farther."

Alvarado tilted his head back and gazed into the entrance over his bottom eyelids. There was something about the dark that he couldn't explain. No light seemed to penetrate it, even to illuminate the doorsill or the floor just beyond the threshold. It was as if sunlight itself was afraid of going any farther.

The general's right foot slid forward a few inches. Then his left. They moved almost on their own, without his even thinking. With each step, his stride grew more emboldened. In less than thirty seconds, he passed Carlos and drew nearer to the entrance.

"General?" Carlos asked, reaching out a hand to stop his commander. "What are you doing? I would suggest we throw some torches in there first to make sure it's safe."

Alvarado didn't respond. He was mesmerized by the darkness. It called to him, begged him to come forward and taste what it had to offer. He swallowed unconsciously. He'd not even realized it, but Alvarado had been holding his breath for nearly a minute. Or had he been breathing without his knowledge.

It didn't matter. All that mattered was the darkness and what secrets it kept.

"Sir?" Carlos said again, concern swelling in his voice.

"It's fine," Alvarado said, putting up a hand to silence his second in command.

The general stepped closer, ever closer to the entrance.

A breeze rolled through the area, washing over the pyramid as

Alvarado neared the opening. The wind grew stronger with each step as if warning him to turn back.

His eyelids narrowed to protect his eyes from tiny bits of debris and dust flying at his face. He put one hand up to his face to block the onslaught as the wind continued to increase. His body twisted sideways to be more aerodynamic.

Alvarado was only a few long steps away when the howling began. It started as a high-pitched shriek and grew louder as he drew closer. The noise sounded like a hundred wolves shouting at the moon.

The general put his forearm over his face as he pressed forward. His staunch determination wasn't shared by his men as they all retreated toward the gate, terrified of what they were hearing.

Only Carlos remained, unwilling to leave his commander.

He watched as the general pressed ahead.

Alvarado lifted his foot. Gravity seemed to be working doubly hard now. His body felt heavier than usual, and it seemed as if his boot was filled with lead. He strained hard until his foot crossed the threshold and landed on the stone just beyond.

Suddenly, the howling ceased. The wind instantly dissipated. Leaves and dust hung in the air for a moment before they began drifting to the jungle floor.

Alvarado was overcome by an eerie silence. Then as abruptly as the chaos ended, something far worse began.

A shriek like the screeching of a thousand banshees filled his ears. He clamped his palms against them to keep out the noise, but it was futile. Then he saw it. At first, it was nothing more than a needlepoint of light in the darkness ahead. He peered into the vast abyss, curiosity taking its hold, overpowering the growing sense of fear in his mind.

The light swelled faster and faster like an oncoming flood until it flashed with the brilliance of the midday sun.

The general flew backward, struck by something more powerful than he'd ever experienced in all his days on the battlefield. He hit the ground and slid to a stop near the feet of his second in command.

Carlos instantly sank to one knee. Concern covered his face as he checked the general from head to toe for any signs of injury.

Alvarado lay on his back. A blank stare filled his eyes as he gazed up at the canopy, unblinking, unwavering. His chest was perfectly still.

"General?" Carlos said, his voice beginning to fill with panic. He turned and looked over his shoulder for the others, but they'd run back to the creek.

"General!" he shouted again.

Without thinking, Carlos raised his fists and brought them down like sledgehammers to Alvarado's chest. They struck the unconscious man with more force than Carlos realized.

Alvarado's torso surged up. Carlos wrapped his hand around the man's back to keep him from falling to the ground again. The general coughed. His eyes blinked rapidly as he turned his head one way then the other, trying to get his bearings.

"General? Are you okay?"

Alvarado's breathing slowed to a steady, normal pace. He looked into the eyes of his subordinate with absent curiosity.

"I'm...I'm fine. What happened?" Alvarado asked.

Carlos sighed.

He stood up and helped the general to his feet. They made their way back through the two boulders and found the rest of the men standing sheepishly on the riverbank.

Carlos helped the general to a seat on a nearby rock and looked the other men in the eyes. They were all waiting for orders, hoping Carlos and the general didn't punish them.

Rafael was the only one with enough courage to speak.

"What should we do now, sir?"

Alvarado was still in a state of shock and couldn't answer. So, Carlos did for him. He looked back over his shoulder through the stone gate. "Destroy it. Cover it up."

"Sir?"

"Do it," Carlos commanded. "Wipe it from the face of the earth."

Chapter 1

WASHINGTON, DC

The young woman rolled onto her side and padded over to a pile of clothes she'd left by the congressman's bedroom door. He propped himself up on his elbow and watched as she got dressed.

"Enjoying the view?" she asked in a flirty tone.

"I always enjoy the view," he said. "One of the perks of this line of work."

"I doubt your wife would call it a perk," she said as she pulled her white satin blouse over her auburn hair and creamy skin.

"Ouch," he said, retracting his head a half inch. "Why do you have to bring her up at a time like this?"

She stepped into her skirt, slipped it around her hips, and zipped the zipper on the back. "I like to push your buttons," she said. "It's one of the perks of my job." She flashed a dangerously flirtatious grin at him that sent the blood pulsing through his veins again. After letting him stare for a moment, she put on her white blouse.

He sat up and pulled on his shirt that was fortuitously close by. "You are, without a doubt, the best intern in this city."

"Do all the interns do this sort of thing with their bosses?"

He stood and pulled up his boxers. A second later he put on his slacks. "I have no idea."

"Oh come on. It's like a tradition in this town: politicians sleeping with their secretaries or interns or whoever."

He made his way over to her, wrapped his arm around her waist, and kissed her on the neck. "Are you complaining?"

She spun around and faced him, staring into his blue eyes. Her head shook from left to right. "Not at all." She pressed her lips against his. "But it's late. You probably need to get home. And I need to get some rest. My boss makes me get to work early and stay late, so I need some sleep."

He pulled his head back and faked a frown. "He sounds like a real piece of work."

She nodded in the cutest way she could. "Oh, he is. But the job has its benefits."

She smirked and stepped away, grabbed her purse, and headed for the door.

"Bright and early tomorrow morning, Miss Jones," he pointed a finger at her, feigning the threat.

"Yes, sir, Congressman Haskins."

"Unless you'd like to stay and have a cigar with me," he motioned to the cigar on the desk in the next room. It was his best effort to tempt her. He knew it wouldn't work.

"Goodnight, Congressman," she said with a smile.

He watched as she slipped out the door and closed it behind her. The intoxicating scent of her perfume still lingered in the room, filling his nostrils.

Tripp Haskins looked down at his desk. A box of cigars sat next to a picture of his wife and two children—the latter two were off living their lives in other parts of the country.

Mariam Jones—his current intern—was just the latest in a long string of women he'd slept with during his seemingly never-ending tenure in Washington. He'd been smart enough about most of them, keeping the affairs out of the public eye. The last girl, a brilliant brunette named Casey, had made a few empty threats about blackmail.

Those threats ended up costing her dearly. Police raided her home and found more drugs on the property than a Mexican cartel safe house. She went to prison for her crime, which was nothing more than threatening a man with power.

Every politician in Washington was connected to someone. The people with whom Tripp Haskins was aligned were more powerful than others. And they didn't take kindly to outsiders threatening their horse.

Mariam wouldn't be so foolish. She knew the score and was smart enough to enjoy the ride while it lasted. If she played her cards right, she'd be taken care of for years to come, possibly even find herself as a member of an advisory committee or even someday as a representative. The latter was unlikely, but it was a carrot to dangle.

Haskins flipped open the cigar box and thumbed through the collection until he found one he wanted. They were all the same brand and all equally good. Searching through the sticks was more of a ritual than anything else. He tipped the cigar up, pressed his thumbnail into the cap, and peeled it back. Some people preferred cigar cutters. Others chose to use a hole punch. Haskins liked to do it the old-fashioned way, the way many of the older cigar dons did it.

He tossed the cap into the trash bin by his desk and picked up the torch next to the cigar box. Methodically, he spun the cigar in his fingers while the blue flame touched the tip, searing it into a bright orange glow. Bluish-gray smoke circled into the air until there was a thin haze surrounding the congressman. He set the butane lighter down and gently blew on the tip before putting the cigar between his lips and taking a long, slow drag. He puffed the smoke out of his mouth in little rings that floated toward the ceiling before dissipating.

The building was a strict no-smoking zone, but Haskins didn't care. It's not like he could be fired for it. He was an elected official. Besides, when he decided to retire or someone beat him out in an election—unlikely—a cleaning crew would come in and scrub down the entire place anyway.

Haskins eased into his leather chair and leaned back. He was
living the dream. Fine women, fine cigars, and a boatload of money
coming in every month from his allies. Selling his votes, sometimes
he wondered if he made it too easy. Their pockets were deep. It's not
like they couldn't afford a little more. He wasn't greedy, though, and
had no intention of killing the golden goose.

As long as he had some semblance of power, he was fine.

He took another puff from the cigar and blew it out into the air.

His cell phone suddenly vibrated on the desk, startling him for a
moment. Haskins set the cigar in a square black ashtray and picked
up the device. He sighed after he saw who'd sent the message. He
also noticed the time.

It was nearly 11:30 at night.

"No wonder she's messaging me," he said. His voice cut through
the dead silence of the cavernous office.

"Honey, it's late. When are you coming home?" He read the text
silently to himself before responding.

Sorry, sweetie, he typed on the keypad. *We've been working on this
new energy bill all day. I'm having a cigar before I come home. Just trying
to unwind and let my brain recoup. Be home soon. Love you.*

He hit send and set the device back on his desk. A minute later, he
got the response. It said, *"OK. Be careful. Love you, too."*

His wife, Cindy, was a good woman. She'd stuck by him through
the tough times when he was just getting started as a city council-
man. Back then, they didn't have much money and definitely no
influence. Together, they'd clawed their way to the top.

Was it immoral of him to habitually cheat on her? Probably. But
she reaped the benefits of his hard work. She drove a hundred-thou-
sand-dollar car, lived in a beautiful home, got to take vacations to
exotic places whenever she wanted, and had an unlimited amount of
funds for shopping if she was so inclined.

Cindy was taken care of, at least that's how he justified it.

Could he stop and just be a loyal husband? Probably not. After
all, it was just so easy. The young, ambitious women who walked
into his office begging for jobs basically threw themselves at him.

And if they didn't, he didn't give them the time of day. He was smart enough to not give chase. That's how lawsuits and scandals happened. Haskins had no intention of losing what he'd worked so hard to gain.

He took another pull from the cigar and held the smoke in his mouth for a long three seconds, enjoying the nutty, spicy flavor before letting it seep out of his lips. With every drag, he could hear the tobacco sizzling in the quiet of the room.

A noise out in the hall startled him, and he instinctively reached for the ashtray before remembering he wasn't fifteen years old, smoking in his parents' house.

"Mariam?" he said in a loud tone. "Is that you? Forget something?"

There was no answer. He leaned to the side and stared at the door. Nothing happened. For a moment, he expected a knock or maybe for someone to push it open.

Must have been something mechanical, he thought. *That or I'm hearing things.*

He laughed to himself, then stood up, spun around, and stared out the huge window behind his desk. Haskins had one of the better views from the Capitol Building. He could see the Washington Monument across the mall, the red lights on top flashing in the night. In front of it, the lights from the Lincoln Memorial illuminated the dark sky.

He placed one hand on the windowsill and let out a long sigh. The room felt warmer than usual, and he unbuttoned the top button on his shirt to loosen the collar. Maintenance didn't usually cut off the air conditioning until around midnight, but maybe they'd decided to try to save a little extra money and do it half an hour sooner. Then again, he thought with a chuckle, he could still just be hot from the amorous activity from earlier.

A bead of sweat formed on his temple. His throat itched, only slightly at first, as he swallowed. He took a deep breath and tried to relax. Something wasn't right. He twisted his head from side to side.

His mouth was suddenly dry. He looked at the cigar and figured it had to be from the tobacco. It wasn't uncommon to need a drink with a good stick.

Haskins turned around and picked up a bottle of water he always kept on the side of his desk. He poured half of the contents down his throat and wiped his lips. Why was he so thirsty all of a sudden?

The room continued to get hotter. His stomach burned, and the scratching in his throat turned to fire. His eyes watered, and tears streamed involuntarily down his cheeks.

"What is...wrong with me?" he said out loud.

The muscles in his legs turned to Jell-O, and he had to press his hands against the surface of the desk to keep his balance.

The internal pain was overwhelming now. It felt like his esophagus and stomach were filled with lava. Something was horribly wrong, and Haskins couldn't figure out what it was.

He knew his bodyguard was down in the car, waiting as he'd been instructed. The man's name was Carl, and he'd been with Haskins ever since the congressman arrived in Washington. Carl was like most of the other bodyguards in the nation's capital. They knew the rules, especially the number one rule: Never interfere with a politician's personal interactions unless those interactions could bring harm. In this case, Carl had been ordered to wait in the car as he always did when Haskins was entertaining one of his girls.

Carl, Haskins thought. *I have to reach Carl.*

The pain in the congressman's abdomen wrenched his body, and he doubled over, nearly hitting his head on the surface of the desk. His fingers slipped, and his legs gave out. Gravity pulled him to the floor. He'd never felt anything so horrible in his life.

All Haskins knew was that he needed help. A sudden surge of bile rose in his throat, and he vomited on the floor behind his desk as he crouched on all fours, trying to regain his balance.

Blood and foam splattered on the carpet. "What the...." he spat.

Haskins dug his fingernails into the desk and dragged his torso up enough so he could see the phone just a few feet away to the right. He grimaced as another round of burning wracked his insides. He clenched every muscle in an attempt to fight the agonizing pain, but it was of little use.

He reached with every ounce of strength he had left, desperately trying to get to his phone so he could call for help. Another surge of fire shot through his stomach. The room felt like it was ablaze. His body wrenched again and he lost his grip on the desk. His left elbow hit the ashtray, knocking it to the floor. As he fell sideways, his hand struck the phone, and it landed a few inches from the smoldering cigar.

The screen displayed the last text message from his wife amid the trickle of gray cigar smoke. He read the words again as the burning sensation suddenly turned to ice.

"I love you," he gasped and surrendered to the darkness creeping in around the corners of his eyes.

He never heard the door to his office open, the footsteps crossing the floor, and the mysterious figure exit a few moments later.

Tripp Haskins was already dead.

Chapter 2

ATLANTA, GEORGIA

The crowd's roar came through the walls of the apartment three seconds before Sean and Tommy saw what happened.

They stared at the television mounted to the wall as the Braves' batter swung. The ball cracked off the bat and soared high into the air. The announcer's voice escalated as he called the play.

"It's a high drive to deep center field. Back. Back...it's gone! Home run! Braves win on a walk-off home run!"

Sean pumped his fist and then clapped his hands on his knees. "Wow! What a game!"

"I told you we should have walked over there and got tickets," Tommy said as he shook his head.

"I can't believe you didn't," Adriana said from the kitchen as she poured a smoothie into a tall glass. "That's half the reason I got this place."

Adriana Villa had Old World money from her family's wine and coffee businesses. She'd grown up in the outskirts of Madrid but rarely went home anymore. Most of her time was spent traveling or in the Southeastern United States with her boyfriend, Sean Wyatt.

"What was the other half?" Tommy asked.

She rolled her shoulders and took a sip of the smoothie, not answering until she'd swallowed the chilly clump of fruity ice. "I just like the area."

"Oh." He had expected a more interesting answer.

The Battery Atlanta was an area constructed just north of the perimeter to give the professional baseball team a new home and a community around the park. The restaurants and bars were top notch, and the living quarters were second to none with modern amenities, retail centers on the sidewalks, and easy access to the interstate.

Even though Sean and Tommy each had their own places in the city, they were both excited about using Adriana's new apartment as their postgame crash pad during the summer.

Tommy Schultz was the director and founder of the International Archaeological Agency based in Downtown Atlanta. Sean was his best friend and a former government agent turned head of antiquities security. The agency's mission was simple: find and recover lost artifacts for governments and occasionally private entities and deliver, research, and restore them to share with the world.

It sounded easy enough in theory, but the work was often fraught with difficulty and danger. The latter was why Sean and Tommy always carried weapons when on the job—just in case.

Tommy pulled his phone out of his pocket and tapped on the email icon while Sean made his way to the kitchen and grabbed a bottle of water.

Scrolling through his email, Tommy stopped on the sixth one and frowned. He stared at the subject line and then tapped the message to open it. The subject line read, *An Unusual Request.*

"Things sure have been slow lately," Sean said from the kitchen. "Good thing you don't do this gig for the money, huh?"

"Yeah," Tommy said absently. He only half heard his friend's comment as he continued reading the email.

"What do the kids do during stretches like this?" Sean asked as he pressed the water bottle to his lips and chugged half the contents in a few big swallows.

The kids to whom he referred were Tara Watson and Alex Simms. They worked for Tommy at IAA headquarters, spending most of their days on research or prepping artifacts for display at various exhibits.

"I dunno," Tommy said, still not paying much attention to Sean's line of questioning.

Sean realized his friend wasn't listening and continued to press him. "I was thinking about setting June up on a date with a buddy of mine if you don't mind."

Adriana nudged Sean's shoulder despite letting out a short chuckle. June was Tommy's girlfriend and now the butt of a joke.

"That sounds great," Tommy mumbled.

He finished the email and then looked up from his phone. "Wait. What?"

Sean and Adriana burst into laughter.

"Nothing, Schultzie," Sean said. "What were you reading that had you so dialed in?"

Tommy snapped his head from side to side, clearing his thoughts. "Oh, an email. Kind of a strange one."

"Oh yeah?" Adriana's eyebrows perked up. "From who?"

"A congresswoman. Name's Lilian Pike. You ever heard of her?"

Sean shook his head. He grabbed a piece of dark chocolate, pulled off the wrapper, and popped the candy into his mouth. "No. Should I?"

"Beats me. I don't know her, either."

"There are so many of those politicians in Washington. It's hard to keep up with who's who anymore."

Tommy unconsciously shuffled backward until he felt his calves hit the back of the couch. He eased onto the sofa again and tapped on the search app on his phone. His fingers tapped on the miniature keyboard until he'd entered the woman's name and job title.

A few seconds later, the results page filled the screen and he tapped on the first one.

"Says here that she's a congresswoman from Alabama," Tommy said.

"That's not far from here," Adriana chimed in. "Surprised you haven't heard of her."

Atlanta was situated about forty-five minutes east of the Alabama border, so the distance wasn't far—as she'd suggested. That didn't necessarily mean they knew their neighbor's business.

"We have a hard enough time keeping up with what's going on in Tennessee and Georgia," Sean commented.

The two friends had grown up in Chattanooga, Tennessee, just eighty minutes north on I-75. Sean still had a second residence there despite being gone most of the time. His south side condo was a getaway from the crazy pace of the big city.

"Looks like she's been in the headlines quite a bit lately," Tommy said, interrupting the other two. "Seems to be a staunch proponent of environmental protection and reform."

"Oh yeah?"

"Mmmhmm. She spearheaded a bunch of new environmental bills. A few of them even passed. She's big on green energy and renewable resources."

"I bet the big oil companies just love her."

"No kidding." Tommy's eyes narrowed as he read farther down the page. He frowned at what he saw. "Oh. That's awful." He put his hand over a wide mouth.

"What is?" Adriana asked with a sudden look of concern on her face.

"This says her son was killed by a pipeline explosion near their property several years ago. Apparently, there was some kind of leak they didn't know about. The boy was out playing in the field and must have set off a spark that ignited the gas."

"Ugh," Sean said. "That's terrible. How old was he?"

Tommy sighed. "Only nine."

Adriana shook her head. "How sad."

"Makes sense that she's taking on those fossil fuel companies, then," Sean added.

"This article says six months later, her husband killed himself. Apparently, his grief was so bad he couldn't take it anymore."

"That poor woman sure has been through it."

"You got that right. I can't imagine losing a child and a spouse, much less within six months of each other."

The apartment fell silent for a minute as the three contemplated the tragedy Lilian Pike had endured. It was fairly miraculous she came out of it with her sanity. Making things better for the rest of the world, it seemed, was a motivator that must have pushed her through.

"What was it she emailed you about?" Sean asked after enough time passed. "You said she reached out to you?"

"Oh right. Yeah, she emailed me about something she'd like me to take a look at. Said it's an old book that I might be interested in."

"Book? What kind of book?"

"Email didn't say. All it said was that she acquired an old diary, and she thinks it might have something to do with a lost city on the Yucatan Peninsula."

Sean's right eyebrow shot up. "Not another lost city of gold thing. We get at least one of those every week."

"Not lately," Tommy said.

"True."

"Wait," Adriana cut in. "She said it might be connected to a lost city? A Mayan lost temple?"

Tommy nodded. "That was who occupied the area for the longest period of time. The oldest Mayan ruins go back as far as 1800 BC. If there's a hidden temple to be found on the Yucatan, it's a good bet it belonged to the Mayans."

"This better not be another one of those city of gold quests. We've already done our time on those," Sean said.

Tommy skimmed over the email again. "Nothing about a city of gold. Just says a lost temple. That, and she'll tell us more when we get to Washington."

"Washington?"

"Yeah. She said it's not safe to transmit all the information online, and she wants to tell us more about it in person."

"That sounds a little sketchy," Sean said. "Although the internet isn't exactly the most secure place."

"Maybe she's worried someone will steal the information and find this temple before she or anyone else has the chance." Adriana's comment made sense. Still, there was something fishy about the email that the two guys couldn't pinpoint.

"What do you think, Schultzie? Wanna fly to Washington?"

Tommy took a deep breath through his nose and exhaled slowly. "I guess," he said, putting his hands out wide. "Things have been kind of slow lately. Would be nice to do a little investigative work, even if it turns out to be nothing."

"Agreed," Sean said. "I like visiting DC." He twisted around and looked at Adriana. "What about you? Want to tag along?"

"It sounds like fun, boys, but June and I are having a girls' weekend, remember?"

"Oh, right," Sean said. "The spa thing."

"Yes. Putting up with you two can be stressful, so we're going to get massages and treatments and sit by a pool for forty-eight hours while you two run around the globe playing cowboy archaeologists."

Tommy cocked his head to the side. "Come on, we're not cowboys."

"Most of the time we're not even archaeologists," Sean added with a wink.

Chapter 3

WASHINGTON

Detective Smalley shook his head. He'd been reading through the forensic report for the better part of the last hour.

His partner, a skinny thirty-something with the last name Robards, sauntered up, munching on a candy bar as he approached.

"What's the matter Smalls?" he asked, using the pet name he'd come up with years before, much to Smalley's chagrin.

"It's this Haskins case," he said. "The thing's driving me crazy."

Robards frowned. "Crazy? Did you get the forensics report?"

Smalley held the file up so his partner could see it.

"Oh. That bad, huh?"

"Doesn't make any sense. There's not a trace of forced entry. The cameras didn't pick up any unusual activity."

"Toxicology said he was poisoned, though, right?"

Smalley nodded. "Yeah." He ran his fingers over his high forehead and through his thinning hair. "The report said his cigars were laced with it."

"Hmm," Robards grunted. "They say tobacco will kill you...."

Smalley fired him a chastising glare.

"What? Too soon?" Robards put up his hands.

"Anyway, we know *what* killed him. We just don't know *how* it got into the cigars."

Robards pulled up a nearby chair and plopped down in front of his partner's desk. Phones rang nonstop on every other desk. Officers huddled with each other, some talking about work, others about personal things, everyone's shoulders hunched from tension. To the unaware observer, it would have looked extremely busy. While everyone was trying to simply go about their usual routines and do their jobs, the truth was the mood of the station reflected a growing anxiety among the brass about the Haskins case. This spreading fear that DC's finest were outmatched by the congressman's assassin, of course, filtered down to the sergeants, detectives, beat cops and desk jockeys. Everyone was on edge—and it was beginning to show.

"Well," Robards said, "you're not going to like this, either."

"I can't tell you how much I love hearing that sentence. If I had a nickel for every time my ex-wife said those exact words..." Smalley's voice trailed off.

"Tragic. Anyway, we interviewed all the custodians, maintenance people, security, everyone and anyone who works there at the Capitol."

"Even the politicians?"

"Even them," Robards said with a nod. "No one saw anything."

Smalley sniffled and ran his index finger across the bridge of his nose. "How in the world could no one have seen anything? Seriously? A man was murdered. Right there in his own office. And there wasn't a single witness who saw anything out of the ordinary?"

"Seems that way."

"Unbelievable." Smalley threw a hand in the air. He was frustrated, hungry, and worn out. He needed sleep. Well, that and a tall drink. "How is that possible?"

"I don't know, Smalls. There are cameras all over that building, inside and out."

"I know."

"Seems like if someone went in there and tainted the congressman's cigars, someone else would have seen something."

"I know!"

"What about the girl?" Robards asked, hoping to shine a sliver of light to the case.

"What girl?"

"Haskins's intern. Security said she left pretty late last night, was the last one there."

"She's being detained as we speak," Smalley said. "Honestly, though, I don't think she's a suspect."

"How so?"

"Call it a hunch. I don't know. Security cameras saw her leave. Then there was nothing. Not even a blip on the footage."

"Makes you wonder what she was doing there so late, huh?" Robards guffawed as his own humor.

"We both know what she was doing there. That's the only thing they found."

"What? Samples?"

"In his slacks and underwear. They'd definitely just had sex."

"Okay, so she slipped the poison into his cigar box when he was getting dressed."

"No. If she was going to do it, she would have done it sometime during the day. Based on the video footage I've seen, the only times she went in there this week were when Haskins was in the office, too. He'd have seen it if she tried to poison his cigars."

"Unless he was distracted."

Smalley flashed the most derisive glare he could muster. "Seriously? Have you seen that girl? She's like an eleven on a scale of one to ten."

"She is pretty," Robards said in a lonely tone. "Okay, so let's say you're right. We rule out the intern. Who would have had a motive to kill the guy?"

Smalley's shoulders raised up for a second and then dropped. "He's a politician. The guy's probably got enemies all over the planet."

Their conversation died down for a minute as the two men considered the quandary. Every case was different, but every single one Smalley had ever worked came with a crack someone missed before. He just had to find it.

"Where does he get his cigars?" Robards asked abruptly.

"A local shop called Cigar Smiths. We already checked there. The guy was clean. No motive. In fact, he said Haskins bought a few thousand dollars' worth of cigars from him every month. No way he'd give up a loyal cash cow like that."

Robards sighed. "It was worth a try, I guess."

Then he sat up a little straighter, doing his best to look professional.

"What?" Smalley said.

Robards gave a single nod in the direction of the door behind Smalley. "Feds."

Smalley rolled his eyes. He leaned back in his chair and waited for the newcomers to arrive. He didn't have to wait long.

"Detective Smalley?" a woman's voice said.

Smalley put his hands behind his head and spun his chair around. The woman in front of him was a tall, slender brunette—probably in her midforties, though it was hard to tell.

"I've already met with the people from the FBI. We're working on this case together, Miss...."

"Starks. Emily Starks." She folded her arms across her chest. "And I'm aware of your cooperation with the FBI. I'm not with them."

Smalley's eyebrows perked up. "Oh no? Who you with then, CIA? NSA? Some other screwjob fed group? Look, lady. We've done everything the feds have asked us to do. They're just as much at a loss over this investigation as we are."

"Which is why I was called in to assist you," she said in an even tone.

"Who are you with?" Robards asked.

"Not the agencies you mentioned."

Now Smalley's curiosity was piqued. "Who, then?"

"Let's just say that my agency answers only to the president. Plus, we're not based in Washington. I got the distinct impression he wanted a new pair of eyes on the case."

"The president?"

"Yes. The president. You know, most powerful man in the world and all that."

"Wait a minute," Robards said, pointing a finger at her. "I've seen you with President Dawkins on television. You're his girlfriend or something like that."

Emily cocked her head to the side. "In this case, I'm not his girlfriend. I'm the director of the Axis agency. And I've been ordered to look into the murder of Congressman Haskins."

"Look into?"

She sighed. "I mean, I don't like to say that I'm taking over your investigation. That's just rude. I prefer to think of myself as a sort of consultant here to help you guys move a little faster."

"Fine," Smalley said. "If you came here expecting a fight from me, you're going to be disappointed. We've spent the last two days trying to figure this thing out, without any luck. So, knock yourself out, Director. If you can do better, hats off to you." He plopped the file down on the edge of his desk near her hip.

"Thank you, Detective." The back of her left hand nudged the file farther onto the desk surface. "I've already looked at the file. And before you tell me about everyone you've talked to or all the work you've done, I know about all that, too."

Robards's eyebrows raised, and he looked at his partner with a surprised glance.

"I've seen everything you've done for the last forty-eight hours to solve this case. You spoke to the man's intern, the wife, coworkers, and everyone under the moon. The one thing you haven't done is compiled a list of potential enemies."

Smalley put his arms in the air as if he was helpless. "That could be a million people, Director. You know how these politicians are. Or maybe you don't since your agency is based in Atlanta. That's right. I know a little about Axis. I know you guys moved your HQ down south several years ago."

The stern look on Emily's face grew more menacing. Her eyes flared, but she kept her gaze locked on Smalley.

"Do not mistake our location for ignorance, Detective. We know how things work here in Washington. I spent most of my career here. Get me a list of the top one hundred people who have a grudge or might have a grudge against Congressman Haskins. And if those one hundred people check out, get me the next hundred. You've turned over every stone you could think of. Now it's time to turn over the stones I tell you."

She reached into her pocket and fished out a business card. Emily didn't say anything else. She simply dropped the card on Smalley's desk and walked away.

"Where do you want me to send the list?" he shouted over the noisy room before she reached the end of the aisle.

"Look at the business card," she said without turning around. A second later, she was gone.

Smalley looked down at the card with her name, number, and email on it. There was nothing else.

"Why's the president getting involved with this?" Robards asked. "He wasn't friends with Haskins."

"No," Smalley said. "He wasn't. He hated Haskins."

"Hated? That's a strong word. I didn't think the president hated anyone."

"Let's just say they weren't on speaking terms, then."

"Okay, but that still doesn't answer my question. Why's he getting involved?"

The answer wasn't immediately evident. Who knew with these politicians? It could have been a move by the president to make it look like he cared about Haskins. That wasn't the president's style, though, to be fake like that. It was one of the things Smalley admired about the guy. So, if the president wasn't trying to expedite the investigation for political reasons, why would he stick his nose in when there were plenty of good people on the case? Maybe he was actually looking out for the best interests of the nation and the friends and the Haskins family.

Smalley wasn't sure. In the end, it wasn't his job to worry about those kinds of things. If he was honest, he was glad to have a little extra help from Starks. The additional work she'd requested wouldn't be fun or easy. In that regard, Smalley wished he could completely pass it off to the Axis director. At least now, however, he wouldn't be held responsible. One more thing off his plate. There was a sort of peace that came with being an underling. He'd not felt that peace in a long time.

After being in the game for two decades, he'd burned out on this sort of stuff. He only had six more years until he could retire with a full pension, and Detective Smalley had no intention of taking the blame for a stalled murder case.

That could fall on Director Starks.

Chapter 4

WASHINGTON

Tommy and Sean waited patiently in the deep leather couches that faced Lilian Pike's desk. The room felt like every other politician's office they'd been in before. The smell of polished wooden furniture filled the air and mingled with the scent of corporate America that seemed to occupy every boardroom across the nation. It was a smell that seemed a mix between a bank and a library.

The only emotions the room evoked came from the pictures of Pike and her family. The son she lost and the husband who'd killed himself took up space in most of the picture frames. There were few exceptions: images of Pike with other politicians at fundraisers, galas, and other high society events. In most of the pictures, she tried to appear happy, though there was a distant sadness in her green eyes.

"I wish this didn't take so long." Tommy broke the silence.

They'd been sitting in the room for nearly twenty minutes, waiting on the congresswoman to arrive. She'd been delayed by a sudden meeting and was running late due to no fault of her own.

"That's the way it is in this town," Sean said. "Sometimes things come up, and the people she works with aren't the types who take no for an answer."

"Oh, I know those types all too well."

Their eyes wandered around the room again for the umpteenth time. More pictures hung from the walls. Some featured Pike in exotic places like the Amazon rain forest, Costa Rica, Africa, and Alaska. A shelf to the right of the window held several awards she'd received through the years for her work on environmental issues.

The door to the left suddenly opened, and Pike appeared, walking briskly across a thick, burgundy rug to meet the men. Her shoulder-length reddish-brown hair waved gently in the air as she moved.

"Gentlemen, I do apologize for the delay. It's been a hectic morning."

Before the two visitors could stand, she extended a hand to Sean.

He was impressed with her firm grip, but not surprised. Women had to be strong in Washington. It was a playground where boys had pushed girls around for far too long, and to get respect, girls had to push back even harder.

She shook Tommy's hand and gave a curt nod.

"Unfortunately, we're dealing with a difficult issue right now. Please, sit down," she said.

The two did as instructed, sitting at the same time like grade-school children.

"Difficult issue?" Sean asked.

Pike looked somewhat surprised and cocked her head to the side. "Yes, the murder?"

The two guests scrunched their faces and shook their heads.

"Congressman Haskins?"

Their heads turned side to side once more.

"Oh, I see you two don't bother to keep up with the news."

"Beg your pardon, ma'am, but we hopped on a plane and came right up here. Haven't had much time to check on current events," Tommy said.

"Ah yes. Of course. Well, Congressman Haskins was murdered last night, right here in this very building. Police said it was poisoning."

"Any leads?" Sean asked, suddenly more interested in the murder investigation than the original reason they were there.

"Not that I know of," she said. "The authorities have been working around the clock but so far have nothing."

Tommy's head shrank back as he scoffed at the idea. "With all the cameras and security they have here? They couldn't find a thing? I'd think the killer would have had a tough time staying hidden, much less getting in and out of here."

"Well, it seems they found a way. Haskins is dead. His intern was here late last night, but they've already dismissed her as a suspect."

"Why's that?" Sean asked.

"Right now they don't have a motive or proof. Whoever poisoned the late congressman did so by lacing his cigars with the chemical."

"Was anything missing from his office?"

Pike scowled at the line of questioning but went ahead and answered. "Not that I know of. And before you ask, yes, the congressman had many enemies. He wasn't exactly a straight-and-narrow kind of guy. If you ask me, he was probably sleeping with his intern, as he'd done with her predecessors. But the toxin the killer used is extremely rare. It would have been difficult for someone like her to acquire. There were no traces of the substance in her vehicle or in her home. Now, if that answers all your questions about the death of one of my colleagues, I'd appreciate it if we could move on to the reason you two are here."

Sean and Tommy gave a shrug and then nodded.

"Sure, go right ahead," Sean said.

Pike stepped around behind her desk and eased onto the leather seat. She assumed a power position, like a CEO of a major corporation, folding her hands on the desk with elbows propped on the edge.

"First, I need to thank you for coming on such short notice."

"Happy to, Congresswoman Pike," Tommy said. "When I received your email, I was a bit surprised."

"Do you not normally get requests like that?"

"No, we do."

"Then why the surprise?"

She was friendly but direct. Sean liked her immediately.

"I guess...I..." Tommy stumbled to find the right words.

Her bright green eyes pierced through him and unnerved him to a level he'd not experienced in quite some time.

"We usually get requests from governments, museums, historians, or archaeologists," Sean answered after seeing his friend stumped for some reason.

"Ah I see. You don't normally get them from an individual."

"Right," Tommy said.

"Well, gentlemen, I apologize if I didn't go through the proper channels, but based on what I've heard, you two are the best."

"The best at what?"

She grinned. "I appreciate your modesty, Mr. Schultz. Let's just say your organization has a stellar reputation for recovering things that have been missing for a long time."

Tommy had worked hard to make sure IAA kept that good reputation. He knew that the agency was respected around the world, and he had every intention of keeping it that way.

"In spite of that good standing, I did a little checking first to make sure you two were the men for the job."

"Checking?"

Sean sat quietly for the moment, listening to the conversation between the other two.

"Yes. I asked around. Turns out you two have a penchant for solving riddles. It seems your expertise in foreign languages, cultures, history, and even code breaking have resulted in some incredible discoveries."

"I wouldn't say we're experts in code breaking," Tommy said. "The guys at the NSA are much better at that sort of thing than us."

Sean perked up in his seat. "I'm sorry, Congresswoman, is that what this is, some code you'd like us to figure out? Because if that's the case, Tommy's right. I'm sure the people over at the NSA could knock it out much faster than we could."

Pike leaned back in her seat and folded her hands across her lap. Her expression never changed, remaining serious.

"I am aware of the many talents that organization has to offer, gentlemen. With this matter, however, I feel discretion is in order."

Both of the men leaned forward, eager to hear what had this woman of power so spooked.

"By now, I'm sure, you're dying to know what it is, and I'm afraid I've been keeping you far too long. You must understand, though, that there are people out there who might try to take what I'm about to show you and use it for personal, selfish gain."

A million guesses ran through Sean's and Tommy's brains, but they kept their thoughts to themselves, choosing to let her finish.

Pike only forced her guests to wait another few seconds before she stood up and sauntered over to a wall to her right where a bookshelf stood next to the shelf displaying several awards. There were dozens of volumes occupying the shelves. Some were books on politics, history, and cultures. There were a few that had old, dusty looking spines. Others appeared to be brand new.

She put her hand out and pried a small book from the collection. It had a tattered leather spine and looked more like an old journal than anything in the rest of her modest library.

The cover, too, was cracked and weathered. Whatever it was, the two visitors assumed it to be quite old.

"This," she said, holding out the book for Tommy to take, "is a diary or journal, if you will."

"Looks old," Tommy said as he took it from her. "Who did it belong to?"

"It *is* old," she said with a nod. "Nearly five hundred years old, to be precise."

Tommy's body tensed, and he nearly dropped the book. "Did you say five hundred?"

"Yes. Don't worry. I've taken much better care of that than whoever had it before me. I made sure the leather was restored as best as possible. The pages, I fear, are on their last legs, which is why I had the entire contents stored digitally."

"Digitally?"

"We took hundreds of pictures and saved them to multiple hard drives."

"Oh right," Tommy said, feeling stupid.

Sean leaned over the armrest and gazed at the worn cover.

There was a cross burned into it.

"Spanish cross," Sean said.

"Yep," Tommy confirmed his friend's assessment. "This belonged to a Spaniard five hundred years ago?" His mind already started connecting the dots. "This wasn't the journal of Cortes, was it? Because we already have one of those."

Pike let a grin slip across the right side of her lips. "Very good, Mr. Schultz. I am impressed. It seems your reputation was spot on."

Tommy smiled with pride.

"Not Cortes, though," she corrected. "It belonged to one of his generals, a man named Alvarado."

It wasn't a name that rang a bell, but that didn't mean much. Throughout history, the greatest leaders stood on the shoulders of people who were often greater. The books and scholars never spent much time on those who lifted up others, and so their names were frequently lost to antiquity.

"Okay," Tommy said. "What's this got to do with us?"

"Open it," she instructed, hovering over him with her hands behind her back.

Tommy looked up at her with uncertainty in his eyes. He really didn't want to without the proper tools, gear, and a contained environment.

"Do you have some gloves?" he asked. "I'd really rather not mess this thing up."

Pike sighed. "Mr. Schultz—"

"Tommy. Call me Tommy."

"Very well, Tommy, do you know where I acquired that book?"

He shook his head.

"It came from a book dealer in Barcelona. I was there for a conference a few months ago and wandered into a little side street where I discovered the book shop. I went in hoping to find something interesting, an old first edition of something famous, perhaps. While the store did have some things of that nature, I was drawn to a bin in the back where there were lots of old books like this one, some newer, some probably from the same era. I asked the store owner how much he wanted for them and he said they weren't for sale because no one would buy them. He explained that they were mostly just old diaries."

"So...how did you get it?"

"I made him an offer...a very generous offer. After that, he was more than happy to part with the books."

"So you brought a bunch of old books back to the States?" Sean asked.

"No. I leafed through them while I was there and picked out a few I thought were interesting. That one," she pointed at the journal in Tommy's hands, "was particularly fascinating."

Tommy reluctantly opened the cover and stared at the faded writing on the first page. It was difficult to make out the signature, but he could see enough to make out the name Alvarado.

"I assure you, Tommy," Pike said, "if I'd found that book in better condition, I would have taken every precaution to ensure it remained in good shape."

Tommy nodded. He'd heard enough to believe the woman despite the fact that he still cringed every time his fingers touched the paper.

He looked over the first page and then cautiously turned to the next. "It's just the ramblings of a soldier," he said after poring over the second page.

"I'm glad you're able to read Spanish," Pike said. "I was beginning to worry you only knew ancient languages."

Tommy and Sean looked up at the woman. She flashed them a playful grin. "I'm kidding, Tommy. Please, keep reading. The initial few pages are just what you said, the ramblings of a soldier during his time in the New World."

Tommy continued looking over the lines, turning pages until he came to a point in the middle of the journal where he stopped. His eyebrows furrowed, and he hovered his finger over a paragraph to make sure he wasn't reading it incorrectly.

"This is what you mentioned in your email," he said. His voice cut through the silence.

"That's correct." She turned and wandered over to the big window behind the desk. She stopped and looked out at the mall. People were running around with their children and pets. Some were taking pictures of the historic buildings. Others were sitting in the shade, seeking relief from the warm sun.

"Alvarado speaks of a lost temple," she went on. "According to the account, it gave him and his men quite a scare."

Tommy's eyes moved faster now as he read through the document, turning the pages more carelessly than he did before.

"It says there were howling sounds, wind, and a great flash of light." Tommy looked up from the pages and stared at their host with questioning eyes.

"I know," she said. "Quite the imagination the author must have had."

"That or he saw something out of the ordinary," Sean said.

Pike raised an eyebrow. "The things he described in that passage sound almost...supernatural." She was loath to use the word; at least she sounded that way.

"No offense, Congresswoman—"

"Please, call me Lilian."

"Lilian," Sean corrected. "Tommy and I have seen our fair share of stuff we couldn't explain. There's probably a reasonable explanation behind what this Alvarado guy wrote in his diary, but that doesn't mean you can blow it off. There's still so much out there that humanity doesn't understand or can't explain."

The congresswoman's eyes narrowed. Her lips creased. "Good. That's what I was hoping you'd say." She turned her attention to Tommy once more. "Alvarado goes on to speak of a great power, something that was hidden in this ancient place."

Tommy listened as he continued turning the pages. He stopped near the end of the book and gazed at the pages.

He pointed at a spot in the text and looked up. "What is this?"

Sean craned his neck to see what had stumped his friend.

The two pages were filled with a sequence of nonsensical letters and numbers.

"Because it looks an awful lot like a cipher," Tommy said.

"That is exactly what I believe it to be," Lilian said.

She turned and walked over to the left-hand wall where a coffee pot steamed atop a long counter. She picked up the pot and poured the hot liquid into a nearby ceramic mug.

"Coffee?" she asked.

"No thanks. We already had some."

She shrugged and set about pouring a few tablespoons of creamer into the cup.

"Alvarado," she said, "went crazy for a while."

Sean and Tommy shot each other a sidelong glance, wondering where the change of subject was going.

"He was so traumatized by whatever he saw there that his men had to carry him back to their camp. He was taken back to Spain where he later recovered from what they could only describe as a kind of shock."

"Then he wrote all this down?" Sean asked.

"We believe so, yes. You'll notice a distinct difference in the handwriting from the beginning of the journal and the end."

"Did someone else write in it?"

"That was something I considered, but after careful analysis, it was done by the same hand. The changes were subtle, not surprising after the strange occurrence Alvarado described."

Something was still bothering Tommy about all this. "I guess my big question is, why did he document all this? I mean, it sounds like the kind of thing he'd want to keep secret. Did they find anything in that temple? Gold? Jewels? Anything else?"

Lilian shook her head. "They were unable to enter the temple. Alvarado goes on to say that his second in command, a man named Carlos, ordered the temple destroyed and buried so that no one would ever be able to find it again."

"Seems kind of extreme," Sean said. "Sounds like that Carlos guy was pretty terrified of whatever they found."

"Indeed. Alvarado thought the same thing. He spent the rest of his life trying to relocate the temple but could never get back to its location. By the time he returned to the Yucatan, several years had passed. The jungle takes over quickly down there. Constant rain and warmth cause the vegetation to overrun everything."

"So, he never found it," Tommy said, more to himself than the others.

"No. Even on his deathbed, Alvarado kept speaking about the temple and the strange power that dwelt there."

"And you want us to find it," Sean said with a dubious glare.

"Mr. Wyatt, I realize that what I'm saying may sound crazy or even dangerous."

"Neither of those really bothers us."

"Then what's the issue?" She folded her arms across her chest.

"The issue is that this guy Alvarado couldn't find it. We hear stories about these lost cities and lost temples all the time from that region all the way down into Peru, Brazil, even Argentina. Even with the latest satellite technology, it's nearly impossible to find anything in those rain forests and mountains."

"Well," Tommy cut in, "there was that kid who thought he found a lost pyramid."

"Sure, there are exceptions," Sean went on, "but that isn't the norm. How are we supposed to find this place without any sort of points of reference?"

"That, gentlemen, is why that book is so important. Just before he died, Alvarado realized he didn't have much time left. So, he put down as much information as he could remember into that journal. His intention was that someday someone would come along and be able to figure out the temple's location."

"He sure didn't make it easy," Tommy said.

"No. He didn't. That diary is a map, but not just anyone can decipher it. It takes someone with a knowledge of those kinds of things."

Tommy twisted his head to the side and stared at the encoded message. "We'll need a key," he said. "Can't do anything with these kinds of ciphers without the key."

"I'm sure you're more than capable of figuring out how to do just that. This temple Alvarado speaks of could be the key to unlocking unlimited free energy for the entire world. I'd say that's a worthwhile cause. Wouldn't you?"

Sean snorted. "We've stumbled on a few things like that before."

"I'm well aware of your exploits and discoveries."

"Then you're also aware that politicians like yourself and others blocked usage of those technologies until further investigation and research could be done." Sean used air quotes for the last part of his comment.

Lilian did her best to look offended. Maybe she really was. "I am nothing like those animals," she protested. "I have championed renewable energy sources for years."

"Fine," Sean said, putting his hand up to apologize. "I'm sorry. Please, go on."

She drew a deep breath and collected her thoughts. "This temple clearly had some kind of incredible energy. I want you two to find it. It goes without saying that you will be well rewarded."

"It should go without saying that we don't do it for the money," Tommy said.

"Yes, Tommy. I know you don't do these kinds of things for profit. That doesn't mean you shouldn't have your expenses covered."

She could see the two still weren't convinced. "Look. Worst-case scenario is you find some ancient ruins with a bunch of artifacts inside."

"No, the worst-case scenario is we end up finding nothing and wasting a bunch of time in the process."

She conceded to the last statement. "I understand. I suppose I could find another agency to look into this for me, but you two were my first choice."

"Now hold on a second," Tommy said. "I didn't say we weren't going to take the job. I just want you to have appropriate expectations. This sort of thing usually doesn't yield the desired outcome. If it looks like a dead end, you need to be ready to accept that."

A wry smile creased Lilian's lips. "I'm well aware of the risk involved. If, and I realize it's a big if, this temple holds what I suspect it might, it will be worth it."

Chapter 5

WASHINGTON

Lightning flashed, and clouds churned in the boiling pot of the night sky over western Virginia. Congresswoman Margaret Monroe looked out from the railing of her balcony while she sipped a warm brandy.

From the looks of the forecast, the storm was supposed to skirt the edge of the city and continue north, narrowly missing the capital on its way toward the Northeast.

She didn't mind the storms. She enjoyed them, in fact, especially from her balcony. It was one of the simpler pleasures her role as a member of Congress provided. The AMG in her garage was another one, although it hardly qualified as simple.

Monroe had been in Congress for just over a decade. She'd won her first term running unopposed. After that, she'd dismantled a slew of mediocre candidates who offered nothing in the way of a positive change for her constituents. The one who had presented a challenge ended up fighting a sex scandal that essentially took him out of the running before the election even happened.

It paid to have powerful friends.

That was a lesson Monroe learned early on in her career. She'd come to Washington with a list of things she wanted to change and a heart full of admirable ideals. It didn't take her long to see that those things weren't what made things go in the nation's capital. Those were the kinds of traits that got someone pushed out before their second term.

Initially, she'd figured playing the game was the best way to make a difference with the things she cared about. For the most part, that had been proven true. Her initiatives had saved tens of thousands of lives in Africa and Haiti, providing medical care, food, and education to those who needed it.

But the cost had been high.

To serve what she believed was the greater good, she'd made a deal with the devil. Every day was a battle with her conscience, though the little voice in her head that tried to steer her down a more righteous path had grown quieter over the years. She'd grown accustomed to the good life as well as the way things had to be done.

In the beginning, she gave herself pep talks every night, reminding herself that this was what had to happen in order to best serve her voters and the rest of the world. Those talks stopped years ago.

Her husband wouldn't be proud of what she'd become, but he was dead, killed six years before in an automobile accident.

She'd always wondered if it really was an accident. The tragedy occurred at a time when she was being asked to vote a certain way on a new energy bill. Monroe had waffled on the bill, thinking it was too much to ask. The people with whom she'd aligned herself, however, weren't the kind to ignore. After her husband's death, she voted as requested, albeit with great hesitation.

Getting reelected that year had been the easiest of all. The sympathy vote along with the massive contributions she received from her allies made certain no one could challenge her seat.

Monroe took another sip of the brandy and leaned over the railing. Now she was fifty years old and one of the more powerful members in the House of Representatives.

Her cat, a Russian blue, stepped out onto the balcony and rubbed its side against her legs. She'd ditched her usual business suit in lieu of a white terry cloth robe, so the cat's fur was soft against her skin.

"You want something to eat?" she cooed like it was a toddler.

The cat offered a short meow in response.

She took a deep breath through her nostrils and sighed. "Oh all right." After another sip of brandy, she set the snifter on a patio table by the railing and stepped inside.

Monroe padded downstairs and into the kitchen, removed a can of cat food from the walk-in pantry, and scooped the wet pâté into a little white bowl that read Albert on the side. The cat eagerly dove into the food, licking the meat at first and then biting off chunks as it purred.

"You like that, huh?"

Monroe tossed the can in the garbage bin and started to head back up the stairs when she caught sight of something outside. Her eyebrows lowered as suspicion rose in her mind. She leaned to the right and looked out the window.

A bird suddenly zipped by, and she jumped back, startled. She let out a sigh and shook her head.

She knew her security guard, a young man named Blake, was sitting in his SUV outside. If anyone tried to get in, he'd see them first. Just to be safe, though, Monroe walked over to the window and pulled back the curtains. Sure enough, Blake was sitting at the steering wheel, peering into the darkness.

Monroe didn't know how those guys did it, especially the night shift guards like Blake. She'd have passed out multiple times on a shift like that.

She let go of the curtain and started back up the steps.

The death of Tripp Haskins had unnerved most of Capitol Hill. Maggie Monroe had taken it especially hard.

It wasn't because she was particularly fond of the congressman, though she'd enjoyed a night of passion with him once after too much champagne at a fundraiser. His tastes were typically much younger. She'd dismissed the occurrence as a mistake and moved on, only occasionally finding conquests of her own when she felt the need.

No, the death of Congressman Haskins didn't bother her because of their relationship or even their one romantic encounter.

Monroe and Haskins were on the same team. They'd been hand-picked by a group of powerful, wealthy people to lead things in a certain direction when it came to voting on bills related to energy and the environment.

She remembered her first meeting like it was yesterday. She was young—relatively—an energetic and ambitious member of the House, hoping to make the world a better place.

She'd returned to her office and found the man waiting for her. He didn't give his name, phone number, or even an email. He'd simply placed an envelope on her desk and told her there'd be more deliveries like that made every month for the rest of her life if she decided to play ball.

At first, Monroe balked at the offer. Then he showed her a picture.

Rounding the top of the stairs, Monroe felt a chill go over her skin at the thought. She shivered away the goosebumps and walked softly back to the balcony where her drink waited on the table where she'd left it.

Her thoughts remained on that first meeting with the mystery man and the picture he'd shown her: her daughter, sitting under a tree at her university, reading a book.

The guy hadn't made any threats. He hadn't warned her what would happen if she didn't do what she was asked. He didn't need to. The danger was implied.

"What am I supposed to do?" she'd asked.

"You'll be told when the time comes" was the only response he offered.

After that, she didn't see him again for almost six months. The envelopes kept coming, though, stuffed with stacks of cash the likes of which she'd never imagined before.

When so much time had passed, she wondered if the man was

ever going to reappear again—or if the instructions he claimed were forthcoming would ever arrive.

Then it happened.

One day, she'd come in from a session on an oversight committee when she found something else inside the envelope of money. There was a piece of paper with one sentence typed on it.

No on 32.

It took her a second to realize what the line meant. Then it hit her. Proposition 32 was a bill to reduce the number of new refineries in the United States by 10 percent every year for the next five years. The goal behind it was to start pushing the big oil companies and other fossil fuel corporations to pump their money into alternative and green energy research and development.

The bill seemed innocent enough, and she didn't yet understand what it would mean for the massive companies it would affect most. What pushed Monroe over the edge with her vote was the thing attached to the note.

It was the same picture of her daughter.

After that, she got more frequent requests from her anonymous benefactor: a vote here, a filibuster there, nothing condemning—at least not in this life.

She stepped back out onto the balcony as another blast of thunder rolled through the soupy sky in the distance. Off to the right, the bright lights of the Capitol Building blazed in the middle of the city. A warm breeze wrapped around her and held her in its embrace. Then it died just as suddenly as it had arisen.

The floor creaked inside her bedroom just beyond the double doors, and Monroe spun around to see what made the noise. The bedroom was empty, lit by the lamp on her nightstand and more light pouring into the space from the bathroom on the other side of the room.

She peered into the dim bedroom, her senses on full alert. After five or six seconds, she turned back around to enjoy the view and her drink.

Monroe scooped up the glass and put it to her lips, letting the golden liquid fill her mouth for a moment before she swallowed. It was her second drink of the night, so the burn that came with the first few sips was gone, leaving nothing but the brandy's natural flavor notes she loved so much.

She enjoyed the last sip so much, she decided to go ahead and finish this drink and get one more refill before heading to bed. She tipped the glass back, poured the rest of the contents into her mouth, and turned around to make her way to the bar in her upstairs study.

As she pivoted, she felt something brush against her back. A strong hand forced her forward against the rail while the other wrapped its fingers around her throat. The jarring contact with the wrought iron jiggled the glass from her hand, and it fell into the grassy lawn below with a quiet clink.

Monroe tried to scream, but the hand around her squeezed so tight she could barely gasp for air.

She felt the intruder shifting their right hand, working it quickly, near her waist, but couldn't see what was happening. Monroe realized what was happening when the abrasive noose slipped around her neck. When the attacker let go of her neck, she instinctively bent over, gasping for air and clutching at her throat—both to remove the rope and to ease her breathing.

The next second, she felt two strong, slender arms wrap around her legs just below the knees. Monroe's feet left the balcony floor as the intruder lifted her up and over the railing.

Her arms flailed, and her legs kicked wildly as she toppled over the railing. She started to scream for help, but her plea was cut short. The rope abruptly jerked and went taut. Monroe's neck popped, but it didn't break.

She kicked her feet harder and clawed at the rope crushing her throat. Her watery eyes bulged out of their sockets. Her face reddened and swelled as if about to burst. The lungs in her chest ached for air, air that wouldn't come.

As she surrendered to unconsciousness, the darkness crept in from the corners of her eyes. Her head slumped forward. Her body shook and gyrated for another thirty seconds before it finally went limp, twisting and turning as she hung from the balcony.

The killer stood on the balcony and watched for another minute to make sure the woman was dead. Then, like a ghost, the shadowy figure vanished into the night.

Chapter 6

ATLANTA

"It's authentic," Alex said as he placed the diary of General Alvarado on the lab workstation in front of Tommy. "Although I don't know how much longer it's going to last being exposed to the elements like this. I'm pretty amazed we can even still see the writing."

"I am, too," Tommy said. "Incredible it didn't fade more than it has."

"Any idea about the cipher?" Sean asked.

"Not really," Tara said as she leaned over the item with her hands pressed firmly onto the desk. "We need the key."

"And there wasn't anything in this document that alluded to a key?"

Alex and Tara shook their heads simultaneously.

Tommy put his hand to his mouth, covering his lips with the index finger. His thumb pressed into the right cheek and rubbed it as he considered the problem.

"What if the cipher's key is encoded within the book itself?" he asked.

The other three frowned.

"What do you mean?" Alex asked.

Tommy flipped open the diary and thumbed through the first few pages. "Occasionally, these kinds of things have the key put into what would otherwise be unnecessary information. It could be a dedication, a comment that seems out of place, something like that."

"So, it could be that the key is hidden inside a message in the journal," Sean said.

"Right. We just have to find the fluff. That's where I've seen other cipher keys in the past."

Tara raised a dubious eyebrow. "How many of these things have you seen?"

Tommy fired a look that told her all she needed to know.

"That many, huh?" she said. "Well, it's worth a shot. We can set up some parameters in the computer and have it analyze all that in just a few minutes."

Tommy snorted a laugh and shook his head. "That would have taken days, maybe weeks twenty years ago."

"Heck, maybe even fifteen years ago," Sean said. "Unreal how fast these things have gotten."

Tara plopped into her rolling chair and scooted over to her workstation where a keyboard sat in front of a 30-inch monitor. A second later, her fingers were flying across the keyboard at a dizzying pace.

Sean shot a sidelong glance over at Alex. "You type that fast?"

"Doesn't everybody?" Alex asked with a cynical grin.

"I guess us old timers take things a little slower."

"You guys aren't even forty yet."

"Getting there," Sean said as he watched Tara work.

The three guys hovered around the workstation until she'd finished putting in all the information.

"Okay," she said after fifteen minutes of furious typing. "It's done. The system is going to check for anything in the rest of the text that has a similarity to what you described: things that might match up with the weird symbols in the back of the journal."

"And it's going to do that pretty fast, huh?"

"Yeah," Tara said, pointing at the screen.

The monitor filled with bars going from left to right, displaying all the different actions the system was running at the same time.

"This computer can process billions of pieces of information and combinations per second."

"Our last setup was awesome. This one is an upgrade," Alex said. "Our systems are about six months ahead of about 99 percent of the world."

"That's impressive," Sean said.

"You're welcome," Tommy chirped.

Something dinged from the computer, and an image popped up in a new window. It was one of the symbols from the cipher and the letter R.

"See?" Tara asked. "We got a match. Once it goes through the entire Spanish alphabet, we should be able to decode the cipher."

"When that happens, will the computer give us all the possible combinations for words and sentences as well?" Sean asked. "These things can sometimes be like a jumbled word puzzle."

The computer dinged again and displayed the letter E at the top.

"Yes," Tara said. "We will get all of that in the results. Once we have those, it will take a human touch to figure out which one the author intended."

The lab fell silent, embraced only by the gentle whirring of the computers and the air conditioning pouring through the vents above.

They stood around for several minutes before Tara excused herself to get some coffee. When she returned with a cup for her and Alex, Sean and Tommy noted the flirty smile she offered.

"So...things going well for you guys outside of work?" Tommy asked.

Sean wanted to nudge his friend's shoulder, but he refrained, hoping that Tommy's lack of subtlety would be missed.

"Yeah, things are good," Alex said.

"Same here," Tara added.

"Good," Tommy said. "That's good." He raised up on his tiptoes and back down a few times, shoving his hands deeper into his pockets.

He couldn't have been trying to make things more awkward.

Fortunately, the kids didn't seem to get what he was hinting.

"Anything interesting happen lately?" he pressed.

Now Sean didn't want to nudge his friend. He wanted to push him through a wall.

Alex looked up to the ceiling as he thought for a moment. Then he shook his head. "No, not that I can think of. Been pretty boring around here. Although I did just try the new burger place in the Westside Provisions District. It was really good. The line was out the door, down the stairs, and onto the street."

"So, the burgers are good?" Sean asked, hoping his question would cut off Tommy's prying.

"Amazing. One of the best I've ever had."

"Did you go over there by yourself, or did some friends tag along?" Tommy pressed.

"You know what," Sean cut off Alex before he could answer, "I think we could use a cup of coffee, too. Schultzie, why don't you come with me? We'll be right back."

"I don't need any coffee," Tommy said. "Besides, you can carry two cups."

"Yes, I *could*, but I don't know how much milk or cream you want. And I really think you need a cup."

Tommy was about to ask his friend why he was acting so strangely, but Sean grabbed him by the arm and yanked him away while Alex and Tara continued watching the monitor.

"What is wrong with you?" Tommy asked as Sean dragged him toward the door.

Once the door closed behind them and they were safely in the next hallway, Sean spoke up. "Me? What's wrong with you, asking all those questions like that? Let those poor kids be."

"What? I was just seeing how things were going."

"You were being nosy, probing around for information. You going to a sewing circle later, too?"

"I don't see the harm in trying to find out if they're involved romantically. What's the big deal?"

Sean started walking down the hallway toward the breakroom.

"It's just kind of rude, that's all."

Tommy's social skills weren't the best in the world. His style of interaction with others was a direct result of spending so many hours absorbed in books and other forms of research.

"I don't see how it's rude. Heck, people post their relationship statuses on social media for the whole world to see. So, what's wrong with just asking?"

Sean's head turned side to side as he turned into the breakroom with Tommy just behind. "Did you stalk their social media profiles to find out if they're dating?"

Tommy scowled. "No. What? No, I didn't. Okay?"

Sean chuckled as he reached the coffee machine and grabbed a paper cup from a stack next to the refrigerator. "You probably should have. At least then they wouldn't be annoyed with your version of twenty questions."

"I'm not going to stalk their social media accounts."

Sean poured a cup of steaming-hot coffee into the cup and scooted it to the side. "Coffee?" he asked.

"No. I already told you I didn't want any coffee."

Sean shrugged. "Suit yourself. Just do me a favor, and don't ask them about their personal life when we get back in there. Okay?"

Tommy made a little hole in his lips as if about to whistle. He blew air out of the opening. "Fine. I won't ask. I don't see why wanting to know if your friends are dating or not is an issue."

"Well, it is," Sean said as he retreated back to the door. "So, leave them alone about it."

They returned to the lab and sidled up next to Alex, who was leaning over Tara. Both of them stared at the screen, watching as the bars continued to fill.

"Almost done?" Tommy asked. He looked across his shoulder at Sean. "That okay for me to ask?" he mouthed.

Sean clenched his jaw.

"Yeah, it looks like it," Tara said.

The computer dinged again, and a green checkmark appeared on the screen.

"And...now it's done."

The screen blinked a few times, and then a printer started running on a nearby shelf.

"What's it doing now?" Tommy asked.

"Printing out all the possible combinations for the solution to the cipher," Tara said. She read the results on the screen. "Looks like there are 110 of them."

"One hundred and ten?" Sean asked Tommy. "Is that normal?"

"It's a little above average, I'd say. I mean, if there was such a thing as an average for ancient ciphers. Pretty sure there isn't."

The other three stared at him like he had a spider crawling on his face. "Okay, yeah, it's a lot. I suggest we split it up to work faster."

"Okay," Alex said, "but how will we know what we're looking for?"

That was something Tommy had been considering for some time. While the computer was doing its thing, he'd wondered about what the right answer would be. Based on what Alvarado's diary said about the lost temple, it was a good bet they'd be looking for something in the Yucatan region of Mexico. On top of that, he could only guess.

"Look for anything that has to do with the Mayans," he blurted. "We'll narrow it from there."

Alex stepped over to the printer and grabbed the stack of sheets from the tray. He counted them, divided them, and passed them out to the other three.

Sean pulled up a chair at the big table next to Tara's workstation and started scouring the lines of text.

Tommy sat across from him and began doing the same. His eyes shifted from left to right over and over again, like watching a tennis match. He was the first to finish his stack and shoved it forward to the center of the table.

"Anything?" Sean asked when he noticed his friend was done.

"No," Tommy said and shook his head. "You?"

Sean ran his finger along one of the sentences and then skipped down to the next one. "No, not yet."

He was in the midst of reading when Alex stopped him.

"I've got something," Alex said, perking up instantly.

Sean and Tommy slid their chairs over to where Alex was working. Tara rolled closer, leaning in over Alex's shoulder.

"Right here," he said. "Look at this line."

Alex pointed to the sentence and waited for the others to read it.

Under the cliff ruins by the sea my journey began.

"Not very specific, huh?" Tara said.

"No," Alex agreed. "That could be anywhere."

Tommy frowned and scratched his chin. "Not necessarily." He thought for a minute, pacing back and forth. "Oh come on. I know this one. Why can't I think of it?"

Sean started to offer a smart aleck answer, but Tommy cut him off. "Shut up," Tommy said. His order caused Sean to laugh.

"You two are like an old married couple," Alex said.

Tommy gave him a glare that said the same thing he'd said to Sean. Then he stopped and looked at the computer. He stepped over to it and started typing.

"What are you doing now?" Sean asked. "Doing an internet search?"

"I thought I knew it, but there's no sense in wasting time when I could just do a quick search. Right?"

"That was going to be my suggestion," Tara offered.

Tommy hit the return key and waited. "I didn't want to cheat," he said. "I should know the answer to that."

The results populated on the screen a second later, and he scanned through them.

"It's Tulum, isn't it," Sean said before Tommy could speak.

"Dang it," Tommy said abruptly. He stood up straight and eyed his friend suspiciously. "You knew that, didn't you."

"I like to watch you squirm," Sean said with a shrug.

Tommy chuckled. "Jerk. Yes, it's Tulum."

"What's Tulum?" Alex asked, appearing a bit lost.

"Well now, Tulum is a resort town on the coast of the Yucatan. Think Cancun but smaller."

"And with less of a spring break PCB feel to it," Sean added.

"Right."

The kids looked more confused than before.

"Wait," Tara said. "So, we're looking for a clue to this lost temple in some Mexican resort? Because if that's the case, I'm packing my bags and coming with you guys."

"Not exactly," Tommy said. "Tulum is a resort town, yes, but we're more interested in the ancient ruins there than anything else."

"Note the odd comment about it being under the ruins," Sean said. "Cave of some sort?"

"Maybe. I'd say that all of those places have been well-searched through the years. If this Alvarado guy left us a clue of some kind, it's probably carved into the rock. If he buried it or tried some other way of hiding it, whatever was there would be long gone by now."

"Of course, it could already be gone."

Tommy scoffed at the comment. "We take that risk every time we go after something like this. You know that."

"True. So, what's the plan?"

Tommy scratched the thick brown hair on the back of his skull and thought for half a second. "We're going to Mexico," he said.

"And we're coming with?" Alex asked with more than a hint of hopefulness in his voice.

Sean and Tommy twisted their heads and exchanged a knowing glance before turning back to Alex.

"No," Tommy said.

"Aww, man. I knew you guys weren't going to let us get out of here and go anywhere fun."

Tommy's eyebrows lowered. "You love it here in the lab. You willingly choose to spend most of your time here."

"He's got a point," Tara said. "I mean, sure, a beach trip sounds nice, but then you have to deal with all the sand and the sunburn and we don't know if the accommodations will be nice."

"I guess so," Alex said, doing his best to sound dejected.

"Tell you what," Tommy said, "when we get back, if you want to go down there for a little vacation time, you're welcome to."

"Full vacation pay?" Alex asked, suddenly hopeful again.

Tommy sighed. "Of course."

Chapter 7

WASHINGTON

"Shut it down."

The president turned his head, shifting his gaze from one person to another until he'd met every eye in the boardroom.

"Sir, we can't just—" one of the men at the table started to say.

"You can and you will. It's not like it hasn't been done before."

"Yes, but when it was done before, it was due to other factors, not an ongoing murder investigation." The wrinkled, white-headed man put both hands out with palms up as if that would help solidify his point.

"He's right, Mr. President. Not to mention that shutting down the Capitol will put everyone into a state of panic."

President Dawkins sighed. He'd faced more than enough challenges in his term as the leader of the free world. Most of the time they were of the international variety: hostage situation, another country invades a neighbor, or threats from potential enemies. Through the duration of his first term and into the second, he'd managed to get through every trial that was thrown his way.

This, however, was different.

"Two members of the United States Congress have been

murdered," Dawkins said. "I'm not talking about shutting down the government for an extended period of time. Just a day or two until we can increase security and everyone has done a thorough evaluation of their personal security details. That's all."

The guy with white hair seemed to accept the explanation. The blowhard from South Carolina—a guy named Steve Morrison—sitting next to him wasn't so accommodating.

"Sir, if we shut down now, it will show significant weakness, not only to the murderer but to the entire world. Our enemies will see how easy it is to throw our government into a panic. Besides, the police haven't called Monroe's death a murder. For all we know, she killed herself."

Both were points the president had considered. He'd called the meeting to make a suggestion since ordering the government shutdown would require official channels. He figured the men in the room would agree—for the most part—with him and spread the word to the members of the House and the Senate that precautions needed to be taken. In regards to the comment on Monroe's possible suicide, he decided not to say anything.

"Then tell your people to keep it quiet," Dawkins said. "No talking to the media, no leaking information about what's going on. All I'm asking for is twenty-four hours to make sure everyone is safe. That's it."

Morrison sighed. "That's a lot of lips to keep tight. Besides, the media is already speculating on the very thing you're asking us to do."

"He's right," a middle-aged woman with dark blonde hair said from across the table.

Her name was Sandra Cummings. She was a senator from the hills of Wyoming. Growing up on a bison ranch had hardened her, made her a strong person Dawkins knew he could trust. He also knew that strength made her extremely opinionated.

"No way we can keep everyone quiet," she added.

"Fine," Dawkins relented. "What do you suggest we do? Keep going on with business as usual? How many people have to be murdered before we take this seriously enough to do something?"

"What's going on with the police? Do they have any suspects, any leads? How's the investigation progressing?" Morrison asked.

Dawkins took a deep breath and exhaled through his nose. He kept his fingers folded atop the desk in a contemplative gesture. "The investigation is ongoing, but as of yet they have no suspects and very few leads."

"How can they not have any leads? Isn't that their job?" Mr. Blowhard roared, startling some of the sleepier people at the table. "What about our guys?"

"The FBI has done all they can to help," Dawkins reassured. "Whoever the killer is—and I believe we're dealing with the same person here—they're very good. They haven't left a shred of condemning evidence. And they've circumnavigated security details and cameras in the process."

"What's your plan, then?" the white-haired man asked.

"I've called in a favor. I figured the authorities could use all the help they can get."

"Who?"

"Just know that I'm doing everything in my power to help bring the killer to justice. That's all I can tell you right now."

The woman from Wyoming frowned. "So, you won't tell us these additional measures you're taking? If I didn't know any better, I'd say you think this might have been an inside job. Do you think it was one of us?"

The president looked down at his table and then back up at her. "I don't know who it is. I wouldn't dream of accusing any of you. The fact, however, is that everything about this case makes it look like whoever is behind it has insider knowledge and probably access to all our security measures. Think about it. How did they distort the camera views in the Capitol? They'd have to have known the wiring schematics, where the cameras were positioned, where the feeds went. And they'd have known the exact hours they could find their targets, and where."

Dawkins shook his head as he considered it all. "Yes, I think it's an inside job, but I don't know who or why. No one does yet."

Everyone around the table went silent. An uncomfortable suspense filled the room.

"Again," Dawkins reiterated, "I do not want a witch hunt to ensue over this. So, don't start looking at each other, wondering if this person or that person might be the killer. That's partly why I want to shut things down for a day. It will give everyone a chance to take care of themselves and keep things from escalating."

Morrison let out a dramatic exhale. "Fine, Mr. President. We'll shut things down for twenty-four hours. I hope whatever backup plan you've put into place can help us figure out just what is going on. Before someone else dies."

The president dismissed the meeting and waited around until everyone had left. Morrison waited around at the door, saying his goodbyes until he and the president were alone with one of his guards.

"Need something, Steve?" Dawkins asked.

The South Carolina representative gave another look out into the hall to make sure everyone was gone before he spoke.

"John, you and I go back a long way," Morrison started. His deep Southern accent filled the room with a smooth, buttery tone. "Do you really think it's an inside job, that a politician is killing other politicians?"

"I think it's a distinct possibility, Steve."

Morrison turned his head from side to side. He rubbed the skin just above his eyebrows, as if the comment stressed him out more than he had been already.

"We're not in a Third World country here, John. That's not how Washington operates."

"Tell that to the four presidents who were assassinated in office."

"Those were exceptions to the rule, and you know it. Not to mention those men were killed by outsiders. They weren't hits ordered by political rivals."

"So far as we know."

"Fine," Morrison said. "Let's say you're right, that there's a rogue senator or congressman out there killing other representatives. Why? What's the motivation?"

"I'm not a cop, Steve. That's their job."

"And apparently, the job of someone else you brought in to help. Who is it, John?"

"Someone who knows every building, every room, every secret passage in the city." He raised his gaze to meet Morrison's.

"You brought in Emily?"

Dawkins gave a single nod.

The news hit Morrison like a piano falling from the sky. He slumped into a chair and stared at the table. "So, you brought in the big guns. You must really be worried."

"I'm worried for the people I work with and for the security of our nation," Dawkins said. "It's important we find whoever is doing this and take them down, by any means necessary."

Morrison took a deep breath. "Do you think it's one of those serial killer things?"

"I don't know. I don't want to speculate. Like I said, that's the job of the experts."

"Well," Morrison said as he stood, "I guess I've got a few announcements to make and some planning to do."

"Planning?"

"You said we need to beef up our personal security. I have no intention of getting killed at my home or office. Thanks for looking out for us, Mr. President."

"Just trying to do my job, Steve."

Morrison left.

When he was out of sight, Dawkins rubbed his hands over his face. Another door opened from the other side of the boardroom. Emily walked in wearing a gray jacket and skirt. Her dark hair was done up in a bun and held in place by a silver clasp.

"So, what do you think?" Dawkins asked as she approached.

She eased into the seat closest to him and touched him on the leg. The Secret Service agent to his left averted his gaze.

The two had grown accustomed to the nearly constant presence of the presidential bodyguards. Dawkins barely even gave it a second thought. For Emily, it took some getting used to, but she was coming along.

"I think you need a vacation," she said. "You look tired."

"This job ages you," Dawkins said. "You come in looking like a young man and leave looking like you put on thirty years."

"I know. It's stressful, which is why I'm doing my best to help with this investigation. The last thing I want is for you to have more stress on your plate."

"Thank you," he said. His hand slid under the table and interlocked his fingers with hers. "I know I disagree with a lot of these politicians. Heck, some of them are downright horrible people. I know that, but I don't want anyone to die."

"The police really are doing all they can," Emily said. "I honestly don't know how much more helpful I'm being."

"I'd be lying if I said having you here isn't a nice bonus."

She leaned closer, so near that her perfume overpowered him with an intoxicating scent of flowers and fine Italian leather.

"Is that the real reason you put me on the job?"

He snorted a laugh. "No. Just a cherry on top, that's all."

She grinned at the response. "Well, I'll keep working on it," she said and pulled away.

He ached to pull her back close, but he restrained himself and stuck to business. "Anything so far?"

"Possibly. I mean, we don't have any suspects at this time. So far, the crime scenes have been clean, too clean. Not a hair or drop of blood or even an eyelash was dropped, much less fingerprints."

"So...what *do* you have?"

"Common interests."

"Such as sports, fishing, candlelit dinners, walks on the beach?"

Emily chuckled. "No. I mean they both had some similar allies—rich allies—in their pockets. Or they were in the allies' pockets. Unfortunately, it's hard to differentiate. Right now, it could just be a coincidence."

The president nodded. "That sounds like a good starting point."

"Well, to their credit, the FBI was already snooping down that trail. It was only a matter of time before the cops did, too. We'll see what we can do, but right now, there isn't much to go on. I think your plan to shut everything down for a day or two and let everyone regroup is a good idea."

He appreciated her approval—though he didn't like the fact that the plan had to be put into action.

"I just wish there was more I could do," he said.

"You're doing everything in your power to protect the leaders of this country. And you need to make sure you keep yourself safe, too. They may be working their way up the food chain."

"I'm not worried about that," Dawkins said with a smirk. "I've got good people taking care of me." He motioned to the guard at the door. The man didn't even flinch, keeping his eyes locked on the wall ahead.

"Still, be careful."

"I will," he said and patted her leg. "Unfortunately, I've got this feeling in my gut that the killer isn't finished yet."

Chapter 8

TULUM, MEXICO

Sean shielded his sunglasses with a hand as he looked out over the scene.

The resort beach town of Tulum buzzed with activity. Tourists milled about in the open-air market, picking out fresh fruit, fish, and anything else they thought might be good for a snack or perhaps a romantic dinner by the sea.

Many posed for pictures taken on their phones. Seconds later, they were busily posting them to social media or texting jealous friends and family back home.

Tulum was a haven for American tourists and expats alike. Far from the reaches of the drug wars and corruption of northern Mexico, Tulum was like an oasis of peace on the edges of a vast desert.

"I've gotta say," Tommy spoke up, "this sure seems like a nice town."

"It's a resort town that attracts a lot of retired Americans."

"Cancun is pretty nice."

"As long as you stay close to your hotel. It's a different animal. Too close to the drug war. It's right in the backyard."

Sean thought about his one visit to Cancun. He swore he'd never go back. People had warned him to stay in the resorts, but he figured things would be fine considering he knew how to handle himself.

That mistake had led to a brawl with some local drug smugglers who wanted to use his corpse as a means of transporting cocaine across the border. Americans who died in Mexico had to be sent back to the States, which made perfect targets of tourists who'd wandered from the safety of their hotels. Then it was just a matter of getting the right escort for the body.

The four men had jumped Sean as he strolled by an alley between a saloon and a taqueria. They pulled him into the side street and immediately went for the jugular in the most literal sense of the word.

Two of the men had knives. The others were armed with baseball bats. Sean knew right away that the guys were low-level functionaries for the local cartel. Only the ones higher up the food chain were given the best weapons. Occasionally, a pistol would be handed out to a newbie, but not usually. Besides, the cartels wanted the men doing the dirty work to instill an element of fear into the government, its citizens, and the cartels' competition. That's why so many beheadings seemed to happen in the bigger cities—and occasionally in a place like Cancun, though they tended to avoid the resorts and only deal their punishments in the outskirts.

Sean dispatched the men, albeit with a struggle. They'd caught him off guard, but he reacted fast as old instincts and training snapped into action. He knew to take out the biggest threat first. That was the biggest guy with a knife. Once he was down, taking out the other three clowns hadn't been difficult. One of the men ended up dead. The other three were severely injured and most likely were executed by their employer upon returning to their compound—if they ever made it that far. The cartels didn't accept failure. If one of their underlings ended up in a hospital, they often didn't make it out alive.

"I can't believe I've never been here before," Tommy said as they strolled by an older woman selling fruits and vegetables. The vendor at the cart next to her was selling bread and tortillas, filling the air with the aroma of fresh-baked goods.

"Me, either," Sean said. "I never really thought about it."

"To be fair, Mexico isn't the first place on my list of places to take a vacation."

"Same. I mean, there's nothing wrong with the Gulf Coast. I just have my favorite places, like Destin, Rosemary, Grayton Beach. Although I've heard good things about the coast of Serbia."

"There's nice coastline all over the world. West Africa has some good ones not many people know about."

"As long as the governments stay stable."

"Same story with Nicaragua, Belize, Costa Rica."

"Yep," Sean agreed. He pointed through an archway in a building to the right. "Looks like we get to the beach through here."

"Lead on, sir. Your guidance is as good as mine," Tommy said.

Sean weaved his way through the throngs of people that bottle-necked in the pedestrian thoroughfare. Tommy did his best to keep up, but it seemed like most of the people were going the opposite direction. Once they were on the other side of the building, the side-walk opened up again and there was plenty of room for them to walk side by side again.

"Over there," Tommy said, pointing to his left.

Up on a hill behind Tommy's finger, the Americans saw the ruins of Tulum. There didn't appear to be much. A few small buildings littered the tall grass and sand around the area. Up on the peak over-looking the cliffs rested a larger building. It was made from gray lime-stone and appeared to still be in good condition despite being several hundred years old—perhaps more.

"Not a whole lot to it," Sean said.

"This place was sacred to the ancient Mayans," Tommy said. "They had a strong respect for the sea, which isn't something that's mentioned a great deal when people discuss their history. From what I read, this temple was a place where people could come to worship not only their regular deities, but the gods of the ocean as well."

"Looks like it also faces east, so it was probably a place of sun worship," Sean added.

Tommy puckered his lips and nodded. "I'm impressed. Look at you with a little knowledge there."

Sean narrowed his eyes. "Shut up. I know almost as much about all this as you, remember?"

Tommy chuckled. "Come on. Let's take a closer look at this temple and see what we can find."

He motioned for Sean to follow and started out down the roped path leading up to the ridge where the temple ruins overlooked the sea.

Hundreds of tourists trod the worn trail that meandered to the temple. Some took pictures of each other with the ruins in the background. Others chose to use their phones and cameras to snap images of the beach and the sea beyond.

They made their way up the gradual slope, bypassing all the other sightseers and gawkers, focused on the mission at hand.

It only took five minutes to make the journey up to the hilltop where dozens more people were admiring the view from the temple or simply taking a moment to appreciate the ancient construction.

The breeze coming in from the ocean blew through Sean's hair, and he ran his fingers through it again to keep it out of his eyes. He set his bag down on the ground and fished out a baseball cap to make sure the wind didn't bother him anymore.

Tommy shook his head. "Such a diva now, aren't we?"

"Shut up. Let's take a look around," Sean said as he slung the bag over his shoulder once more.

The men walked around the interior of the temple first, scanning the walls for any signs of something that might be a clue from Alvarado. All they found were a few glyphs from the Mayans who'd occupied the area so long ago. The temple was essentially empty save for the people there to see it.

"The cipher said that Alvarado's journey began under the cliff ruins. Should we make our way down to the beach?" Tommy asked.

"Yeah," Sean said. "I don't think there's anything here."

The two made their way back out of the small structure and back down the path. They veered left onto another trail that led through the grass to the white-sand beach beyond the dunes.

They made another left and walked back toward the cliffs that rose dramatically from the beach, giving the temple ruins a spectacular view of the sapphire-blue water of the gulf.

Sean was glad he'd decided to wear sandals. The sand poured through his toes and under the soles then sifted back out of the openings and onto the beach once more. Wearing shoes to the beach was a huge pain, a fact Tommy had become painfully aware of the last time he visited Sean in Destin.

Sean laughed to himself, unable to keep his friend from hearing.

"What?" Tommy asked as they neared the cliffs directly underneath the ruins. "What's so funny?"

"Oh nothing," Sean teased. "Just remembering the time we went to the beach in west Florida and you thought it would be a good idea to wear shoes."

"Ugh, don't remind me. You know I eventually just threw those things away. I never could get all the sand out of them."

"Believe me, I know."

Sean stopped and looked up at the jagged rocks leading to the base of the temple. The afternoon sun had already dipped behind the hillside, leaving the area of beach under the ruins in cool shade.

"I didn't realize how hot it was until we got to this shade," Tommy said. "I'd be just as happy to park my rear right in this spot for the afternoon."

"Yeah," Sean agreed, "if we didn't have a job to do. Let's keep looking. I don't see anything here."

The two split up and moved closer to the cliff. Most of the beachgoers were sunbathing away from the shade, leaving only a few older people sleeping in their beach chairs under the hill's shadow.

It didn't take much time for the two to realize that there was no opening in the cliff that came even remotely close to what General Alvarado described in his journal.

The two men met back in the middle of the shadows and looked around at the people walking along the beach or sunbathing next to coolers and umbrellas.

"What now?" Sean asked. "I don't see anything like a cave around here."

Tommy rubbed the back of his neck for a second and then looked over at a grassy area blocked off by ropes. "Let's take a look over there."

The two waded through the loose sand until they reached the corner of the rocky outcropping. The cliff continued back until it merged with the hill, sloping down into the dunes.

They stopped short of the ropes and looked around toward the back side. There in plain sight, was what Alvarado must have been talking about in his journal.

The temple had been built upon the rocky cliff to give it a stable base. Part of that base jutted out to the north, providing a sort of natural roof over the ground. It wasn't anything spectacular. No tourists hovered around the opening, wondering what was hidden inside. Sean and Tommy speculated that it probably only went back a dozen feet or so under the ruins. That being said, this had to be the place.

"Looks like we can get in there easily enough," Tommy said. "It's only about five feet high but plenty wide enough. Just have to crouch down and go in low."

Sean noted a man in a Mexican military uniform standing on the path off to the right.

"Except if we cross this rope, we'll probably end up in a Mexican jail."

Tommy followed Sean's gaze and realized the trouble. "Oh, good point. Nobody wants to go to jail in Mexico."

"Yeah, it's not pretty."

"You've been?"

Sean turned his head and gave his friend a *don't ask* glare.

"Right," Tommy said. "So, what do we do? Wait for that guy to wander away on his patrol or something?"

Sean watched the soldier with keen intensity. The man didn't appear like he was going to be moving anytime soon.

They stood there in the sand for nearly five minutes, occasionally looking out toward the water and pointing to other areas of interest lest the soldier become aware that he was being watched.

When five minutes had passed, Sean spoke up again. "He's not going anywhere. If we try to get in there right now, he's going to give us trouble."

"So, what do you suggest we do?"

"The ruins close later when it gets dark, but the beach doesn't. I say we come back tonight when everyone is gone and take a look then."

"You sure about that?" Tommy asked. "I mean, we'll have to use flashlights. Flashlights kind of draw attention when it's dark out."

"Only if there's someone around to see them."

"Granted, but how do we know there won't be one of those guys standing around when we come back?"

"We don't. It's that or take our chances right now. The only difference is right now we know he can see us."

Tommy exhaled in frustration. "Fine. I guess we come back later after dark and try to sneak in. So, what are we going to do with the next six hours until the sun goes down?"

Sean peered over his friend's shoulders. A man in sunglasses with jet-black hair and a dark tan was looking in Sean's direction. He'd noticed the stranger before but hadn't paid much attention at first, thinking he was just another random guy on the beach.

One thing that triggered Sean's senses this time, however, was the fact that the man was wearing white linen pants and a matching shirt with black sunglasses. There weren't many people wearing similar outfits, so the guy stood out like a compound fracture.

"Sure is a pretty spot here, huh, Schultzie?" Sean pointed out to the sea. He covered his mouth with his bicep as he pointed. "Don't look now, but we're being watched."

Tommy's head instinctively started moving to the right.

"I said don't look now."

"Sorry," Tommy apologized and then quickly put a smile on his face as he pretended to admire the view. "Who's watching us?"

"Guy in a linen outfit about a hundred yards to your right, in front of the entrance to the beach. He's been trying to play it cool, but for the last few minutes he's been keeping a close eye on us." Sean lowered his arm and made the last comment through his teeth, keeping his lips as immobile as possible.

"Any idea who he might be and why he's watching us?"

"Your guess is as good as mine. Did you tell anyone else we were coming down here and what we were doing?"

"No. Just the usual people." Then Tommy was overcome by a sudden concern. "You don't think Lilian would—"

"Set us up?" Sean turned his head to face his friend for a second and then returned his gaze to the blue waters. "No. That wouldn't make any sense."

"Unless she had a vendetta."

"Okay, now you're just being silly. Why would she have a vendetta against either one of us?"

"I don't know," Tommy said as he rolled his shoulders. "Crazier things have happened. Come to think of it, why am I more suspicious about this than you? Aren't you normally the paranoid one?"

It was true. Sean usually *was* the one who was always on full alert about everything. The idea that Lilian Pike would send them to Mexico in search of a lost temple only to have them followed, watched, or otherwise harassed didn't add up. Tommy was right, though: they had seen stranger things.

"Whoever that guy's working for," Sean said, "I doubt they have our best interest in mind."

"Unless they're just monitoring our progress."

"Then why would we need to call Lilian with updates?"

"Are we supposed to do that?" Tommy looked at his friend with a sincere curiosity on his face.

"I assumed."

"Well, we have nothing to update at the moment. Maybe after tonight we will."

"Yeah," Sean said as he eyed the guy down the beach. "Looks like we'll need to watch our backs, too."

Chapter 9

WASHINGTON

Congressman Brody Ambrose stared down into the nearly empty glass of whiskey between his fingers. He'd already powered through four drinks and was about to leave for his home. His driver/bodyguard was waiting in the car, though after the events of the last several days he wondered if the guy should be in the bar with him. His guard, a guy named Chris, had even offered to do that.

Ambrose didn't like being babysat. He reassured Chris that he could take care of himself if the need arose, although he wasn't entirely sure about that. Two members of Congress had been murdered in the last week. It had resulted in the president issuing a request that the House and Senate take a twenty-four-hour leave of absence. The official reason given to the media was that there were some renovations that needed to be done at the Capitol.

No one was buying that line.

Everyone knew why they'd taken the day off. Ambrose, along with all the others, were told to tighten up their personal security while systems at the Capitol Building were checked and rechecked to ensure everyone's safety.

A lot of good it did Tripp Haskins and Maggie Monroe.

Ambrose took another swallow of whiskey. He didn't even wince as the warm liquid fell down his throat.

He'd worked with Haskins and Monroe on a few different projects. There was one, in particular, that was more demanding than others. He knew whom he was working for and where the money came from. Haskins had known, too. Maggie, on the other hand, may have been in the dark. She definitely was in the beginning when they'd recruited her. Surely, she'd been brought into the loop at some point.

Not that it mattered now.

Ambrose shook his head and stared at the wall full of bourbons, sour mash whiskeys, scotches, tequilas, and vodkas. There were a few bottles of Irish whiskey thrown in for good measure among the rest.

He'd ramped up his personal security detail at his home in Georgetown, but he knew that wouldn't be enough. It was all so obvious to him. The people he and the other two had been serving so dutifully were coming after them, eliminating them one at a time.

Ambrose didn't know who'd be next. He only knew he was on the list, and that sooner or later, his number would be up.

He'd wondered: Why now? Why take out the people who had worked so hard to pave the road? The thought made him angry. He'd done everything they asked of him. Why they were eliminating the people who'd stuck their necks out to help was beyond him.

One thing was certain: Ambrose had no intention of going quietly. He'd put together files along the way, making sure that if something like this ever happened, he'd have a way out. He could blackmail them, tell them he'd go to the press, even to the president himself with what he had. Ambrose would blow the lid off their entire operation. He'd throw everyone under the bus, including his associates in the House. Whatever it took to save his own skin, Ambrose would do it. It was nature's way. Or, at least, his way.

Involuntarily, he patted his suit jacket around his waist to make sure the pistol he'd packed was still in the holster. The weapon was just one more way to ensure his personal safety.

Ambrose had grown up in the Louisiana bayou country. By the

time he was eleven, he'd killed all sorts of wild game, including a few gators. His parents were fishermen. Depending on the year, they had an overflow of money, but sometimes almost none at all. He'd left and attended LSU to pursue a degree in political science. Eventually, he found himself in the state legislature with his sights on rising much higher.

Survival was second nature to Brody Ambrose. If someone was coming after him, they'd be in for a fight.

"Another round, Congressman Ambrose?" the bartender asked as he approached, wiping down a beer mug with a towel that probably hadn't been cleaned in a month.

"No, I'd better call it a night, Marvin. I appreciate it, though."

"Yes, sir. Want me to settle up on your card?"

"Yes, please. Thank you."

The bartender scurried away to the other end of the bar and started typing on the keypad.

Ambrose loved the little dive. It was in a neighborhood far enough away from all the trendy places that few people visited, but not so far that it was in one of the sketchier sections of town.

The entrance had a dark green awning with crimson stripes that had probably been there for forty years. Old neon beer signs hung in the windows with logos that were at least three generations behind the current ones. Even the seats inside were relics of the 1960s—dark red vinyl with high backs and buttons riveted intermittently.

"Here you go, Congressman Ambrose," Marvin said as he set the congressman's receipt on the counter. "Have a good evening."

The bartender lingered for a moment, which was unlike him. He had a grave look of concern on his face.

"Something bothering you, Marvin?" Ambrose asked as he wrote down the tip and the total on the receipt.

"It's just that...well, do the cops have any leads on these killings everyone's been talking about?" He stammered the question and immediately looked like he regretted asking.

"Not yet, Marvin. They'll find them eventually." Ambrose slid the receipt across the counter and stood up.

"I heard they don't have any leads or suspects yet."

"Don't believe everything you hear, Marvin. That stuff will drive you crazy."

"Yes, sir, Congressman Ambrose. You have a good night, okay? And be careful. I don't want to read about anything happening to you. You're one of the good ones."

"Will do, Marvin. Will do."

Ambrose collected his card and slipped it into his money clip. He strode out of the bar with an arrogance in his gait.

He liked Marvin, though the proprietor of the establishment had certainly missed his guess when it came to the congressman's disposition and his character in general. Ambrose was not a good man. Not even close. And he knew it.

He got what he could while he could because he was acutely aware that no one was going to give him anything in this life. He had to take what he wanted.

Ambrose wasn't concerned with power like others in Washington. He was there to make as much cash as he could and then retire to some small island or perhaps a ski lodge in Colorado or Wyoming. If he worked hard enough, perhaps both.

His associates—the ones he now feared were going to come after him—had given him an incredible head start on those lofty goals. The money they'd provided cut his time to retirement in half, and as long as the checks kept rolling in, that time would be reduced to almost nothing. Then he could get out of the political arena and take it easy for the rest of his days.

He deserved it. At least that's what he told himself. After growing up in a shack on the bayou and never knowing if they'd have enough to eat, he looked forward to the possibility of never having to think about finances again.

Ambrose was almost there. He figured one more term would do it, and then: a life of leisure and luxury.

He pushed through the door and stepped out into the warm Washington evening. The summer had been hotter than expected so far, and he was a little caught off guard by the humidity. Being from southern Louisiana, he was no stranger to damp air. He often laughed when he heard locals complaining about it.

"Don't go to Louisiana," he'd joked with someone before. "You'll drown in the air down there."

It only took him a second to acclimate to the muggy evening, and by the time he reached the black SUV on the sidewalk he already felt like he was back home in the swamps.

He opened the back door and climbed in behind the driver's seat and fastened his seatbelt.

"Thanks for waiting, Chris. I appreciate it."

The driver nodded and stepped on the gas, steering the SUV out onto the street.

Ambrose didn't have to thank his guard. That was—after all—the guy's job. He was paid to stand around and wait on the congressman without questioning anything.

Chris had been a good bodyguard for the better part of four years. He'd stood in the rain while the congressman took care of personal matters with one of the many high-end escorts Washington provided. Ever since then, Ambrose insisted Chris wait inside the car so he wouldn't get wet.

Not that the congressman cared about Chris and his human dignity one way or the other, but the smell of wet clothes lingered in his vehicle for days after that. Now, wherever they went, Chris stayed behind the wheel unless otherwise notified.

The SUV veered to the right and sped along the street. Ambrose pulled out his cell phone and checked his messages. He'd received a request to attend a meeting the following morning. The other representative made it seem like they had a great deal of catching up to do as a result of the shutdown.

Ambrose shook his head. The only thing that moved fast in this town was the news. Everything else crept along at a snail's pace. That's the way government worked.

He tapped the phone's keyboard and sent a response, saying he'd attend but that he had another commitment that overlapped so he might be a few minutes late. Ambrose wasn't lying. He preferred to start his day with his favorite intern, a young blonde go-getter from Providence named Lucy.

She wouldn't sleep with him despite his numerous attempts. That didn't mean he wouldn't keep trying. She was feisty and energetic, two huge reasons why he'd brought her on board.

The fact that she denied him only caused his desire to burn that much more, like a westerly wind blowing through a forest fire.

Ambrose checked the time on his phone. It wasn't too late to send her a text. He had no interest in a late-night meet up, but there was no reason not to set a little spark to the fire.

He found her number in his notes app and then tapped it to pull up the messaging option. Rule number one of having any indiscretions was to never leave a paper or electronic trail of evidence. He was diligent about deleting anything he ever sent that could have been incriminating.

His fingers flew across the keypad as he sent her a quick message asking if she'd be in early the next day.

Once the message was sent, he waited eagerly for the reply.

Suddenly, the driver carefully pulled the wheel to the left, guiding the SUV onto a bridge that crossed the Potomac.

The driver's eyes flicked to the mirror for a second to make sure he was occupied with whatever he was doing on his phone.

Ambrose was so preoccupied with the potential for a flirty response that he didn't notice the driver was taking him on an alternate route until he heard the tires clacking on the seams between sections of asphalt on the bridge.

The noise startled him, and he looked out the window.

"Um, Chris? You do realize we're supposed to be going back to my place, right?"

"Mmm," was the only response he got.

The tone was different. Ambrose realized that even though the driver didn't speak. He looked into the mirror, but it was too difficult to see the face.

"Chris, where are we going? I need to get back to the house. Long day tomorrow."

The SUV reached the other side of the bridge and continued on. The bright lights of the district disappeared behind thick stands of trees and bushes that lined the river.

As soon as the city was out of view, the driver pulled off on a side road.

"Good," Ambrose said. "Just turn around here. What's the matter with you tonight? Are you sick? Something wrong with your voice?"

Then the driver shifted the vehicle into park and opened the door. Only when the driver stepped out did Ambrose see the person's face. It wasn't Chris. It was a woman with hair cropped short, much like Chris. Her thin, dark eyebrows seemed permanently pinched together, mirroring the scowl on her face.

"Who are you?" Ambrose asked, still not feeling threatened.

The woman slammed the door and started walking away into the dark trees near the river, passing the front of the SUV as she moved.

"Hey!" Ambrose yelled. "Where are you going? Where is Chris?"

He reached for the button on his seatbelt buckle and pressed it. The mechanism didn't release. He pushed it again and again, harder each time, but still nothing. He was trapped.

"Hey! What's going on here?"

Ambrose stuck his hand into his jacket and wiggled his body enough to free the weapon in its holster. He pulled the gun up and pointed it at the window and the shadowy figure beyond.

"I'll shoot!" he yelled.

His finger tensed on the trigger.

"Get back here right now! Do you have any idea who you're messing—"

He never finished the sentence.

A sudden pop from under the SUV erupted into a loud bang. The explosion consumed the vehicle in a flash of white light just before it turned into a raging orange inferno.

It took five minutes for the initial sirens to whine in the distance, another three before the first responders arrived on the scene. By then, the killer had already left on a boat she'd moored on the riverbank.

Chapter 10

TULUM

The two Americans stood just inside the little corridor that led from the market sidewalk to the beach. The waves crashed in a constant rhythm that would put even the most stubborn insomniac to sleep.

They'd spent the last several hours planning their return to the beach and then took the opportunity to get some rest, exchanging nap times in case the guy who'd been watching them at the beach decided to break into their hotel room.

No such intrusion occurred, though, and once the sun was down and the stars were twinkling in the clear night sky, they left the hotel and made their way down to the street.

It was a short walk to the beach entrance where the Tulum temple ruins overlooked the sea.

"Coast is clear," Tommy said as he peered out to the dimly lit sand.

"Literally," Sean quipped.

"Really?"

"I almost never say that. In this case, I think it applies given the context of your clichéd statement."

Tommy let out an exasperated sigh and rolled his eyes. "You done?"

Sean cinched his bottom lip and gave a nod. "Yeah, I think so."

"Good," Tommy hissed. "Because I'd prefer not to loiter here in plain sight. Those soldiers could still be hanging around."

"I'd say it's a solid bet they are. Not to mention our friend."

"Exactly. So, keep an eye out."

"Do you really think you need to remind me of that?"

"Just...fine, shut up. Let's move."

Sean cracked a smile as his friend moved out from his hiding place and started creeping down the beaten path toward the shore. He loved pushing Tommy's buttons. It helped that he knew all the right ones that would drive his friend crazy.

He followed Tommy out into the open, both keeping to the edge of the roped trail and staying low as they crept ahead.

"You think maybe we shouldn't look like we're sneaking around?" Sean asked as they passed a sign that told them the ruins were closed after dark.

Tommy stopped and looked back at his friend with a questioning glance.

"I'm just saying," Sean went on, "two dudes creeping around in the dark looks kind of suspicious."

"And two dudes out for a casual stroll on the beach doesn't?"

"We're going for a stroll on the beach? I had no idea you were so romantic."

"Oh my goodness. It never stops, does it?"

"It's a big reason why you love me."

"It's also a reason I want to put a muzzle on you." Tommy shook his head in frustration. "You might be right, though. Just don't try to hold my hand."

"You're such a tease," Sean said as he straightened up.

The two continued along the path, doing their best to look like a couple of sightseers who didn't know they weren't supposed to be there.

"So, what's our angle?" Tommy whispered. "You know, if we get caught? Better to ask for forgiveness than permission?"

"Always."

"Think that will translate down here in Mexico?"

"Only one way to find out."

"I was afraid you'd say that."

The sound of the waves crashing on top of themselves grew louder as they approached the beach. The moon reflected on the rippling water out beyond the shelf where the ocean floor dropped off into the deep abyss below.

They cut to the left and kept moving. Their heads were on swivels, constantly turning one direction and the other, eyes peering into the darkness to make sure they weren't being followed—or watched.

There was no sign of anyone save for a young couple a few hundred yards down the coast. They were wrapped up in each other's arms, enjoying the warm night air and a little alone time. The two didn't pay any attention to the two Americans as they found their way over to the underside of the cliffs.

Tommy stopped at the closest rocky corner and looked back down the beach. The couple was still focused on whatever they were doing, and by now they were so far away that if they made a fuss, Sean and Tommy could get away. Neither of the friends figured that would happen, and so they kept going until they reached the other side of the cliff.

A quick peek around the corner told them the soldier was no longer at his previous post. The guy was probably gone for the night with no replacement being sent.

"Keep a lookout," Tommy said as he raised one foot and crossed the rope barricade.

Sean continued turning his head from side to side, sweeping the area for any sign of trouble. They were still the only people in the area as far as he could tell.

Tommy climbed up the short slope, keeping one hand on the rock wall to his left to maintain balance. It took less than twenty seconds for him to reach the opening. Once he was at the threshold, he looked out over the area and then motioned for Sean to come up.

Sean followed the same line until he arrived at the overhang where Tommy was crouched down, looking inside.

"Need to keep our lights as low as possible until we're out of plain sight," Sean said.

Tommy gave an understanding nod. "You want to...." He made a side motion with his head toward the dark underbelly of the rocks.

Sean rolled his eyes. "Yeah, sure. I'll lead the way."

He bent down and shuffled his feet sideways, making sure he didn't bump his head on the rough ceiling above. He felt the sand give way to hard rock underfoot and continued moving slowly until he couldn't see the beach or the sea any longer.

Then he switched on a flashlight he'd taken from his gear bag. The tight beam put a bright circle on the wall ten feet across from him. He pointed it toward the rear of the shallow cave and ran it along the walls and ceiling. A moment later, Tommy joined him and switched on his light.

The two scanned the rocky surface, panning over it one direction and then the other for any sign of a clue left by Alvarado.

"See anything?" Tommy asked.

"Not yet."

They continued the search, scouring every inch of the wall until they'd gone around the entire room.

Tommy put his hands on his hips and let out a frustrated exhale.

"Any thoughts?" he asked.

Sean tilted his flashlight up and focused the beam on the ceiling. He moved it toward the back of the cave and stopped after only a few seconds.

"Got it," he said.

Tommy's demeanor perked up. He cocked his head back and stared at the ceiling. Sean's light illuminated several symbols carved into the wall and highlighted with a faded black paint.

"They look just like the ones in the cipher," Tommy said.

"Yep. Quick, get your phone and take some pictures. We need to send this back to the kids so they can analyze it and give us the next location."

Tommy hurriedly set down his light and fished the phone out of his pocket. He focused on the symbols and snapped several shots before shoving the device back in his pocket.

Then Tommy continued to stare at the bizarre markings. "You know," he said, pointing at a familiar shape, "we saw one of those in Alvarado's journal, too."

"It's a Mayan serpent," Sean said.

"I know what it is. You must think I'm some kind of idiot."

Sean shrugged and ticked his head to the side. "Your words."

"Anyway, I wonder what it's doing here. Seems a little out of place."

"Not sure," Sean said. "Maybe Alvarado found it and decided it was a good spot to put his clues. Would make sense since we're trying to find a lost Mayan temple."

"I don't know," Tommy said. "I feel like maybe it's deeper than that."

He craned his neck and tilted his head to the side to get a closer look at the serpent head. The black eyes were prominent, more so than the rest of the outline. The mouth, too, seemed to be darker than the head surrounding it.

"The serpent," a new male voice said from the cave entrance, "was a highly revered beast in Mayan society."

Sean spun around, ready to draw his weapon in the blink of an eye, but the stranger warned him and brandished a pistol of his own. "Stop right there, Mr. Wyatt."

Sean sighed and slowly lowered his hand. He kept the flashlight shining on the guy in the doorway.

"Who are you?" Tommy asked, standing just a diagonal step behind his friend.

"And what is it with you guys calling me Mr. Wyatt? My dad was Mr. Wyatt."

The stranger ignored the question.

"I'm sorry, but you two must not be permitted to go any farther.

Too many innocent lives are at stake. Were you to continue your search and succeed in finding the lost temple, humanity would suffer the consequences."

Sean raised a questioning eyebrow at the man. He was tall, probably an inch or so taller than Sean, and had a muscular frame, dark tanned skin, and a thick black mustache.

It was the same guy they'd seen on the beach earlier that day.

The man kept his weapon aimed at Sean, but his flashlight highlighted both of the Americans. The piercing bright beam caused them both to wince for nearly a minute until their eyes adjusted.

"What are you talking about?" Tommy asked.

"You can play stupid all you like, gentlemen, I know you're trying to find the temple. And I know you have the diary of General Alvarado." The man's accent was distinctly Mexican with the *G* in general pronounced with a heavy *H* sound.

"Diary?" Sean asked in his most sincere, clueless tone. "What diary?"

"Do not take me for a fool, Mr. Wyatt. I know what you and your friend do for a living. I also know why you are here. Now, please, stop wasting my time. The diary, now." He shook the weapon in his hand to emphasize the urgency of the moment.

"I'll have to get it out of my bag over there," Sean said, pointing to his gear bag on the floor nearby.

The stranger took a long breath and exhaled through his nostrils. "Move away," he ordered, motioning to his left. "You continue to assume I am unintelligent. I know you must keep weapons and many other things in that bag of yours. I will retrieve the diary. Then the two of you will die in this place."

"Die?" Tommy said, suddenly sounding afraid. "Why? We're just a couple of archaeologists searching for a missing piece of history. What did we do wrong?"

"Move away from the bag," the stranger said again, his voice rising.

"Do as he says, Schultzie."

"Why?" Tommy protested. "You heard him. He's going to kill us anyway."

"No," Sean argued. "He's not going to kill anyone tonight. He knows we're the good guys. And you're a good guy, too, aren't you Mr. —"

"I protect the location of the temple. If that makes me a good person, so be it. I truly do not care. What I care about is making sure the power that lurks in that unholy place remains hidden for all eternity."

"Sounds like you're one of the good guys to me. I mean, bad guys typically don't care about the pain and suffering of others. Right, Schultzie?"

"Yeah, I guess. Although the gun he's pointing at us doesn't help your argument."

Sean ignored his friend. "I still didn't catch your name."

"I didn't give it," the stranger said as he took a step closer to the bag.

Sean and Tommy inched their way to the right, shuffling carefully to ensure they didn't accidentally make a sudden move that would startle the intruder and cause him to fire. Even if he missed, in this small space a ricochet would be deadly.

"Oh, I noticed. Rude, by the way. I mean, what's the harm? If you're going to kill us, shouldn't your victims know the name of their killer? It's the least you can do."

The man stopped just short of the bag and lingered for a second, contemplating Sean's request.

"My name is Sandoval."

"Is that your last name or your first name? Because I gotta be honest, that sounds more like a last name. If it's your first name, I'd probably shorten it to something like Sandy." He turned to Tommy. "Am I right?"

"Definitely. That has to be his last name."

"It *is* my last name!" the gunman roared. "Now, both of you shut up and stand in the corner."

He bent down and picked up the bag, keeping his eyes and the gun in his hand trained on the two Americans as they eased their way to the back of the room.

"I am sorry," Sandoval said. "Truly, I am. But you have left me no choice. If it makes any difference, I don't want to kill you. It is, however, for the good of humanity."

Suddenly, a figure stepped from the shadows behind the gunman. He never saw the rifle butt swinging toward him. The hard edge struck Sandoval on the back of the skull. The fleeting thought that ran through his head before he succumbed to unconsciousness was simply acknowledgment of the pain. Then he collapsed to the hard floor, smacking his face against the surface as he landed.

Sean let out a sigh of relief. "Cut it close much, Greg?" He bent over at his waist and removed Sandoval's wallet from his back pocket. "He wasn't lying," Sean said as he stared at the guy's ID. "Pablo Sandoval. Gotta admit, kind of an amateur move carrying his real ID around like that."

"What did take you so long, Greg?" Tommy asked, ignoring Sean's wallet investigation. "If you'd waited a second longer, that guy was going to kill us."

Greg stepped from the shadows and grinned. He wore a black silk shirt with a gold chain hanging from his neck. His gray slacks completed the outfit, making him look like a drug dealer from the 1980s.

"You know," Greg said in his sharp English accent, "you boys could just say thank you. They ever teach you Yanks any manners?"

"We're from the South. We learn lots of manners when we're young. We just don't use them on riffraff like you," Sean said. Then his stone expression cracked, and he let out a grin.

Greg chuckled. "Fair enough."

Sean and Tommy crossed the room. Sean picked up the gunman's weapon and checked the magazine. It was full of hollow points, a deadly round that would have made quick work of him and his friend.

"Seriously, Greg, thank you," Sean said as he tucked the sleeping man's gun in the gear bag. "How you feeling, you know, after that whole affair in France?"

Greg shrugged and worked his right shoulder back and forth. "I was doing fine until you two showed up on my doorstep a few years ago. I'm lucky that guy shot me where he did. Docs said half an inch in either direction and I'd be dead."

"We know all that, Greg."

"Yeah," Tommy agreed. "We know the whole story. That's how we knew where to find you down here."

"Oh. Right. Well, anyway, glad I could help out a couple of old friends."

Greg Pilkington was a British ex-pat. In his former life, he'd been an art collector. To pay for his expensive taste in wall decor, he made a living running a vast smuggling empire. Sean and Tommy never asked what kinds of products he dealt, though they both had their suspicions. During a particularly hairy adventure, Greg had helped his friends escape and hide out until the trouble dissipated. Shortly after, he'd been shot in the chest and nearly died. After everything that went down, he left everything behind and moved to the coast of Mexico where none of his old enemies would bother looking.

Sandoval groaned, and his head rolled for a moment.

"What do you guys say we take this little reunion on the road? I'd rather not be around when our friend, Sandy, here wakes up." Sean looked at the other two with a sense of urgency.

"Wait," Greg said. "You're not going to kill him?"

Sean glanced down at the unconscious stranger. Then he shook his head. "No. It's not my style to kill someone while they're out. And besides, something tells me he's not a bad guy."

Tommy frowned. "Seriously? He was about to kill us, like, gangland execution style."

Sean drew a deep breath. "It's hard to explain. Call it a gut feeling." He eyed the gunman with curiosity. "Sometimes people aren't what they seem."

Chapter 11

WASHINGTON

"I need answers, gentlemen. And I need them two days ago." Emily's voice boomed through the trees and echoed out over the Potomac.

Police had blocked off the road during the early morning hours until the majority of first responders were off the scene. When the police realized the vehicle belonged to Congressman Ambrose, they knew the Axis director would have to be notified.

Emily hadn't slept much the last few days. The bags under her eyes gave that away. The night before had been like the others. She'd tossed and turned in the hotel room bed, unable to get comfortable.

She knew she'd sleep better at the White House with the man she loved, but they'd kept things quiet—and out of the public eye—so far. No sense in destroying that now.

She could wait a little longer until his last term was over.

They'd discussed his plan after the presidency ended. He'd promised to move to Atlanta where they could start a new life together, still in the public eye but without political intrigue or distractions from the national media.

For the time being, those beautiful future days seemed an eternity away.

She stared at the charred husk of the congressman's SUV as the first rays of daylight peeked over the buildings to the east. Three members of the House had been killed this week. And no one—not a single person—had a clue as to who was responsible.

"We're doing the best we can, Director Starks," one of the forensic detectives said.

His comment snapped her back to the moment.

"I know," she said, running her fingers through a loose strand of brown hair to pin it behind her ear. "But that's not good enough."

The young man looked discouraged—as did the rest of the cops and federal agents hovering around her. A few of them appeared angry, but she didn't care about that. Their fragile egos weren't her problem. Finding the murderer, however, was.

"I'm not doing a good enough job, either," she said. "None of us are. We're missing something. We have to be. No one pulls off three murders like this without leaving a crumb along the way."

"They can if they're careful," Smalley chirped. His head bobbed when he spoke, like a toy bird with a spring for a neck.

"No," she said. "Eventually, killers like this always screw up."

"So, it's clear we're dealing with a serial killer situation," Robards said, jumping into the conversation for the first time. "Right?"

"All signs point to that," Smalley agreed.

"Maybe," Emily said.

"Maybe? Come on, Director. It's a clear cut serial case. Three members of Congress. Three murders. Whoever the killer is, they're targeting members of the House. No senators have been killed. Tell the president to get all these politicians back to their respective districts until we can figure out who is doing this."

It was an extreme measure the detective was suggesting. President Dawkins had already requested the Capitol be shut down for a day. Getting them to take a mandatory leave would be difficult considering the time of the year. They were in the middle of an extremely important session. Immigration bills were at the forefront of their activity, and the fate of millions hinged on those laws. Dawkins had promised to have that issue taken care of in a timely manner. Any delay would cause an uproar. That didn't include the other big items, such as the student loan situation and the issues with the health care industry.

"That's not going to happen," she said.

Smalley rolled his shoulders. "Then we should just go home, get some rest, and wait for the next call to come in because I can guarantee you there will be another murder in the next forty-eight hours. And spoiler alert: it's going to be a member of the House."

Her phone started buzzing in her jacket pocket. She reached inside the fold, pulled it out, and looked at the screen. "You'll need to excuse me. I have to take this."

She turned away from the men in front of her and stepped away, walking back toward her car. After a quick look over her shoulder, she hit the green button and put the device to her ear.

"What have you got for me?"

"Good morning to you, ma'am," the voice on the other end said. There was the slightest hint of an Irish accent.

"Sorry if I'm not in the mood for pleasantries, O'Rourke. Please tell me you've got something."

Collin O'Rourke was one of her top anti-terrorist agents. Usually, he worked in the field in undercover roles. The grandson of Irish immigrants, he'd changed his last name from O'Connor to protect his family, taking on his mother's maiden name instead. Collin had a knack for digging up information on people, things that others would miss.

"Oh I do. There's a link between all three of the victims."

"You mean other than the fact that they were all members of Congress?"

"Yes, other than that. Come on, Director. You don't actually think I'd waste your time with obvious information like that, do you?"

"One never knows with you, Agent O'Rourke."

"That hurts, ma'am. It really does. No, I'm not calling about that. Turns out your three corpses all had a similar voting pattern."

Emily raised an eyebrow.

"Go on."

"It was tricky to detect at first because their votes, historically, have been all over the place. I wasn't positive until I looked at Ambrose's votes, but his eliminated any doubt in my mind."

"What's the connection, Agent?" she asked, trying to hurry him along.

"These politicians each had different agendas, but they did find agreement on one issue. They all voted the same way when it came to major fossil fuel bills, especially the ones concerning the big oil companies."

Emily's eyes narrowed. "So...they voted against the big oil companies, and you think that's who is behind this?"

"No. They voted in favor of the bills. Those new laws ended up bringing a windfall of money to the oil companies."

Emily's forehead wrinkled as her tired frown deepened. "So, why would they go after their own puppets?"

"Precisely. I'm not entirely sure it was a hit from the fossil fuel guys."

"They certainly have the resources to bring in a top-notch assassin like the one who did all this."

"Right, but it doesn't feel like they're the ones who did it. I think we're looking for someone else."

She hesitated to say the words for fear Smalley and the others would hear. "Are we talking about a serial killer?"

"I don't know. Maybe. Could be some extremist tree-hugger who wants to save the world. Or they might want to make an example to put all the others in line."

"I never heard of a hippie going to such lengths to save the environment."

"Stranger things, ma'am. Stranger things."

He was right, of course. In her line of work, Emily had most certainly seen more bizarre things than what O'Rourke was suggesting. Unfortunately, that still left too many questions unanswered.

The agent seemed to read her mind. "The real problem you need to solve is; who will they hit next?"

Emily stood still for a moment. She realized she'd been biting the fingernail on her index finger and quickly dropped the hand to her side.

"We have to warn anyone who has been involved with the big oil companies."

"Yeah, probably, but how?"

She let out an exasperated breath. "I have no idea. The president isn't going to shut things down again. And even if he wanted to, there's too much happening in the political arena for everyone to take more days off. The next scheduled break for Congress isn't for another month."

"Lucky for you, I'm on your side."

"Oh?"

"While I was running the analysis of the votes and voters, I went ahead and put together a comprehensive list of everyone who's voted in favor of the oil companies the last four years. It's as current as I could make it, but it's a good starting point. If you wanted, you could reach out to every single one of those people and warn them. That way, you'd keep it out of the media and not cause a citywide panic in the capital."

"Do I ever tell you how much I appreciate having you at Axis?"

O'Rourke chuckled. "Not necessary, ma'am."

"Well, I do. Send me that list as soon as you can."

"I just did. Should be in your inbox within a minute."

"Thanks, O'Rourke. Good job."

"More than welcome, ma'am."

Emily ended the call and tapped on the mailbox icon on her phone's screen. It took less than ten seconds for the new message to appear. She scrolled through the list of names, recognizing several prominent political figures in the document.

"So many in the oil companies' pockets," she whispered to herself.

She was glad Axis headquarters was in Atlanta. At least there she was somewhat separated from the constant games going on in Washington—well, other than the fact that her boyfriend was the president. Now and then, that fact put her front and center with some of the things she longed to avoid. Just one more reason for her to be thankful his term would be ending in a couple of years.

"Director?" Smalley said, interrupting her thoughts.

She spun around and saw him and the others still huddled close to the scene, waiting for answers.

"I know that our responsibility is to find this killer," she said. "But we also have to find a way to protect the representatives until we can find whoever is behind this."

"We'd need to know who they're going to hit next. How we gonna do that?"

"I have a list," she said. "So far, everyone who has been murdered was a person who voted sympathetically for the oil companies. The three victims we have so far all voted the same way on bills that specifically benefitted Big Oil."

"Okay," Smalley took the bait. "Why would they go after the very people who were helping them?" He asked the same question she'd wondered just minutes before.

"We aren't sure that's who is behind all this. For now, we have to make certain that everyone on this list is protected. Each of you will take a section of names from the list and personally see to it that everyone is safe." Then a thought popped into her head. "While you're at it, see what you can find out from every person you see. Maybe we'll get lucky, and someone will have some answers."

Chapter 12

TULUM

"What's your status?"

The woman's voice sounded stressed, full of concern.

"And a cheerful good morning to you, too, Congresswoman Pike." Sean displayed the cheesiest grin he could muster just to annoy Tommy, who stood a few feet away in their hotel room.

After leaving the unconscious man in the cave by the beach, the two Americans had rushed back to their hotel, collected their things, and checked into another place in town. The move was pretty standard in a situation like the encounter with Sandoval. Odds were he had someone stationed at the hotel in case something happened.

When they left to find a new location, however, no one followed them—at least not that they could tell.

"Lilian," she corrected Sean for the formal use of her last name.

"Yes, Lilian. My mistake."

"Do you have an update for me, or are you just calling to say hello?"

He wasn't accustomed to dealing with someone like her: bossy, commanding, and straight to the point. Emily was like that in a way, but they'd been friends long enough that Sean didn't even notice anymore. He was also unaccustomed to being forced to report on the details of a mission. It had been years since Sean had to do anything remotely close to that.

"I do have an update, ma'am," he said. "We were able to find a set of strange markings along the coast underneath some ruins. Our research team back in Atlanta has been analyzing the information. We're confident we will be heading to the next location soon."

"Next location?"

"Yes. We knew it wouldn't be as simple as showing up to a Mexican tourist information center, knocking on the door, and asking for directions to the lost temple. Someone wanted to make sure this thing was never found again. The guy who left the diary had actually been there, and he still couldn't find his way back. All this is to say this could take some time."

"But you do have a lead?" Pike asked.

"Yes, we've got something. Should know more in an hour or so. I'll keep you updated as things progress."

"So, what you're telling me is that as of this moment, you have nothing." She didn't try to hide the irritation in her voice.

Tommy snickered in the corner.

"No, that's...no, we do have something. I just thought you'd like to know—"

"Sean, I am a very busy woman. While I appreciate your effort to keep me informed on the goings on with your mission, perhaps in the future you could only call when you have something important to share. Okay?"

"Yes, ma'am," Sean said with a hint of dejection in his voice.

"Good. Have a good day."

Before he could return the well-wishes, she ended the call, leaving him holding the phone to his ear. "Okay...you have a great day as well," he said, even though he knew she was gone.

Tommy shook his head. "I tried to tell you not to call her yet."

"She said she wanted updates. I gave her an update."

"Deep down, you're still a secret agent—always reporting to the higher-ups to make sure they know every little detail about what is going on."

"You don't know these political types like I do. They want to micromanage everything."

"Which is why you don't call them. And if they call you, don't answer unless you've got something really important to share."

Sean set his phone down on the desk and plopped onto the edge of the bed. "That's information I could have used ten minutes ago," he said.

Tommy took on an offended expression. "I tried to tell you not to call her. In fact, calls like that one are the reason I almost never take on a private job. I learned a long time ago that when someone makes a request for IAA to come in and try to recover or find something, that they understand we run our own ship. I don't tolerate that sort of thing."

Sean smirked, and his eyebrows pinched together. "I don't usually see this side of you, Schultzie."

Tommy looked surprised. "What do you mean?"

"I mean, usually you're just happy to help out or tag along or whatever. I'm not used to seeing you so adamant about something, so commanding."

Tommy cocked his head to the side for a second as he shrugged. "It took only one time to unfold like that for me to know I was never going to let it happen again. Hence, why you made the call instead of me."

"And you let me."

"Best way for you to learn."

Sean's shoulders shrugged as he laughed. "Thank you so much, sensei."

Tommy's phone started dancing on the desk, interrupting their conversation. He glanced at the screen then tapped the green button.

"Hey, guys. What's up?" He mouthed, "It's the kids," so Sean would know who was on the line.

Tommy turned toward the balcony door and shuffled over to it as he switched the device to his other ear.

"Well," Alex said on the other end, "we have a match on the new markings you two found—although it's kind of sketchy."

"Sketchy? What do you mean? Was the translation not clear?"

"No, it was clear. In fact, this one wasn't too difficult to decipher. The problem isn't the translation. It's the location where it says to go."

Tommy frowned as he stared out through the glass at the quiet little town. It was still early, and most of the citizens hadn't awoken yet. The tourists definitely hadn't, probably still sleeping off the tequila and beer they'd consumed the day and night before.

"What's wrong with the location?" Tommy asked.

Sean's ears perked up as he sat on the edge of the bed, trying to decode the conversation.

"It's in a bad area."

"Bad area? You mean like in a dangerous part of town?"

"No," Alex said. "I mean like a dangerous part of the jungle."

"Jungle? No big deal. We've been in dangerous jungles before."

Sean's renowned fear of heights was only one of his weaknesses. He also had a healthy fear of spiders and snakes as well, both of which Tommy shared. That hadn't stopped the two of them from venturing into some of the most untamed wilderness on the planet in search of historical relics.

"This isn't normal jungle I'm talking about, Tommy. Along with all the wildlife you'll have to avoid, there are other problems."

"Okay?" Tommy was anxiously waiting for Alex to get to the point, a point the younger man was clearly trying to avoid.

"That part of the jungle is swarming with cartel. It's one of the biggest havens for cocaine manufacturing, along with marijuana. That sector is the epicenter of the Mexican drug trade."

"I see." Tommy sounded despondent, which caused Sean to put out both hands with palms up, begging to know what was going on.

"I guess we'll have to be on our toes, then," Tommy said.

"That's not all," Alex cut back in. "There are also guerrillas in the area."

"Like big monkeys or like the kind who are trying to overthrow the government?"

"The latter, although there might be some monkeys, too. I wasn't really looking into that part."

"Guerrillas in Mexico?" Tommy turned around and looked at his friend.

Sean heard his friend ask the question, sat up straight, and gave a nod. He'd heard of the small roving bands that occupied small areas of the rain forest in Mexico. They weren't as prominent as in some of the other Central American countries, but they were equally dangerous if outsiders crossed their path.

"So...I don't suppose you can give us their exact coordinates so we can avoid their camps?" Tommy asked.

"Unfortunately, no."

Tommy was afraid Alex would say that.

"Their camps are well camouflaged to avoid satellite detection, as well as any aircraft that may fly over," Alex explained. "Not that it matters. A good chunk of the police force down there are on the take anyway."

Tommy knew Alex was right. Corruption had reached new heights in Mexico through the last few decades. The cartels wielded a power that even some of the highest-ranking politicians in the land feared. It made sense that the guerrillas were hiding out nearby. If the government wouldn't touch the cartels, they could blend in and operate in the shadows next door.

"Sounds like we're going to need to take some weapons."

"And then some," Alex said.

Tommy realized the conversation had diverted away from its original purpose. "Now that you've warned us, what is this place we're looking for?

"Oh right. I almost forgot. Sorry about that. The cipher said you're to go to a place called Cascada del Diablo. It says the devil's mouth speaks lies and truth."

"Devil's waterfall? Lies and truth?"

"Yep. No offense, but this whole mission sounds dangerous, even for you two."

Tommy thought hard for a minute. He didn't recall a place called

Devil's Falls, but that didn't mean anything. There were probably a thousand places in the Western Hemisphere he'd never heard of. That was part of the job.

"How do we get there?"

"I'm sending you a map now," Alex said. "It's due southwest of where you are in Tulum. You'll be able to take an SUV to the edge of the jungle, but you'll have to hike several miles in to reach the falls."

"How many is several?"

"As far as I can tell, the closest road is about fifteen miles out."

"Fifteen miles? We're going to hike fifteen miles through the jungle?"

Sean's eyebrows shot up in surprise.

"Yep," Alex said. "So, I suggest taking some supplies, you know... for camping, backpacking, stuff like that."

"Thanks. I get it. Just so we're clear here, there isn't a closer way to get to the falls? How do all those drug smugglers get their supplies out of the jungle?"

"I don't know. I guess they take unmarked roads or paths. Maybe they use donkeys or something. Look, even if you could find one of their roads, you don't want to go that way. It would take you straight into the lion's den."

Tommy fell silent for a moment as he considered the problem. They could get supplies. That wasn't the issue. He and Sean had faced considerable obstacles in the past. This one, however, carried an elevated level of danger.

"Okay," he said. "Anything else I need to know?"

"Not that I can think of. Just be careful. Who knows, you may get lucky and have a straight path to the falls."

Tommy knew better than to expect that. Things were never so easy.

"Okay, Alex. Thank you. And tell Tara thank you as well. We'll see what we can do."

"No problem. Just be careful. I really don't want to have to get a new job...you know, if you die."

Tommy chuckled at Alex's attempt at humor. "Thanks. I'll be in touch soon."

He ended the call and slid the phone into his pocket.

"What was that all about?" Sean asked. "I mean, I heard most of what you said."

"We're going to a place called Devil's Falls," Tommy said, shortening the literal English translation.

"Sounds exciting."

"Alex said there are guerrilla fighters in the area."

"I heard you say that."

"And the cartel occupies the forest there, too. He said there are cocaine and marijuana manufacturing camps all over the place."

Now things started to make sense in Sean's mind. "Oh I see." He thought for a second. "You said we have to hike fifteen miles into this place?"

"Yep."

"Which is why you were asking about an alternate route."

"Correct."

"We wouldn't want to do that anyway. We'd walk right into one of their camps."

"That's exactly what Alex said."

Sean scratched his scruffy blond hair and then folded his hands, resting his elbows on his knees as he leaned over and pondered the situation.

"Usually," he said, "drug smugglers operate close to an airstrip. They use any number of methods to get the drugs to the planes, but the planes are the key. If we can find that airstrip, maybe we can plot out a route that will keep us out of their way."

He stood abruptly and took a step over to the entertainment unit where his laptop was sitting. He grabbed the computer and flipped it open. His fingers flew across the keys. A moment later, he clicked on a map result in the search directory and zoomed in on the Yucatan.

"Where did he say this place is?"

"Due southwest of here."

Tommy's phone dinged and he pulled it out of his pocket. He turned the screen toward Sean so his friend could see the message.

Sean noted the coordinates on the phone and entered them into the computer. The map zoomed in to an exact spot on the map. The satellite image displayed a thick forest canopy, making it impossible to see anything on the ground.

He moved his finger along the mouse pad, dragging the map to search for anything that remotely looked like an airstrip, but found nothing. The only thing that stood out in the otherwise smothering forest was a thin strip of water just to the south. Almost unnoticeable, it appeared to be nothing more than a narrow creek.

"What's that?" Tommy asked. "A river?"

Sean narrowed his eyes and peered closely at the screen. He'd zoomed in as far as the image would allow. "Could be," Sean said. "Doesn't look very big, although the trees could be blocking out the riverbanks. Some smugglers do take their goods downstream via boat. It's possible there's an airstrip near the water somewhere. Unfortunately, I can't find anywhere on this map because I don't know where the river goes. It disappears after this little clearing here." He tapped on the screen to pinpoint the area.

"Based on the coordinates Alex gave us, that's close to the waterfall. Makes sense there's some kind of runoff or river or something."

"It's also a really good bet that the cartel camp is somewhere close by." Sean frowned. "The more I think about it, the more I think it's likely that they're using the water for transport. Even if it's not very deep, they could use canoes outfitted with small motors."

Tommy nodded. "I've seen those before on the Amazon." He paused for a moment. "So, I guess we need to get some gear."

"We have a few things, but we'll need a tent, sleeping bags, backpacks, the whole nine."

"And more ammo," Tommy said. "You know...just in case."

Sean took a long breath and sighed. "The bad news is if we run into a cartel camp out there, no amount of bullets will help us."

Chapter 13

WASHINGTON

Lilian shuffled through the last papers on her desk, collected them in both hands, and then tapped the end of the stack on the surface to get all the documents neatly in line.

It was already dark outside when she picked up her laptop bag and turned off the lights for the day.

She'd been working in the Capitol for several years now, and most of her days were as long as this one: waking at the crack of dawn and leaving long after the sun disappeared over the horizon to the west.

Her bodyguard, a middle-aged man named Mitch, was standing outside the door waiting for her as she stepped out into the long corridor leading to the exit.

"How was your day, Congresswoman Pike?" Mitch asked politely, as he always did as she left for the evening.

She gave her usual response, telling him it was fine and that she'd been productive. The truth was she'd stopped caring about the work long ago. Washington was beyond corrupt. She'd learned that long ago. Making a difference was almost impossible with the current structure. Being productive meant she was able to delay laws that she felt would not be in the best interest of the country, but it was rare she stopped anything. The few items she'd been able to get pushed through were so watered down they were almost as ineffective as not having them at all.

Her black skirt fluttered in the breeze as she strode down the hallway, her shoes clicking on the hard surface with every step.

Mitch's head was on a swivel. He and all the other personal security guys in Washington were on high alert after the three mysterious murders in recent days. Men just like him had been taken out along with the people they were protecting. While his sense of duty to guard the congresswoman was at the top of his list, he had no intentions of being killed on his watch.

He'd been in this business a long time, nearly twenty years after doing a short stint in the military. While it wasn't the same as being on the battlefield, it came with a more sinister threat: complacency.

The two passed through the metal detectors and out the doors into the muggy Washington night. Most of the other representatives had already left, returning to their homes for supper with their families. Lilian knew some of them were making pit stops on the way home to dabble with a few vices before making their way to the family hearth.

She winced at the thought.

She'd been a loyal wife and loving mother. As far as she knew, her husband had been the same way right up until the moment he took his own life.

And if she were being honest with herself, suicide seemed like the easy solution. There were plenty of nights when she wished she'd had the courage to put a bullet through her head. More than a few times—after a bottle of wine—she'd nearly done it.

Lilian recalled the occasions she'd actually put the pistol's muzzle against her chest and tensed her finger on the trigger. She could never go through with it, and there was a small part of her that regretted her weakness. She almost felt guilty because of it. No, she did feel guilty. It wasn't right that her son and her husband were both dead while she kept on living. She should be in the ground with them.

Something, though, deep down inside kept pushing her forward.

Was it her sense of purpose? Was it her calling? She didn't know. All Lilian Pike knew was that her role in government was becoming less and less effective and that the changes she'd hoped to make in the world were nothing but a distant memory.

She descended the steps of the Capitol and followed Mitch around the corner, beyond a row of small trees and bushes that lined the sidewalk on the way to the reserved parking area.

Once inside the back of the SUV, she leaned her head back and sighed, hoping the pain in her heart would flow out of her nostrils and mouth to leave her nothing but relief and peace.

Those two things never came.

Mitch fired up the engine and steered the vehicle out onto the street.

Lilian watched as the lights along the sidewalks whirred by, only slowing to a stop each time her driver came to an intersection. They passed late-night joggers and couples strolling along hand in hand. The couples laughed and smiled at each other, enjoying a happy evening walk.

Lilian remembered those days. Before they'd had their son, she and her husband had enjoyed many evening walks like that. She recalled taking her son to the park with her husband. They would run in the grass until they collapsed, and then they'd rolled around until their skin itched and their clothes were covered in dirt and grass stains.

Those days were gone. They'd been gone for a while. Sometimes she wondered if she'd ever shake the memories and be able to live a normal life.

Mitch turned through an intersection and onto the street leading to her townhouse.

She pressed her head against the window and stared blankly out into the night. She no longer noticed the details or the people. Everything became a blur up to the moment Mitch stopped the car in their usual parking space and shifted the transmission into park.

Lilian didn't move for a moment, mired in her thoughts of how things used to be. Mitch waited nearly a minute before he said anything.

"Congresswoman Pike? We're home."

Mitch knew all about her past. He'd been good to her, never asking too many questions and always willing to listen—not that she talked much about the tragedies. It was easier to keep everything locked inside, at least that's what she told herself.

She snapped out of her daze and opened the door. "Thank you, Mitch. I appreciate how much you take care of me."

"You're more than welcome, ma'am."

A black luxury sedan approached from the opposite direction. Both Mitch and Lilian eyed it with suspicion. Every politician in the city had been on edge because of the killings.

The sedan passed safely by, and Mitch surveyed the area to make sure everything was clear while Lilian retrieved her laptop bag from the seat. She slung it over her shoulder and walked around the SUV to where Mitch was waiting.

"I'll be out here until Scotty arrives to take over. If you need anything—"

"I know, Mitch. Just ask. You know, you always say the same thing to me every night you drop me off."

"And you never take me up on it." He let his stone face crack a frail smile.

She knew he wanted her. It was obvious from the way he acted, the overly chivalrous things he did, the way he looked at her. Had things been different, she may have done something about it. There were moments, times when she was lonely, when she felt like calling him into her home and wrapping his strong arms around her. That could never happen. She wouldn't allow it. Her feelings of loyalty to her dead husband and child always got in the way of fleeting passions.

"You know I can't, Mitch. Thank you for always taking care of me."

"It's my pleasure, Congresswoman Pike."

A shadow shifted from behind one of the cars across the street.

Mitch's smile vanished, and his hand moved in a blur to the holster inside his jacket. "Lilian! Get down!"

He pulled out his weapon and raised it like he'd done so many times in training. A loud pop echoed from the other side of the street. It was followed by several more.

The first rounds found Mitch's chest and abdomen. The third struck him in the shoulder. Another hit his leg, dropping him to his knees.

He squeezed the trigger, but his weapon wasn't close to being lined up with the target and the bullet pounded harmlessly into the townhome's brick wall. Mitch slumped over and raised his weapon again, desperately trying to get off one good shot at the shadow across the road.

The figure was gone.

Mitch searched the area, but he couldn't see the shooter. Blood oozed from his leg and shoulder. His vest had stopped the shots to his chest and gut, but the points of contact ached nearly as bad as where the bullets missed his armor.

Lilian watched in horror as her guard was shot over and over. Knowing there was nothing she could do to save him, she turned and ran down the sidewalk. She clutched her laptop bag and pumped her legs as hard as she could in heels. When she reached the corner, she risked a look back and saw the dark figure standing behind Mitch as he tried to crawl to the other side of the road where he thought the shooter was still hiding.

The shadow fired, sending the round through the back of Mitch's skull. His torso fell to the asphalt.

"Mitch!" Lilian screamed.

The killer's head turned toward her. Lilian's eyes went wide, and she knew she'd made a mistake by yelling. She veered left down the busy street, waving her free hand at every passing car.

"Help!" she yelled. "Please! Someone help!"

She saw a police car parked along the sidewalk on the other side of the road and kept screaming at the top of her lungs.

At first, the cop in the front seat didn't hear over the sound of traffic and whatever noises were going on inside his car. Then he saw the panicked congresswoman waving her arm and jumping up and down.

He immediately got out of the car and looked around then held up his right hand to slow traffic as he crossed the street.

"Help! Please help!" Lilian screamed once more.

The cop hurried across the street and skidded to a stop in front of her. His eyes scanned the sidewalk in both directions before addressing her directly.

"What's wrong, ma'am? Are you okay?"

She swallowed and thought for a second. Then she nodded. "I...I think so."

He looked down at her arm and grabbed it gently with his fingers. She followed his gaze and saw a trickle of blood coming out of her suit jacket. Her legs went weak, and she started to waver.

The cop wrapped his arm around her and lowered her to the sidewalk. Once she was securely on the ground, he pressed the button on his radio. He spoke fast, using a short code for the emergency and requested backup and an ambulance.

Most of what he said was a blur to Lilian. The world spun around in her eyes.

"Stay with me," the cop said. "You're going to be fine. It's not bad. Just a flesh would."

"They...they killed Mitch." It was all she could get out.

"Who's Mitch? Ma'am? Ma'am?" he said with a heightened sense of urgency. "Who is Mitch?"

"He's my...my bodyguard...my friend."

Her eyes closed, and the cop felt her body get instantly heavier in his arms as she went limp.

Sirens blared in the distance. It would be another thirty seconds before backup arrived. Not that it mattered. The assassin had already vanished.

Chapter 14

CHIAPAS, MEXICO

"I have never—not even in the hottest, most humid summer—experienced anything like this in the South," Tommy whispered amid panting for breath.

He stopped on the side of what passed for a trail and leaned against a tree, grabbing the water bottle out of his backpack for what must have been the tenth time that hour.

"Nope," Sean said as he gasped for air. "Makes things worse that we have to wear long pants and shirts. It's necessary unless you want to get eaten alive by the bugs out here."

"No doubt," Tommy said after taking a huge gulp from the bottle. "I bet there's stuff out here that really could eat you alive."

Sean didn't want to freak out his friend, but he knew that was exactly the case. Some of the wildlife in the Mexican rain forests was the stuff of legends. He was no biologist, but Sean had read and seen enough to know not to fool around with the local creatures.

Tommy stuffed the bottle back into his backpack and trudged ahead to catch up with Sean. Each carried sidearms on their hips and semiautomatic rifles slung over their shoulders. Getting the more powerful weapons had taken a bit of doing and a considerable financial investment, but Greg had been more than helpful and connected them with a local guy who took care of the rest.

They'd loaded up their packs with enough rounds to start a small war. The tent and other gear came from a local outfitter in Tulum. While it wasn't top-of-the-line camping equipment, it would do the job and definitely beat having no shelter. The last thing Sean wanted to do was have to build a lean-to of sticks and leaves out in the rain forest.

They marched on, using their machetes carefully and only when they needed to knock a stray branch out of the way. The entire time, their free hands remained on the rifle grips with a finger ready to squeeze the trigger at a moment's notice.

Most of the world's jungles were dangerous places. This one was near the top of the list. There were dozens of varieties of wildlife that could kill a human. Adding the cartel and guerrillas made it that much more inhospitable. Even the most alert, well-trained bushman could meet his end out here.

Something squawked high up in the canopy to the right, and both men spun in that direction. A second later, they let out a relieved exhale.

"Just a bird," Sean whispered. "Let's keep moving. We need to get to the falls before the sun goes down."

They pushed ahead for another thirty minutes until another short hydration break was needed. The men had brought enough water for the journey in, plus purification tablets and filters to refill their bottles when they reached the falls.

Sean stuffed his water back into the backpack once more and pulled a map out of the cargo pocket on his right pant leg. He unfolded the piece of paper and checked their position in relation to the dot he'd made on the map the night before.

"So, we are here," he said, tapping on the point he estimated they were standing. "That means we have...another four miles to go." He folded the map and shoved it back into his pocket. "Getting close, my friend." Sean's tone was irritatingly cheerful, but Tommy couldn't help but share a little of the joy that their journey was almost over—

for the moment. There was still the hike back they'd have to endure tomorrow. Neither was looking forward to that.

"We should be there way before sunset," Tommy said. "We've made good time. Glad I put in all that effort to get in shape. I probably couldn't have made it this far a few years ago."

Sean didn't add anything to his friend's comment other than to give a humoring nod.

"Off we go again," Sean said. "Keep your head on a swivel. The closer we get to the waterfall, the better chance we have of running into trouble."

"You think?"

"Yeah. That's where I'd be if I were them."

Tommy's fingers tensed on his rifle just to be safe.

They trudged forward for nearly an hour, moving as quickly as they could while remaining silent. At one point Sean noticed a snake dangling from one of the trees about a dozen feet off the path, but the serpent didn't bother them since they weren't going anywhere near it. More than a few times, Sean had to hack his way through huge spiderwebs—a task that sent goosebumps over his and Tommy's skin. The worst part about the spiderwebs was not finding the spiders. That always caused the instant assumption that the arachnids had found their way into the men's hair or clothing.

Nearing the end of the next hour, Sean stopped abruptly in the middle of the narrow path. He held up his hand for Tommy to halt and listened closely to the sounds of the jungle.

Tommy was tempted to ask why they were stopping, but he soon heard the reason.

It was a faint, distant sound, but distinct. There was no questioning what it could be.

"Waterfalls," Tommy whispered.

Sean nodded. "Not far now, Schultzie. Keep a lookout. We've been lucky so far. Last thing we want to do is run into some—"

A twig snapped in the leaves to their left, and both men spun to face the threat, their trigger fingers ready to unleash a volley of hot metal that would shred the enemy in seconds.

There was nothing in sight.

Sean frowned as he surveyed the area.

"You heard that, right?"

"Yep," Tommy said.

Sean took a wary step off the trail, sweeping his weapon around in a wide arc. Tommy narrowed his eyes as he peered into the forest, hoping to catch whatever made the noise and blast it.

Then he felt a hand wrap around his mouth while a pistol muzzle pressed hard into the side of his head. He wanted to make a sound to warn his friend, but all he could do was make a low moaning noise.

Someone in dirty, tattered clothing stepped by Tommy and rushed at Sean. The second attacker made a mistake and stepped on a stick lying near the path. The little piece of wood snapped loudly under the man's weight, and Sean spun around to find his friend being held hostage while another guy was charging his way.

Sean aimed his gun at the second man's chest and readied himself to pull the trigger.

"Put the gun down." The man holding Tommy spoke in perfect, albeit heavily accented English. His mouth and nose were covered with a ragged, stained strip of cloth. The skin that showed was darkly tanned, a lighter version of his deep brown eyes.

Sean didn't have a move. He could shoot the guy who'd frozen mid-attack, but then the man holding Tommy could easily end his friend's life. Then there was the matter of the other four men in the group, all who had weapons aimed at Sean.

With no options, Sean nodded and eased the rifle strap over his head and shoulder and dropped it on top of the weapon before standing up straight and putting his hands in the air.

"The pistol, too," the man in charge ordered.

Sean swallowed and did as told, removing his sidearm from its holster and placing it next to the rifle.

"And the machete."

Sean let out an annoyed sigh and tossed the blade on the ground. "Anything else?" he asked in a tone layered with irritation.

"Is there anything else I should know about?"

"I've got a crap load more ammo and a few explosives in the backpack."

"I appreciate your honesty. Set it on the ground as well." The man's Spanish accent was refined, smooth. He sounded like someone who'd been raised in an affluent home.

"What are you two doing out here?" he asked. "This is no place for a couple of gringos like yourselves."

Two of the other men disarmed Tommy and shoved him toward Sean.

"Sightseeing," Sean said. "We've been thinking of opening a zip line course out here through the canopy."

"It's a million-dollar idea," Tommy said. "You wanna invest?"

The leader chuckled. "You are funny, gringos. Very funny. I have to say, your response is both original and humorous."

Then he raised the pistol and pointed it at Tommy's face. "Now tell me why you're really here. Two heavily armed Americans in my jungle? My first guess is that you're with one of the drug enforcement agencies. The only problem is in my jungle you have no jurisdiction."

"We're not with any agency," Sean said. "Well, not technically. I mean, he runs an agency."

Tommy turned his head and scowled at his friend.

"Relax, Schultzie," Sean said. "These guys don't care what we're looking for."

The leader's curiosity was piqued. "Looking for?"

"It's nothing," Tommy insisted.

The man shook the gun, and Tommy instantly quieted down.

"We're archaeologists," Sean said. "We brought all these guns because we heard there are dangerous animals in the area, along with a band of rebels."

The man in charged cocked his head to the side and gave them a skeptical glare. "Do you really expect me to believe two archaeologists are carrying around automatic weapons, pistols, and explosives? You must think I'm stupid."

"No. No, sir. No one said you were stupid," Sean said. He did his best not to sound desperate.

"Then who are you, really? Are you working for one of the other cartels? If you're not with the American government or the Mexican government, that must be the answer, and if that's the answer...you're still going to die."

"Why would one of the cartels hire a couple of gringos like us?" Tommy asked. "Seriously? Is that something you guys do, bring in a few ringers from up north?"

The question momentarily stumped the leader. "No. That is not how things are usually done."

One of the other men stepped close to the head guy. He was shorter, at least by three or four inches, and had a wide bush hat on his head with dark camouflage paint on his face. He bent the leader's ear and whispered something.

A second later, a sinister grin crossed the leader's face as he spoke. "My associate here has a good idea for you two."

He turned and started barking orders in Spanish. Either he didn't realize the two Americans spoke the language, or he didn't care.

The rest of the men grabbed Sean and Tommy and started marching them down the slope toward the growing sound of the river. They didn't have to hike long before the camp came into view.

Sean noted the layout. He knew it would be his only chance to reconnoiter the vicinity before they were stuffed in a cage.

The tent city covered a broad area under the trees. All the canvas shelters were also covered with additional camouflage netting for protection against any aerial surveillance from their government or from Uncle Sam.

Most of the residential tents were on one side and circled a central area where there was another tent filled with tables, a large fire pit, and chairs. Sean immediately knew that was the makeshift mess hall where all the workers could eat.

Off to the left side of the camp were the processing tents. Dozens of people—women and men—were busily cutting cocaine, packing it tightly into cellophane wrapping or weighing the product. One of the other tents housed what looked like an old-school chemistry lab filled with Bunsen burners, glass bulbs, tubes, and an assortment of other equipment.

The workers—for the most part—were more diminutive than the men surrounding the processing stations. The cartel had a nasty reputation for rounding up illegal immigrants from Guatemala and forcing them into work camps like this one. The women—acquired via human trafficking—were typically used for carnal tasks unless they were older, like the ones scooping white powder onto the weighing scales. Whoever ran this camp had clearly continued the tradition of bringing in Guatemalans as slave labor.

"Any ideas how we're going to get out of this one?" Tommy asked as he and Sean were shoved forward toward a row of cages set in the mud between the residential tents and the big-top processing tents.

"Not yet. I'm working on it."

"Well, work faster. You heard what that guy said."

"Yeah, I heard him."

The leader had made no effort to disguise his ploy. Sean and Tommy were going to be held for ransom. For every week that passed without payment, one of their appendages would be cut off and sent back to the States.

Based on what was being said by the other men in the group, the clock was already ticking.

Chapter 15

WASHINGTON

The blurry light blinked in and out for a moment in Lilian's eyes. All she could hear was the sound of something beeping in a steady rhythm. She tried to move her head but found every muscle was sluggish. Her head slowly rolled over with some extra effort. She forced her eyes to stay open for a second and saw a couple of figures looming over her.

It was difficult to tell—at first—where she was. Then she noticed the surroundings: the wires, the bed, the room, the IV sticking into her arm. She was in a hospital.

Her eyes blinked faster until her vision cleared. Then she was able to focus on the tall brunette standing over her and the man to the right. Two cops stood on either side of the door just beyond the threshold.

"I'm in the hospital?" Lilian asked.

"Yes, Congresswoman Pike. You were shot. The wound isn't fatal. You were lucky."

Lilian looked around, still dazed from the drug-induced sleep. "Mitch. Where's my bodyguard, Mitch?"

The brunette woman did her best to look sympathetic. "Congresswoman Pike, your bodyguard was fatally shot in the back of the head by the killer."

Tears welled in Lilian's eyes. Her head tossed back and forth on the pillow as she tried in vain to fight off the flood of emotions rolling into her chest.

"No. No, that...that's impossible. Not Mitch. He was a good man."

"I know, Congresswoman Pike. I'm sorry for your loss, and I cannot convey my sympathies deeply enough. What I can do is try to find the person responsible for this."

Lilian tried to sit up, but the room spun around in her eyes and she collapsed back against the pillow.

The brunette reached out her hand and pressed it to Lilian's shoulder. "Congresswoman Pike, please, you need to rest. You've had a traumatic day. My name is Emily Starks. I'm leading the investigation to find the person who did this, the one we think is responsible for the recent murders and who shot you and your bodyguard."

More emotions washed over Lilian, and she coughed amid the stream of tears. "I know who you are, Miss Starks."

"Then you know I'll do whatever it takes to bring this killer to justice." She paused for a second before pushing her line of questioning. "You...you didn't happen to get a good look at the shooter, did you?"

Lilian took a long breath through her nose and exhaled slowly. She shook her head as she recalled the events of that tragic evening. "No. Everything happened so fast. Mitch...Mitch had just driven me home from the office. He was going to drop me off like he usually did. Only this time, there was someone waiting for us on the other side of the street. The shooter stuck to the shadows. I never saw their face. I didn't even see them shooting at me. I did the only thing I could think of. I ran down to the other end of the street where there were lots of cars going by. I guess I figured the killer wouldn't follow me to a busy road like that."

"That was good thinking," the man on the other side of the bed said. He wore a navy-blue windbreaker and button-up shirt with the top two buttons undone. "Like Director Starks said, you were really lucky. You're the first person to survive an encounter with this killer."

Lilian averted her gaze to the foot of the bed. She stared at it for a long moment before saying anything again. "I...I don't feel lucky," she said finally. "My friend Mitch is dead."

"I know, ma'am," the detective said. "I promise you, we are doing everything in our power to bring this person to justice."

Lilian sighed. "I know. I'm sorry I can't be of more help. I just didn't get a good look at them. If I hadn't run away—"

"You'd be dead right now, Congresswoman Pike," Emily interrupted. "You did the right thing. There was nothing you could have done to save Mitch. That killer is singling out members of Congress. We don't know why they targeted you, but we will find out."

Emily looked over at the detective and motioned with her head that they needed to leave. Then she turned her attention back to Lilian. "Get some rest, Congresswoman. Take it easy. You'll be safe here. We'll have around-the-clock security watching your room. No one is getting in here."

"Thank you," Lilian said. "I...I appreciate all you've done."

Emily gave a curt nod and then motioned again to the detective to head toward the door.

Once they were outside and beyond earshot, Emily turned and looked back at the two officers at the door.

"You vetted those guys, right?" she asked.

"Yes, ma'am. We were very thorough." The detective did his best not to sound condescending.

"Sorry, Smalley. You and your men are doing a good job."

Emily stopped at the end of the hall near the elevators and paused before pressing the down button.

Smalley appreciated the kind words. It was the first time he'd seen any sort of sensitivity from Emily. She'd been hard on him and his men since taking over the case. If he was honest, he'd have been the same way.

"You seem pensive," he said, noticing the blank stare in her eyes. "What's up?"

She reached out and pressed the button. "I don't like it."

"Like what?"

Emily watched the arrows over the doors as she waited. "How much do you know about Lilian Pike?" she asked.

Smalley rolled his shoulders. Keys jiggled in one of his pockets as he did so. "I know she lost her son and husband a few years back. Sad story. No way anyone will ever beat her in an election because of that." He noted the dubious expression on Emily's face and quickly made an addition to his comment. "Not that she would ever want that or use that to her advantage."

"No," Emily said just above a whisper. "That's not what bothers me."

"Oh?"

The bell dinged, signaling their ride had arrived. The silver doors opened and they stepped in. A few seconds later, the doors closed again, and they began their descent.

"No. How much do you know about her politics?" Emily asked, now speaking at a normal volume.

"Not much," Smalley said. "I've lived here so long, I stopped listening to the rhetoric years ago. That's all it is to me now. I don't even watch the news much anymore."

"You and I have that in common."

The elevator dinged, and the doors to the main floor opened.

They stepped out and walked briskly through the lobby toward the exit. Emily held her thoughts until they were outside in the cool morning air. A dense fog wrapped around the building, but the sun was already rising high over the horizon, doing its best to burn off the moisture.

"Why do you ask?" Smalley wondered.

"Because Lilian Pike is pretty much the polar opposite of the other victims. They were all allies for the big oil companies. She's a big proponent of environmental issues. One of her major things is green energy."

Smalley frowned. "That doesn't jive with our case."

"No. No, it doesn't. This throws a huge monkey wrench into everything."

"Maybe...maybe the killer did it to throw us off. You know, make us look the other way. If they knew we were zeroing in on their targets, that might be a plausible explanation."

Emily shook her head. "I considered that. It could be, but I doubt it. There has to be something else. We need to see if there's any connection between the other three victims and Congresswoman Pike."

"Still don't think it's a serial thing, huh? That whoever is behind this is just trying to take out as many politicians as they can?"

"No. Although this one does make me wonder. See what you can dig up about her voting history. I'm pretty sure you won't find anything, but we have to cover all our bases. See if you can track down campaign contributions, lobbying activity, all of it. I want to know as much about her as we can dig up. Who knows? Maybe we'll get lucky."

"I'll see what I can find, Director Starks."

"Thanks, Smalley."

They split up as they reached the parking lot, Smalley returning to his sedan and Emily to hers. She got in the car and looked down at her phone to check the time. Smalley wouldn't find anything in his search. She knew that much. It was a dead end, but every angle had to be examined.

The attack on Lilian Pike had thrown the entire investigation in the toilet. Emily was, effectively, going to have to start over from scratch.

Chapter 16
CHIAPAS

The late-afternoon sun sprayed a smattering of rays through the canopy above, throwing bright spots on the ground around the cage. Sean and Tommy didn't waste their energy begging for release. They knew that wouldn't change anything, and they needed to conserve energy since there was no telling when they'd get a chance to eat or drink again.

"Who is this guy?" Tommy asked as the two watched the busy camp through the makeshift bars.

Sean's eyes were level as he gazed into the processing area where the slaves continued their tedious labor.

"His name is Osvaldo Martinez," Sean said. "He's second in command for his brother's cartel."

"Okay, first of all, I was just kind of taking a shot in the dark there. I didn't actually expect you to know the guy's name. Second...how do you know the guy's name?" Tommy had to be careful not to shout the question.

Sean took a deep breath and exhaled. "I remember seeing something about him back when I was with Axis. He was much younger then. We both were. His brother, Tito, had just taken over one of the midlevel cartels here in Mexico. From the looks of things, they're not midlevel anymore. These guys are in the major leagues now. I'd say they've got at least a quarter million in blow alone. Figure in the weed they're moving, and this is a multi-multimillion-dollar operation."

Tommy didn't know what to say at first. He let the information set in.

"They're part of a growing problem in this country," Sean went on. "Most of the bigger cartels operate out of Guadalajara or Juarez. It's swelling to a breaking point between the decent citizens and the criminals. It's unfortunate."

"Unfortunate? Interesting choice of words. Because right now, I'd say we're the unfortunate ones."

"Maybe."

"Maybe? Um, we're in a cage, in the mud, in the middle of a Mexican rain forest, surrounded by drug smugglers and guerrillas."

Sean snorted. "To be fair, we haven't seen any of the rebels yet."

"Yet."

"Hey, I'm just trying to be half-full here."

"Well, while you're trying to look on the bright side of life, maybe you can come up with a plan to get us out of here."

Tommy stood up as tall as he could. His head nearly hit the top of the cage. The confines were just high enough for him to stretch his spine and he took a few steps to get the circulation back in his legs. His feet stuck in the mud with every step, and he finally gave up due to the strain.

"Relax. We're going to be fine."

"Fine? They're going to cut our heads off, Sean. Or worse."

"They're not going to do anything of the sort."

Tommy raised a skeptical eyebrow. "You sound pretty sure about that. Care to share why?"

"They're going to take us into that tent over there," Sean said, pointing at an army-green shelter on the far side of the camp. "They'll question us, maybe even torture us a little."

"I don't like the sound of that."

"I don't either, but they're not going to kill us. Especially if you tell them who you are."

"Me?" Tommy asked with wide eyes. "Why?"

"They can do a quick internet search for you and see we're not lying."

"What if they search for your name? I don't think they'll appreciate your previous line of work should that come up in the search results. Part B of the problem with your plan: How are they going to do an internet search out here in the middle of nowhere?"

"They have a rudimentary satellite link in the same tent where they'll do the questioning."

"How in the wide, *Wide World of Sports* do you know that?"

Sean chuckled at the reference. "I noticed it on the way in. There's a small dish in the back of the tent. I could see it from the slopes up there." He motioned to the hill with a toss of his head. "It isn't much, but it does the trick and is still probably faster than dial-up."

"Is there anything else you noticed on the way in? Maybe an omelet bar?"

Sean snorted. "No, no omelet bar. But I did see where they put our gear."

"Same green tent?"

"Actually, no. It's in the—"

"Gentlemen," a familiar voice cut Sean off, and the two prisoners looked to the right.

Osvaldo Martinez was stalking toward them like a hunter who'd just snared some big game.

"I'm so sorry to interrupt, but we need to conduct some business."

Four men were following close behind Martinez. They carried a hodgepodge of automatic weapons slung over their shoulders.

"Taking us in for questioning?" Sean asked. He already knew the answer.

"Very astute of you. Yes. We'll be conducting our interview over in that green tent on the other side of camp."

Tommy cast a sidelong glance at his friend, wondering how he could have possibly known that.

Sean didn't return the look, instead staring straight ahead at Martinez.

"We already told you everything you need to know," Sean said. "You know...you could dispense with torturing us for answers and just do a quick search online for my friend here. You'll discover everything we said is true. He runs an archaeological agency in Atlanta. Once you do that, you'll know we aren't lying, and you can let us go free."

Martinez laughed from the bottom of his belly. He put his hands on his hips and leaned back, looking up at the trees as he enjoyed the moment. Then the laughter died, and he peered deep into Sean's eyes.

"Do you think that's why I'm keeping you? Because you might be with one of our government agencies? I'm not keeping you for that. You're here because the two of you are worth a hefty price. Based on what you just told me, I'd wager I can get even more than I originally thought."

"If you think anyone's going to pay for my head, you're gravely mistaken," Sean said. "No one wants me."

Martinez cocked his head back, gazing at Sean over his bottom eyelids. He was clearly sizing up the American to see if there was an ounce of truth in what he said. Not that it mattered. Martinez had no intention of letting the two Americans go. If he couldn't sell them, he'd just shoot them and toss their bodies in the river.

"Just because no one wants you doesn't mean we shouldn't try, eh?" Martinez said.

"Eh? What are you, Canadian now?" Tommy joked.

The smuggler clearly didn't understand the joke, so he ignored it. "I have to admit, the two of you have courage. We'll see how much courage you have once we begin cutting off your fingers, legs, and arms and sending them back to your loved ones. Or you could be honest with me and tell me what you're doing here, and maybe I don't cut off anything."

"I already told you," Tommy started to explain.

Sean cut him off. "We're looking for an ancient treasure. There. Happy?"

Martinez looked skeptical. "Treasure? What kind of treasure?"

Tommy shook his head. "Don't tell this buffoon about the treasure, Sean. We've worked too hard to give up and let an idiot like him take it."

The smuggler did his best to look offended. He tilted his head to the side and stared at Tommy with curiosity. "You know, Tommy, it's rude to say things like that to your host. I gave you two my best cage, and this is how you repay my generosity?"

"I'd hate to see what the worst cage looks like," Tommy muttered.

"Ignore him," Sean interrupted again. "Yes, we are here looking for a treasure. Okay? Do a quick internet search on him. You'll see that's what we do all the time. We travel the world and hunt down lost treasures. It's kind of our thing."

"Is this true?" Martinez asked Tommy, who stood against the side of the cage with his arms crossed.

Tommy sighed. "Yes. Okay? You happy, Sean? Now he knows why we're here."

Sean's eyes were fixed on a tent thirty yards away. He'd been watching it the entire time since being put in the cage. He pulled his gaze from the tent and put it squarely on Martinez.

"You mean in general or with our current situation?" Sean asked in his best smart-aleck tone.

Tommy spun around and threw a right hook. His fist smashed into Sean's jaw and knocked him to the muddy ground. Sean winced and sat there for a moment in disbelief. He rubbed his cheek to ease the pain as he stared at Tommy with confusion in his eyes.

"What was that for?" Sean asked.

"You've ruined everything! Now this guy is going to get the treasure, moron!" Tommy jerked a thumb at Martinez, who stood on the other side of the cage bars with a dumbfounded look on his face. "You always do this, Sean. You always take things so lightly. Well, I hope you're happy! Because we're going to die out here, and he's going to get the treasure we worked so hard to find."

"This treasure," Martinez interrupted. "Where is it? Perhaps you tell me, and we work out a deal. What do you say?"

Tommy's eyes narrowed. "What kind of deal?"

"Let's just say if this treasure is worth it, maybe I can let you two live."

Tommy didn't like the way the smuggler said it, but he was in no position to bargain. Or was he?

"Let us out of here, and we'll show you where it is."

Martinez laughed hard. "We both know that you are in no position to bargain."

Tommy snorted.

"What's so funny?"

"What you just said. Those were the exact words in my mind."

Sean had pulled himself off the ground and leaned against one of the bars. "Good luck, Tommy. You can count me out. I can't believe you hit me—and for no reason."

"I'll do it again if you don't shut up. I'm tired of it, Sean. All our lives, you've been the class clown, never taking anything seriously. You'd better get back on the ground or I'll *put* you back on the ground."

Sean had never heard his friend sound so menacing, so serious. He slunk back toward the back of the cage, putting both hands up in the air in surrender.

"Fine, Martinez. We'll cooperate. But I want a cut of the treasure."

The smuggler's eyebrows shot up. "A cut? You're lucky I don't cut you right now. You'll get nothing, except perhaps, your freedom...or at least a chance to earn it."

Tommy didn't like the way the guy said that last part, but he didn't have a choice. "Fine. We'll show you the way to the treasure in the morning. No way we can find it now that it's getting dark."

"Very well. I'll allow you two to sleep here in the cage tonight to work out your problems." He fired a disgusted look at Sean. "I wonder, are you always such whiny little baby?"

Sean said nothing and slumped down onto a dry patch of ground with arms crossed.

"We leave at dawn tomorrow morning. How far away is this place?" Martinez asked.

"Not far," Tommy said. "We're close to it right now." He hoped they hadn't looked over the maps in their gear bags, although he doubted they'd be able to pinpoint the exact location of the next clue.

"Good. Because if I start to sense you two are leading me off course as part of some crazy escape plan, your torture will be far worse than anything you've ever imagined."

Martinez turned and walked off toward the fire in the center of the camp. Tommy watched until the guy was out of earshot and sitting next to some of his men before speaking.

"You think he bought it?" Tommy asked.

"I'd hope so," Sean said as he shuffled back to the front of the cage near where Tommy stood. "You actually hit me kind of hard."

Tommy grinned. "I had to make it look real."

"Yeah, but you didn't have to make it look *that* real. And what was all that you were saying about me being reckless? You didn't have to embellish that much."

"Who said I was embellishing?" Tommy spun around and sauntered to the back of the cage.

Sean chuckled, still rubbing his jaw.

"So, let me get this straight," Tommy said. "We're going to lead Martinez to the waterfall, blow up the camp, and take out his men? Sound about right?"

"Yep. That's the plan."

"And you're sure that when you set off the explosives that you're not going to hurt our gear?"

"Our guns are in that tent over there," Sean pointed to a tent to the left of the campfire. "They took our explosives over to that tent." He pointed to another structure on the opposite side of the camp.

Tommy shook his head. "How do you know all that?"

"I pay attention," Sean said. "And I feel like we've had this talk already. While they were bringing us in, I watched what they did with our bags. I knew they initially took them into the first tent I showed you, but then I saw a guy emerge with the ordnance I brought. They probably want to keep that stuff separate in case there's an accident."

"An accident we're going to help happen."

"Exactly."

Chapter 17

ATLANTA

Erika Forsberg watched through the tinted window of her sports coupe. She'd been staking out IAA headquarters for several hours, waiting for everyone to leave the building before making her way inside.

She knew there would probably be two occupants in the building until late into the night. Based on the intel provided by her employer, a young woman and young man were typically there early in the morning and stayed to almost midnight. They were primarily researchers, which wouldn't be a problem.

She'd managed to kill three congressmen along with a few security guards as well. The task would have been a challenge for some assassins. Erika, however, was no ordinary killer-for-hire.

After dedicating four years of her life to climbing the ladder at Interpol, she realized she'd never achieve her ambitions. She was passed over for promotions and raises. She'd even succumbed to sleeping with one of her bosses after hard work and dedication to the job didn't do the trick.

Still, nothing.

In fact, the man respected her even less after the night of less-than-stellar passion.

So, after four long years, she put in her notice and branched out on her own as a freelancer. It didn't take long for Erika to find work on the other side of the law. It started out as contract security jobs for some of Europe's biggest criminals. Then the slippery slope led to her first paid killing.

The guy she murdered wasn't a good person, which made it easier. In some ways, that's how Erika justified it. It wasn't like she was killing children or blowing up churches. The people she eliminated were dirty. If they needed to be removed from the earth, she had no problem getting paid for the job.

Thanks to both her skills and her ruthlessness, her reputation grew in the criminal underworld. There were whispers in the shadows about the woman who could get into any building, bypass any security system to eliminate her targets.

When her current employer discovered her, Erika was a little surprised by the offer.

One hundred thousand dollars, just to hear the proposal. If she decided not to take the job, Erika could still keep the money.

There'd been initial suspicions, certainly. After all, when something sounded too good to be true....

But Erika was no fool. She also wasn't stupid enough to turn down a hundred grand. Those kinds of gigs only came around every so often. When they did, her end goal, which was sitting on a beach somewhere with a margarita and zero responsibilities, grew rapidly closer.

Her goals were lofty, although they were getting closer with every job she pulled. Only a few more and she'd drop off the map for good.

Erika's time in Interpol had taught her every trick in the book. She knew how to navigate police at every level, what security strategies were most common, and how to get around some of the best security systems in the world. Thieves would pay a fortune to get inside her brain.

Her secrets, however, would remain hers.

The last lights in the IAA building went dark, and a couple of minutes later a man in a blue polo walked out the main entrance.

"That's the last of them," she said to herself.

Erika waited until the man disappeared around the corner to where he'd parked his car before she turned her attention to the black case in the passenger seat. Her fingers made quick work of the latches, and she flipped open the lid to reveal twin 9mm pistols, four magazines, and an extra box of shells.

With only two potential targets—both of whom were likely unarmed—Erika doubted she'd need so much ammunition, but it was always better to have too much than not enough, especially if it didn't weigh her down.

She slid the weapons into their holsters, shoved the spare magazines into two slots on the back of her belt, and grabbed a pair of sunglasses from the console. When the eyewear was resting on her nose, she pressed a tiny button on the side that activated an augmented reality system.

The two lenses displayed the layout of the IAA building. She'd done the research ahead of time in order to program the lenses and make it easier to navigate through the many corridors and rooms.

Her main objective was illuminated by a bright red dot against the blue grid of the building's framework. Based on her analysis, the target was in the belly of the building, hidden deep in a vault on the second basement floor.

Initially, Erika had been shocked at the level of security this archaeological agency possessed. After reading a little deeper into what they did, she understood. The second basement level was where the more dangerous artifacts were kept. Things that displayed unexplainable tendencies were put there behind walls of three-foot-thick concrete.

She assumed such measures were taken because of fear of radiation, though there was no way to confirm that suspicion. She dismissed the notion, figuring there wouldn't be anything of that nature in the building.

Erika walked around to the back of the car and opened the trunk. Inside was a black gear bag that she slung over one shoulder.

Loaded up and ready to go, she slammed the trunk shut and strode down the sidewalk.

On the other side of the street, people loitered by the fence that wrapped Centennial Olympic Park. Others were inside walking around, hand in hand, enjoying the peaceful evening.

Erika didn't pay any attention to them, and she knew the lack of care was reciprocated.

Once she was around the back of the building, she found the rear exit and switched off the augmented lenses. Two cameras—mounted high on the corner wall—were honed in on the back door. She set the gear bag down on the ground next to a stack of pallets. After unzipping it, she pulled out a small device that looked much like a cell phone. This unit wasn't made for texting or making phone calls, though. It was designed for one purpose: hacking security systems.

She had several in her possession, but this one served a specific purpose. She could plug into security camera feeds and automatically loop the displayed images as long as the device was within a certain radius.

Erika glanced over her shoulder at the pallets and then stuffed the jamming unit through one of the wooden grooves so no one would see it.

From here, the device would send a signal through the external cameras and into the monitors in the security room, thus making it look like things were normal.

The feed spread like a virus, hijacking every camera in the building.

Once more, her years at Interpol proved to be useful. She'd learned more about security systems than nearly anyone else on the payroll. While that knowledge never translated into more rewards for her at the agency, it was paying huge dividends for her now.

The red bar at the bottom of the device screen turned green, signaling that the camera feeds had been successfully altered.

She reached into her bag of tricks, as she liked to call it, and pulled out a black box. There was a seam in the middle of it that divided the thing into halves. She pulled the halves apart, revealing two metal rods in the center attached to two miniature clamps.

Erika took a step back and surveyed the rear wall until she found what she was looking for. A box painted to look the same as the building's exterior was situated flush against the wall on the far corner. Two matching tubes protruded from it and plunged into the concrete.

Erika hurried over to the small box. She was wary enough to consider that the exterior wall unit might also be hooked up to some kind of alarm. She carefully slid a knife tip under one of the seams and lifted it a millimeter or two. Nothing happened. Satisfied the box itself wasn't rigged to trigger an alarm, she removed a set of bolt cutters from the bag and snapped the padlock keeping the panel shut. The lock clanked on the concrete and she dropped the tool back into the bag.

Inside the box was a mess of wires and two blinking lights. It was a system she'd seen before despite how new it was. Erika made it her business to stay in the know when any new tech hit the market, especially in the security industry. She found the two wires she needed and pulled them out, stripped the coating from the copper inside, and pinched the clamps from her black box against the wiring.

She waited for a second to make sure the alarm didn't go off, but she knew it wouldn't. That little box could easily sell for $50,000 in the criminal underground, but then she wouldn't have an edge when it came to bypassing an alarm system.

With a sense of urgency, she rushed back to where she'd left her bag and pulled out something that looked like a string of Play-Doh. Erika pressed the odd string against the door, making a half circle that encompassed the lock and latch. Then she stuck a detonator into the center of the clay-like substance and moved back around the corner.

She took another device out of her bag and knelt down on one knee. She pressed her back against the wall and mashed the lone button on the device. There was a low popping sound, a fizzle, and then a cloud of acrid smoke wafted by her. A heavy clunk came from the back door, signaling that her explosive had done its job.

Erika set the box back in the bag and stepped around the corner. More smoke drifted by her. There was a hole in the door, precisely where she'd placed her compound. The door had swung open slightly.

"Too easy," she whispered.

She slung the bag over her shoulder and rushed into the building, pulling the door closed on her way in.

Inside, she scanned the dark room for a moment before switching on the augmented lenses once more. The red target was down below, in the middle of the building's second basement.

From the looks of it, she was in some kind of delivery and holding room. Huge stacks of boxes were arranged across the floor. She assumed they contained artifacts that had been brought to the building for research or to be put on display in the small museum.

Erika put a wedge under the bottom of the door to make sure it stayed closed and then hurried across the room. If a security guard came through the place, he might not see the hole where the door's lock used to be but would almost certainly notice a door swinging wide open.

She pushed through the next doorway into a long corridor and ran ahead until she reached a pair of elevators. One had a single massive door that split in the middle and opened up to a big freight lift. The other was for people. She had no intention of taking either.

Just down the hall next to another door was an entrance into the stairwell. She pushed through the door and stopped just on the other side, letting the door close softly behind her.

A set of stairs went up to the right. To her left, a doorway with a card reader and a keypad led to a set of steps that descended into the bowels of the building. She reached into her tight black tank top and produced an ID card. She scanned the bar through the slider and then entered an access code when the little LED screen prompted her.

A second later, a green light appeared, and the door clicked in three places. She pushed through and paused on the other side to let the door close before continuing.

Getting the ID card had been easy enough. Disguised as a courier, she'd delivered a package to one of the logistics guys in the building. A little coffee spilled onto his pants and the guy jumped up in a panic, making it easy for her to steal his card, replace it with a fake, and get out of the facility without him ever knowing what happened.

The access code was somewhat more difficult, but she'd planned ahead for that as well.

When the guy jumped up from the scalding hot coffee, Erika knew he'd have to run to the restroom to clean up the mess. She'd told the guy she'd wait until he finished cleaning himself before getting his signature.

The unwitting victim had no idea he'd just inadvertently given access to his computer to one of the most dangerous women in the world.

She watched until the guy disappeared around the hallway corner before sliding into his seat and pulling up the access codes for everyone in the building. His name was easy enough to find. Once she had it, the numbers for the code seared into her memory, and she returned the screen to where he'd left it.

Erika pulled her weapons out of their holsters and made sure a round was chambered in each. Then she began the descent into the depths of IAA headquarters.

She passed the door for basement level one and kept moving. While she wondered what might be on that floor, she knew the goal was farther down. With every step she took, the red target in the middle of her lenses drew closer and the angle to it shallower.

The staircase ended on a concrete landing, and she faced another doorway. This one didn't have any additional security measures, which she found to be odd. Then again, if the people who ran the place believed the previous door was enough, why would they install additional measures?

She pulled the door open and stuck her head into the room. Long bright lights flashed to life on the ceiling high above. For a second, she thought someone might be inside, but she realized the lights were on an automated system, probably designed to save energy when someone left the room.

Erika snaked her way through the door and into the huge space on the other side. The room was like a small warehouse. The ceiling stretched up to nearly twenty feet high and the far wall was at least 120 feet away. Unlike the cardboard boxes she'd seen upstairs, this room was filled with glass cases, each containing priceless artifacts from all over the world.

She walked by the first row of cases and stopped in the middle of the room. She reached up, switched off her lenses, and placed the glasses in her gear bag. There, on the far wall, was an upright, narrow case with a glass cube at the top. Inside it, the relic glowed with a bizarre light.

Erika had been told the object produced a strange glow, but she didn't believe it, at least until now.

She walked by more cases, mesmerized by the artifact. When she reached it, she slid the bag down to the floor and stood up straight, staring at the object inside its protective display.

When her employer requested that she steal this item, her boss hadn't given her any details regarding the relic, only what it was and where to get it. When Erika learned the artifact's name, finding information on it had been easy enough, though no one seemed to understand its true power. That was part of the reason it was stored at IAA headquarters, to undergo further investigation.

Erika reached out and touched the glass, partly out of admiration and partly to test her override systems. Nothing happened, and she clenched her jaw, ready to finish the last part of the mission.

She dipped into her bag once more and retrieved a device with two suction cups and a spinning diamond blade attached to a metal disc. It looked like a high-tech pizza cutter, but this tool could cut through almost any glass in the world.

She started to attach the unit to the display case when she heard a voice from the stairwell.

Immediately, a frown crossed her face. She stuffed the cutting tool back into her bag and yanked it up off the ground as she ducked behind a long, wide display case to her right.

A second after she dropped from sight, the door swung open, and two people walked in.

Erika couldn't see their faces, but she heard their voices.

"Why are the lights on?" a man said.

"No idea," said his female counterpart. "Don't they normally shut off when nobody's here?"

"Supposed to."

Erika deftly bear crawled over to the other end of her hiding place, holding one of her pistols in her right hand. She peeked over the top edge and saw the agency's primary researchers standing in the doorway with confused looks on their faces.

She lined up her weapon's sights with the guy, putting the right side of his face squarely in the middle. From this distance, sidearms could be inaccurate. Erika, however, could shoot a fly off a horse's back from that range with a stable base.

Her finger tensed on the trigger, ready to put a round through Alex's head.

Chapter 18

CHIAPAS

"You know," Martinez shouted, "I think patience is overrated!"

Sean and Tommy roused from troubled sleep. Sean was leaning against the bars in one corner of the cage while Tommy had slumped to the ground and was resting his head on his forearm.

Sean blinked slowly, trying to adjust to the blinding flashlights Martinez's men were shining into their miniature prison.

"What are you going on about?" Sean grumbled. "Can't you see we're trying to get some sleep in here?"

"Yeah," Tommy agreed. "And can we get some new pillows in here? This is worse than that hotel in Mumbai a few years ago."

"I'm glad to see you two are in your usual humorous form despite the fact that you're both my prisoners," Martinez said.

"Well, you know us," Sean said. "Always looking to please."

"That's good, amigo. Because we aren't waiting until morning for you to show me this treasure. We're going tonight."

Sean and Tommy exchanged frowns.

"Tonight?" Tommy asked. "What's the problem, Osvaldo? Couldn't sleep?"

"Like a child on Christmas morning," Martinez said.

"Oh that's right. You guys celebrate Christmas, too," Sean cut in again. "What's it like around the holidays at the old cartel stronghold? Do you guys sit around singing Christmas carols and exchanging presents?"

"Hey, what did you get Julio?" Tommy said with a chuckle. "Oh nice. A kilo of blow! Awesome!"

Martinez ignored their little play-for-two and motioned to one of his men standing close by. The guy stepped forward with a ring of keys befitting a bank manager and fumbled through them until he found the right one. A second later, the cage door swung open and the man stepped back, resuming his position near the boss.

"Please," Martinez said, motioning with one hand. "Lead the way."

Sean hesitated, thinking for a second that maybe they were being duped. Then he reminded himself that being inside the cage wasn't any safer.

He stepped out, stretched his arms, and kicked his legs out a few times to get the blood going.

"Sorry," he said, "foot's asleep."

Tommy followed him out into the open and waited with arms crossed.

"Would you mind giving us a couple of those flashlights?" Sean asked. "It's awfully dark out here."

"My men will light your path," Martinez said as he brandished a pistol. He pointed the gun at Sean's face. "Move."

"I need my map," Sean said without flinching. "It's in my gear bag, back in that tent over there." He pointed to the canvas shelter across camp.

Martinez kept a stoic expression on his face, never taking his eyes off the prisoner. "Diego," he said to one of his men. A diminutive guy with an automatic rifle slung over his shoulder stepped up immediately. "Run and fetch their map," he said in Spanish.

"It's in my rucksack you guys took earlier," Sean said.

Diego frowned, not understanding. He spun around and took off at a jog. Sean watched until the man disappeared into the tent and then returned his attention to Martinez.

"We need the map," he said and rolled his shoulders.

Diego reappeared from the tent, holding the map in one hand. He hurried back across the camp and presented the rolled-up piece of paper to his employer. Martinez clutched it with a firm fist for a second before handing it over to Sean.

"Thank you," Sean said and snatched the map.

He unrolled it with Tommy looking over his shoulder. Martinez shifted his position so he could also see what the two Americans were examining.

"We're going to a place called Devil's Falls," Tommy said so Martinez could hear.

"It's right here," Sean said, tapping on a place on the map.

"I know where the waterfall is," Martinez said, irritated. "You could have just asked."

"Yeah, I figured, but I really like this map," Sean quipped.

Martinez didn't seem amused. "The waterfall is this way, just over the next ridge." He turned and issued orders to the men hovering around. "Watch these two very closely," he said. "I don't want them trying to do something stupid."

The group started marching into the darkness with two armed men in the lead, followed closely by the two Americans and then five more guys, including Martinez.

"The joke's on him," Tommy whispered into Sean's ear as they trudged forward. "We do stupid all the time."

Sean gave a nod. "Yep, and it's about to get even stupider."

Tommy glanced over his shoulder at the two guards behind them. They didn't speak a lick of English. "So...you gonna let me in on this plan of yours?"

"No. I think I'm just going to let it play out while you watch."

"I already know part of the plan; at least I think I do."

"Just keep in mind it's fluid. Things can change. And then there's always the possibility that we don't find what we're looking for at these falls."

"Believe me, I've already considered that."

"Good," Sean said, keeping his eyes forward. "Because if that happens, they may kill us right there."

Tommy swallowed and kept moving.

Once the procession was out of the camp, their speed slowed as they climbed the nearest hill. The narrow path wound its way up the slope from left to right to make the grade less steep, but it also made the walk a little longer. As the group got closer to the top, the sound of the waterfall grew louder. By the time everyone reached the top, they were all breathing a little heavier, and the sound of the water crashing into the little river was the only thing they could hear.

A hole opened in the canopy above the waterfall and allowed moonlight to fill the immediate area, bathing the pool and churning white foam in its pale glow.

Tommy stared out at the scene. "I wonder why they call it Devil's Falls."

Sean peered through the darkness at the illuminated waterfall. "I suspect it has to do with those two rocks at the top looking like horns. And if you look close enough, the rock formation the water pours over looks like a skull."

Tommy leaned forward and narrowed his eyes to get better focus. "Oh yeah. You're right. I can see that."

"Shut up, both of you," Martinez rumbled from the back of the line. "You're here. Now what?"

"I can't believe we were this close," Tommy muttered. "It's right in their camp's backyard."

"I said silence!"

Tommy slowly spun around and faced the cartel leader. "And you also asked what we're supposed to do next. So, it's kind of a catch-22, telling us to shut up and also asking what our next move is supposed to be."

Martinez raised his weapon and aimed the barrel straight at Tommy's right eye. "The treasure. Where is it?"

Sean stared at the map and recalled discussing the solution to the cipher with Alex. He'd said that inside the devil's mouth there were lies and truths. Sean raised his head and looked at the waterfall. He traced the skull outline on the rocks and found what he believed would be considered the eyes, which were really nothing more than a couple of symmetric recessions in the upper part of the rock face. Below that, he couldn't see anything that resembled a mouth, but that didn't mean it wasn't there.

"We'll need to get closer," Sean said. "It should be down there." He pointed at a spot next to where the white water poured into the pool.

Martinez looked skeptical, but he gave a nod to the men in front to keep moving.

The convoy continued down the other side of the ridge, winding their way down the path until they reached the bottom where the narrow river lapped against the shore. There was no way up to the rocks from where they were standing, which meant they would have to cross the stream. It was only thirty feet across at most, but it was difficult to tell how deep the water was. On top of that, there could be anything lurking in the murky darkness.

Sean surveyed the area, looking for some kind of a way across that didn't involve climbing to the top of the waterfall. He found what he was looking for downstream where a series of rocks jutted out all the way to the other side.

"Looks like we can cross over there," he said, pointing at the makeshift bridge.

"Cross?" Martinez asked. "I don't think so. Why don't you tell us where the treasure is, and we'll go check for you?"

Sean rolled his eyes. "Because, Osvaldo, we are probably going into some hidden chamber or something where there will be booby traps and ancient symbols you have to decipher. So, unless you want to end up crushed under a giant boulder falling from the ceiling—or pierced with ancient blow darts dipped in a neurotoxin—I'd suggest letting us take the lead on this one."

Sure, he embellished a little, but there was no sense in leaving room for doubt in Martinez's mind. The more he believed he needed the Americans, the better.

"Fine," Martinez relented. "Let them cross, but keep an eye on them." He turned to Sean and Tommy. "If you try anything foolish, they will cut you down like grass."

"Like grass?" Tommy asked. "That's your big threat? Or was that supposed to be a metaphor?"

Martinez wasn't amused. "Move, before I change my mind and order my men to kill you right here."

"Fair enough."

Sean led the way down the riverbank until they reached the place where the narrow row of rocks stretched across the water. If he didn't know better, he'd have said those stones had been deliberately placed there a long time ago.

He and Tommy paused for a moment, eyeing the rocks suspiciously. Then Sean stepped down the steep embankment and pressed his boot onto the first stone. He tested his weight and, happy it seemed stable, took a step over to the next rock. When he was several steps away, Martinez sent one of his other men behind Sean and then ordered Tommy to go; that way they could keep a closer eye on the men as they crossed the river.

The going was slow and methodical. While the water certainly wasn't cold, the best-case scenario was that they'd end up with wet socks and boots for the remainder of the venture. Worst-case scenario was they'd fall in the water and get eaten by something.

Sean didn't notice any predators lurking about, but that didn't mean they weren't there. This part of the world was swarming with things that could kill a human in minutes.

Halfway across the river, one of the men behind Tommy slipped on wet rock and his boot plunged into the water. The sound caused everyone in front of him to look back. The man clumsily lost his footing in the river as well and fell backward onto his rear, splashing in the water loudly once more.

His arms flailed like he was being attacked by something, but the reality was he was just trying to get out of the water as fast as he could. The guy behind him reached out a hand and helped his comrade back to his feet. Before they knew it, the soaking-wet gunman was carefully crossing the rocks once again.

Sean reached the other side and waited on a narrow path cut into the side of the slope. As the others arrived, he moved upstream to make room for everyone until all the others had made it and were ready to proceed.

"Okay if we head toward the falls, boss?" Sean asked, his tone slathered in sarcasm.

Martinez gave a single nod, either ignoring the way Sean asked or simply missing it altogether.

"Point the light this way," Sean said to the guy behind him.

The gunman didn't speak English, but he knew what Sean was asking and pointed his flashlight along the path leading to the falls. Sean kept a close eye on the ground as he moved toward the falls. When he noticed something in the corner of his eye, he didn't twitch his head that direction. Instead, he shifted his eyes to the left and moved his head so slightly that no one behind him would notice.

There it was again.

Something was moving in the forest on the other side of the river. It was too dark to tell what it was. He glanced back down at the path and then again where he noticed the movement. Nothing.

Whatever it was, it either went into hiding or it was doing something more sinister: hunting.

Chapter 19
ATLANTA

Erika squeezed the trigger a little tighter, ready to put a round through Alex's head when the young man suddenly shifted his position. He reached into his pocket and pulled out a phone, looked at the screen, and then answered.

He stepped back out into the stairwell, leaving Tara alone in the big storage room.

Erika let out an irritated sigh and switched her aim to the young woman by the door. Killing Tara first or Alex first didn't matter. They were both going to die.

The door popped open again, and Alex beckoned her to come with him.

The two disappeared into the stairwell, leaving Erika by herself with all the display cases.

When the door clicked, she stood up from her hiding spot, keeping her weapon still pointed at the entrance just in case the two decided to come back.

She moved backward until she reached the end of the long case she'd been using for cover and shifted to her right. Satisfied the two young researchers weren't coming back anytime soon, she turned her attention to the tall vertical case holding the artifact she'd been sent to steal.

The lights in the ceiling above abruptly switched off, plunging the intruder into near-pitch darkness. The only light in the room that remained was the strange glow from the artifact and from tiny points along the wall. She knew what those were.

Lasers. The two meddlers must have reset the system. That meant she'd have to deal with the beams to get out. She pushed aside the fury raging in her head and focused on the solution.

She stood perfectly still in the darkness, taking inventory of as many of the dots as possible. Then she bent down and pulled out another device from her bag. She pressed a button on the side of the little metal box and set it on the floor.

An instant later, smoke started spewing out of both ends, filling the lower part of the storage room with a billowy white fog. Red beams appeared in the smoke, making it much easier to identify where to move and what areas to avoid.

Unfortunately, the case she'd targeted was surrounded by laser beams. "I do enjoy a challenge from time to time," she whispered to herself.

Deftly, she raised one foot high and stepped over a beam. Again and again, she twisted and contorted her body until she'd reached the back of the vertical display case. She pulled the cutting tool out of the bag again and attached the suction cups to the glass.

Funny, she thought, *that the lasers meant to protect the treasures in this room are giving me the light to see what I'm doing.*

Not that she needed them. Erika had an assortment of lights on hand from glow sticks to flashlights to flares. Working in the dark was better with the lasers, though, because light had the tendency to drown out the beams. The last thing she needed was to trigger the security system. She guessed the room was equipped with a setup that sucked the oxygen out if there was a fire or other emergency. If she triggered that kind of alarm, she'd be dead in no time.

She'd seen systems just like this one. It would take at least three minutes to unlock the door and override the alarm. Holding her breath wasn't one of Erika's strengths. She could make it a minute, ninety seconds tops. Then she'd be done for.

Erika took another glance over toward the entrance and listened. Still no sign of the young researchers.

She flipped a switch and then pressed a button to start the cutter. It took almost a minute for the hole to be punched through the glass. When the device finished, Erika pulled it off and carefully placed the piece flat on the floor.

Staring into the glass box, she tilted her head to the side. Just as she suspected from her intel: The artifact was resting in a metal stand atop a pressure-sensitive base. If she snatched the relic now, all the alarms she considered before would be set off. Of all the steps she'd taken thus far, this one was going to the most difficult.

She reached into the bag and pulled out her last two tools. They were both gray boxes the size of a television remote. Each had a narrow calculator-like display on the top with three buttons beneath. On the end of each was a pair of metal clamps.

Before staking out the building, Erika had done as much searching as she could for information about this artifact. One of the publicly released tidbits was the size and weight of the thing.

Knowing the exact weight was crucial. The pressure system IAA had in place was accurate to within one gram. With the information in hand, she'd purchased a custom-weighted piece of lead to use for the heist.

She fished a tiny cotton pouch from her bag. She poured the weights into her palm and then slid the hooks she'd attached before through one of the clamps. Few things made Erika nervous, but as she reached the first device into the glass case, she could feel her heart pounding in her chest. One mistake, and she'd be dead.

With the other hand, she inserted the second device into the case and centered the clamps around the artifact. Using her thumb, she pressed the button on the left, and the clamps started gradually closing. This move was going to be tight. If she so much as nicked the relic and altered the weight distribution in any way, the alarm system would be activated.

She focused on her breathing, keeping it in a smooth, even rhythm. Her hands remained steady, almost perfectly still, while the clamps wrapped around the artifact. After what seemed like an hour, the mechanism stopped. The metal pinchers were securely gripping the object. Now came the hardest part.

Erika pressed the center button on the other device with her thumb, and the LED screen turned on, displaying the weight of the lead attached to the clamp. She let out a breath and touched the platform with the weight, careful to make certain the digital scale on the LED screen didn't change. Let one gram go too quickly, and the sensors inside the platform would trigger the alarm.

She watched the narrow display as the first milligrams started to tick away. As they did, she lifted the device with the artifact ever so gently to make sure the milligrams she was losing on one screen were matched by the other.

The task was half art, half science. She'd practiced the tactic in her hotel room, but time had been limited. This real-life run at it required total focus.

Each minute crept by like sap oozing from a maple tree. Her arms ached from being frozen in the same position. Even though the weight at the end of each device wasn't substantial, keeping her arms out like that started to take its toll. Her muscles screamed to move and stretch, but she couldn't. One twitch in the wrong direction, and it would be curtains.

Sweat rolled off her forehead as the readouts neared their goal. Her breath came quicker from fighting the muscles in her arms and shoulders. A bead of perspiration trickled into her right eye, stinging like a burning needle. She winced and noticed the scales went slightly off balance. Erika corrected the mistake immediately.

Her head trembled, and it was all she could do to keep her hands from doing the same.

Finally, after what seemed like an eternity, the device on the left hit the number she was looking for. A split second after that, the one on the right matched it. She carefully slid the counterweight off the clamp, leaving it sitting upright on the base within the glass box.

Then she raised the other hand so the artifact would clear the lip of its metal stand and then pulled it out through the opening.

Her arms and shoulders rejoiced at finally being able to resume normal circulation.

Erika let out a breath of relief as she placed the two devices in her bag, along with the artifact. She closed the bag and slung it over her shoulder, securing it tightly against her back so it wouldn't swing round too much and damage the item.

She gazed out at the array of laser beams between her and the exit.

One leg after the other, she stepped over the low beams and ducked under the high ones. Her body twisted and contorted to avoid cutting through one of the red lights. Fifteen feet from the door, a stabbing pain shot through her left calf. She grimaced in agony as the muscle bound up.

The bag slipped off her shoulder and nearly dropped through a laser on its way to the floor. Erika reacted immediately, though, and whipped her left hand out in time to catch it on the interior of her elbow.

She jerked the arm up and adjusted the strap on her shoulder to keep the bag from slipping again.

That was close, Erika thought.

She stepped over the last few beams of light and reached her hand out to the door. Her hand pressed against the bar, and the door opened, letting in the fluorescent glow from the stairwell. The lights above flickered on again, and the lasers automatically shut down.

Erika waited for a moment to make sure the alarm didn't go off. She glanced around the room, checking for any signs that's she'd triggered something, but the area remained silent.

She let out a weary sigh and stepped into the stairwell. Suddenly, a painfully loud siren started blaring just over her head on the wall.

"Really?" she said out loud.

Even as her feet flew up the stairs, taking them two at a time, she recalled what must have gone wrong for the alarm to go off. It didn't take her long to come up with an answer.

The system reset itself after the two researchers returned to the main floor. That, or they reset it manually when they left. Not that it mattered. The fact of the matter was that the alarm was going off, and soon the entire building would probably go into lockdown, not to mention the cops that would be showing up in the next few minutes.

Erika reached the first basement floor in under ten seconds. Her legs burned as she arrived at the next level another ten seconds later. She barged through the door and rushed into the next corridor just as Tara and Alex reappeared at the other end. They frowned and pointed her way, realizing what had caused the system to go off.

She didn't wait around for introductions. Erika turned to her left and sprinted down the hallway away from the two young people standing in her way. There had to be another way to get back to her initial point of entry. Although maybe that wasn't necessary. Any security personnel remaining in the building would be on their way to the underground storage bunker.

If she could get to the front door before the police arrived, she could escape to her vehicle and disappear into the night.

It would be close, but as she dashed through the passage it became clear that going out the back way wasn't going to be an option.

Erika hung a left at the next corridor intersection and ran by a series of offices, two bathrooms, a water fountain, and a breakroom.

A hulking security guard unwittingly stepped out in front her just as she was about to round another corner. She ran into his brawny chest and bounced off, knocking herself a step backward.

The man reached for his weapon, but her reactions were quicker. Erika snapped her right foot up in a quick kicking motion and smacked his hand away from the holster. He reached for the radio with his other hand, but she jumped up, pressed a foot against the wall to gain elevation, and then swung the same foot around in a wide arch. The base of her shin struck him in the side of the head.

She dropped to the floor, landing on her feet as the stunned guard toppled over backward with a huge thud. His stunned eyes stared lifelessly up at the ceiling. She jumped over the body and kept moving. No reason to take the time to see if he was dead or just unconscious. The guy was out of the way, and that's all that mattered for now.

Erika pushed ahead, sprinting toward the next door she knew led into the lobby. She burst through and found herself standing in an atrium. The black marble tiles and matching support columns made the room seem even darker than it already was. The receptionist desk to her right was empty, as was the waiting area.

She trotted over to the glass doors leading outside and started to push the handle when she halted. Her hand rested on the bar as she gazed out at the street. *Were those sirens?*

Erika winced in anger. Then she looked out at one of the buildings on a perpendicular street and knew the cops would be there in less than a minute. She looked out at her car on the opposite street and knew if she made a run for it right now, she'd probably not make it. Her calculations could be incorrect, but the sirens grew louder.

What to do now?

She spun around and surveyed the area. *Elevator.* No one would expect her to go deeper into the building. She could hide out until the authorities left. Maybe there was a way to get into the ventilation system It might be a long night, but it was better than being caught.

No. No way she could hide herself like that. Sooner or later, they'd figure out that she was still in the building.

"Freeze!" a woman shouted from the other end of the lobby.

Erika swallowed and put her hands out by her sides, slowly raising them. She cursed herself. Hesitation always resulted in bad things. She knew better, yet she'd hesitated with her escape. Now she was caught.

"Turn around, very slowly," the other woman ordered.

Erika shuffled her feet inch by inch until she'd spun all the way around and was facing the speaker.

Tara stood on the other side of the big room with a pistol in her hand, pointing it straight at Erika's chest.

Erika processed the situation immediately. Tara was still far enough away to make a miss highly probable. She didn't know anything about the other woman's marksmanship, but it was difficult for most people to be accurate from that range.

Tara took a step closer.

Erika leaned back ever so slightly and felt her backside touch the bar on the door. She stared into Tara's eyes, sizing her up to see if she had what it took to shoot someone.

"Stay right there," Tara ordered. "Alex? Got her in the lobby!"

There was no response. "Alex?!"

The corner of Erika's mouth creased. She pushed her butt against the bar and fell back.

The door opened behind Erika's weight and she tumbled through as Tara opened fire.

Rolling backward for a second, Erika went head over heels into the warm evening air. Bullets smacked into the door's glass but didn't puncture it.

"Bulletproof glass," she said to herself.

The sirens grew louder, and she instantly realized she'd gone from the pot into the fire.

Blue lights flashed everywhere. The cops would have the place surrounded in no time.

No more hesitation. She pumped her legs hard, running for her car off to the left. She was twenty feet from her vehicle when more gunshots erupted. There was too much space between her and Tara now. Even so, rounds pinged off the asphalt and plunked into the other cars nearby.

She skidded to a stop as the first squad car rounded the corner and turned into the parking area in front of the building.

Erika deftly slung the bag over her shoulder as she opened the sedan's door and slid inside. The engine revved to life, and Erika stole a quick look through the windshield.

Tara was standing in front of the building with her hands up and the pistol at her feet. Erika shook her head and cracked a devilish smile.

She pulled out of the parking space and did a U-turn, heading in the opposite direction.

No sooner had she steered the car onto another street and left IAA headquarters out of sight than two more squad cars pulled in behind her with their blue lights flashing brightly.

Escape, it seemed, wasn't going to be as easy as she hoped.

Chapter 20

CHIAPAS

Cool mist poured over the men as they shuffled their feet sideways toward the back of the waterfall. Their clothes had gotten soaked in no time.

"Reminds me of Australia," Tommy said as he inched his way to the left with one of the guards just in front of him. "Remember?"

"How could I forget?" Sean asked.

Flashlight beams played off the water in the pool below their feet. Occasional stray beams flashed across the face of the white foam falling from above.

The crashing sound of the waterfall was overwhelming and only grew louder with every step.

Martinez yelled something from his position on the wall, three men down, but the Americans couldn't hear him over the noise.

They kept moving, an inch or two at a time with their heels hanging over the narrow ledge, their hands pressed firmly against the wet rock wall. Tommy's nose nearly rubbed the stone as he moved. None of the men wanted to fall in the water even though they were already wet.

Falling would delay things, and moving across the shelf was slow and methodical. But no one wanted to start over, and considering

Martinez's trigger-happy posse, they might not get a do-over if Sean or Tommy fell.

The first guard disappeared behind the falling white water. Tommy followed and found the narrow edge and saw it turned into a wide landing with a shallow cavity cut into the rock. The next guard arrived, and then Sean stepped into the little alcove. He rubbed a hand through his hair and shook off the water.

The ground was wet, but most of the mist billowed out away from the rocks.

Martinez and the rest of his men made it onto the landing and stopped for a second to look around.

"Where is it?" Martinez asked the second he was on secure footing. He searched the shallow alcove, but there was nothing of interest.

"Looks like you two gringos lied to me," he said, raising his weapon and pointing it straight at Sean's forehead. "Maybe I won't ransom you two after all. I think killing you might give me more satisfaction after you wasted my time this evening."

"You can do that," Sean said. "Honestly, I'd appreciate it if you did. I'm getting a little tired of your attitude and your lack of patience."

Martinez barely shook his head, gazing at Sean in disbelief. "There's no treasure. So, either you lied, or you're too late. Either way, there's nothing here." He lowered his weapon and pointed it at Sean's foot. "Maybe I just take off one of your toes as punishment."

"Up there," Tommy interrupted. He didn't know if Martinez was really going to blow off Sean's toe or not, but he figured it was as good a time as any to let the drug smuggler know their mission wasn't over yet.

"What?" Martinez asked. Then he followed Tommy's eyes up the rock wall to a place where there was another indentation in the stone. Above that one were two smaller cavities.

"This is just the chin of the skull," Tommy explained. "The eyes and mouth are up there. The riddle said the next clue is in the mouth of the Devil's Falls. If there's anything to be found in this place, it's up there."

Martinez eyed the rocks carefully. It would be a dangerous climb, and only a few men could manage it at once. From his initial assessment, he picked out two routes with enough ledges and grips for a person to scale the wall. The stone, however, was wet and would definitely be slippery. He turned to the two men standing closest to him and ordered them to go up to the next opening.

The men obeyed, slung their weapons behind their backs, and began the ascent. Martinez had picked the two skinniest guys, but from the way they scaled the wall it might have been because they had climbing experience. The two easily made it up to the opening in less than four minutes.

Sean and Tommy were impressed but wondered what the smuggler was trying to do.

The two men disappeared inside the mouth of the cavity. They were gone for a few minutes, their lights dancing around on the outer edge of the entrance or waving across the falling water now and then.

They reappeared, motioning excitedly for the others to come up.

Martinez wasn't so sure just yet. "What did you find?" he yelled in Spanish.

"Markings," the one on the left said. "Strange markings. We don't know what it means."

"Another cipher," Sean whispered, more to himself than anyone else.

Martinez turned to the Americans with a scowl on his face. "What is that supposed to mean? Markings? Do you know what they're talking about?"

Tommy shook his head slowly. "No, but if you let us up there, we might be able to figure it out."

"You said there was a treasure here. You said this was the place." The drug smuggler waved his gun around recklessly at the prisoners. "You know what I think?"

"Good hygiene is overrated?" Sean said with a smirk that begged to be slapped off his face.

Martinez ignored the barb, possibly because he didn't understand the context. "I think you two are trying to stall for time. Maybe you believe someone is going to come rescue you or come to take us out. I have news for you, amigo. No one is coming. No one is going to stop us. So, tell me where the treasure is or I start shooting."

Sean didn't have to think long about what to say. "Let us go up there," he said. "If those markings are anything like the ones that led us here, it would mean we're really close. The treasure could be anywhere around here, even down in that water." He motioned to the natural pool under the falls.

The other men standing around all looked down into the water, their eyes filled with curiosity. Even though they didn't speak English, they picked up enough to get the gist.

The drug smuggler wasn't stupid. He had the look of someone who'd grown up in a tough situation, possibly even on the streets. Even if he hadn't, the streets had probably taught him a few things, and getting into the cartel game only further enhanced his experience. There'd be no fooling him.

"I asked you two if the treasure was here, and you said yes."

"To be fair, there's no way we could have known that for sure," Tommy said. "I mean, if we knew exactly where it was then we'd probably have retrieved it already."

"That or you're lying." Martinez pointed his weapon at Tommy's right knee.

"Take it easy," Sean said. "We're not lying. Let us go up there and read what's engraved on the rocks. We might be able to figure it out—and if we do, there will be more money and power than you've ever imagined."

Sean was speaking to the guy's desires now. These types were almost always the same. They wanted to live like kings. The cartel money was great, but the power and respect that came with being in charge was what really motivated Martinez.

"I have money. And power." Martinez turned to his men and then back to the Americans. "If I didn't know better I'd say you two are leading me into a trap or some kind of ambush."

"How in the world would we be setting you up for an ambush?" Tommy asked. "You took all our gear. We haven't been in contact with anyone. And if you had enough money and power, why would you have come out here with us in the first place?"

He made a good point, one with which Martinez couldn't argue.

"Come up there with us," Sean said. "Climb to the skull's mouth, and we'll show you."

The man thought about it for another minute before making his decision. "Fine," he relented. Then he looked at the other men around him. "Keep your weapons on them. If one of them even so much as slips, shoot him in the back."

"That's a little extreme," Sean commented. "Okay for me to start climbing now?" Martinez gave a slow nod and moved over to the right where the other man had gone up the rocks.

He stuffed his pistol back in the holster and reached up to the first ledge. Sean also started up, cautiously pulling himself higher as he scaled the wall. Just above fifteen feet high, he stopped looking back down at the onlookers and focused exclusively on the next grip and foothold. A slip from here would either get him shot or break some major bones. Neither sounded like a good idea.

Sean reached the top ledge a few seconds before his captor and slapped his hand onto the moist landing, relieved to be done with the tiring work. The two men at the top rushed over to help pull up their boss, leaving Sean to scramble over the lip on his own.

He stood up and moved away from the edge, the old fear of heights doing its best to make him dizzy.

He looked into the recess but couldn't see what the men had found since it was nearly pitch dark.

"You!" Martinez yelled down at Tommy once he was safely above. "Climb!"

The other men below jabbed Tommy with their rifles, urging him to hurry.

"Fine. Take it easy." Tommy put both hands in the air as he stepped to the wall.

Tommy had no trouble making the climb. His workout routine included lots of pull-ups, rowing, and several other back and arm exercises that made doing something like this a breeze.

It hadn't always been that way. Tommy had to overcome some personal challenges to get into shape, but he'd done it in an amazingly short period of time and was now able to endure almost any physical challenge.

Sean stuck out a hand to help his friend over the lip and hoisted Tommy up to the landing.

Tommy slapped his pants and then looked around the half room cut into the rock.

The two guards were shining their lights into the back, pointing at something in the corner.

"It's back there?" Sean asked in Spanish.

One of the men looked at his boss and then nodded.

"May we?"

Martinez gave a nod and then motioned for his men to keep a close watch on the Americans. As the other four made their way back to the rear of the little cave, Martinez stole a quick glance over the edge at his men below to make sure they were still in position. Seeing them standing there looking up at him, he acknowledged them with a short wave and then hurried to catch up to the others.

The dome-shaped cavern only went back about thirty feet, maybe a little more. Centuries ago, it may have been used as a shelter by some of the locals, although with so much mist floating in from the falls it would have been difficult to keep things dry.

The men had to bend down a little to keep from hitting their heads on the back of the cave. Sean tilted his head to the side and looked up at the rock where the guards were shining their lights.

Martinez and his men were distracted, so Sean took a second to put his hand in his pocket to make sure the remote detonator was still there. He felt the smooth metal device and then took his hand out again so as not to raise suspicion.

He looked up again at the bizarre symbols on the wall. They were the same style as the ones they'd found before.

"I need one of you to take a picture with your phone," Tommy said.

Martinez looked at him like he was crazy. "What?"

"You guys have cell phones down here, right? I mean, I doubt you have coverage, but surely you have the devices."

The drug smuggler's scowl remained in place like a permanently irritated statue. Then he reached into his pocket and fished out a cell phone.

"What picture would you like me to take?" Martinez asked.

"Just have your men shine the light on these carvings and take a few pictures."

"Why am I doing this?"

"When we get back to the camp, we'll need to analyze them and make sure we understand where to go next." Tommy lied, but he did it in an extremely convincing way.

Martinez sighed and relented. He took several quick photos and then shoved the phone back into his pocket.

Sean noted that the guy didn't lock his device.

"Now what? You two going to find another way to waste my time?"

"No," Sean said. "It will be easier to make notes and analyze these writings with our gear back in the camp."

Martinez motioned for the Americans to head back to the edge. The two guards followed close behind. When they got to the lip of the landing, the leader looked down over the ledge to where his men had been standing just a few minutes before.

His face instantly twisted with a frown. The men were gone.

Chapter 21

ATLANTA

Erika knew she had to get out of the city. Downtown would be on lockdown within minutes. All the narrow streets and corridors would be closed off, and the cops would squeeze her in like a boa constrictor.

She stepped on the gas and accelerated up over a hill toward the city's center. Peachtree Street would be the most open, the best option, but there would also be the risk of regular traffic there, even at this hour of the night. Her best bet would be to make a break for the interstate, though that came with its own set of problems.

Once there, she'd have no way of getting off until she ran out of gas or found an exit that wasn't blocked by the police. The latter would be unlikely since the cops would radio ahead to every exit and have a blockade in place for just such a maneuver.

Right on cue, she reached a line of stopped cars filling all the lanes running north on Peachtree Street toward Buckhead. She cut the wheel to the right and turned onto 14th going east.

The car zoomed down the hill. Old businesses and abandoned buildings whirred by. A few pedestrians stared in wonder at the speeding sedan and the squad cars pursuing it.

Erika glanced back in her mirror at the flashing blue lights. Up ahead, she saw the reflection of similar lights bouncing off the brick buildings on a perpendicular side street.

"Reinforcements," she muttered.

In a few seconds, the cops would pull into the intersection ahead, effectively blocking off her escape. She noticed a gravel parking lot to the right. Without knowing anything about the lot, she immediately guessed there had to be another way in and out.

Erika took the chance and pulled the emergency brake while she spun the steering wheel to the right. The car fishtailed expertly into the parking lot entrance. She corrected the steering easily and accelerated into the dusty gravel lot while one of the squad cars behind her slammed on the brakes and missed the turn. The other car's driver saw her maneuver and was able to slow down in time.

She'd already increased the gap between her vehicle and the cops, but that could change in a hurry, especially since they had radios. She jammed the gas pedal and sent gravel and dust shooting out behind her.

The lot was filled with old school buses, fire trucks, electric company vans, and decommissioned government vehicles that had been retired long ago.

Erika jerked the wheel to the right and slid her car between two US Postal Service Jeeps. She stepped on the gas again and surged through on the other side as the cop behind her had to slam on the brakes, back up, and hurry to try to make up ground.

A quick turn of the wheel and Erika was heading toward the back of the lot again. She stole a glance in the rearview mirror. She could see more blue lights reflecting off the buildings and old vehicles behind her.

The squad car reappeared, now farther behind. She reached the end of the row of vehicles and turned the wheel sharply to the left. This time, she shot by the last car in the row and rocketed across the aisle toward a series of rows. The lot was larger than she'd anticipated, covering several acres of junked vehicles. The place was a labyrinth—a huge maze of metal, rubber, and glass. Dust plumed into the air behind Erika's car as she kept racing toward a hill on the other side.

The lot was in a sort of basin, surrounded on three sides by a ridge that wrapped around the property all the way to the main entrance. A chain-link fence protected the property with barbwire pointing out over it. Unfortunately, there wasn't another exit as she'd initially believed and the hill was slightly too steep for her to hit it head on. The front bumper of her car would dig straight into the dirt and grass, and her little escape would come to a sudden and painful halt.

Two more cop cars appeared in the rearview mirror, joining the first pursuer. Then she had an idea. She couldn't hit the hill directly, but it was sloped just enough that if she steered onto it at the right angle, she could drive up it.

It was her only hope—that or try to lose the cops in the maze. That could only work for so long until they blocked off every possible turn. It wouldn't take them much time to figure out she was trapped. Then it would become a waiting game.

She flipped the wheel to the right. Gravel spat out from the back wheels amid more dust clouds. The back end swung one way and then the other before she expertly corrected the steering again.

Erika kept her foot on the gas as she veered the car toward the steep embankment. If she'd missed her guess, her getaway was going to end much sooner than she planned.

The left wheel hit the hill. She gunned it through the gradual curve until both left-side wheels were on the grass. The car was tilted at a sharp angle to the side. Then she felt the right side wheels leave the gravel. Instinctively, she leaned her body to the left, as if that would keep the car from flipping over on its side.

Up ahead, the end of the parking lot approached rapidly. If she was going to get out, she'd have to make her move now or crash violently into the oncoming embankment.

She grimaced as she turned the wheel sharper to the left. The car shook and bumped along the dirt, but it kept going up, higher and higher toward the fence along the top.

Behind her, the first cop tried to follow behind and hit the hill at too steep an angle. His front-right quarter panel dug into the dirt and brought his pursuit to an immediate and horrific stop. His car's momentum lifted the trunk off the ground for a second before it slammed back to the ground in cloud of dust and smoke.

The driver of the squad car directly behind him crashed into the back of the first, unable to react fast enough to avoid the collision.

The third cop veered around the other two but was rapidly running out of space. He deftly steered his vehicle onto the grass and stayed in the chase, climbing at a steeper angle than Erika's car.

She took one quick glance back and saw the cop coming after her along with three others blocking the main exit down below.

Erika smirked. She wouldn't be going out that way, and there were no other cops in sight, not yet at least.

Gravity pulled at her vehicle, doing its best to pull her off course so she would smash into the hill to her right, but she held the sedan true and reached the top just in time. The sedan left the ground and took flight, sailing into the middle of the fence and crashing through it. Her head jostled back and forth as the car landed on the asphalt of the upper street. The front bumper scraped asphalt but hung on as she stepped on the accelerator and steered the car onto a dark street leading to the east side of town.

The last cop behind her struggled against the steep hillside, desperately trying to get his car to climb. His angle was too sharp, though, and as the vehicle lost momentum, the back wheels started spinning uselessly on the dirt and grass. Before he knew it, he was sliding backward down the slope to the bottom.

Erika wasn't out of the woods yet.

Sirens sounded in the distance above her engine's groan. Blue lights flashed down the corridor of abandoned warehouses and buildings to the right. It was time to ditch her car and pick up another ride.

At the next intersection, she pulled on the hand brake and whipped the car down the street to the left. An old knitting mill on the right and a warehouse on the left were surrounded by chain-link

fencing that had seen better days. Many of the bricks on both buildings were covered in graffiti.

There. On the left, the warehouse gate was open. A rusty chain
hung from one side, broken long ago by intruders or simply by time
wearing it down.

She jerked the wheel and steered the car into the parking lot,
guiding it toward the loading area where 18-wheelers used to load
and unload cargo. A ramp off to one side ended in an opening that
looked just big enough to fit her vehicle.

Blue lights continued splashing on other buildings to the right
and left as the cops kept up their search for the thief.

Erika's foot touched the floorboard as she gave the car all it could
handle. She raced across the lot toward the warehouse door, only
letting off when the front wheels hit the ramp.

The car bounced hard, and the bumper took another hit, this
time nearly coming free. She kept the sedan straight, though, and it
zoomed up the ramp and through the rubber flaps that blocked the
entrance.

Inside, she slammed on the brakes. The tires squealed on the
slick concrete floor. Her eyes went wide. A forklift that had been
sitting there for decades was right in front of her, the huge forks
pointed directly at the windshield.

She pumped the brakes harder, desperate to keep the sharp steel
from taking off her head.

The car lurched forward, but the brakes stayed engaged, yanking
the sedan to a stop mere inches before the forks touched the windshield glass.

Erika let out a sigh of relief and then switched off the engine.
Cops would certainly see light coming from an abandoned warehouse. The last thing she needed to do was to make it easy for them
by drawing attention to herself.

She got out of the car and grabbed her gear bag. She took a quick
look inside to make sure the amulet was still there. The bizarre glow
escaped through the zipper, telling her it was still intact.

After zipping it closed again, Erika slung the bag over her

shoulder and strode toward the ramp she'd come up just a few moments before. She pulled back one of the rubber curtains and peeked out into the night.

Sirens were blaring all around. A squad car raced by with its blue lights flashing wildly. The cop kept driving up to the next street and then turned right. She'd made it to the warehouse in the nick of time.

Erika stepped out of the warehouse and jumped down from the platform. She kept close to the building, sticking to the shadows in case another patrol came around. She also crouched low as she skirted the building and rounded the corner toward the street. Sirens screamed again as another cop sped by.

It would only be a matter of time before they started checking every one of the industrial buildings. She had to get out of there immediately.

Across the street was a rundown church that looked like it hadn't held a service in a decade or more. Behind that were small residential homes, probably built in the 1950s based on the architecture—or what was left of it.

Erika burst from the shadows and ran across the drive to the fence. She took shelter next to a huge oak tree, peeked out from behind it to make sure no one was coming, and then sprinted to the other side of the street.

Once there, she plunged into the shadows by the church and ran to the back, where she took a second to catch her breath. Her heart pounded in her chest, partly from the exercise and partly from nerves.

She took inventory of the area and noticed a truck that looked like it was thirty years old. No way it was going to run. Rust on the side and on the hood, flat tires; that thing wouldn't go a hundred feet even if it *would* start.

Erika knew she couldn't just hop in a car and drive happily to safety. There would be roadblocks on every thoroughfare between where she was standing and the interstate.

The only thing going for her was the fact that no one knew what she looked like. The mask covering half her face took care of that.

Now that she was away from the car, the mask made things worse, so she ditched it in the bushes behind the church.

There was a short concrete wall directly behind the building. From there, a chain-link fence ran along the top, blocking two adjacent yards from the church property.

She climbed the wall and flew over the short fence with ease. There were lots of fences between the houses and their property. She glanced up to make sure no one was on their back porch. As far as she could tell, no one was, but she'd have to keep an eye out. The last thing Erika needed was to get popped in the back by some random person thinking she was a trespasser.

She ran through the darkness, staying close to the fence on her left as she worked her way up the street between the homes. No chance she was going to hit the streets or sidewalks until she'd put some distance between herself and the cops.

Chapter 22

CHIAPAS

"Where are my men?" Martinez roared.

He stared down at the bottom of the waterfall where they'd left two guys to keep watch. There was no sign of them anywhere.

Martinez pointed his weapon one way and then the other, sweeping the landing below in case the one responsible showed their face. One of the remaining gunmen with him also checked the area, waving his weapon around in a similar fashion while the others kept an eye on the Americans.

"Did your boys get lost?" Sean asked.

Martinez fired him an angry sidelong glance.

"Get down there, and see what's going on," Martinez ordered one of his men. Then he motioned to another to do the same. "You, stay here with me, and keep an eye on these two."

The men nodded, and the two he'd told to climb down began their descent.

Martinez kept his weapon ready as he watched the men carefully climb back down the rock wall. He also kept his eyes on the entrance to the secret landing in case an intruder came through. Maybe he was being paranoid, but his men knew better than to abandon their posts.

Such a mistake would be punished severely. Martinez had drowned men for less than that.

The first two made it to the bottom and swept the immediate area to make sure there was no threat. They gave the all-clear sign and motioned for the rest to come down.

Martinez narrowed his eyes, still searching for the missing men. Then he motioned with his pistol to the two Americans.

"Nice and slow," he said. "Or I will shoot you myself."

Sean and Tommy cast each other a knowing glance. Something was going on, and they believed the disappearance of Osvaldo's men was the work of guerillas.

They carefully lowered their feet over the edge and started the tenuous descent. The wet rocks made it even more difficult going down than going up. It was also much harder to spot the right places to grab or place a toe, and the lights from the men below weren't helping a great deal.

When Sean felt his boot hit the ground, he let out a breath of relief. Tommy touched down immediately after him, and the two men stepped back away from the wall while their guards kept watch. One of them pointed his flashlight up again so the last two could make their way down safely.

Martinez moved fast, working his way deftly down the wall until he reached the bottom. His head was on a swivel the second he touched the ground. He waved his gun around on full alert, wary there was trouble near.

Still no sign of his other two men. Martinez's growing concern wasn't for the missing gunmen. Those types were easily replaced. His was concerned for his own personal safety.

Paranoia swelled in his mind with every passing second he didn't find the two guards. Had one of the governments finally sent someone to take him down? Was it the Mexicans or the Americans? Or was it someone else, a rogue hit by someone with revenge on the brain? Perhaps it was one of the other cartels coming to level a score or take over the operation.

He shook off the thoughts and flicked his head up at the Americans. "Get them back to their cage."

Sean felt the little diary still stuffed in the front of his pants. He knew if Martinez and the others found it, he'd never get it back. Climbing the rocks would have exposed it if he stuffed it in the back of his belt, so the front was the only place.

Moving around was awkward to say the least, but it had done the job even though at one point he feared the book would slide down one of his pant legs.

He shifted uneasily, making sure it was secure, and then fell in line behind one of the guards in front as the man led the way back across the narrow ledge to the riverbank.

"I hope this is not your doing," Martinez said as he climbed on to the ledge behind the last of his guards.

The first to arrive on the other side pointed his weapon at Sean, who was focused exclusively on the rock wall two inches from his nose. One by one, the men traversed the rocks until they were all safe on the other side. It was only then that the skinny guard in the rear spotted something in the water.

"Boss," he said in Spanish, pointing at the pool of water lapping the sand and pebbles along the shore. "Look." The guy had fear written all over his face as he stared down into the black liquid.

Martinez followed his finger and realized the problem immediately. The two missing guards were floating facedown in the pool.

"Get them out of there," Martinez ordered in a panicked rage.

The skinny guard and one of the others hurried down to the water's edge, leaving the two Americans with the boss and one other guard.

Sean and Tommy knew this was their chance. They'd been waiting for the opportunity to present itself. Now they'd received their wish.

Martinez, momentarily losing his focus, watched as the two bodies were dragged from the water and flipped over. The men's throats had been cut from ear to ear.

"What happened?" Martinez said out loud.

He started to turn to Sean, ready to threaten him again, but Sean's fist crunched into the smuggler's jaw before he could fully face him.

The blow knocked Martinez off balance, and he nearly tumbled down the slope to the water. The only thing that stopped him was Sean grabbing him by the arm and pulling him back for a second dose.

The other guard saw the sudden movement and swung his gun around to shoot Sean, but Tommy lunged forward, jumping on the guy's back. He wrapped his arms around the guard's throat and squeezed while the gunman shook, twisted, and spun around in a wild attempt to throw Tommy off.

The two guards by the water saw what was happening and took aim with their weapons, but the odds of hitting their allies were as good as hitting the enemy.

Martinez swung his pistol around and fired just as Sean ducked and delivered a fist into the guy's midsection. The breath escaped Martinez's lungs, and he doubled over just in time to catch Sean's knee in his nose.

The smuggler yelped as his face was turned into a bloody mess with crimson leaking from his nostrils, which now resembled a busted pipe.

Tommy's guard was losing consciousness, spinning slower and slower now. Desperate, the gunman pulled the trigger, firing rounds aimlessly into the darkness.

Sean instantly hit the ground, fearful he might catch a bullet. The two men down by the river weren't so lucky. Hot metal splashed into the pool all around them before tearing into their chests, legs, and arms.

Sean poked his head up to see what happened. The two other gunmen fell back into the water, faces looking lifelessly up into the night sky.

He started to push himself off the ground, but the right side of his jaw was met with the top of a boot. Blunt pain shot through Sean's face and head as he rolled through the leaves and came to a stop in a shallow depression in the ground. Martinez stalked toward him, gun still in his hand. He shook his bloody head dramatically as he reached Sean, who was struggling to get up again. This time, he drove the tip of his boot into Sean's ribs—then again into his abdomen, ribs again, then midback.

Each blow rendered pain worse than the one before and made getting up more difficult. He winced and tried to roll away, but Martinez grabbed him by the hair and made him look up into his eyes.

"It was a good effort. I'll give you that, but now you're gonna die." He pistol-whipped Sean across the face, blasting the American into a haze.

Sean's fingers scratched at the dirt and leaves. The toes of his boots dug into the earth. He tried to fight the pain and get up, but everything hurt.

Martinez raised his weapon and aimed it at Sean's head. "Goodbye, Señor Wyatt."

His finger tensed on the trigger.

Tommy's guard collapsed to his knees and then fell over prostrate with the big American still wrapped around him. Tommy looked up and saw the scene unfolding twenty feet away.

"No!" he yelled.

Martinez shuddered and turned toward Tommy with a confused, horrified look on his face. Tommy didn't know what the guy was doing until he was fully facing him. Then the American saw the arrow protruding from his neck. Martinez's gun went off. Then it fired a second and third time before the man dropped the weapon and started clutching at the projectile in his throat.

Someone had shot him through the back of the neck, narrowly missing his spine. Not that it mattered. The wound was mortal.

The drug runner fell to his knees, still desperately feeling at the bloody wound with soaked fingers. His eyes said it all. He was dying and he knew it. Maybe a lifetime of regret flashed through his memory, or perhaps it was just regret for not killing the Americans.

Either way, the moment only lasted a few seconds before he toppled over onto his side, dead.

Tommy stood up and nudged his guard's body to make sure he wasn't getting up. The lifeless corpse remained still. Tommy's next priority was checking the area. Someone had shot Martinez in the neck with an arrow. The other four guards were down in the water or on the shore. They all appeared to be dead.

Who'd shot the arrow? And why?

Tommy ran over to his friend and helped him to his feet. Sean grunted and put his hands on his knees for a second, catching his breath and letting his stiff muscles recover.

He stood up straight and grimaced again, grabbing at the ribs on his right side. "That guy really packed a wallop," Sean said, looking down at the dead smuggler.

"Where'd the arrow come from?" Tommy asked.

Sean's head turned one way and then the other as he probed the dark forest for an answer. "I...I have no idea."

"I do," an oddly familiar voice said from the shadows.

Sean sighed, both from irritation and from the pain still throbbing through at least seven parts of his body.

"Where you been, Pablo?" he asked before he even saw the man. "I was just asking Tommy here what happened to you." He looked at Tommy. "Isn't that right?"

"Yep," Tommy agreed. "We were worried about you."

Pablo stepped from the darkness amid a thick stand of trees. He was holding a black compound bow that matched his cargo pants and military-style tactical jacket.

"You left me in a cave," Pablo said in a menacing and irritated tone.

"Oh come on, Pablo," Sean said. "It wasn't that bad. You were on a beach."

"Not to mention the fact we could have killed you right there if we wanted," Tommy added.

"Then you should have done so," Pablo said. "It was a mistake leaving me alive because now I have to kill you both."

Sean's face scrunched into a confused frown. "If you were going to kill us, you would have already done it. You saved us—well, me—from a ruthless drug cartel leader. So, thanks for that."

Pablo dropped the bow to the ground and pulled out a pistol from his jacket. He aimed it at Sean's head. "I saved you so you would know it was I who would be taking your life. I told you no one is permitted to locate the forbidden temple. It must stay hidden forever."

"Forever?" Tommy asked. "That's a long time. You really think you can—"

"Silence!" Pablo tightened his finger on the trigger.

"You know, Pabs," Sean said, disobeying the order, "you might want to rethink killing us just yet. Looks like the natives are a little restless."

Pablo followed Sean's gaze. He was looking through the jungle toward the camp where, apparently, the rest of the cartel's troops were rallying. Lights danced in the darkness, and voices soon filled the air.

"I guess the gunfire got their attention," Sean said. While Pablo was looking the other way, Sean slipped his hand into the pocket where the little metal device was still sitting in the bottom.

Pablo's eyes flared in the moonlight coming through the opening in the canopy above. "I don't need your help to escape," he sneered.

"Maybe not," Sean said, "but we're going to offer it anyway."

He pressed the button, and the night suddenly erupted in a bright flash of orange-and-yellow flame. The concussion rocked the trees surrounding the camp and blew some of the tents over.

Fires blazed instantly in several places as the highly flammable canvas tents sparked to life.

The lights coming toward the two Americans suddenly disappeared as Martinez's men turned around and rushed back to the emergency.

Pablo nearly jumped out of his shoes at the explosion. He spun around to see what happened, momentarily losing track of his captives. The second he realized he'd made a mistake, he turned back to face them, but it was too late.

Sean had used the distraction to grab Martinez's gun and held it out at arm's length, the sights lined up straight at Pablo's forehead.

Pablo bit his lower lip and sighed, frustrated.

"Now," Sean said, "drop the gun."

Pablo hesitated, so Sean cocked the hammer. It was an unnecessary display but one he felt reinforced the fact that he would kill the other man if he didn't play along.

The point hit home, and Pablo let his weapon fall to the ground.

Tommy rushed over and grabbed it, stuffing it into his belt as he rushed around to collect some of the other weapons.

"You are making a grave mistake, Sean Wyatt," Pablo said. "You can kill me, but if you find the temple and unleash its power, you and everyone else on the planet will die."

"Did he mention that before?" Tommy asked, looking at Sean.

"You know what? I think he did. Now, Pabs...mind if I call you Pabs?"

Pablo looked incredulous.

"I'm gonna take that as a yes. Anyway, you're not going to like this, but I only have two options here. One, I shoot you in the face and leave you here to be jungle food. I'm sure some jaguar or giant lizard would love to chow down on you, but I'd rather not do that.

"Of course, I could leave you here, but then you'd be caught by the cartel's guys over there as soon as they figured out what happened. Maybe you slip away and don't get caught, but it's also likely you could be captured by the guerrillas, who I believe aren't far from here."

Pablo's eyes narrowed, still full of fury but now more curious than before. "Then what?"

Sean ran back and fished a phone out of one of the dead men's pockets. It was the same device they'd used to take pictures of the code in the waterfall. A quick check revealed that the man didn't use a password to protect his phone.

Sean hurried back to the other two and glanced at Tommy, exchanging a knowing look.

He faced Pablo once more. "You're coming with us."

Chapter 23

WASHINGTON

Emily roared and threw a stack of files off her desk. The papers inside flew around like giant snowflakes until they fluttered to the floor in a pile.

Smalley and the other detectives rubbed their foreheads or averted their eyes, not wanting to get caught in the line of fire.

"How in the world do we have zero leads?" she stormed.

"This person is a pro," Smalley said. "It's rare to get someone this good in a case of any kind, much less a high-profile one with government officials."

Emily shook her head and put her hands on her hips. She'd not slept much during the week since arriving in Washington. Eating had also been optional. She hadn't checked, but if she had to guess, Emily would say she'd probably lost a couple of pounds.

And the bags under her eyes showed her fatigue. It was the most stressful case she'd ever worked, and after all her hard work and the efforts of the men in the room, they'd managed to turn up nothing.

"When Kennedy was killed, they found the man responsible that same day, and they didn't have half the technology we have now. So, I ask again: How is this possible?"

A young man in a white button-up shirt, loosened blue tie, and black slacks rolled his shoulders. "We know it's a woman," he said. "That's not nothing."

"So, what if we know it's a woman? That narrows the field of suspects to about three and a half billion."

He bowed his head impishly, embarrassed he'd even mentioned it.

Her phone started buzzing on the desk. She sighed and looked at the caller ID. It was coming from IAA headquarters in Atlanta.

She muted the device and set it back on the counter. No time to talk to Tommy right now.

"What else do we have, people? Do we even have a plan of where to go next?"

Smalley and the others sat silently. Most stared down at the floor, not wanting to make eye contact with Emily. A few looked out the window behind her.

"We've analyzed every bit of evidence we could find," Emily said. "We've exhausted the few leads we could get. We're at a dead end."

Her phone started ringing again, dancing on the desk surface.

She looked at the screen and saw once more that it was the number for IAA. She let out an exasperated breath and picked up the phone.

"Hello?" she said. "I'm kind of busy right now, Tommy. You think this can wait?"

"It's not Tommy," Tara said. "We can't get ahold of him and thought maybe you knew where he and Sean were and how to reach them."

Emily's audience saw her face contort. If she'd been a cartoon, steam would have billowed out of her ears. As it was, her skin flushed deep red.

"Tara, I don't mean to sound rude, but I'm sort of in the middle of something important here in Washington. I'm sorry, but I have no idea where Tommy and Sean are. I have to get off the line. I apologize."

"It's okay," Tara said. "Sorry to bother you. Our vault was just robbed. Some woman broke in and stole something extremely valuable. It's a pretty sensitive subject."

Emily didn't need Tara to tell her the kinds of things they kept in the vault at IAA headquarters. Almost everything there was priceless. They housed a collection of artifacts unlike any in the world. Most were things people didn't know even existed.

Emily frowned and motioned to the team in her office to take a five-minute coffee break.

The men and women filed out the door. When they were gone, she closed the door and started talking again.

"I'm sorry, Tara. I'm in the middle of a murder investigation. Did you get an ID on the thief?"

"No. She was wearing a mask that covered her face from the nose down and a black baseball cap. Whoever this woman is, she's a pro and knows how to get in and out of places with minimal detection. She shut down all the cameras in our facility. We found a device in the back of the building she used to hack the system and distort the images for about an hour."

Emily's interest was piqued. "How do you know what she looked like, then?"

"One of our guards saw her. Cops are still looking for her. As of now, they have no leads."

Emily's eyebrow lifted. "When did this happen?"

"A few hours ago. We were trying to get in touch with Tommy to let him know what was taken."

"What was taken?"

"An amulet. We've been analyzing it for months, trying to understand where it gets its power."

Emily knew a little about the amulet though she was fuzzy on the details. Sean had been a bit vague on how they came by it.

"Why would someone steal it?" she asked. "Other than the obvious that it's probably worth a lot of money?"

"How much do you know about that amulet?"

"Not much," Emily admitted. "Just that the guys brought it back a few months ago and they were trying to keep things around it pretty hush-hush."

Tara took a deep breath and paused. "Emily, we believe that amulet has the power to grant life to whoever possesses it."

"Grant life?"

"Immortality. As far as we can tell, something about it can heal pretty much any disease, any injury; it can even stave off death from a wound that would be considered mortal."

Emily hadn't heard that part. "I would think something like that should be at the CDC or perhaps in a government research facility somewhere."

"That's why Sean and Tommy wanted it kept here. They figured if the government got their hands on it, that would be the last anyone ever heard about the amulet."

She wasn't wrong about that. Emily kept secrets as part of her day-to-day routine. She'd seen any number of things in her career that were dubbed unsafe for the public and were subsequently marked as classified. There'd been cover-ups galore—some she approved of and others that made her scratch her head.

Emily didn't need Tara to tell her the reasons behind keeping the amulet a secret. Sean and Tommy knew all too well what could happen.

Unfortunately, the other bad thing that could go wrong—did.

What intrigued Emily about the amulet heist wasn't just the stolen article. The moment Tara described the thief, big red flags went off in the Axis director's head.

She wandered back to her side of the desk she'd been using and flipped open the only remaining file that wasn't on the floor. It contained a picture. All this time she'd been in Washington, working the case for the president, it was an image that had confounded her.

She stared at the picture for a moment. There wasn't much to go on. It was just a shot from a traffic camera in Washington taken on the night Lilian Pike was attacked. It featured a woman in black with a matching mask over her face and a baseball cap that cast her eyes into shadow.

"You said this woman was wearing a black mask and baseball hat?" Emily asked again, just to be sure.

"Yes, but that's all we have to go on." There was another pause. "Why do you ask?"

"I'm working on something here...I can't give you all the details over the phone because it's of a pretty sensitive nature. Would you and Alex have time to meet with me tomorrow morning and answer a few questions?"

"Sure. Of course. Anything we can do to help."

"I'll need that security guard, too. Make sure he stays safe tonight."

"All right," Tara said, sounding a little befuddled.

"I'll be on a plane tonight and there at your office first thing tomorrow."

"Sounds good, Emily. Thank you."

Emily ended the call and gazed at the picture in her hand. Finally, she had a connection. The woman in the image looked exactly like the description Tara gave her. Sure, it was a stretch. There could be a thousand thieves who dressed the exact same way. She'd need to talk to the security guard to be sure. Even then, she doubted they'd get a positive ID on the woman. At the very least, however, there was a sliver of hope.

Chapter 24

CHIAPAS

Sean, Tommy, and Pablo hurried along the ridge, cutting their way through brush and dangling branches.

Down below, the lush river valley stretched out between the mountains, running far off and eventually to the sea. Smoke rolled up from the jungle behind them where the cocaine mill still smoldered from the night's explosion and fires.

As far as the Americans were concerned, they couldn't move fast enough.

At first, Sean and Tommy thought Pablo would put up a fight, but apparently their trust in him and willingness to drag him along meant something. That didn't change the fact that at a moment's notice he might turn on them and try to kill them.

On the hillside across the way, another column of smoke rose from the canopy. Sean noticed it and stopped in his tracks to get a closer look. The others halted right behind him and gazed out into the wilderness.

"Guerrillas," Pablo said, gasping for air. "I passed their camp on the way in."

"How'd you get by them?" Tommy asked.

Pablo shot him a disparaging look.

"Fine," Tommy said. "Just trying to have a friendly conversation."

Pablo shook his head. "You two fools don't understand. I cannot let you unleash the power that's buried in that temple."

Sean sat down on a rock and wiped his forehead with the bottom of his shirt. They hadn't had any water since the day before, and their mouths were dry as a desert lake bed. The humidity and heat were pushing their bodies to the limit. Sweat rolled off their foreheads and soaked their clothes.

"I know, Pabs. You've mentioned that a few hundred times already."

"Three times," Tommy corrected, trying to be cordial. "Look, Pablo, we're not the bad guys, here. If there's something dangerous in that temple that's capable of doing what you say it is, Sean and I are the best people in the world to find it and make sure it stays locked down for all eternity."

Pablo didn't seem sold. "You two are nothing more than treasure hunters. I know about your exploits. You run around the world digging up ancient relics that the rest of history forgot. Then you parade around in your suits, throwing big exhibit parties to show off what you've done. Believe me when I tell you, if you find the lost temple...it will be the end of all things. You don't know what you're dealing with."

Hearing the threat again spiked Sean's curiosity.

"You've said that a few times, too, Pablo. Tommy's right. We aren't looking to get rich from some lost treasure here. As to your comments about our exploits, some of those you may find in the media are highly exaggerated."

Pablo seemed to consider the comment.

"I'm telling the truth. If there's something sinister down there, we need to make sure it stays there. Now, we were told that whatever is in that temple is the source of great power, power that could be harnessed to give free energy to billions of people. It could change the world for the better. Why wouldn't you want to at least see if that's true?"

"Who told you this?"

The two Americans exchanged a glance and then looked back at Pablo without saying a word.

Pablo snorted a derisive laugh and shook his head. "El Templo de la Muerte is not a source of energy that can be harnessed by humans for fuel. Whoever told you this is a liar."

Sean rolled his shoulders but kept his comments about politicians and deception to himself.

"As the story goes," Pablo went on, "thousands of years ago, the first Mayan settlers discovered that place. It was unlike anything they'd ever seen before. They marveled at it and wondered what could be waiting inside." There was a tone of sadness in his voice.

"Some believed treasures awaited. Others thought it could be a gateway to the realm of the gods. There were a few who warned everyone that something evil lurked inside, but that didn't stop their king from sending men in to investigate."

He stopped and looked out over the land.

"What happened?" Tommy asked, fully sucked in to the story.

"They all died," Pablo said. Not a single man the king sent into that place was ever seen again." Then he motioned to the diary Sean held in his hand. "The man who wrote that saw firsthand what the temple is capable of. He tried to enter it and was thrown back by the power inside. Some would say he was lucky not to be killed. Then again, he obsessed over it for the rest of his life, always close to finding El Templo de la Muerte again but never succeeding."

Sean and Tommy let Pablo's words linger for a moment in the muggy air. Thick gray clouds rolled up the mountainside across from their position, bringing a steady rain to the area. Thunder rolled in the distance.

"The woman," Sean said abruptly as he shook the diary, "the woman who gave us this has been a major proponent of green energy for a long time. She did her research on this. If she'd found anything like what you're saying, she would have warned us."

"This woman," Pablo said, "would have no way of knowing the things I know. Long have we kept the secret of El Templo de la Muerte out of the minds of mankind. You won't find it mentioned in

any history books, any lectures, or any specials on the History Chan-
nel. For all intents and purposes, it doesn't exist. It must remain
that way."

The Americans fell into silent contemplation for a long moment.

Exotic birds squawked and chirped in the trees above. The sound
of rain sweeping down the opposite hillside filled the air with a
steady pounding as millions of droplets splashed on leaves and earth.

The men had no intention of moving yet. The cooling rain would
feel good on their sweat-soaked skin.

"You said everyone who entered the temple died," Sean said,
breaking the relative silence.

"Yes."

"But Alvarado...he didn't die."

"He was unconscious when his men took him away. According to
the story, he barely made it beyond the entrance to the temple."

"Yes, but you're saying that whatever is down there could bring
about the end of the world. If Alvarado went in there—heck, if the
ancient Mayans who found it went in there—you see what I'm getting
at here, right?"

Pablo nodded. "Yes, I understand your question. Why didn't the
world end if those people went in. Effectively, on a grander scale,
nothing bad happened."

"Exactly."

Pablo rested his hands on his knees for a few seconds while the
rain began its steady climb up the hillside toward where they sat.

"Have either of you ever heard of the fourth Mayan prophecy?"

Tommy and Sean looked at each other and then shook their
heads.

"Is that the one—" Tommy started to ask.

"No. The fourth prophecy has nothing to do with the end-of-days
prophecy that had everyone on the planet freaking out in 2012. And,
as we all know, the world didn't come to an end."

Tommy shut up, feeling a little stupid for bringing it up.

"The fourth prophecy is one of seven the Mayans recorded during
the height of their civilization. These prophecies have different mean-

ings, different calculations worked into each one. The fourth prophecy is directly related to the lost temple."

"How so?"

"It was discovered more than a hundred years ago, written on a stone pillar outside one of their temples."

Thunder boomed as the storm drew closer. The first drops of rain spattered around the men.

"Written on a pillar?" Sean asked. "I never knew anything about that."

"The pillar was removed shortly after so that no one could read it and interpret its meaning. It was there as a warning to any who dared to search for the temple. My predecessors believed the warning would make more people aware of the lost ruins. That's why we destroyed the pillar. The temple entrance hasn't been seen since the time Alvarado and his men visited there. His second in command had the place covered so no one could find it."

"Yeah, I think we were already told that part."

"No one must be allowed to unearth it. I am one of the last of my order. When I die, I will pass on my knowledge to another who will watch over the secrets of the lost temple, as was done for me when my mentor died."

Something had been on Sean's mind during the entire conversation, and when Pablo stopped talking he decided to bring it up. "You said you've never been to the temple before. Is that true, or were you just telling us that so we wouldn't force you to take us there against your will?"

Pablo nodded. "You're right to question that. No, I have never been there. There is no one on earth who knows the way to the lost temple. It is not visible from the sky or from the ground. It has been covered for hundreds of years."

"You say covered," Tommy said. "What do you mean, covered?"

"I honestly don't know. When Alvarado's second in command issued the order, he left no record behind."

Sean felt the phone in his pocket, knowing what it contained in its memory. The pictures within would—hopefully—help them unlock the location of the lost temple.

"We have to try to find it, Pablo," Sean said. "You can't simply tell us that there's a lost temple somewhere in the Yucatan and that it holds an ancient magical power, then expect us to just walk away."

"He's right," Tommy said. "That's not how we operate. Finding ancient stuff that may or may not be dangerous is kind of our thing."

"Then you will both die," Pablo said. "I have sworn to protect the temple."

"You don't even know what or where it is. Shouldn't your concern be protecting the people of Earth? Because it feels a little like you're getting the mission confused."

Pablo's eyebrows pinched together. "They are one and the same." He didn't sound convinced.

"Are they?" Sean asked. "It's possible that whatever is down there in the belly of that temple could kill us. But what if it's something that could help the world? What if it could help heal diseases, give free energy to people who had none? We can make a difference. Don't you want to be a part of that? Isn't that the real purpose behind what you do? Whatever that is."

Pablo thought long and hard. The two Americans made a good argument. If he'd been honest with them, he'd have said there'd always been a deep curiosity buried inside him that wondered what the temple really was, what it could do. But he'd never admit that to Sean and Tommy.

And, he thought, now was his chance. If he helped them and it turned out to be a good thing, no harm. On the other hand, if it turned out to be some kind of cataclysmic engine that brought about the end of the world, would he really want to be the one responsible? Perhaps there was a way to satisfy both his curiosity and his sense of duty.

"Very well," he said after weighing the variables. "I will not get in your way. If we find the lost temple and something starts going wrong, we bury it and never go back."

Sean and Tommy were skeptical. Their new associate had changed his mind fairly fast.

"Why the sudden change of heart?" Sean asked.

"I've protected the symbols for many years," Pablo said. "I've spent so much time watching for those who would try to find the location of the temple that...I guess I just...I want to see. I want to know what's there, what's been hiding in the jungle all this time. Plus, I figure if there really is something horrible deep down under that temple, you two might need a little help shutting it off...you know, in case you activate some kind of doomsday device."

Sean and Tommy glanced at each other and then grinned.

"Glad to have you on the team, Pabs," Sean said.

Pablo nodded. "Perhaps you can give me one of those guns now since we're in dangerous territory." He motioned to one of the rifles Tommy had slung over his shoulder.

"Don't push your luck," Tommy said with a wary eye.

"Was worth a shot."

"We need to get moving, guys," Sean interrupted. "It doesn't look like this storm is going to let up anytime soon. The quicker we can get somewhere to figure out this next part of the riddle, the better."

"Yeah," Tommy said with a hint of trepidation in his voice. "The only problem is; how do we find our ride? We left the cartel camp in a different direction than we took going in. Without our map, we're lost."

Sean's shoulders sagged. He scratched his head and looked out over the landscape, trying to recall the path they took the day before.

"It's okay, amigos," Pablo said. "I know where your car is."

The man stood up and started walking down the slope away from the valley where the guerrillas were camped.

Sean and Tommy looked at each other with puzzlement in their eyes.

"Why didn't you tell us that before?" Tommy asked.

Pablo looked back over his shoulder with a smirk on his face. "You didn't ask."

Chapter 25

ATLANTA

Emily strode through the IAA main entrance and flashed her badge to a cop who was standing just inside the lobby, blocking the way in. He waved her through and resumed what she figured had to be one of the most boring jobs in the world.

Detectives were scouring the place for clues as to who the thief had been that broke through IAA security.

She walked through the lobby and over to a pair of double doors where a second cop was standing guard. She flashed her badge again, and after a short glance at it, the man waved her through just as the other had done.

Emily passed through the double doors and continued down the hall until she reached another pair of doors, this one with windows built in. She pressed her nose to the glass and peered inside. The lab was full of all kinds of research equipment: tubes, vials, and tech gadgets.

There was movement along the far wall in the corner. Tara, wearing goggles and a mask, was clearly deep in work. Emily pulled open the door and stepped inside. She cleared her throat when the door closed.

Tara spun around, startled, then relieved to see Emily.

"Oh hey, Emily," Tara said, excited. "Give me one second, and I'll be right there."

"No problem." Emily gazed around at all the stuff. "Alex here?"

"He should be back any second. Went to get coffee. Did you want some?"

"No, thank you. I had some earlier."

Tara flipped a switch and a machine started whining softly. She removed the goggles and set them on the table next to her white lab coat.

"What are you working on?" Emily asked as Tara walked across the room, meeting her guest at the door.

"Nothing major, just analyzing the compounds from an artifact the boys brought in. It demonstrates some strange properties, so we thought we'd check it out."

"Strange properties?"

"Yeah, you know, stuff that isn't easily explained by science. That particular item has the tendency to spontaneously set things on fire."

Emily suddenly looked concerned. "Really?"

Tara chuckled. "No. I'm kidding. But it does have some strange properties. What can I do for you?"

Emily was relieved to hear the building wasn't going to burn down, at least not from whatever Tara was analyzing in the corner. "The security guard," Emily said. "You know, the one who saw the thief get away. I'm here to speak with him."

"Oh right. Silly me. I've been so busy I completely forgot. Come on," she said with the wave of a hand. "Follow me. He should be in the back."

Tara led the way out the lab door and down the hall. The two made a sequence of turns that made Emily's head spin. Her office at Axis headquarters was confusing the first time she arrived in the building, but she'd grown accustomed to it quickly. She doubted she'd ever get used to the labyrinthine IAA layout.

"Security office is just down here," Tara said with a cheerful smile. For someone that kept long hours and slept very little, Tara acted like she had enough energy to power the entire continent.

Just being around her was kind of exhausting.

They reached a white door at the end of a long corridor. A black sign with white lettering read, *Security.*

Tara rapped on the door a few times and then stepped back to wait. It didn't take long to swing open.

"Oh hey, Tara," a middle-aged man in a uniform said with a smirk. "How are you?"

"Hey, Cliff," Tara said. "This is the lady I told you about, Director Starks. She's the one who wanted to ask you a few questions about the break-in."

Cliff was a big fellow with a bulging belly that belied too many beer and burger joints he'd visited in the past. His thinning hair was cut close to the scalp so the receding line blended more naturally. He had a round, chubby face atop a fleshy neck. The security uniform looked like it was stretched to its maximum capacity. For a moment, Emily wondered how the guy ever stopped anyone. Then she reminded herself not to read a book by its cover.

"Cliff, Emily Starks. Pleasure to meet you." Emily extended a hand and shook Cliff's vigorously.

He gave a curt nod. "Nice to meet you, too, Director. Please, come on in."

He spoke with an accent that suggested he was from somewhere in New York City, though Emily couldn't pinpoint which borough.

The inside of the security office wasn't quite what Emily expected. In truth, she wasn't sure what to expect. She half figured it would be a plain white room with a coffee machine, soda machine, and a giant box of donuts sitting on a counter in a compact kitchenette.

A quick look to the right told her she'd not been wrong about the donuts and the coffee machine. Both were sitting out on a counter next to a stainless steel refrigerator. *Two out of three,* she thought.

The wall opposite the doorway was covered in flatscreens, each showing a different angle of dozens of areas inside and outside the building. Another security guard, this one much more diminutive and slender than Cliff, was watching the screens with close attention.

Cliff led the two women over to a small white table in the corner and offered them a seat. He helped himself to one and eased into it. The legs creaked, straining under the weight, but the chair held strong.

When the two women were seated, he folded his hands on the table and gazed expectantly at Emily. "How can I help you today? Tara said something about you wanting to ask me some questions about the burglary?"

"Yes," Emily said with a nod. "And thank you for taking time out of your day to see me. I really appreciate it."

"Not a problem, ma'am. Not much for us to do right now, what with all the cops and detectives hovering around. No one would dare try to break in here again. Not to mention we're overhauling our security measures to make sure this sort of thing doesn't get repeated."

Emily hated chitchat or small talk. That's what she felt like they were doing, like two old friends catching up after not seeing each other for a decade. She knew the social convention required it, but that didn't mean she had to like it.

"Good idea," she said, hoping it wouldn't lead to more idle chatter. Fortunately, he simply nodded and took a sip of water.

Before he or Tara could start off on a new tangent, Emily went ahead with the reason she was there.

She set a file on the table, pulled back the metal tab keeping it shut, flipped open the cover, and pulled out a black-and-white picture. She slid it across the table to Cliff.

He scratched the side of his head and looked down at the image, grasping it with a finger and thumb. The image resolution wasn't great.

"This taken by a traffic cam?" he asked, looking up from the picture for a moment.

"Yes," Emily confirmed. "Unfortunately, those cameras aren't always the best for clarity."

"Yeah, but you can definitely tell it's a woman."

"Do you think it's the same woman who broke into this building the other night?"

"It's hard to say, but yeah, if I had to guess I would say that's the same girl...er, woman." He tried to correct himself so as not to offend.

Tara waved it off. "We're all just girls and boys, Cliff. It's fine."

"But you think that's her?" Emily asked again, seeking certainty.

"Yep. Looks like her. Same hat and face mask. Body type looks the same, too. The burglar even had on the same kinds of clothes. If I had a million bucks to stake on it, I'd say they're the same person." A curious expression washed over him. "What did the woman in the picture do?"

Emily frowned and sighed. She wasn't allowed to say exactly what, although it wasn't like it was a huge secret. Half the country knew Lilian Pike had been attacked.

"I'm working on a murder investigation. We think the woman in this picture is the killer. Apparently, she's moved on from assassination to stealing priceless artifacts."

Cliff frowned. "I'm no investigator, but that seems like an odd jump."

"You're right, Cliff. It is an odd jump, but if you say the woman in this picture is the one from the other night, then there must be a connection." Emily stared down at the image, tapping her finger on the surface. "There has to be a connection," she said. "We just have to figure out what it is."

"If this woman stole the amulet," Tara chimed in, "it's possible that she needs it for...some kind of disease or something."

Emily and Cliff turned their heads to face Tara.

"Since that amulet seems to be able to cure diseases and heal severe injuries," she went on, "maybe she wants it for personal reasons. Of course, it could be that she wants it because she thinks it will make her immortal. That rumor was going around for a while."

The room dipped into a deep silence.

"It can't, though, right?" Emily asked.

"No, we don't think so. Hard to know for sure. We've only had one test subject so far. That was Sean, and it was hardly done in a controlled environment. Although we have seen some pretty interesting results with lab mice."

"Interesting?"

"Yes," Tara said with a nod. "They have demonstrated longer-than-average lifespans since being exposed to the amulet."

"Exposed?" Emily asked.

"All that is required is touching the amulet. The longer you touch it, the faster the effects take place. It's all been extremely fascinating to observe."

"What would a murderer want with something like that?" Emily asked out loud, intending to keep the thought to herself. Then another idea came to her. "This woman is working for someone else."

"What?" Tara asked.

Emily shook her head. "Sorry, was thinking out loud. The woman in the picture; we think she is working for someone else."

"So she's a hitman...er, woman?" Cliff asked.

"We believe so, yes. That means if she's working for someone, it's possible that she stole this amulet for that person as well. The question is; who has the kind of money to throw around on a high-end assassin/thief that may also be suffering from a chronic illness?"

The other two stared blankly at her. Nothing came to mind.

It wasn't the definitive answer Emily was looking for, but it was a piece to the puzzle she previously didn't have. There had to be a connection.

Her phone started vibrating in her pocket, and she pulled it out to check who was calling. It was Detective Smalley.

"Please excuse me," Emily said, standing up and stepping away from the table. "I'll be right back."

"No problem," Tara said cheerfully.

Emily put the phone to her ear. "What's up?"

"So, I was doing a little research on the victims."

"And?"

"I went back through our list of common enemies because I thought it was weird there weren't any real connections."

"Okay?"

"I started wondering if we needed to go through old footage. It took a while; I'm talking hundreds of man hours."

"Get to the point, Detective."

"We missed something before," he said plainly. "There's no way we could have found it without going through old tapes from the Capitol. Lilian Pike."

He let the name dangle for a few seconds.

"What about her? She was attacked last week."

"Yeah, that threw me for a loop, too, Director. But something about that whole hit bothered me. I thought it was strange that the murderer had been able to take out the other three with such precision, such perfection; why would they suddenly screw up with Pike? The bodyguard was killed with ease. Doesn't seem like the type to let a target simply run away with nothing more than a flesh wound."

He made a good point. It was one Emily had considered but figured it was nothing more than her imagination starting to run wild, desperate to find some link to the killings.

"Are you suggesting that Lilian Pike is the one behind all this?" Emily asked bluntly.

"I'm not saying anything definitively, Director. I'm just brainstorming here."

Emily sighed.

"Pike is a beloved politician, if that sort of thing is even possible," he continued. "After her son and husband died six months apart, she became a sort of darling in this town. Then when she found out she had cancer, no one could believe it. Poor woman can't get a break. Forget I brought it up, Director. You're right."

"No, wait. What did you just say?" Emily suddenly stiffened.

"Which part? About her not getting a break or me being sorry?"

"Neither. You said she has cancer?"

"Oh yeah. Apparently, she doesn't have much longer. The story got a lot of press around here for a week or two, especially when she said she wasn't going to do chemo. Said she wanted to treat the disease with other methods. Some people thought she was just trying to kill herself, you know, like life's beaten her up enough already. I don't know; maybe she really is trying to cure the illness."

There was the link Emily had been missing. The entire story started falling into place.

Lilian Pike hated the big oil companies. She'd dedicated her career to taking them down and bringing clean energy resources to the forefront. Her son's death and the subsequent suicide of her husband were all the motivation someone would need if they were patient enough to see it through over the course of several years.

Emily's mind spun. The connection was all too clear now. Pike had cancer; that explained sending the thief to get the amulet. She must have found out about its healing properties. It was a long shot, but Emily knew that if someone was desperate enough, they would go to almost any lengths to stay alive.

"She's been plotting this all along," she muttered. "The attack on her was a diversion to throw us off the trail. She must have known we'd be looking at potential enemies the earlier victims had. So, she told her assassin to make it look like a hit gone wrong, one where she narrowly escaped."

"Yeah, but come on. She was shot for crying out loud. You'd have to be pretty anguished to take a bullet like that. One wrong move, and it's curtains."

"Only someone with nothing left to lose would do that. Pike fits that description."

"She's got her political career. Doubt she wants to lose that."

"No," Emily shook her head. "She doesn't care about her career. She only cares about revenge." Emily thought for a second. "Where's Pike now?"

"I...I don't know. We can find out. You want us to lock her down?"

"Yes," Emily said. "Find her, and bring her in. Last thing we need is her slipping through our fingers again."

Chapter 26

WASHINGTON

Cameras flashed all across the room. A half-dozen reporters were lined up in chairs in the front row, all with phones, tablets, and even a few still using pen and paper.

The rest of the room was full of supporters, friends, and a few stragglers who couldn't get a seat up front.

They'd all gathered to hear an announcement from Congresswoman Lilian Pike. Rumors were flying around. Some said she was dying and only had a few weeks to live. Others claimed she was going to announce her candidacy for the presidency in the upcoming election two years away, though Pike had never said anything about that in public. It was, after all, Washington: a place where the rumor mill was always running and hot new stories were a dime a dozen.

Lilian waited behind a dark blue curtain with her speechwriter and two other assistants. They had tears in their eyes as they waited for her to step out and make the announcement.

She put her arm around one intern's shoulders. The young girl was only twenty years old, but had shown a tremendous amount of potential in her short time with Pike. Evidently, she didn't want to lose her mentor.

"Erin," Lilian said in a comforting tone, "this is only temporary. Okay? I promise, I'm coming back. I just need to take a little time off."

Erin nodded and wiped away a stray tear.

"Now, time to speak to the press," Lilian said. "Wish me luck."

Lilian stepped out from behind the curtain and placed her hands on the podium. Cameras popped and flashed all over the room again. The reporters all straightened up and hit the record buttons on their phones, ready to catch every word of the announcement. While it wasn't necessarily huge news, it was better than nothing. Whether it made the front page or not was up to the editors.

"Thank you all for coming today," Lilian started. "It's been a rough couple of weeks for me. Actually," she choked back a laugh, "it's been a rough decade. But that's life, isn't it? It's not easy for anyone."

She looked out at the gathering. Her eyes panned the room, taking in all the faces, every anxious pair of eyes.

"When I first started this job, I had lofty goals. I wanted to make a difference in the world, especially here in the country I love. I know it's cliché, but that's how I felt. That was my driving motivation. It kept me going when times got tough.

"Washington tried to beat me down. There were those who did their best to suppress my goals, the things I wanted to get done. And while I wasn't always successful with everything, I feel like we've been able to make a difference. It might not be a big difference, but a difference nonetheless."

A few heads nodded in the audience amid more camera flashes.

"The events of the last few weeks have caused me to rethink some things. No, I am not quitting my job. I want to put that out there right off the bat. I will continue to serve my constituents and the people of this great country with every ounce of strength I have. However, due to my physical condition, I'm going to have to take a leave of absence to get treatment. This doesn't have anything to do with the shooting that happened a few days ago. I have recovered from that incident. My mind is strong and I will eventually continue to do my job with the same resolve I've used for so long. This decision to step away for a short amount of time has to do with my cancer treatments."

She took a deep breath before continuing. "I've not shown any signs of improvement with my therapy and have decided that to get the best results, I need to take some time off from the stress and day-to-day grind of the office. My doctors have agreed that stepping away will improve the results of my treatments. Again, this is not a resignation speech." She flashed a playful smirk. "Now, if any of you have any questions, I'll do my best to answer. But before you begin, I'll put one question out of the way immediately. No, I am not running for president anytime soon."

The room erupted in an uneasy but rousing fit of laughter.

Lilian spent the next ten minutes answering questions about the kind of therapy she was undergoing, what she expected from it, where she'd be going after she left Washington, and a dozen other things that she knew were trivial but had to be asked.

When she was done, she stepped back behind the curtain to a group of proud, smiling faces.

Her assistants and interns escorted her back to her office, where she collected a few personal things and said her goodbyes, once more reassuring them she'd only be gone for a short time and that the circumstances were only temporary.

After they'd all left the room, she took a deep breath and looked around the office. It had been her refuge, her home away from home for so long that it was like a part of her.

Lilian wasn't so sentimental that she'd shed a tear over an office, even though she'd lied to her assistants and everyone in the press room.

It wasn't going to be a temporary leave of absence. If everything went according to plan, she'd never come back to Washington again.

When she slid into the back seat of her car, her driver looked into the rearview mirror. He was wearing a pair of aviator sunglasses, much like the ones her previous driver used to wear.

"Where to, Congresswoman Pike?"

"The airport. I'm going on a little vacation."

She watched as he pulled out of the parking area and onto the road leading away from the Capitol. The pristine white building that symbolized power, freedom—and to many, corruption—would soon be a shambles.

Lilian Pike couldn't wait to watch it all burn.

Chapter 27

CHIAPAS

"You disabled our ride?" Tommy asked, incensed.

He stood next to the SUV with his hands on his hips. The two right-side tires were flat. Sean couldn't help but laugh at their predicament even though he knew it could prove to be their undoing.

"I didn't want you to get away this time," Pablo said with a shrug. "After the way you slipped through my fingers in Tulum, I didn't want to make it easy on you."

"Little did you know it would make things harder on you as well, huh?"

"Not to worry."

Tommy's frown deepened. "What do you mean, not to worry? How are we supposed to get out of here?"

"Open the doors and I'll tell you."

The key was one of the few things Tommy'd been able to keep from the drug smugglers when they were taken. The only reason the cartel didn't find it was because it was in the bottom of his pocket with no keyring attached.

He fished out the key and unlocked the doors.

Pablo opened the back hatch and reached inside. He pried open a panel on the right-hand side and revealed an air compressor.

"How'd you know that was there?"

"How did you not?" Pablo fired back with a mischievous grin.

Sean laughed. "So, you didn't pop the tires. You just let the air out?"

Pablo confirmed the answer with a nod.

He rushed around to the front of the car and opened the passenger door, leaned inside, and plugged in the compressor. Then he knelt next to the front right tire and attached the hose before turning on the switch.

The little black box rattled loudly as it slowly poured air into the flat tire.

Pablo stood back and watched with arms crossed as the tire gradually began to rise.

Tommy was tempted to remind their new friend that none of this would be necessary if he'd not let the air out in the first place, but decided to keep his lips sealed.

"That thing sure doesn't work fast," Tommy said. "It's going to take forever at this rate."

"Beats walking back to civilization," Sean said. He stepped around to the back of the vehicle and sat down in the cargo area. He set the diary on the mat and placed the dead gunman's phone next to it.

"Yeah, but it's going to be dark soon. I'd like to be out of this jungle before that happens."

"Agreed."

Sean tapped on the phone screen and flipped through the pictures they'd taken inside the cave at the waterfall. He studied the images for a few minutes and then started turning the pages of the diary until he'd come to the last the little book had to offer.

Inside the folds of some of the pages were notes he'd made from earlier translations along with the coded sequences they'd discovered at the other sites. His eyes darted back and forth as he compared the symbols to ones from before.

Tommy stepped around the back of the vehicle and looked inside at what Sean was doing.

He snorted a laugh. "Are you trying to figure that out manually?"

"Our phones are gone and we're out of range, so even if we had them they wouldn't be of any use. When Alvarado created this code, he didn't do it with the knowledge of computers from the future. He designed it to be decrypted by a human mind."

Sean got out of the back and walked around to the front door.

"Where you going?" Tommy asked, concerned he'd somehow upset his friend.

"To get a pen."

Sean looked in the glove box but found nothing but a manual and a map. He checked the center console and found what he wanted.

He returned to the rear of the SUV, proudly holding up the ballpoint pen and set back to work on the cipher. Then he wrote on the back side of one of his previous notes, putting the symbols and letters next to each other for reference.

"Now that we have most of these symbols already decoded, getting the last sequence shouldn't be too difficult," Sean explained as he continued working.

Pablo hovered close by, listening to the conversation and watching Sean writing furiously.

After several minutes, the first tire was full, and Pablo unplugged the hose and attached it to the rear tire. The machine groaned in protest for a moment and then picked up its usual humming rattle.

"What are you doing?" Pablo asked, looking over Tommy's shoulder.

Sean kept working while the other two continued staring into the back of the SUV. "It's a code, Pabs. I'm trying to figure out what it says."

"I realize it's a code. But why are you writing down all the letters from the other sites? I would think they each stand on their own."

"That would certainly make things a lot trickier," Sean said. "In this instance, Alvarado used one sequence for everything."

"Thank goodness," Tommy added.

Sean kept scribbling on the notes while Pablo looked around at the tire. It was almost full.

His eyes narrowed, and the skin on his forehead wrinkled. "Did you guys hear that?"

Tommy looked up at their new associate. "Hear what? All I hear is that compressor."

"No," Pablo shook his head. He tilted to the right to try to hear better. "There's something else," he said in a quiet tone.

Sean looked up from his work and listened. Concern washed over his face. "He's right. Someone's coming."

"Someone's coming?" Tommy asked. "Who?"

Sean hurriedly collected his notes and the diary. "If I had to guess, I'd say it's guerrillas."

"Or the cartel is out for revenge, and they're trying to hunt us down," Pablo offered.

"Thanks for that. Yes, it could be the cartel. Either way, we need to move."

Tommy rolled his eyes. "Just one time I'd love for it to be easy."

He ran around to the driver's side of the SUV and climbed in. Pablo unplugged the hose on the tire and flung the compressor onto the front floorboard on the passenger side. Then he opened the back door and slid onto the seat while Sean rushed to the front and clambered in. He hadn't even closed the door when he told Tommy to punch it.

Tommy revved the engine and gunned it. The vehicle's rear wheels spun in the mud, spitting brown goop into the forest behind them.

"What's wrong?" Pablo asked. "Why aren't we moving?"

"Mud," Tommy answered. "The wheels can't get a grip."

Sean glanced back in the side mirror and saw the first sign of trouble. "They're here, buddy. Anytime you wanna kick this bad boy into four-wheel drive, I'd be grateful."

Tommy looked back and saw a beat-up old Toyota pickup rumbling toward them down the jungle road.

"Good call." Tommy reached over and pressed the button to

engage all four wheels. He stepped on the gas again, this time with a little less force, and the SUV surged forward.

The pickup behind them closed fast. Pablo was looking back at the oncoming threat. Two masked gunmen were in the truck bed, taking aim with their rifles.

"Must go faster. Must go faster!" Pablo said with sudden urgency.

Sean looked back again. "Yeah, those are definitely guerrilla fighters." He pulled up the gun he'd taken from Martinez and rolled down the window.

"Might want to take the other side, Pabs," Sean said. "Don't want to accidentally hit you."

"Right."

Pablo slid to the opposite window and drew one of the automatic weapons they'd taken off Martinez's men. He pulled back the slide to make sure there was a new round in the chamber and then rolled down the window.

"I hate these child safety windows," he complained when the window stopped halfway.

"Break it," Sean said.

"What?" Tommy and Pablo asked simultaneously.

"Break it."

"Then we'll have to pay for it," Tommy said.

Sean flashed an *are you serious* glare at his friend. "Dude, you're worth like a hundred million dollars."

The SUV hit a bump in the road and went flying through the air. The front tires slammed into the mud again about thirty feet down the track, just before a curve in the trail.

"Waste not," Tommy said as he jerked the wheel to correct the vehicle from spinning out of control.

Sean turned to Pablo. "Break the stupid window!"

Pablo didn't hesitate again. He rammed the butt of the gun through the glass, raining it down onto the dirt road as they sped through the jungle.

He started to poke his head out and open fire when the sound of metal plunking into the rear hatch caused him to shrink back and take cover behind the seat. The gunmen in the pickup truck poured a relentless stream of bullets at their quarry as the driver did his best to keep the vehicle steady on the bumpy, irregular road.

Sean leaned out his window and squeezed the trigger. He didn't hit anything but trees and mud. The shots, however, caused the pursuing driver to tap his brakes and lose ground for a moment.

"Which way?" Tommy shouted.

"What?" Sean turned around and looked out the windshield at a fork in the road ahead.

"Left or right?"

"I don't know. We didn't come this way before."

"Go left!" Pablo yelled from the back.

A second later, he poked his weapon out the window and opened fire.

The pickup veered right then left. The driver lost control, and the truck slid sideways on the trail. A second later, the right-side tires caught in a rut, and the pickup flipped off the ground. It tumbled through the air, one side over the other, throwing the truck bed's occupants into the jungle and onto the road. The horrific crash seemed to happen in slow motion until the top of the pickup's cab smashed into the ground and rolled to a violent stop.

Pablo retreated to his seat with a proud smile on his face. "They won't be a problem anymore," he said amid a trickle of acrid smoke seeping out of his gun's barrel.

"Nice job, Pabs," Sean said. Then he took another look in the side mirror. "Unfortunately, they had backup."

Two more pickups appeared in the mirror, lined up one behind the other. Like before, gunmen in the truck beds took aim with automatic rifles and opened fire.

Bullets whizzed by the SUV as Tommy spun the wheel to the right, accidentally going down the wrong road at the fork.

"I said go left!" Pablo shouted.

"In case you hadn't noticed, they're shooting at us!" Tommy defended. "I'm just trying to not get shot!"

Pablo stuck his head back out the window and started firing again.

Sean did the same, carefully squeezing the trigger one pull at a time to maximize accuracy. His weapon popped, and a round found the left headlight of the truck directly behind them. He fired again. The round zipped through the windshield, the vacant headrest, and into the gunman's knee standing behind the cab. The guy grimaced and dropped into the truck bed. Sean couldn't see what happened from his vantage point, but he figured the bullet must have hit the guy somewhere for him to disappear so suddenly.

Pablo resumed his attack, recklessly spraying hot metal into the jungle behind them, occasionally hitting the mark. It only took him a few seconds to empty the first magazine. He climbed back inside and set the weapon down in the back, trading it for the other one that still had a full complement of rounds.

"Pabs," Sean said, ducking back inside for a moment. "Hand me the other rifle."

"Are you sure? I was going to—"

"Pabs," Tommy interrupted, "you really do want to let Sean handle this."

The truck jumped over a bump and cut to the left as the trail veered in a sharp 90-degree turn.

"Fine," Pablo relented.

He passed the second rifle to Sean, who took it and pulled the slide back. Sean stuck the barrel out the window and was about to lean out to open fire when a barrage of bullets cracked through the glass in the back and pounded the metal tailgate.

Sean sprawled back inside for cover while the gunmen in the truck behind them emptied their magazines. The second pickup wheeled around the first as the men reloaded.

Sean had no intention of giving them even a fraction of a second to resume the attack. He popped out of the window, locked his sights on the driver and tensed his finger on the trigger.

Suddenly, he felt momentum pulling him forward. His back rammed against the door frame as Tommy stomped on the brakes.

The SUV slid in the mud, and Tommy had to let off the pedal, opting to feather it rapidly until the vehicle came to a controlled stop.

"What are you doing?" Sean asked, doing his best not to sound condescending.

Tommy didn't answer. He didn't need to. Sean twisted around and looked at the road ahead. Four more pickups were blocking the path along with a dozen armed guerrillas.

"Oh no," Sean said.

"That," Pablo said, "is why I told you to go the other way. This trail goes right through a guerrilla camp."

Chapter 28

WASHINGTON

"What do you mean she's gone?" Emily roared. Her voice echoed through the conference room and out into the hall beyond. "Where did she go? Please tell me you have her location."

Heads turned in the room as each person looked to another for an answer. Smalley was the closest to Emily. He cleared his throat before speaking when he saw no one else was going to say anything.

"We...um...we don't know where she went, Director." He stammered, struggling to find the right way to give her what was the ultimate bad news. "We're working on it. Apparently, she took a private jet to Belize, but our people on the ground there said there's no sign of her."

"No sign of her?" Emily couldn't believe what she was hearing. "How is that possible? In this day and age, when we can track almost everything and everyone on the planet, especially a high-profile politician, how in the world did she just disappear?"

Smalley drew a long breath while he collected his thoughts and carefully pondered what to say next. The last thing he wanted was to tick her off more.

"Director Starks, we're working around the clock here. We did what you asked and sent people to her office and her home. When we learned she wasn't there, we put out an APB. It wasn't until it was too late we found out she'd left the country."

"She gave a press conference, Detective. On national television."

"Yes, ma'am. We know. We weren't aware she was going to be making an announcement of that kind until after the fact. There's no way any of us could have known that." He put his hand out to both make a point and plead for a little leniency. "Heck, you, me, none of us even considered her to be a suspect in all this until earlier today."

Emily put her hands on her hips and hung her head. He was right. It wasn't entirely his or anyone else's fault. They'd been too slow to identify Pike as a suspect. One of the thousands of questions racing through her head was whether or not Pike knew they were going to come after her or if the timing of her announcement was mere coincidence. If it wasn't coincidental, that meant there was a leak in her team. She looked up at the eyes staring back at her, searching for the one who may have given up the information. No answers came.

She let out a long sigh and shook her head. There wasn't a mole. No one in that room would have told Pike what was going on. If the congresswoman held a press conference, that meant she'd planned it in advance, at least by a day or so. That meant no one would have been able to alert her to what was happening.

Still, it was a shady coincidence. Maybe Pike knew eventually the house of cards would crumble and she'd be implicated in the murders. That wasn't out of the realm of possibility, though the plan had been enacted so carefully, with such precision, it would have been surprising if the congresswoman had lost faith so quickly.

No, leaving the country had to be part of the overall scheme. Everything had been timed perfectly. If Pike really was the one behind all this, she'd planned it with the utmost care. Nothing would be left to chance.

"It's not your fault," Emily said after letting the room simmer in uncomfortable silence. "It's none of our faults. There was no way we could have seen this coming. None of it. Not the fact that Pike is now our primary suspect or that she was going to leave the country. No way we could have anticipated all that. If we could, it's my fault for letting her slip through our fingers."

"Don't be so hard on yourself, Director," Smalley said. His kind words were a bit of a shock. Up to that point, Emily thought he resented her for coming in and taking over the case. "Like you said, there was no way to know this was going to happen. But it's not like we don't have any leads. We know what part of the world she fled to, if she was indeed fleeing the country. We've got eyes and ears on the ground down there in Belize, Mexico, and Honduras keeping a look-out. If she pokes her head out, we'll have her in custody before she can say the word *attorney*."

Emily stepped over to a window looking out toward the Capitol. She stared for a long moment, keeping her thoughts to herself.

Why Belize? The question kept rising to the surface in the ocean of questions that flooded her mind.

"Everybody, take the rest of the afternoon off. I'll see you all tomorrow." She didn't turn around to see everyone exchanging confused expressions and curious glances. When the noise died down and she was alone, she slumped into the closest chair and put her head back against the headrest.

She ran a hand through her hair and then tightened it into a ponytail. "What are you doing in Belize?" she said out loud. "Do you have a summer home there?"

It took a second to hit her, but as soon as it did she pulled out her phone and did an internet search for Belize. When the results popped up, she tapped on the map and zoomed out.

Belize was on the Mexican border, next to the Yucatan.

Sean was down in the Yucatan. At least, last she checked. There was no telling where he was now. When he and Tommy were working on a project, they could bounce from one country to the next at a moment's notice. One day they'd be off the coast of Mexico, and the next they could be in the middle of the Arctic Circle.

She pulled out her phone and called Sean's number. It went straight to voicemail. She figured he was either out of range or too busy to answer.

"Hey, Sean," she said after the beep. "It's Emily. This is sort of a random, short-notice call, but I was wondering if you might be able to help me with something. I know you were down in the Yucatan with Tommy. Maybe you're not there anymore. If you are, give me a call back. I'm in a strange little pickle right now, and I was hoping you could help me out. No, I'm not trying to get you back into the agency. I just have a question about a person who fled the country and might be down in your neck of the woods. Anyway, call me if you get a chance, and if not, no big deal. Just thought I'd take a shot in the dark. Hope you're well."

She ended the call and set the phone down on the table. Standing alone in the conference room, she stared out through the windows at the busy office. People rushed around, performing their routine police tasks. Emily remembered when she was like them, taking orders from the higher-ups, doing menial tasks she didn't really understand. She'd been fully submerged in the red tape at that point in her life. Now the responsibilities were much more significant, but at least she was in charge—for the most part. There was only one person to whom she answered directly.

The phone started ringing, and she looked down at the screen. She frowned. "How does he do that?"

It was the president, calling from a number only she had.

"Yes, Mr. President?" she answered, putting the phone to her ear.

"You know, I've told you more times than I can count that you don't have to call me that,"

"I know, sir. And I've told you more times than I can count that when I'm on the clock, that's what I'm going to call you."

He chuckled. "I respect that, Emily. When I retire in two years, though, you'll have to cut it out."

"We'll both be retiring, so that shouldn't be a problem."

She'd already made the decision to call it quits at Axis, though she hadn't told anyone yet other than the man on the phone.

Emily had served the agency for a long time, though she wasn't even close to what most people considered retirement age. The truth was, she could still do the job effectively for another decade or so if she wanted, probably more. The job was mentally, physically, and emotionally taxing, but she'd learned how to deal with that through the years.

The real reason behind her early exit was the man on the line with her. She wanted to spend time with him, time she was denied while he was president. They had to play things cool. On top of that, the guy was almost never in one place for very long. He was constantly traveling or deeply entrenched in a meeting that involved who knew how many political agendas.

She'd learned how to deal with being the president's girlfriend, but Emily looked forward to the day when they were just John and Emily.

"It's funny," she said. "I was just thinking about you, and then you call."

"We must have that connection."

Emily knew what he was talking about. They'd discussed it before during a wine-induced conversation that drifted into spiritual philosophy.

"Hmm," she agreed with a smile. "That we do." Then she remembered she was talking to her boss and he was likely calling for other than personal reasons. "What can I do for you?"

"Something just happened in Mexico. I think you should take a look into it."

"Mexico?"

"Yes. There was an explosion. It wasn't much, but big enough that one of our task forces noticed it on satellite imagery. The area is a hot spot for cartel activity, so we do a good amount of surveillance there to try to keep the drug runners in check."

She wondered why they hadn't simply bombed the area if they knew it was a drug cartel compound. Then again, that sort of action would have repercussions, especially since Mexico was an ally. Probably best she wasn't the president.

"I know you're working on this murder investigation, but I thought you'd want to know about this since our mutual friend is down there."

Emily couldn't remember if she'd told the president about where Sean was going or if he'd found out some other way. Not that it mattered. He knew.

"Yes, sir. I was just trying to get in touch with him. We think our prime suspect may have fled to that area of the world."

"Prime suspect?" he asked.

"Yes. We believe that Lilian Pike may have been the one pulling the strings behind the killings."

She waited for half a minute before he responded.

"So, you think she faked the attack on herself, including the gunshot wound?"

"I've seen crazier, so yes, we believe she may have been the one who orchestrated everything."

"And you have evidence to prove it?"

"I have a suspect who just left the country with very short notice to the rest of Capitol Hill. Seems kind of sudden after being attacked just a few days ago."

"I'm not questioning your motives or your thoughts on the matter. Just surprised, that's all. If you think Pike is the one behind all this, then by all means, bring her in for questioning."

"We were about to, and then she had a press conference announcing she was taking a leave of absence. Before we could get to her, she'd already left. We believe she flew into Belize, but who knows where she is now."

"So, she anticipated your move."

"That's the only thing I can figure."

"Well," he said, "perhaps you need to pay a visit to the Yucatan. I'm concerned about Sean and Tommy. I know they were going to be in the area where that explosion happened. The Mexican government isn't helping us out with this one. They won't even send a unit over to investigate. So, we'll have to do it ourselves. Only downside is that we'll be there illegally."

"Not if we're there on vacation," she said with a playful smile.

He let out a chuckle. "I wish we could, my dear. I wish we could. Won't be long now. No, I was thinking you could send someone down there to check it out. Now that you've told me about Pike, I'm even more inclined to issue the order."

Emily thought about it for a second. "I do have an agent available I could put in play down there if that's what you're suggesting."

"I don't know," he confessed. "At first, I was just thinking maybe have your people keep an eye on that area. But we're already doing that. It might be good to have eyes on the ground to recon the cartel camp and see what you can dig up."

Emily nodded. "I'll put someone on it right away, sir. I need to find Pike anyway. Now I can kill two birds with one stone."

"Okay. Sounds good. Thanks for doing this, Em...I mean, Director Starks."

"You're welcome, Mr. President."

Chapter 29

PLAYA DEL CARMEN, MEXICO

Erika closed the door as quietly as she could. She had no trouble picking the lock to the beach home overlooking the Gulf of Mexico. The security guards had a regular patrol path they walked that was easy enough to time to avoid detection.

She surveyed the dark living room and the kitchen just beyond to make sure no other guards were in place. The last thing she needed was to be accidentally shot by some rent-a-cop.

Satisfied no one else was in the house, she turned and went up the stairs to her left, tiptoeing as she went to stay as silent as possible. At the top of the stairs, she turned right and made her way stealthily down the hall until she reached a door on the left.

It was closed, though Erika suspected it was unlocked. She reached out, grabbed the doorknob, and gave it a gentle twist. Sure enough, it wasn't locked. She cautiously turned it all the way until the bolt came free of the plate and then gave the door a tenuous push.

It swung open with only a minor creak, but it was already too late. The owner of the house was sitting in the corner, wide awake, with a gun in her hand laid across her lap.

"I was wondering when you'd show up," the woman said from the shadows.

"It took longer than I anticipated," Erika said.

"Yes. I saw you had trouble getting away from the authorities in Atlanta."

"It went according to plan. I have the amulet."

"I'd hardly call it according to plan, but yes, you accomplished the mission objective. Well done."

Erika stepped all the way into the room and closed the door behind her. She took the amulet out of her jacket and walked over to the bed. After setting the glowing object on the edge of the mattress, she stepped away and stood by the wall opposite her employer.

"I've already wired the money to your account," the woman said.

"Yes, I saw that. Thank you. A big leap of faith considering I had what you wanted. You're very trusting."

The woman in the corner let out a long sigh and leaned forward, revealing her face. "Trust," Lilian said, "is something this world needs more of. Besides, you wouldn't cross me. You know what I'm capable of."

"You know what I am capable of as well."

"Indeed. Our mutual respect for one another breeds a necessity of trust, wouldn't you say?"

Lilian stood up and walked over to the bed. She set the pistol down next to the amulet and then lifted the jewelry to examine it more closely.

"It's beautiful," she said in a mesmerized tone.

"What makes it glow like that?" Erika asked.

Lilian flicked her eyebrows. "No one knows for sure. I'd bet those imbeciles at the IAA were trying to figure it out. With all their resources, though, I doubt they came up with any answers."

"When I found it, they had it in a storage vault under the main building. It was housed in a glass display case, like they were going to put it on exhibit sometime soon."

"Or perhaps that was just their way of protecting it. Lot of good it did them. Now, however, with this relic I will be unstoppable."

Lilian wandered over to the window and looked out at the foaming white waves of the ocean as they crashed onto the shore.

The night was perfectly clear; not a cloud in the sky. The nearly full moon hovered over the water, casting its pale reflection onto the rippling gulf.

"What's our next move?" Erika asked, watching her employer as she gazed out upon the sea.

"We wait for now."

Erika was puzzled. "Wait? Wait for what?"

"My puppets are deep in the Yucatan jungle right now, searching for the last piece of the puzzle. I heard from them a few days ago but told them not to call unless they had a legitimate update for me. They'll be in touch soon."

"How can you be so sure?" Erika asked, narrowing her eyes.

"Because Sean Wyatt and Tommy Schultz are the best. They always get the job done. That's why I chose them. I could have sought out any number of archaeologists or historians. I even have friends at the Smithsonian I could have called, but I chose them because only they are capable of going into dangerous situations and coming out unscathed. All the others would have balked at the offer. Those two are action junkies. They live for this sort of thing."

"What happens if they fail, if you don't hear from them?"

"I have a backup plan in place; however, I won't need to use it. They won't fail. Failure isn't part of their vocabulary."

Pike gazed at the amulet again. Now she possessed a relic with the power to grant eternal life. The only person on the planet that even had an inkling of her plans was the woman in the room with her. Erika had been told the goal behind the ultimate plan.

With no ties or emotional connections to anyone else in the world, Erika had signed on without hesitation. While some people wanted to make the world a better place, Lilian Pike had a plan. It was lofty, but a plan nonetheless.

Now that they possessed the amulet, they could begin setting the final pieces in motion and no one would be able to stop them.

Chapter 30

CHIAPAS

"Are we getting rusty?" Tommy asked as the three men were marched into a camp in a river basin deep in the jungle.

"What do you mean?" Sean asked as he tried, with hands bound with twine, to swat at a mosquito.

"Two times in as many days we've been captured by ruffians. Just wondering if we might be losing our touch."

"Ruffians?" Sean said with a laugh. "I don't know if we're losing our touch, but that's an interesting word to use."

"What?" Tommy asked, sounding a little offended. "How else would you describe these guys?"

A gunman behind Tommy jammed him in the kidneys with the barrel of his rifle, causing the American to grimace.

"Hey, watch it. That thing could go off," Tommy warned.

"This is not a good situation," Pablo said. "These men are ruthless killers. There will be no escape this time—unless of course you have some other miracle hidden up your sleeves."

"Well, if it's the end of the line, it's been a good ride," Sean said in an almost cheerful tone.

"I, for one, don't share his optimism," Tommy said. "But then again, I'm a worrier."

"He really is," Sean agreed. "Always has been."

"Death comes to us all," Pablo said. "Sooner or later, that is. So, why worry about it?"

"I just have a lot to live for," Tommy said. "Would rather face my fate later rather than sooner. That's all."

The gunmen marched the three into a camp that was eerily similar to the one run by the cartel. The procession wound its way through the outlying tents and into the central area of the camp, then left toward a huge tent covered in camouflage netting. Even with the thick green canopy above, these guys weren't taking any chances.

They walked through the entrance to the tent between two guards standing on either side with automatic rifles in their hands and menacing glares on their faces. The men were dirty and had a look of desperation in their vapid eyes.

"If I had to guess, I'd say it's probably going to be sooner than later," Pablo said.

"Run into these types before?" Tommy asked as they entered the dark tent. Only a few lanterns illuminated the room. A big wooden pole was in the center holding up the primary part of the roof.

Pablo shrugged, not exactly answering the question at first. "I may have had a run-in once or twice."

Tommy and Sean both raised their eyebrows and glanced at Pablo with surprise.

"It's not my first time in the jungle, you know."

"Quiet," one of the gunmen ordered.

"Oh, so you speak English?" Sean asked the diminutive gunman.

The guy didn't answer, which made Sean think maybe he only knew the one word. The man immediately started barking orders in Spanish, telling the others to line them up to meet their leader. He clearly didn't think the Americans knew what he was saying. That or he didn't care, which seemed to be a common theme lately.

The three men stood side by side, staring at the other side of the sparsely decorated tent. There was a wooden chair and a matching desk in the corner that looked like something left over from World War II. A narrow cot sat alone in the opposite corner. Other than that, there were only a couple of stools and other chairs in the room for occasions, Sean assumed, like this one.

"What are we waiting on?" Tommy asked, not that he expected an answer.

"Silence." The same guy from before gave the command.

"We're waiting for their leader," Sean said as he stared ahead at the place in the tent where the fabric parted. At the moment, it hung together, but he knew that soon someone would be coming through to issue their fate.

Sean knew he'd used up most of his tricks. He and the other two had no weapons, no explosives, nothing. The only thing that could save them now was a miracle.

"Leader?" Tommy asked.

His question led to a rifle butt to his lower back. Tommy grunted and doubled over for a second, instinctively trying to reach to where the pain pulsed, but his hands were tied and getting to it was impossible. He coughed several times before he could stand up somewhat straight.

Sean shook his head. "If I had a nickel for every time he's been hit in the kidneys with a gun."

Pablo turned his head and looked at Sean with a puzzled gaze.

The tent fabric in front of them parted, and two men with similar weapons to the others stepped in. One held the flap open for someone else to pass through, but it was impossible to see who it was at first.

First, the prisoners saw boots, then legs in military fatigues. Whoever was coming to greet them certainly had a flare for the dramatic. He walked slowly, letting each footstep hit the ground in a deliberate, threatening way to let the prisoners know he meant business.

As the man stepped into the light of the tent, Sean's concern turned to shock. The sweat on his forehead dripped to the ground as he scrunched his eyebrows together to make sure he wasn't seeing a ghost.

The tent flaps closed and before them stood a man with tanned, freckled skin, dirty blond hair, and one of the smuggest grins they'd ever seen.

"You killed two of my men," the leader said with a stone-cold expression on his face. His accent was American, probably Southern California.

"Which two?" Sean asked.

Pablo turned his head and fired a look at Sean that begged him not to be a smart aleck, not at the moment anyway.

"The two in the back of the truck. The driver survived."

"That's good. Maybe the other two shouldn't have been shooting at us."

"Maybe you shouldn't be somewhere you're not welcome."

"To be fair, we were just passing through, and my driver here"— Sean motioned to Tommy—"took a wrong turn."

The guerrilla leader put his hands on his hips and took a step toward Tommy. "Is that right? You took a wrong turn?"

"We were in a hurry. And your guys were already shooting at us. So, it's not really my fault."

The man pulled out a gun and held it out, pointing it toward Tommy's gut. "You saying it's my fault?"

"No. No, not at all. Just saying that we wouldn't have come through your territory."

"Shut it."

Tommy's lips pinched together.

The leader turned back toward Sean. "You gotta lot of nerve coming here after all you've done."

"I'm just getting started," Sean sneered.

Pablo and Tommy risked a questioning glance at each other out of the corner of their eyes. They were both wondering the same thing. Did these two know each other?

The leader stopped a few feet in front of Sean.

"You know, I'm glad to see you haven't changed, Sean. It will make crushing you feel so much better."

That answered Tommy and Pablo's question. The next question was, would that bode badly for them? Based on the remark about crushing him, the initial guess was that it would be bad.

"You've tried before, big boy. I don't see why anything would change now."

The leader stepped close to Sean, putting his toes an inch from Sean's. They were both about the same height, though the guerrilla leader probably had fifteen pounds on his counterpart.

"Cocky as always."

"Confident," Sean corrected. "Cocky people talk too much."

"You're talking too much now."

Silence fell across the room. Then the leader handed his gun to one of the subordinates and put his hands out wide. The next second, he wrapped his arms around Sean and patted him on the back.

"It's been too long, my old friend."

"That it has, Jack. That it has."

Pablo's and Tommy's faces curled in confusion.

"Emilio," Jack said, turning to one of the men behind the prisoners. "Get these ropes off of them. These men are my friends."

"Thank you," Sean said.

Emilio stepped over and produced a hunting knife. After making quick work of Sean's bonds, he cut through the other two and then returned to the side.

Tommy wrung his hands to get the feeling back in his fingers while Pablo shook his hands loosely by his hips.

"You men can wait outside," Jack said in Spanish.

The guards in the room immediately turned and walked out.

"You guys going to fill us in on how you know each other?" Tommy asked.

Sean chuckled. "Jack was with the CIA when I was with Axis. We helped each other out with a few things."

"Actually," Jack interrupted, "Sean helped me way more than I think I ever helped him."

"Nah," Sean disputed.

"Don't be so modest. Thanks to you, we took down several serious threats to national security."

Tommy raised an eyebrow. He knew about some of his friend's exploits, but Sean was always deliberately vague on the details.

"What are you guys doing way out here in the jungle? And seriously, did you have to kill two of my men?"

"They were shooting at us," Sean explained. "And I didn't know they were your men."

Jack shook his head and then turned to the other two. "So, who are these guys?"

"This is Tommy and our new friend, Pablo. We picked him up last night."

"Last night?"

"Yeah, we had a run-in with the local cartel. Barely escaped with our lives."

Jack's eyes widened. "So, you're the one."

Sean didn't follow. "One? One what?"

Jack let out a big, booming laugh. "You guys! You're the ones who blew up the Martinez compound. That camp was still smoking this morning. Wow. Nice work."

"Thanks, I think."

"Osvaldo Martinez is a bad person," Jack said. "He's been tormenting this region for a long time. Knocking him down a peg is a good thing, I promise."

"Well," Tommy cut in again, "we didn't knock him down a peg."

"No?"

"No. He's dead."

Jack's shock was written all over his face. "Really? You guys killed Martinez?"

The three visitors nodded.

"You know," he said, "I shouldn't be so surprised. Sean, you always were really good at your job."

"It was out of necessity, I assure you."

"Okay. Look, I don't care. That's one huge thorn out of my side. We've been having to watch our step for the last five years around these parts because of the cartel. Maybe now we can make a little progress."

"Progress? I'm sorry, what is it you're doing here?" Tommy asked.

Jack turned back toward him. "Isn't it obvious? We're running a revolution."

The three guests said nothing.

"Okay, actually, we're not trying to overthrow the government. We're taking down the cartels. Our job is to try to keep them in check as much as possible."

Sean shook his head. "What?"

Jack grinned and motioned for the men to follow him back out through the entrance. When they were all outside, he showed them the camp. "All these men," he said, "lost someone to the cartels. Some of their families were beheaded in the streets right in front of their eyes. Women, children, even pets were executed to make an example. Then they were sold as slaves or forced to work in the factories and cocaine camps around the country. I freed most of the early ones. As our numbers grew, we started taking on more aggressive missions, using hit-and-run tactics on supply trucks, convoys, even some of their airfields."

The three visitors listened in stunned silence as Jack described his operation. When he was done, no one said anything at first.

Sean was the first to break the silence. "That's a dangerous game you're playing, Jack. A very dangerous game."

"I was playing a dangerous game when I worked for the CIA, Sean. You know that. You played the same game. But we played for politicians, for governments who don't always believe in justice. I found these men when I was here on a mission from the United States government."

"Mission?" Tommy asked.

"Yeah, I was supposed to come down here and take down one of the cartel kingpins. Escobar had nothing on this guy, let me tell you. He had an empire that stretched all the way to Singapore."

"Does that mean you killed him?" Sean asked.

"No," Jack said. "Not for a lack of trying. Every time I got close, he was one step ahead. Through the years, we've been working to take down one cartel after another, but he's always remained elusive, dodging us at every turn. Sooner or later, though, he'll get his. He can't run forever."

"Jack Forrest always gets his man, huh?"

"Something like that. Anyway, I still can't believe you killed Martinez. I've had my eye on him for a while, but he runs—or ran—a tight operation. I'm curious how you pulled it off."

"It was less tactical than you might imagine," Sean said. "He captured us."

"Captured?" Jack laughed. "Sean Wyatt captured by a drug smuggler?"

"Happens more often than you might think," Tommy quipped.

"Look, Jack, I'm enjoying this little trip down memory lane, but we're kind of in a hurry."

Jack's expression changed to one filled with curiosity. "Oh? I was going to ask you what you guys were doing down here."

"I don't work for Axis anymore," Sean explained. "I work for him now. Tommy runs an archaeological recovery agency out of Atlanta. I won't get into the details, but we're here in Mexico looking for a lost Mayan temple. We were investigating a clue when Martinez caught up to us. We need a lift back to the nearest city and any weapons and ammunition you can spare."

Jack's eyebrows raised half an inch. He crossed his arms as he considered the request. "Yeah, we can get you to a town about an hour from here. It's on the coast. Lots of expats there, so you shouldn't run into too much trouble. We get most of our supplies there because it's one of the few places the cartel doesn't have a stranglehold." He eyed Pablo suspiciously. "What's with the local?"

"Pablo? We recently became friends. Isn't that right, Pabs?"

Pablo nodded but said nothing.

"Quiet, huh?" Jack asked. "That's okay. I'll have you guys back to civilization in no time. As far as transport goes, you can have your SUV back. Just follow one of my men out of the jungle, and you'll be fine."

Jack motioned for his guests to follow him.

He led the way to the middle of the camp and then hung a right, taking them into another large tent—this one with open walls facing the camp's interior.

"I imagine you boys need something to eat. We don't have much in the way of variety, but what we have will fill your bellies and get you feeling better."

"Thanks, Jack," Sean said.

They passed through one of the openings, and the smell of onions, garlic, and beef filled the air. A man was making fresh tortillas on a table to the side.

"I was wondering," Tommy said, "why is it the cartels don't come wipe you out?"

Jack gave a nod as he turned and looked over his shoulder at Tommy. "Good question. The secret is to make sure you don't leave any survivors."

"No survivors?" Pablo asked, finally finding his voice again.

"That's right. Some might think that leaving a witness or two would be better because then the witness could issue a warning to those in charge. Doesn't work that way. It's much better to let the dead do the talking."

"Yeah, but sooner or later they'll figure out it was you and your group here."

"That's why we leave clues," Jack said.

"Clues?"

"Yep. Make it look like it was the Mexican government doing the dirty work. The cartels have already been at it with the government for a long time. They think we're on the same side. I simply let them keep thinking that."

He grabbed a plate and handed it to Tommy. "Taco?"

Tommy nodded and took the plate gratefully.

The other two helped themselves and continued down the short line where there was a pan of beef, onions, some kind of sauce with cilantro, and a few other items the guests could add to their food.

"So, this thing you're looking for," Jack said, "what is it exactly?"

"We're trying to find a lost temple," Sean said.

"Right. Temple. Where is it?"

"We don't know. We found another clue, but we have to get back to civilization so we can try to figure out where to go next."

"Why civilization? Need the internet or something?"

"Yeah, or something. Why? Don't tell me you have an internet connection out here." Sean was dubious, but he didn't think the camp had anything like that.

"Nope," Jack said with a smile. "I haven't had internet since I came down here. Have to be honest. I don't miss it." He paused for a second. "Should I?"

The other three shook their heads.

"No. It's a mess," Sean said. "Everyone's on social media now, acting like they should get all the world's attention. It's really annoying."

"But the internet is useful, right? I mean, you can find stuff on there."

"Oh sure. It's useful. But being unplugged from it sounds pretty nice. I get away now and then to the wilderness to reset."

Jack nodded that he understood. "It's the best way to live, man. So, you're looking for a temple. Maybe I can help."

Sean and Tommy exchanged a sidelong glance.

"Really? How's that?"

Jack's lips creased into a huge smile. "There are other ways to find what you're looking for."

Chapter 31

CHIAPAS

"Here you go," Jack said. "This is everything we have."

Sean and Tommy looked around the tent, taking inventory of all the gadgets, gizmos, and technological equipment.

Some of it looked like it came from the industrial era when telephones were in their infancy and people were still reluctant to leave Morse Code behind. There were a few old radios along one of the tent walls. The antique communication devices were set up on top of rickety wooden tables and connected to a gasoline generator just outside.

A computer sat on a table along the far wall. It wasn't new, but it was less than five years old. Funny, Sean thought, how context changed one's point of view.

In the United States or most of the civilized world, a five-year-old computer was the equivalent to a few hundred years old. Deep in the heart of the jungle, however, things changed. Any kind of technology was a rare and appreciated blessing.

"You can use that computer to call anyone you need," Jack said, pointing at the rudimentary workstation. "We have a link that feeds

up to a satellite and then filters back down through wireless networks
and cell towers."

Sean raised a dubious eyebrow. Tommy, too, was suspicious.

"How did you manage that with this little operation?" Sean asked.

Jack flashed a mischievous grin. "Do you really want to know the
answer to that, or do you just want to make a call?"

Sean returned the smile. "I'll just make the call. But we have a
little work to do first."

"I thought you'd say that."

He led the way over to the desk and turned on the computer. It
flickered to life despite looking like it was covered in a month's worth
of dust.

"It's charged up and ready to go," Jack said. "The battery is pretty
old, so if you need it for more than half an hour, let me know and I'll
turn on the generator. What else can I get you?"

"Paper. Pen. Maybe a map if you have one."

Jack turned to one of his men and issued the order to get the
things Sean requested. Tommy and Pablo pulled up chairs and
circled around the workstation while Jack remained standing,
watching them over their shoulders.

Sean set down the diary and then placed the phone he'd taken
next to it.

He turned it on and went to the camera app, opened it, and pulled
up the images they'd taken in the cave behind the waterfall.

"Where'd you get that?" Jack asked.

"Took it off one of Martinez's men. He won't be needing it
anymore."

"What is that on the screen?"

"It's the code we've been working on," Tommy said. "This diary
works in conjunction with those engravings. We've found those
symbols in several places. One set leads to another, and as we
progress, the matrix becomes easier to solve."

Jack looked at the grid in the diary, then the image on the phone,
and back to the old book again. "How in the world do you guys find
this stuff?"

Sean rolled his shoulders and snorted a laugh. "This gig was actually a private deal. Someone wanted us to look into this book for her. We're trying to see if this lost temple is actually a source of power."

"Power?"

"Or evil," Pablo added with a heavy layer of cynicism.

"Evil?"

"Pabs is worried we're going to uncover something that might bring about the end of the world. He'd rather us not trigger the apocalypse."

Jack raised an eyebrow. "I'd prefer you not do that, as well."

"Obviously. The thing is, if this temple really does exist and there is something dangerous inside, better we find it than someone else. Right, Pabs?"

Pablo said nothing, but he didn't disagree. They'd already been over that.

"So, you're trying to find some ancient Mayan temple. We've seen all sorts of interesting stuff like that in the jungle over the years. You stumble across ruins pretty frequently. The jungle grows so quickly, I imagine most of the ancient buildings and other structures were probably covered up in a short amount of time."

"Which is why these clues are so important," Sean said. "If we can pinpoint the temple's location, we can avoid any needless wandering around."

"You definitely don't want to do that, the wandering thing. Lots of stuff out there that can kill you."

"Right."

Sean turned his attention to the phone and the diary.

A few seconds later, the guard Jack sent out returned with an old notepad, a pencil, and a folded map. The man laid the stuff on the workstation and returned to the corner of the room to watch in silence.

Tommy took the pencil and paper and started drawing the symbols on the notepad while Sean held the book open and kept the phone's screen from going back to sleep mode.

"It's weird," Tommy said, looking at the phone, "it seems like most of those emblems circle around those three dots in the center."

"I noticed that," Sean said. "Wonder why?"

Once Tommy had copied the symbols, he turned his attention to the diary and the matrix they'd been working from earlier in their quest. He created a new matrix and began working through the code to translate the symbols.

Two-thirds of the way through the translation, he scowled and scratched his head.

"What's the matter?" Pablo asked.

Tommy shook his head. "The translation. It's...it's nonsensical. Just random letters put together."

"Before you pass judgment," Sean said, "finish the code, and let's see what else it contains."

"Fine, but I'm telling you I don't like it. Something is wrong here."

Everyone leaned in closer as Tommy kept working, translating one symbol after another until he'd finished the entire sequence. He leaned back and put the pencil down. Tommy shook his head back and forth.

"I don't get it," he said.

The words on the page looked like a jumble puzzle with mixed-up consonants and vowels. There was no way to make hide nor hair of any of it.

"Maybe we have to shuffle the letters around to make sense of it," Sean offered.

"No," Tommy said, shaking his head. "I already thought of that. There's not enough vowels to make it work."

He stood up and walked to the other side of the room to take a breath and reset his mind. Sean, Pablo, and Jack remained at the table, still poring over the diary and phone images.

Sean frowned as he stared at the phone screen. He tilted his head to the side and narrowed his eyes.

"What if"—he paused for a second to make sure he wasn't suggesting something crazy—"these aren't part of the cipher from before?"

Tommy spun around and waited for further explanation.

"It could be that the cipher ended with the previous clue," Sean went on. "Maybe Alvarado wasn't trying to code this last piece at all but gave us the answer right there on the ceiling of the waterfall cave."

Tommy stepped back toward the workstation. "What do you mean, exactly?"

"Look at these images on the phone," Sean said. "Maybe the last site has a code all its own, a new one we have to figure out based on a completely new key."

"Then where is the key?" Tommy asked. "We can't solve the thing without it."

"It's not another language?" Pablo asked. "I know several different dialects from this region, and it relates to none of those. It could be something foreign."

Sean stood and paced around the room while he thought. Tommy mimicked his behavior along the opposite wall while Jack and Pablo remained by the table, trying to work out what the strange message could possibly mean.

After twenty minutes of working on it, no one could decipher the bizarre message. Jack stretched out his arms and yawned before he moved away from the table.

"You know what helps me when I'm in a pickle like this and can't figure something out?" he asked.

"What?" Tommy wondered.

"I step away from whatever it is I'm working on and take a break for a little while."

"We just started on this like twenty minutes ago," Tommy said.

"I know. And for that twenty minutes you were hammered down on that. Maybe you should take a step back, come out here by the campfire, and let things go for a while. Have some tequila. Try to relax. And maybe it will come to you."

"I think I'll pass on the tequila," Tommy said. "But maybe you're right. It might do us some good to give our brains a little rest. We've been working so hard on figuring this out, running from drug smugglers—"

"Killing my men," Jack added with a wink.

"Still, I'm sorry about that."

Jack shrugged. "Personally, I had my doubts about them. Pretty sure they were plotting to overthrow me. So, if you were going to take out any of my guys, those two were the ones to go."

"That makes me feel a little better," Sean said.

"Come on. It's getting dark outside. We make our own tequila here, and it's very good."

"I'll have some of that," Pablo said, standing up with an eagerness the other two hadn't seen in him since they met. "I need it."

Outside, dusk had already taken over. Twilight filled the jungle, bathing it in a pale darkness that grew blacker with every passing moment. The sounds of wildlife died slowly, leaving only a few tropical birds to fill the air with their exotic songs. In the center of camp a fire crackled, sending sparks and smoke high into an opening in the canopy above. The fire's dancing tongues of orange and yellow licked the air in wild and erratic fashion.

Some of Jack's men were standing guard at various points around the camp while several others took their turn around the fire, pouring each other tin cups full of home-brewed tequila. Jack spotted some empty chairs to the left and led the way over to them where he had a seat and offered his new guests one as well.

Sean and the others accepted graciously, easing into the rickety chairs where they could feel the warmth radiating from the fire. He looked up into the night sky as stars began twinkling in the ever-darkening blanket above. The smell of smoke filled his nostrils, a welcome scent from the past he didn't get the chance to enjoy all that often anymore.

"I miss camping," Sean said out of the blue. "I can see why you like it here."

Jack nodded. "Yeah, I mean, this setup has its challenges, but I don't miss my old life that much. There are times when I miss the little things like a hot shower or air conditioning, but you adjust.

The freedom that comes from living out here far outweighs the cons."

Tommy let their host finish as he stared into the hot coals at the bottom of the fire. Someone passed a jug of tequila to him, and he started to hand it off to Pablo when he realized the man who gave it to him was anxiously waiting for him to take a drink.

"No getting out of this one, Tommy," Jack said. "It would be rude to refuse."

Tommy sighed. "Really? Tequila isn't my thing. I mean, I don't really drink, but if I did, it would probably be bourbon or something like that."

"Tommy...." Sean prodded with a devilish grin.

"Fine," Tommy relented. He took the jug and tipped it up to his lips. The peppery liquid splashed into his mouth, and he swallowed with a grimace. The burn hit his throat as he lowered the jug. He nearly coughed the tequila all over his legs. Somehow, he fought off the urge and managed to keep it down before passing the jug to Pablo.

"Smooth, isn't it?" Jack asked, holding off a fit of laughter.

Tommy was still coughing a little, so he couldn't answer right away.

Meanwhile, Pablo tipped the jug back and took two giant swigs. Only a small dribble escaped down the side of his mouth and over his chin before he passed the jug to Sean.

"That isn't bad," Pablo said with smile. "Warms the soul."

Sean took the jug and passed it to their host.

"Don't want any?" Jack asked.

"I'm good," he said. "I prefer to keep all my wits about me. When you're already working on a brain cell deficit, it's best to hold on to as many as you can."

Jack pursed his lips and nodded, happy to take the jug and pour some tequila into his throat.

"Hey, wait a second," Tommy protested abruptly. "No, sir. You said it would be rude if I turned down a drink, but it's okay if he does it?"

Jack shrugged, holding the jug in front of his mouth. "I was messing with you. These guys don't care if you have a drink or not. More for us if you don't."

Sean and Pablo erupted into a full round of laughter while Jack enjoyed several gulps of the homemade liquor. Tommy shook his head, but he couldn't help joining in the laughter even if it was at his own expense.

The jug made its way around the campfire a few times before Pablo and Jack decided they'd had enough.

"I can see what you mean about the freedom of being out here," Tommy said after a long period of contemplative silence. "But it's got to be dangerous. I mean, the cartels are obviously bad news, but the wildlife here is equally as terrifying."

"Yep," Jack agreed. "It can be if you let it. We keep a pretty good perimeter so the venomous snakes and other dangerous animals usually stay away. Now and then, we spot a jaguar hanging out in the trees, but they typically keep to themselves. And there's always a fire burning at night to make sure any particularly brave animals will think twice."

"What about supplies?" Pablo asked. "You said you go into one of the towns to get things you need. Where do you get the money?"

"Ah," Jack said, holding up a finger. "Nothing gets by this guy. We are privately funded."

"Privately funded? By who?"

"That, my friends, is a secret and one I'm not permitted to share. Just know that we are well taken care of and want for nothing...well, except the air conditioning I mentioned before. This place gets pretty hot and humid."

None of the men had anything to add at that point, so they all fell into a comfortable silence, listening to the background noises of jungle mixed with a few sparse conversations from Jack's guerrillas.

Sean stared up into the sky. It was the first time he'd had a chance to relax in a while. Even though he knew danger might lurk all around them, he allowed himself to switch off and just enjoy the sights, smells, and sounds washing over him from all directions.

He hadn't had much time like that in recent memory. A few vacations with Adriana were his primary conduit for rest, though those were rare. He realized he'd not been in touch with her in nearly a week. Oddly, he hadn't even thought about her that much, though it wasn't without good reason. With everything going on in the lost temple mission, there hadn't been a lot of time to sit down and pine over her absence.

Now, however, he wished she was there, sitting by him at the campfire, enjoying a moment of quiet in the middle of the Mexican jungle. Maybe he had a weird sense of what it meant to relax. He didn't care. It was what he enjoyed, and it went perfectly with his skewed sense of adventure.

He put his palms on the back of his head and continued to gaze up into the night sky. Billions of stars twinkled like miniature lamps burning in a far-off galaxy. He knew some *were* galaxies. Others were stars in other solar systems, and a few were planets he knew well from his time spent studying astronomy.

Sean had taken the class out of pure curiosity. His major wasn't even remotely related, but that didn't matter. He'd always enjoyed looking at the stars as a younger man, even sitting out in his driveway to gaze up into the heavens at the incredible creation above.

He leaned back and soaked it in. They'd been sitting by the fire for over an hour, and he was starting to feel fatigue settling in.

As he stared into space, he cocked his head to the side. Something caught his eye. He turned his head to the other side and peered upward.

"No," he said out loud without even realizing it.

The other men heard him break the silence and looked over at him simultaneously.

"What?" Tommy spoke first. "What is it?"

Sean swallowed and shook his head quickly. He refocused his vision and stood up, still staring into the sky.

"It can't be," he muttered.

"What can't be?" Jack pressed.

Sean licked his lips. His heartbeat quickened. He'd grabbed the phone and diary on his way out of the tent, not because he thought someone might try to steal it but because he preferred to be safe than sorry.

He took the phone out of his pocket and tapped the home button. A few seconds later, he'd accessed the camera again and held it up to the sky. He twisted the device around and looked at the sky, then the image, and back at the sky.

"You gonna let us in on what you're doing, or you just want to keep us in the dark?" Tommy asked.

Sean turned to face his friend. "I think I got it."

Chapter 32

CHIAPAS

Tommy and the others followed Sean back into the big tent where all the tech gear was kept.

Sean strode through the entrance with purpose in his step. He beelined it over to the computer and switched it back on while the others gathered around him.

"Soooo, you think you got what?" Jack asked.

"I'd kill for a satellite link right now."

"Yeah...sorry about that."

Sean's fingers flew across the keyboard as he entered the information rapid-fire.

A few seconds went by before several results came up. He turned to the notes Tommy had left on the table and flipped the page over so it was upside down. Then he clicked on one of the results on the computer and pulled up the third image.

"See anything familiar?" Sean asked, leaning back in the chair.

"Whoa," Tommy said. "I never even considered that before."

Jack's eyes narrowed. "So, the symbols you guys found in that waterfall were actually constellations?"

Sean nodded. "Yeah. I think so. See," he pointed at the screen. "This is Cygnus, the swan constellation."

His fingers tapped away on the keyboard again, and a new set of results popped up. He clicked the first image on the following page, and a new constellation appeared.

"Lyra?" Pablo asked.

"Yep. The harp. And you can see here that it matches almost perfectly."

"And the last one?" Tommy asked.

"Aquila," Sean said before he performed the search. It only took a minute for him to show the others the last constellation. "It's a bird, sort of like Cygnus but shaped differently. Although if I had to guess I wouldn't say the shapes have much to do with the riddle or what we're looking for."

"Why's that?"

"Call it a hunch."

Tommy stood up straight while still gazing at the computer screen. "The ancient Mayans used to build villages, cities, and places of worship based on the stars. They studied the heavens relentlessly. Some people say they placed their buildings as mirrored locations on the planet to please the gods. Others say they did it because of their belief in the sacred connection between earth and sky."

"Whatever the reason they did it, one thing is clear: Ancient civilizations respected the stars. They knew there was some kind of connection between what's in space and who we are. The Hopi traveled thousands of miles to build towns along celestial patterns. The Aztecs and Incas did their construction in a similar way."

"So, you think this lost temple you guys are searching for might be related to these constellations?" Jack asked.

"Certainly seems that way based on the evidence. We just have to figure out which one of these stars represents the location of the temple."

"Yes," Pablo spoke up, "I imagine that will be easier said than done. There are so many stars, even in those three constellations. If one of those stars represents the temple location, how do we figure out which one?"

Sean frowned as he stared at the screen. He shifted his gaze to the paper and the matrix. Then he looked at the diary. There was something he'd not really paid attention to before, but now it seemed to stand out. It was a tiny mark in the bottom corner of the diary's final page. He flipped through several of the other pages to make sure he hadn't missed anything else. Seeing nothing of note, he returned to the last page.

"What are you doing?" Tommy asked.

Sean put his fingertip at the corner of the page where the miniature triangle was drawn. "See this before?"

Tommy leaned in. His eyelids nearly shut, leaving nothing but the narrowest of gaps as he focused on the tiny image. "No. I didn't notice that before. It's a triangle."

"What does that mean?" Jack asked.

Sean took a deep breath and thought. His eyes darted back and forth between the constellations, the notepad, and the triangle on the page. Everything was connected, but how?

He moved the computer mouse around and clicked the search bar again. Then his fingers flew across the keyboard, pecking at them loudly as he entered the terms. After he hit the enter key, another slew of results popped up. He clicked on the first image, then the second, and so on.

"What are you doing?" Pablo asked.

Sean didn't answer immediately. He was totally engrossed in the task at hand. "Trying to find a connection," he said after a minute of intense study.

"Connection to what?"

Sean hit the back button on the computer and then entered another search. This time, his search term was *triangle constellations*.

The screen populated after a long moment. He clicked on another result and stared at the image on the screen.

"Of course," he said after a second. "How did I not see that before?"

"See what before?" Jack asked.

"The Summer Triangle," Sean said. "That must be what the triangle means at the bottom of the page."

"For those of us who aren't astronomy geeks," Tommy said, "maybe you could fill us in on exactly what it is you're getting at here?"

In his excitement, Sean fumbled for the words. "The...the Summer Triangle isn't a constellation. It's a pattern in the sky that links three primary stars."

He opened one of the tabs on the screen he'd been looking at previously. His eyes flashed from the screen to the image on the phone and back again. He checked the picture of Aquila first, then Cygnus, then Lyra. "Oh. My. Goodness," he said.

"Would you please stop doing that and just tell us what's going on?" Tommy begged.

Sean nodded. "The Summer Triangle is composed of three primary stars: Altair in Aquila, Deneb in Cygnus, and Vega in Lyra. Alvarado found the first two sites, places that correspond with the stars, but he couldn't get to the last one before he died." Sean's voice grew quieter to the point of an almost reverent tone. "He was so close." Sean clicked the mouse and dragged it across the screen. Then he hit a few of the other buttons in tandem. The size of the image on the screen changed. He continued altering the dimensions until it was about the same size as the paper on the desk.

"Okay, I'm following you, but how do we know the location of the last star as it relates to a position here on Earth?"

"Simple. Well, sort of simple." Sean took the map on the table and laid it out flat. He found Tulum and pressed his finger on it. A second later, he marked a dot where he'd been holding the place. Then he found the area where they'd discovered Devil's Falls and made a mark with the pencil.

"These are the two we've seen so far. These places contained the clues to the next. To complete the triangle, we have to find the third star."

He returned his attention to the computer monitor and tilted his head to the side. Then he reached over and grabbed the notepad, ripped the next page down out of the binding, and placed it over the screen. He picked up the pencil and traced the lines of the triangle onto the paper, placing dots at every corner.

"That's one way of figuring out the correct angles," Tommy joked.

Sean smirked at his friend's sense of humor. "I didn't think our friend Jack would have a compass and protractor."

"You'd have thought wrong," Jack said. After a second, he started laughing when everyone looked at him to see if he was serious. "I'm kidding. Of course, we don't have those things. I haven't seen those since I was in sophomore geometry class."

Sean shook his head, still grinning. With his rudimentary drawing complete, he took the paper and placed it over the map. Ever so gently, he poked the tip of the pencil through the paper and pressed it down on Tulum. Then he pushed the paper down flush onto the map. He lifted the map to see how it related according to the locations they'd visited and then twisted the paper around until he estimated the dot on the sheet was directly over the dot that represented Devil's Falls. Again, he pressed the paper down flat against the map. This time, he took the pencil up from its place and gently drove it through the last dot on the surface. He wiggled it around to make a mark on the map and then pulled both pencil and paper away.

He stood up and looked at his handiwork with the others crowding around to get a good view.

"That's where we'll find it," Sean said, pointing at the last dot on the map.

Jack frowned. "There isn't much out there. Wild jungle, mostly. Although there are a few inhabitants."

"Cartel?"

"And more. Lots of wildlife in that area. Not to mention the ghosts."

The three guests turned their heads, puzzled.

"Ghosts?" Tommy asked.

"Well, they're not literally ghosts. Not that I know of. I don't believe in that mumbo jumbo. That's just what some of the locals call them. I've only heard rumors, stories about painted men who protect the jungle in that region. If I had to guess, I'd say they're some kind of tribal natives or something. Like I said, though, I've never come in contact with them. We don't typically venture into that sector."

"Lucky for us we don't believe in ghosts either," Sean said.

"Yeah, but that doesn't mean you shouldn't be careful. Anyone who has wandered into that area has never come out."

"Sounds like some kind of urban legend...well, maybe not urban. You know what I mean."

Jack chuckled. "I get you. You just need to be careful if you're planning on going into that part of the rain forest. That's all I'm saying. Keep your head on a swivel."

"We always do."

Sean turned back to the map and eyed it carefully. He ran his finger along the side and then into the middle where the third dot was positioned.

"What are you doing now?" Pablo asked.

"Getting the exact coordinates," Sean said. "It's time we updated our friend on how things are progressing."

"You're going to tell her?" Tommy asked, sounding leery.

"She wanted an update when we had something significant to share."

"Yeah, but—"

Sean frowned. "But what?"

"I don't know." Tommy rolled his shoulders. "I already told you all the reasons I don't like taking on clients."

"You want me to hold off?"

Tommy thought about it for several seconds before he shook his head. "No. Go ahead and call her. It might be good for someone back home to know where we are and where we're going. You know, just in case."

Jack and Pablo listened to the conversation. When the room fell silent, Jack took it to mean they were done.

"I'm sorry," he said with a confused look on his face. "Who is this *her* you guys are talking about?"

Sean and Tommy exchanged a knowing glance.

"You're not gonna like it," Sean said.

Chapter 33

CHETUMAL, MEXICO

Collin peered through his sunglasses at the people passing by. Hundreds of faces moved along the sidewalk on their way to work. Others—tourists—strolled by taking pictures or clutching their beach bags, eager to spend some time in the sand.

It had taken an intense couple of days of research and digging to try to locate anyone with any information on the whereabouts of Lilian Pike. Collin kept an extensive list of contacts around the world for missions just like this one. He'd built up a network in a short amount of time, a network it probably took other agents decades to compile.

He thanked his charisma, but really it was more about persistence.

Collin took a sip of coffee as he continued watching the masses parade by. Chetumal was a small coastal town of about a hundred and fifty thousand people. The pristine white beach ran along water that was bluer than Frank Sinatra's eyes. Situated on the border with Belize, it was the perfect place for someone to sneak across the border, although Collin doubted how much actual sneaking would be involved. A high-level stateswoman would be able to navigate such issues by either using influence or money. In this case, Collin thought it would be the latter, that is, if she came through that area.

Director Starks usually used him for less field work and more intel-type stuff, but all of the other agents were already on other assignments and since Axis only kept eleven on the roster, that meant he was up.

Axis was a strange organization. At least Collin thought so. Small, operating out of the scope of most of the government. When he was first asked to join, he wondered if it was legitimate. The whole thing seemed sketchy—right up to the moment he met the president. Then his mind changed rapidly.

He cut a piece of empanada with a fork and shoved it in his mouth. The cafe where he'd chosen to meet his contact wasn't much to look at: a plain white building with cracks running along the exterior walls and the word *Corusco's* painted on the side above the entrance. If Collin had learned one thing during his travels, it was to never judge an eatery by its appearance. He was pretty sure that it was an unspoken requirement that some of the biggest food gems around the world had to look like their buildings could be condemned at any moment.

He washed down the bite with another sip of coffee. As he set the mug down, he noticed a familiar face coming his way.

The man looked nervous. That was almost never a good sign. His name was Raul, and every time Collin had met him in the past, the guy acted a little unsteady. It was a stark contrast to the rest of the people moving by along the street and sidewalks.

Raul stumbled as he reached the curb and managed to catch his balance before falling flat on his face at Collin's feet. He was panting as he pulled up the other white metal chair at the table. After sitting, his eyes darted around the plaza, watching.

"What's the matter with you?" Collin said as he raised the mug again. "Looks like you've seen a ghost."

Raul swallowed. "You didn't tell me you were looking for a United States congressman."

"Technically, she's a woman, so I think it's congresswoman. Although now that I say it out loud, that doesn't sound right either. Let's just call her a politician."

"Shut up, you idiot," Raul snarled.

"Diplomat then?" Collin sipped the coffee with a grin, clearly not worried.

"Do you have any idea the hornet's nest you've kicked? The cartels will pay generously to anyone who can bring in an American politician. Do you have any idea how much that is worth?"

"So, we're going with politician then?" Collin waited for the reaction, but all he got was a bewildered stare. He snapped his head back and forth to blow off the comment. "I guess we're talking about value for ransom here? Is that what you're saying?"

"Ransom. Execution. Whatever. The cartel doesn't like the American government interfering with their business. If they get ahold of someone they believe is part of that government, it will be bad."

Collin's head twitched to the side. His nose crinkled for a second, and he narrowed his eyes. "What does that have to do with me trying to find Pike?"

Raul gave another look over his shoulder.

"Relax," Collin said. "I'm watching every direction."

Raul wasn't so confident. He remained tense, with thumbs twiddling one over the other. "What does it have to do with trying to find Pike? It has everything to do with it. When you start asking questions about an American government official in Mexico, word travels fast. You can't expect to keep that sort of thing covered up for long. The cartels know she's here, man. They're going after this woman. They might already have her."

"Okay, now you're being paranoid."

"No," Raul said with an intense look in his eyes. "This is their chance to strike back at the American government. I overheard one of the men saying the cartel wants to make an example of this one."

Up to that point, Collin had been able to dismiss most of what Raul was saying. The guy still had a little white powder in the under-

side of his nose from his morning key bump of cocaine, though
Collin had chosen not to bring it up.

If what his Mexican counterpart was saying was true, however,
that could mean trouble. Collin needed to get to Pike first. She had to
be brought in alive. He leaned across the table, folding his hands on
the surface.

"Where is she?" he asked.

Raul took another look over his shoulder. "I don't know. Okay? I
only know where she was going."

"Just as good. Hit me with it."

"She crossed the border yesterday. From the sound of it, she had a
convoy of SUVs. My guy said they have eyes on her, that they're
tracking her movement."

"Tracking her?"

"Yeah, man. That's what I'm trying to tell you. They know where
she is. I'd be surprised if she wasn't already dead or at the very least
being tortured."

"Where is she, Raul?"

"Last they heard she was in a hotel along the coast to the north of
the city. Resort place. The cartel doesn't mess around in that area
much because of the heavy military presence. Can't afford to lose the
tourist money. So, if she's there, she might be safe for now. The
second she leaves the resort, though, they'll nab her."

"You've told me a lot without really telling me anything, Raul.
Where is Lilian Pike?"

Raul slid a piece of paper across the table. Collin picked it up
while his guest continued to look around the plaza with a palpable
anxiety. The paper had the name of the hotel.

"That's where she was last night," Raul said. "I don't know if she's
still there or not. I've told you too much as it is. I'm pretty sure the
others were wondering why I was asking so many questions."

Collin stood up and took a wad of cash out of his pocket. He left
more than enough bills under his coffee saucer. Then he reached into
his other pocket and pulled out another stack of folded bills bound
by a rubber band. He tossed the cash to Raul.

"American," Collin said. "I hope that's okay."

Raul looked at the money with wide eyes.

"You ought to be able to buy a ton of blow with that. Or at least enough to get you through the weekend," he added.

Collin started to turn and walk away, but as he spun around he found himself facing a huge man in a black tank top and jeans that looked like they were from the late 1980s. The guy was easily two inches taller than Collin and had him outweighed by at least twenty pounds.

"Excuse me," Collin said. "Didn't see you standing there."

The man flexed his huge pectoral muscles and cracked his neck to one side and then the other.

Collin spun around and found Raul standing between two other men in white T-shirts and dark blue jeans. Both of the men were holding Raul by the back of the shirt.

Collin turned back to the big man in front of him. "So, I guess my question for you is, stone-washed jeans? Really? You look like you're going to a Def Leppard show."

The man reached out to grab him, but Collin stopped him. "I wouldn't do that if I was you," he warned. "Lot of people standing around. Don't want to cause a scene."

"Shut up and do what he says," Raul snapped. "These guys run this town."

Collin didn't flinch. He stared the big man in the eyes. "Fine. Where would you like us to go?"

The guy motioned to an alley off to the side of the cafe. There were a few dumpsters overflowing with garbage and some sand that must have blown in from the beach over the years.

"Oh I see. Quiet side street where no one will see what you do to us. Makes sense. That's what I'd do, too, although I might prefer taking a victim out to the middle of nowhere. I guess that's not how you guys operate, though, is it? You like to make examples."

The big man drew a pistol out of his belt and pointed it a Collin's chest.

"Okay, fine. I'll go. No need to get testy." Collin directed his next comment at Raul. "Your friends need a lesson in manners."

"Shut up," Raul said again.

Collin waited for another few seconds before he started toward the alley. He walked slow, deliberate, making sure he didn't do anything to startle the gunman, not yet at least.

The truth was, Collin wanted to get out of the crowd as much as they did. The difference was they had no idea with whom they were dealing.

They marched deep into the side street and around a corner between two buildings where no pedestrians could see them. Once they were completely out of view, the other two men shoved Raul over next to Collin.

"What are you going to do?" Raul asked. Fear spilled out of his lips.

"You know what we do to traitors," the big man said.

One of the smaller guys in a T-shirt produced a machete. The blade was old and even had a hint of rust to it, but the edge was sharp as a razor.

"How long has it been since you cleaned that thing?" Collin asked. "Just wondering because I haven't had a tetanus shot in a while."

The three henchmen frowned for a second, puzzled. Collin didn't know if it was the language barrier or the context that threw them off.

"On your knees," the man with the gun said.

Raul shook his head. "No. Please, don't do this. I didn't tell him anything. I swear."

"Then why are you so afraid, Raul? If you did nothing wrong, you should have nothing to fear."

"Please. I'm begging you. Don't kill me."

The guy with the machete motioned to T-shirt No. 2 to put Raul on his knees. He stepped forward and grabbed Raul by the shoulders, forcing him to the ground.

That was the next-to-last mistake he ever made.

Collin grabbed the gangster by the shirt and yanked him over so he was between the gunman and the American. A half second later, Collin's forearm was wrapped tightly around the guy's neck, using the thug as a human shield.

The gunman turned his pistol toward Collin.

"Drop the gun," Collin ordered. "Do it."

He saw the man's finger tense on the trigger and knew what was coming next. Collin had slightly miscalculated the loyalty between the cartel hitmen, but not entirely. He knew there was a chance the guy would light up his comrade. It was hope that caused him to offer the gunman a way out.

Oh well.

The big man squeezed the trigger. Collin shoved his captive forward as the weapon's muzzle spat fire and smoke. Round after round pounded the hapless gangster as he stumbled toward the gun. He collapsed into the gunman and knocked the shooter's hand to the side as he kept firing.

The guy with the machete reacted a tad slow but still fast enough to cause problems. He lunged at Collin with the blade held high over his shoulder and took a wild hack at the American's neck. Collin stepped to the side, easily dodging the attack while driving his knee into the man's midsection.

The attacker doubled over and nearly dropped the weapon, but he recovered well enough to spin around and try again.

Collin saw the gunman shrug off his dead associate, sloughing the body to the ground as he turned and readied to fire again. Collin whirled around and grabbed the guy with the machete as he took another swing, this time at the American's shoulder. He twisted the gangster's arm into an L shape and jerked it up and back, dislodging the shoulder from the socket.

The guy screamed as the blade hit the ground with a clank. Collin spun him around and dropped to the ground a second before the gunman unloaded the rest of his magazine in a barrage of loud gunfire.

Bullets ripped through the gangster's chest, back, and arms as he spun around in a carousel of death before he fell to his knees then onto his face.

Collin rolled to the side, scooping the machete as he moved. The gunman raised the weapon as Collin stood only seven feet away from the end of the gun barrel.

The gunman flashed a crooked-toothed grin. "Adios, gringo."

Collin cocked his head to the side and smiled back. "I'm not entirely sure, but I think you just used up all your rounds."

The big man's forehead wrinkled with a frown as he pulled the trigger. The weapon clicked. It clicked again and again as he tried to fire the gun, but Collin was right. He was out of ammunition.

Collin stepped toward him with the machete gripped firmly in his hand. The guy tossed the gun aside and reached to his hip. He drew a long hunting knife and brandished it menacingly. The shiny blade flashed in the sunlight.

"That's not a knife," Collin said, holding up the machete. "This is a knife."

The guy lunged toward him, whipping the knife tip back and forth, hoping to catch the American in the gut or, if he was lucky, in the neck.

Collin deflected the first swipe with a counter of his own. The second swing was a backhand, and Collin grabbed the guy's forearm and pulled him hard in the same direction, using his momentum against him.

The attacker stumbled forward but maintained his balance enough to stay on his feet. Collin could have followed and ended the fight right then and there, but the sick part of him was enjoying it too much to stop things so quickly.

"Your form's a little off," he taunted. "Make sure when you wage a knife attack that you keep your balance."

The big man grunted as he spun around and charged the American again. Now he was even angrier, more reckless. Collin slid to the side as the guy tried a stabbing lurch. A quick flick of the wrist, and the machete cut the man's right arm as he rushed by.

He yelped at the sudden stinging pain coming from his arm and looked down at the cut. Blood didn't appear for a few seconds, then it came suddenly, oozing freely down the skin and dripping onto the ground.

The wound only angered the man further. He growled and lunged forward again with the knife, jerking the blade left to right in a furious rage. Collin's forearm collided with the attacker's. Both men winced from their bones striking, but Collin reacted faster. He twisted his arm down, knocking the other guy's arm toward the ground, then drove his hand into his own torso just below the rib cage.

The raging Mexican's eyes went wide as Collin forced the blade deeper. The man grabbed at the knife handle with both hands. Collin raised the machete and brought it down on the guy's wrist. The blade was sharper than most machetes he'd seen, and the edge cut through to the bone with ease.

A howling scream escaped the man's mouth, to which Collin finished pushing the knife into the hilt. The guy lurched violently. Collin twisted the blade and then pulled it to the right, knowing an artery was close to the sharp metal.

He knew when he hit it. There was slight resistance and then a clipping feeling, then the crimson liquid flowed from the wound.

The killer dropped to his knees, still grasping at the handle with one ineffective hand as he stared up into Collin's eyes.

The American let him slump over onto the ground and stood there for another minute making sure he wasn't getting up again. Then he turned and looked for Raul.

His Mexican connection was lying on the ground with his back against the wall and his shoulder pressed against a dumpster. A dark hole in his forehead told Collin the story of Raul's fate. In the chaos, the gunman must have accidentally shot Raul.

Collin dropped the machete and walked over to Raul's body. He stared at him for a second and then reached down and fished the wad of money he'd given Raul earlier.

"I guess you won't be needing this," Collin said, doing his best not to be irreverent. Raul was a scumbag. Collin knew that, so he had no intention of mourning the loss. To him, it was like losing a favorite tool from the garage. He could always get another one, but that would be a pain.

He didn't have time to think about replenishing his network. Lilian Pike was his target, and apparently she wasn't far away.

Chapter 34

CHIAPAS

"Shame Jack couldn't come with us," Sean said as he and the others trudged down a hill in the soaking wet jungle. "But I understand. He has other concerns."

"Yeah, I'd say he's busy," Tommy agreed.

The three men kept their heads on a swivel, turning left and right, constantly on the lookout for danger of any kind.

Jack had given them their SUV back along with weapons and ammunition. Sean was grateful for the supplies, though he missed his trusty Springfield at his side. The Kalashnikov in his hands would do, but he'd have preferred something a tad more reliable and far more accurate. In a pinch, though, the AK would work fine.

Birds squawked in the canopy above. Rainwater from a storm that went through an hour before dripped onto the men intermittently. Most of the forest floor was covered in leaves, twigs, and debris, though the animal path they were on had thick patches of mud that drove the men off course for a few yards at a time.

Sean stopped by a huge tree and pulled out the map again. They'd been tracking toward the point he'd drawn the night before, checking every twenty minutes or so to make sure they were still going the right way. The hike had already consumed two hours, and

Sean had initially wondered if they should have brought more supplies, perhaps for an overnight stay in the forest.

"According to the map," he said, "it shouldn't be too far now. Just over that next ridge over there, and we should be right on top of it."

"I hope you're right," Tommy said, wiping his forehead with his forearm. "I gotta tell you, I cannot wait to get back to the office."

Sean laughed and raised an eyebrow. "This humidity is something else, isn't it?"

"I thought you two were from the Southern United States," Pablo said. "Doesn't it get hot there?"

"Yeah," Tommy nodded. "It gets pretty hot. And the humidity is bad in the summer months. It's nothing like this, though. This is next level. I mean, I've been to Charleston, South Carolina, in the middle of July, and it can't touch this."

"At least the rain cools us off here," Sean added. "Come on. Let's keep going. Standing around here talking about it isn't going to make things any better. And we have a temple to find."

Sean stuffed the map back in his gear bag and pressed on down the hill, grabbing low-hanging tree branches along the way to keep from slipping and busting his tail.

The downhill part wasn't so bad, but the hard work began at the bottom of the ravine where they began the difficult task of climbing the steep hill on the other side. It took nearly half an hour for the three to make it two thirds of the way to the top, where they stopped again to drink some water and catch their breath.

The men didn't say much while they recovered. When it was time to get moving again, Sean made a weary motion to the others, and they got going once more.

Arriving at the top of the ridge brought relief to every man's face. Then they were given a small reward for their efforts. The crest rounded at the top, and the thick stands of trees parted slightly to give them an incredible view of the foothills and jungle spreading out over thousands of square miles.

Down the other side of the little mountain, a roundish basin spread out, almost like a giant bowl had been placed there millennia ago to imprint the land.

Sean took a long drink of water and looked out over the setting. "Based on this map, the temple should be somewhere down there in that basin."

"That's a big area to cover," Tommy said. "Could take a couple of days to search all of it."

"The ancient Mayans were extremely precise with their designs and with their construction. If our calculations are correct and this is the right place, the temple should be somewhere in the center of that basin."

"Like a giant dot on the map."

"That's if your conclusions were correct," Pablo said, playing devil's advocate.

Sean grinned at the snide comment. "I like your style, Pabs. Maybe when this is all over you can come work with us at IAA."

Tommy's eyebrows lifted high with surprise.

"Thanks, but I'll pass."

"I know, because you have a duty, and even when or if we find this place, you'll still feel like you have to protect it."

"Actually, I think I'll take a vacation. If this place isn't dangerous, I believe I'll go somewhere milder. Perhaps British Columbia. I hear the weather there is much cooler."

Sean pursed his lips and nodded, appreciating the response.

"Sounds like you've thought about this."

"You could say that."

Sean's eyes caught movement in the jungle below, and he snapped his head to the right. "We're not alone," he said.

The other two looked down into the basin but didn't see anything.

"Get down," Sean said, motioning with his left hand like he was pressing something toward the ground.

He and the other two got on their bellies with weapons out in front of them, ready to fire if necessary.

Sean kept his eyes locked on the place where he'd seen the movement. There was no sign of an animal or another human. Was his mind playing tricks on him? Maybe it was the heat finally toying with his brain.

"You sure you saw something?" Tommy whispered after nearly two minutes of watching the jungle.

Sean nodded.

Another minute passed when they saw something fly from one tree branch to another about two hundred yards away.

"There," Tommy said, almost shouting. He instantly muffled his voice. "There it was."

"Yeah, I saw it."

"What was that thing?" Pablo asked, keeping his voice as low as possible. "Monkey?"

"I don't think so," Sean said. "Looked like a human leg."

"You think it's one of those ghosts Jack was talking about?" Tommy asked.

Sean didn't know the answer, but if he had to guess, that's what he would have thought. "Maybe. This is the area Jack said those guys are guarding. I'm pretty sure that was a human leg, but it was covered in dark gray and green paint. Perfect camouflage for this part of the world."

He kept his eyes locked on the tree where he'd seen the creature land. Minutes passed and nothing happened.

"What is he doing?" Pablo asked.

"Maybe he had to use the bathroom," Tommy offered.

Sean shook his head at the silly comment. "Doubtful."

Something didn't feel right. Sean had experienced the same feeling many times before when trouble was about to strike. The birds no longer chirped or sang in the treetops. There were no signs of any wildlife either. No snakes or mammals crawling through the branches or on the ground. It was almost as if the entire forest had gone quiet. More than that, there was an ominous feeling hanging in the air, like the three men had crossed a boundary into an area where no creatures lived other than the thing they'd seen in the basin below.

"You guys notice you can't hear the birds anymore?" Sean asked just above a whisper.

"Now that you mention it," Tommy said. "Yeah. That's kind of creepy."

Pablo had a fearful look on his face. "We shouldn't be here. This is a place of death. I tried to tell you two not to come here. We should leave."

He started to get up, but Sean put his hand on Pablo's back and kept him down low. "If you go now, they'll see you." Sean eyed him with tempered disdain. Up until this point, Pablo had seemed somewhat brave. And he'd acted with military precision to take out Martinez's men at the waterfall. The sudden look of panic in the man's eyes was disconcerting.

"Remember why we're here," Sean added.

Pablo let out a sigh. His head turned back and forth as he lowered his body to the ground. "I was wrong to help you. This place is cursed. None of us should be here. This place has been untouched for centuries. Why do you think that is? Evil spirits are at work here. We mustn't disturb them."

"They're not spirits," Sean said, pointing into a tree close to the one where they'd seen the leg a few minutes before. "They're just men."

Pablo followed Sean's finger until he saw the target in the branches. Two legs were wrapped around a tree trunk, with feet planted on two opposing limbs. The person's arms also encircled the tree, but they couldn't see the face. Only shoulders and appendages.

"That's no ghost," Sean reiterated. "It's just a man. I've seen tribal types like this before. They prey on your fear. That's their power. Other than that, they're just people."

"So what, you want to waltz down there and eliminate 'em?" Tommy asked. "Looks like an ambush if you ask me."

Sean agreed with his friend's assessment; it smelled like a trap. For that to be the case, though, the men in the trees below would have to know they were coming. How could they? Then again, it was possible that these "ghosts" had been watching them since they arrived in that part of the rain forest. There was no telling how long they'd been under surveillance.

"We need a plan," Sean said.

"You're usually the one who comes up with that."

"I know. Feel free to chip in whenever."

"You've done well enough to keep us alive this long. No need to change now."

Pablo listened to the back-and-forth conversation between the two and finally decided to cut in. "If you're going to do this, you need a diversion."

Sean and Tommy looked at each other and then at Pablo.

"We've used those before," Sean said. "What exactly did you have in mind?"

"One of you could run down the hill and get their attention. Then you run back as fast as you can to draw them in."

"Draw them into what?" Tommy asked.

"To our own trap. We can take them out when they follow you back to here or wherever we set up."

It was a good idea in theory except for one problem.

"That's great," Sean said, "but running back up that hill will be tough. This thing is a small mountain." He motioned to the ridge.

"Well, if you guys have any ideas, I'm open to suggestions."

Tommy stared up into the treetops with wide, glazed-over eyes. "Guys. I think we can forget that plan."

"Why?" Sean and Pablo asked in tandem.

"Because they're looking right at us."

The other two men followed Tommy's gaze up into the trees and realized what had him spooked. Dozens of men with paint covering most of their bodies and faces were standing on tree branches high above. Several had bows and arrows. Others had blowguns held to their mouths, aimed at the trespassers below.

"What do we do?" Pablo whispered. He couldn't hide the sudden returning fear in his voice.

"Retreat," Sean said. "I'll cover you. Go. Now!"

He dug in, took aim up into the canopy, and opened fire. The other two didn't need to be told twice. They sprang from their positions and ran back down the trail. Their retreat was short-lived. Darts and arrows flew in a barrage, sinking into the ground around them.

"They've got us pinned down!" Tommy shouted as he dove for cover behind a dead tree to the side of the trail.

Pablo hurled himself in the other direction behind a huge stump.

Sean hit one of the men in the leg, taking out a huge chunk of flesh. The man howled and fell from his high position and hit the ground with a thud. Sean took aim at a bowman as he loosed an arrow. There was barely time to roll out of the way as the arrow thumped. The second the tip hit the dirt a few inches from Sean's side, he straightened his aim and fired another shot.

The round hit the bowman in the chest and sent him flying backward from the tree limb, down to his death forty feet below.

More darts and arrows followed, and Sean had to scramble to take cover behind a big tree to his right. He looked down at Pablo and Tommy and saw they were trapped as well.

Sean spun around and fired a few wild shots into the canopy before returning to the temporary safety of the tree. In the brief moment he'd looked out from behind the trunk, he saw something terrifying. Dozens more painted men were swinging his way via thick vines. Others were charging up the hill, yelling something in a tongue he didn't understand. He pivoted around again and opened fire at the men coming in through the air. One took a bullet in the shoulder. Another took a shot to the chest. Both fell to the earth and writhed in a heap while the battle continued around them.

Then Tommy and Pablo opened fire. Tommy was more selective, only firing one or two shots at a time to keep the weapon balanced and accurate. Pablo, on the other hand, emptied his first magazine in less than ten seconds. The recoil drove the muzzle up every time he squeezed the trigger, sending rounds of hot metal sailing through the green leaves above.

Out of sheer luck, Pablo struck one of them in the head and caused another two to jump clear of the hailstorm, which proved fatal for one and rendered the other immobilized from shattered bones in his legs and pelvis.

"What's it looking like on your end?" Tommy shouted up to Sean thirty feet away.

"We're not going to have enough rounds!" Sean yelled back. "There are more of them coming!"

"Not good!"

Sean spun around and squeezed off another shot, missing the target by a few feet before he had to return to cover as the tribesmen kept firing their ancient but deadly projectiles.

He knew there was only one option. Looking down from above his companions, he saw that the reinforcements weren't coming from the other direction, only over the ridge.

Sean made a quick decision. "We have to make a run for the truck!" he shouted. "I'll cover you two! Get through the initial wave, and then cover me, taking them out from behind!"

"You sure about that?" Tommy yelled back as he fired another shot from his cover behind the dead log. "They'll pick us off! There are too many of them!"

Sean knew his friend was probably right, but it was their only chance. They couldn't make a run into the basin. That would put them right in the teeth of the enemy.

"No other choice, Schultzie! Too many the other way, and if we don't make a move now they'll have us surrounded on all sides in no time!"

Sean spun around again and fired. This time, he let several rounds loose, spraying a deadly hail of metal at the enemy. Two more of the attackers fell from trees. Then Sean altered his aim toward the men on the ground, who were closing in fast. Several of them carried old spears that looked like they were from the Stone Age. He knew the tips were probably poisoned, as were the blow darts and possibly the arrows.

One nick of the skin from one of those things, and death would come quickly and painfully.

Sean ejected the magazine from his weapon and rapidly loaded a new one. He chambered the first round and took aim at the onrushing attackers who were bearing down in a hurry. The weapon's muzzle flashed as Sean fired round after round at the desperate charge.

He dropped six of the crazed men in seconds. Another popped around his tree, holding a dagger menacingly in one hand. The guy screamed some inaudible word and started to bring the tip of the blade down toward Sean's neck. Sean swung the butt of his gun around and struck the man in the gut. As the injured attacker doubled over, Sean raised his weapon and hit the guy on the back of the head with the same part of the gun, dropping him to the ground and rendering him instantly unconscious.

Another look down in the basin was all Sean needed. The painted warriors were swarming like ants rushing out of a kicked anthill.

"Get back to the SUV!" he shouted.

He fired into the trees to give Tommy and Pablo time to escape. The targets ducked behind tree trunks or danced side to side to avoid being hit. One lost his balance and fell to the ground headfirst. His body twitched next to the trail as Tommy and Pablo ran by it at a full sprint.

Suddenly, gunfire erupted from somewhere else in the woods.

The painted men in the trees fell one after another all around.

Tommy and Pablo skidded to a stop and dropped to their knees, desperately looking around to find the source of the new shooters.

Sean heard more guns popping to his right and left. He didn't have to look long to see where it was coming from. Men in dark green tactical gear were positioned around the outside of the circle the tribesmen had formed around their targets. Now they were exposed from behind with nowhere to run.

"Americans?" Sean said to himself, wondering what the newcomers were doing there.

As long as they were both shooting at the same enemy, he didn't care. Sean spun around and continued to fire as the painted men now tried to turn and run.

The men in the trees behind Sean's position were wiped out in short order as Tommy and Pablo continued the fight, picking them off from the trail while the new support took out the enemy from the side.

When there were no more targets, Tommy and Pablo turned around and returned to Sean's position next to the tree. Emboldened by the sudden change in fortune, the three pushed ahead, forcing the attackers back into the jungle.

The men in the tactical gear charged forward, taking the top of the ridge in a broad line that spanned several hundred feet. The fleeing targets disappeared into the dense foliage, though most of them were strewn about the forest floor. A few were still alive, writhing in pain in the dirt. The vast majority were lying still.

Sean stepped over to one of the dead men and knelt down beside him. The warpaint was fresh. Then he noticed something in the man's tattered clothing. He reached in and pulled out a tiny bag of white powder. Initially, he'd felt guilty about shooting at what he figured was an indigenous tribe. After all, they were just protecting their land. Now Sean realized that wasn't what they were guarding. They were working for a cartel. Which one, Sean had no idea.

One of the gunmen, a guy in a green hat with a thick, black beard turned toward Sean and put a hand up. "You Sean Wyatt?" he asked.

Sean's forehead wrinkled as he tried to place the man's face. "Yeah. I'm sorry, I don't think I know you."

"You don't. Name's Kirk. Todd Kirk. We're here with Lilian Pike."

Chapter 35

CHIAPAS

The smoke from the gunfight still hung thick in the air as Sean watched Lilian Pike stride confidently up the hill. She looked nothing like before when she was dressed in her stately business suit with hair neatly brushed. If she had makeup on, it was minimal.

She had a hat similar to the one Kirk and the rest of his team wore. Her clothes were only slightly different, a black tank top with a green long-sleeve button-up over it and matching pants. Unlike the rest, she only carried a pistol on her hip and no tactical backpack.

"That was quick," Sean said with a hint of suspicion in his tone.

Lilian was honest in her response. "I was already in Mexico when I received your message."

Sean frowned, confused. "Already in Mexico. Why? You on vacation?"

"I knew the general area where you were and wanted to be able to lend assistance if needed." She surveyed the battlefield littered with the bodies of the so-called ghosts. "From the looks of it, I'd say that was a good call on my part."

"Indeed."

Tommy and Pablo stood next to Sean with their weapons hanging from their shoulders.

"I see you picked up another member of your group," she said, motioning to Pablo. "Is he with your agency?"

"No, ma'am," Tommy said. "Pablo is local. We thought it might be wise to have someone with us who knows the lay of the land since Sean and I haven't been through this area." He hoped she bought the lie.

"Good thinking," Lilian said.

She looked around as the rest of her men swept the area to make sure there were no more stragglers.

"So, where's this temple?" she asked. "Your message suggested it was here."

"We figure it's down in the basin," Sean pointed in that direction. "Apparently, those men were guarding it."

"There has to be something important down there if all those guys were willing to die for it," Tommy added.

"You haven't found it yet?" Lilian asked, sounding a little disappointed and surprised.

"No, but that means you'll be here when we do. By our calculations, it should be in the center of that giant bowl."

"Then what are we waiting for?" she asked. "I don't want to spend more time in this jungle than I have to. Just because I grew up in the country doesn't mean I want to be this far off the grid."

"Yes, ma'am," Tommy said. "Follow me."

He motioned down the trail leading into the basin, but Lilian stopped him. "Why don't you let two of my men lead the way?"

Tommy started to protest and tell her he and his associates could take care of themselves, but then he decided against it. What was the point?

"Sure," he said with a thick reluctance in his voice.

Kirk and one of the other men stepped in front of Tommy as the group proceeded down the trail.

Sean didn't let on, but he counted ten men with the congress-woman. Quite a bit of firepower she'd brought with her. That meant she'd not come to Mexico for a quiet getaway. This trip was all business. What he didn't understand was why she'd come at all. Recovering lost items or finding where they were hidden was Sean and Tommy's job. It was why she'd hired them in the first place. She didn't seem like the type that would venture into a dangerous jungle in search of ancient ruins or artifacts. Something didn't feel right, but he couldn't put his finger on it.

Tommy and the others led the way down the trail, through the last remains of acrid gun smoke and past the dead ghosts lying here and there, until they reached the bottom of the hill. A shallow stream cut through the jungle, winding its way between trees through a ditch that divided the foot of the ridge from the rest of the basin.

Sean kept his eyes peeled as the procession crossed the creek, venturing deeper into the forest. They'd not taken out all the ghosts during the fight, and it was likely the painted men had taken up new defensive positions. All the tribesmen needed was for the intruders to mentally switch off for a few seconds to launch a new attack.

Taking a blow dart or arrow in the chest was the last thing Sean wanted at that moment—at any moment. He was glad to see Pike's men were taking every precaution, sweeping every possible angle as they pushed forward.

Sean tucked into line just behind his friend with Pablo behind him. "So, Kirk, how'd you get into the mess? Former beret? Navy SEAL?"

"Army ranger," he said, keeping his voice low. "Been doing private security for about three years now. My team is made up of guys from all kinds of backgrounds. Most of them have been in the military. A few were with government agencies, much like yourself."

Sean couldn't tell, but it almost sounded like Kirk had a hint of disdain in his voice. He didn't infer too much from it. This was no time to be petty.

They marched for ten minutes before Tommy, his hand shooting up, halted the group. He motioned for the others to stop. He peered into the jungle through the thick foliage. There was no sign of a temple or anything that even looked remotely like it could have been an ancient holy place.

"We need to split up," Tommy said. "We'll be able to search faster if we spread out."

"That will also make us susceptible," Kirk whispered. "We took out most of those...whatever those guys were." He motioned over his shoulder where the fight had taken place. "That doesn't mean there aren't more of them regrouping somewhere. I'd suggest we stick together, just to be safe."

Tommy understood. "Fine, but at the very least we need to go wide, cover as much ground as possible."

He turned to Sean. "Let me see the diary."

Sean produced the little book and handed it to his friend. Tommy flipped through the pages until he came to the point where the three symbols were drawn around the three dots.

"Look for anything that resembles one of these symbols," he whispered to Kirk, who signaled the order to his troops. Tommy held up the page so everyone could see.

"Symbols?" Lilian murmured. "Where?"

Tommy shook his head. "I don't know. Just be on the lookout for them. If you find one, it's a good bet we're getting close to the temple."

Lilian took a long look at the page and then turned to Kirk. "You heard him. Spread out. Stay close to each other, but open up your ranks." She smacked a mosquito on her arm. "I want to get out of this place ASAP."

"Yes, ma'am," Kirk said with a hint of reluctance in his voice. He turned to the rest of the men.

Sean watched as Kirk signaled the group to fan out. One of the men in the group had kept his head down since they'd arrived, concealing his face. Sean hadn't really paid much attention to each member of Pike's security team, but now that they were splitting up, this one stood out. He wore a black scarf over his face and an olive green hat pulled down low. His figure, however, was different. Underneath the tactical vest and gear, that soldier was slightly smaller, lither than the others. Sean watched closely, doing his best not to look like he was watching closely. While the group divided into a staggered, diagonal line across the jungle, he saw the mystery soldier's eyes as he tipped his head up.

It was a woman. Her hair was pulled up into the hat, but a single blonde strand had broken free and dangled by her ear. Sean's eyes narrowed. *I wonder where they found her,* he thought. She had to be tough to be a part of this unit.

The woman fell into line close to Pike and lowered her head once more as if she was consciously trying to keep her identity a secret.

When the line was formed, the entire group covered a huge amount of space. From one end to the other, it was over a hundred feet wide. Each person had ten or so feet between them to stay close in case the ghosts returned.

"I assume you know which way to go," Lilian said to Tommy.

He didn't, but Sean had a suggestion. "Move along the creek bed," he said. "We know the temple is in the basin." He didn't know that as a 100 percent certainty, but he was pretty sure.

"Very well," she said and turned to Kirk, who signaled to his men.

The group started moving again, now more methodically than before. Each person was on full alert, watching for any sign that the painted tribesmen might return. Every set of eyes scanned the trees above and the earth beneath. They could be anywhere.

Five minutes crawled by as they pressed ahead. Eerie silence filled the jungle. Not even the sounds of animals outside the basin could be heard, as if they were inside a glass wall surrounding the entire ravine.

A gunshot from the left flank of the line startled everyone. Sean and Tommy were close to the center and immediately broke rank to look over and see what happened.

The female member of the security team was standing ahead of the rest, holding her pistol in two hands, pointing it at the ground. A thin stream of grayish smoke trickled out of the barrel.

Sean and the others rushed over to where she was standing.

Pablo was the first to speak as he looked down at what had caused the woman to fire.

"Hognose viper," he said, staring at a brown snake with a bloody, mangled head. "It's against Mexican law to kill one of those." He looked at the blonde woman with irritation.

"It's also extremely venomous," the woman said.

"You know snakes of the Yucatan?"

"I make it my business to know any dangers I might encounter wherever I go."

Sean detected a Scandinavian hint to her accent. Swedish if he guessed correctly. Maybe Norwegian or Danish. He couldn't tell for certain.

"I think we can let this one go, Pabs," Sean said. He looked up and made eye contact with the woman. "Wouldn't want anyone accidentally stepping on one of those things if we come back through the area."

"It's an endangered species," Pablo insisted.

"Look on the bright side. That one isn't in any danger anymore. Come on. Let's keep moving."

"Hold on," Tommy said.

Everyone turned their heads toward him. He was standing just out in front of the rest of the group, on the other side of the dead serpent. His eyes, however, were turned slightly to the right. They followed his gaze to a large boulder sticking out of the ground. On the side of the rock, almost invisible to the naked eye, was a figure carved into the stone.

Tommy took a cautious step toward the boulder, carefully watching for more snakes. He stopped at the base of the big rock and bent down. He touched the carving with his index finger and ran it along the outline. It was a bird.

"We're close," he said. "This is one of the constellations."

"Constellations?" Lilian asked, confused.

"Yes," Tommy said, suddenly frantic. "Look for two more rocks like this one. We're searching for another bird and a harp."

"Bird and a harp?" Lilian sounded skeptical.

"Yes. I know it sounds weird. Trust me. That's what we're looking for."

Kirk got a nod from his boss and then issued the order to the men. "Be on the lookout for anything that looks like a bird or a harp," he said, sounding foolish as the words escaped his lips. He shook his head and started moving ahead.

The rest of the group pushed forward, albeit with closer ranks than before. Perhaps they were afraid of stumbling across more snakes.

They trudged through the jungle, cutting their way through the overgrowth with machetes in one hand while still holding their rifles steady with the other. All manner of giant leaves, branches, and vines blocked their movement and made progress slow and methodical. Visibility into the forest was less than seventy feet at any given time.

The creek bent to the right and meandered off through the jungle. Sean traced the stream through the valley and noticed something jutting out of the bank next to it.

"Over there," he said to Tommy. "Another boulder. Could be a marker."

Sean picked up his pace, slashing his way back over to the creek where the second boulder stood out from the dirt.

The rest of the group followed him and gathered around the big stone. Sean pointed at the side. "There it is," he said. "Harp."

"Now we just have to find the last marker," Tommy said. He looked down at the diary again and then remembered the map of the Summer Triangle. He turned toward the center of the basin and pointed. "That means the last marker should be somewhere in that direction."

"Why do you say that?" asked Lilian.

"Because all of these clues from the diary point to the Summer Triangle." He could tell from the look on her face that she had no idea what he was talking about. In fact, most of the group didn't, except Pablo and Sean.

"The Summer Triangle is a formation in the night sky that connects three prominent stars from three separate constellations. I'm not going to get into the details about which constellations right now, but the last one we're looking for has to be out there because it's the final point." He thought for a moment and gazed out across the basin. "If I had to guess, I'd say it's that way." He pointed his finger off to the right.

Tommy took the lead, walking out in front of the others, cutting his way through leaves and limbs, moving faster now that he could sense how close they were to their goal. The others followed, falling into a wide line as they cut a swath through the jungle.

Ten minutes into it, Tommy stopped and wiped his forehead. Sweat poured off everyone in the group, even the two women. Their damp clothes stuck to their skin, making things even more uncomfortable.

"You okay, Schultzie?" Sean said as he chopped down another broad leaf with his machete.

"Yeah. I'm so great."

"Reminds me of my days in college when I worked for that family as their lawn care guy."

"They didn't have a jungle like this."

"No," Sean said as he cut through another green branch. "But that guy had me out in the woods all the time, making paths for his grand-kids to walk on. There were a few places that were pretty dense. It was hard work and humid, although not quite this bad."

"I'd kill for Tennessee humidity right now."

Sean huffed and wiped the buckets of sweat from his forehead.

He whipped his blade through the air and sliced through another cluster of huge leaves. Suddenly, the forest opened. The space before them was devoid of most vegetation save for a stand of trees growing sporadically here and there. While it seemed unnatural, the clearing wasn't what struck every member of the group.

It was the two stones jutting out of the ground about thirty feet directly in front of them. One was broken at the base and lying on its side. The other still stood upright. Tommy cocked his head to the left, analyzing the anomaly.

Tommy stared with wide eyes at the two stones. When he spoke, his voice was hushed with reverence.

"This is it. This is the gateway to the temple."

Chapter 36

CHIAPAS

Tommy absently stepped forward toward the two big rocks, still eyeing them with an intense, analytical stare. Sean followed his friend, noting the way Pike's men were staying close, almost like they were there to prevent them from getting away instead of being there for protection. Maybe he was overthinking. Then again, Sean knew his instincts. They'd saved his hide more times than he could count. If something didn't feel right, that usually meant it wasn't.

"These stones," Tommy said. "There was a part of the diary that mentioned stones that acted as sort of an external gate to the temple."

"What's this?" Lilian asked, stepping around the cluster of people to get closer.

"It's a good bet the entrance is around here somewhere." Sean pointed at the stone on the left. "There's the second bird."

"So this isn't it?" Lilian asked, sounding perturbed. "Shouldn't there be some old ruins lying around? A pyramid? Something?"

"We're close," Tommy said. "But if there was anything like that lying around, we'd probably see it by now. It's been several centuries since this place was last documented. I'd say it's likely buried by dirt and other debris."

"Not to mention the fact that Alvarado's right-hand guy had the thing closed off," Sean added.

"Exactly."

"So, how do we know what we're looking for?" Lilian asked.

Tommy stood silent for a moment, staring beyond the two stone gates and into the jungle. Not far away was a mound covered in trees, leaves, bushes, and rocks. It looked like any other mound in the middle of a forest. At first glance, no one would think anything of it. Tommy, however, thought otherwise.

"Don't worry about spreading out your men, Congresswoman," he said. "I think we found it."

The rest of the group huddled together behind him, following his gaze.

Lilian stepped forward to stand next to him. "Are you sure? That doesn't look like a temple. Just looks like a natural mound."

Tommy unconsciously stepped toward the little hill. "That's why it's been so difficult to find. I bet people have walked right by it multiple times through the centuries and never even realized it."

"Assuming they got past the ghosts," Sean chimed in.

His friend didn't even hear the attempt at humor. "So long ago," Tommy said. "It was closed off so long ago."

"Okay," Lilian said. "So, if that's it, how do we get inside? There's got to be some kind of entrance, right?"

"Have your men scour the base of that mound," Tommy said. "Look for something unusual."

"Unusual?" she asked.

"Yeah." Tommy's hands were making different spinning motions as he tried to describe what he meant. "A pile of rocks, maybe a smaller mound of dirt that seems out of place. Any kind of thing that looks out of the ordinary."

"We're in a jungle in Mexico. Everything is out of the ordinary." She turned and issued the order to the rest of the group.

They moved forward, leaving the gate behind and spread out into three columns along an old path leading toward the mound. Something strange stuck out of the ground ahead. Sean and Tommy slowed until they were close. Sean bent down and picked up the object, wary there could be a snake or something else hiding underneath.

"Spanish helmet," he said, showing it to Tommy. "They must have dropped it when they left."

"Which means they left in a hurry," Tommy said.

"Definitely." Something else caught Sean's eye. "Over there," he said, pointing at a breastplate lying on the ground twenty feet away. The armor was partially covered by a couple small bushes. Vines ran around the edges and over the center.

They made their way over to the armor and examined it closely.

"No body," Sean said. "Where's the skeleton?"

"Maybe an animal took it," Kirk offered.

"Possibly," Tommy said. "And if not, they must have been pretty spooked to take off without their gear."

"It's the curse," Pablo said with a tremor in his voice. "I tried to warn you not to come here. This place must not be disturbed. We should leave at once."

Lilian turned to face him. There was a raging fire in her eyes. She raised her pistol and pointed it at Pablo's face. "What are you talking about?"

"The curse," he said. "This place is cursed. That's why no one has found this temple since the time Alvarado and his men accidentally discovered it. We must turn back while there's still a chance."

"No one is going anywhere," Lilian said. "The rest of you, spread out and search for the entrance. If this hill is covering the temple, there must be a way in somewhere."

Everyone in the group did as told and spread out once more and surrounded the mound, scouring the earth for any clues as to the whereabouts of the entrance. Sean and Tommy stood still for a moment, both taken back by Pike's sudden and somewhat disturbing threat against Pablo.

"Congresswoman," Sean said, "put the gun down."

"What?" she sneered with a glance over her shoulder. "I don't know if you realize this, Mr. Wyatt, but I'm running this show. You

and your friend work for me. But if anyone is thinking about bailing
out of the mission, then we're going to have issues."

Sean took a cautious step toward the woman. He'd not seen this
side of her before, although he'd only met her one time prior. Still, it
was something he hadn't expected.

"Pablo is helping us," Sean said. "He's not going to go anywhere.
Just put the gun down before someone gets hurt."

She held it for another two seconds before dropping her hand
down to her side. "See to it that he doesn't. For all we know, he could
have an army of his own hiding out in the jungle somewhere, just
waiting for us to find the temple for them."

And Sean thought *he* was paranoid. He didn't say anything to
Tommy. He didn't need to. The same thought occurred to both of
them at once.

She walked away, staying close to Kirk as he approached the base
of the mound. Tommy and Sean exchanged a knowing glance and
then motioned to Pablo.

"Come on, Pabs," Sean said. "And knock off all that curse business
while you're at it," he whispered.

"You don't understand. I can feel it, Sean. Something is here.
Something terrible. We shouldn't be in this place."

Sean saw the fear in Pablo's eyes.

"We'll be careful. But if you try to run now, these guys will cut you
down before you get back to the creek. So stay close to me
and Tommy."

Pablo's eyes flashed around, assessing his chances of getting away.
He knew Sean was right.

"Come on," Tommy said. "Let's see if we can find the entrance to
this place."

The three made their way along the path until they were at the
base of the hill. The group encircled the earthen structure and
looked painstakingly around the area for any sign of something that
could be an entrance. Some of the men climbed to the top, scouring
the surface. They kicked rocks, leaves, sticks and other debris out of
the way. A few of them turned a log over and rolled it down the side.

After nearly thirty minutes of intense searching, though, they had found nothing.

"Are you sure this is the spot?" Lilian asked from the side of the mound. "We've been here for a half hour and haven't found a thing. It's not like it's a huge area to search."

Sean and Tommy knew she was right. It wasn't a big search zone. If there was an entrance to an underground temple, they should have found it by now, or at least some trace of it.

Sean ran the sleeve of his shirt across his brow to remove the sweat for what had to be the tenth time since they began looking for the entrance.

"This is the spot," Tommy said. He knew it was. Call it a gut feeling. Call it a hunch. Or just call it his stubbornness coming through. They could wander through the jungle for days and never find anything. They were in the right place. He knew it. That didn't mean it wasn't time to consider bringing in some equipment to aid in the search. Ground-penetrating radar was the first idea that came to mind, but getting it to the remote location would take time and a good deal of planning. It might be another week before they could get back. That didn't take into account all the dangers they'd already navigated. Leaving to bring in new gear could mean trying to get through that gauntlet all over again.

Lilian shook her head. "If we don't find anything in the next hour, we're going to need to head back and set up camp. Or we set up camp here."

Sean sensed Pablo was about to protest and quickly cut him off. "Probably better to set up on the other side of the ridge," he said. "Last thing we need is those tribesmen coming back in the night to take us out one by one."

"We'll post guards," Kirk said.

"Yeah, I know. Even so. These guys live here in the jungle. This is their domain." Sean looked around the forest. "I have a feeling that if there are many of them left, they'll find a way to take us out without anyone ever knowing what happened. I agree with the congresswoman. Let's keep searching for another hour, and if we don't find anything we head back to the other side of the ridge and make camp for the night, maybe reassess things."

His idea seemed to satisfy the others, and they resumed their efforts.

"Do you really think we might be in the wrong place?" Tommy asked under his breath so only Sean could hear.

Sean glanced at Pablo, who was nervously looking at the ground, sweeping debris out of the way with his boot. "Not based on the way he's acting. But I do think it would be a good idea to not be here when it gets dark. There's something off about this place, and it isn't just the weird jungle men that attacked us earlier. It's bigger than that."

"I hear you. I think you're right. Let's just keep looking and—"

A scream ripped through the silence, cutting off whatever Tommy was about to say. They both looked up and over toward the mound. Three of Kirk's men rushed to where one of the others had been standing a moment before. A hole had opened up in the ground right under the guy's feet. The opening was fairly large, about eight feet in diameter at its widest point.

Sean and Tommy hurried over and joined the others already looking into the hole. Some of the men's mouths were gaping as they stared into the darkness.

"Reg?" Kirk shouted down into the opening. "You okay?"

There was no answer. "Reg!" Kirk raised his voice even louder. "What's your status?"

No response.

"Get me lights in there," Kirk ordered.

Several of the men produced flashlights and shone them down into the hole. What they found was shocking. Reggie was about twenty-five feet down, lying at an awkward angle on the bottom. A huge stone spike protruded through his chest. There were at least a dozen similar spikes all around him.

Pablo covered his mouth as he gazed into the hole. "I told you we should leave. This place is cursed."

Lilian raised her weapon and pressed the muzzle to Pablo's head. "I told you no more of that curse talk. You understand?"

"And I asked you not to threaten our friend," Sean said. He tapped the top of his rifle with his index finger.

"That sounds like a threat, Mr. Wyatt," she said, glaring at him.

"I'm just asking you to not point guns at people who are on the same team. We're all on the same team here, right?"

She nodded slowly and lowered her weapon. "Yes, Sean. You're correct. We are all on the same team. But get a handle on your lackey. I'd prefer him not spooking the rest of my men. It's bad enough one just died."

She turned her attention to Kirk. "We have ropes, right?"

"Yes, ma'am."

"Then let's tie up. Looks like we just found our way in."

Sean swallowed hard and looked at Tommy. They both had a bad feeling about this whole situation, and it wasn't just because of the deadly hole in the earth. Something wasn't right. And they were beginning to think it had to do with the woman in charge.

Chapter 37

CHIAPAS

Kirk was the last of the group to rappel into the chamber below. The rest had carefully lowered themselves with hand brakes to make sure they didn't suffer the same fate as their impaled comrade.

Some of the men had compact lanterns in their bags that cast a pale glow around the entire subterranean room. The rest pointed their beams around to assess their surroundings. The walls were cut smooth from the rock in the earth. The hole leading to the surface was a perfect cylinder that dropped into a huge dome-shaped room.

"This doesn't look like a temple," Kirk said. "Looks more like a deathtrap."

"Whoever or whatever created this," Tommy said, "it wasn't done by primitive tools. They had some other kind of technology."

"What do you mean?" Kirk asked.

"You can't get that clean of a bore through the rock with a hammer and chisel. I mean, you could, but it would take centuries to get this deep and get it so clean. Not only that, you'd have to have an army of skilled craftsmen to do it. This looks like it was done by a machine."

"What are you saying?" Lilian asked. "That the ancient people who built this had modern tech?"

Tommy rolled his shoulders. "Wouldn't be the first time we encountered something like that."

"Do you think this was put here deliberately?" Lilian asked, staring at the spikes and the deceased man's body.

"Yeah," Sean said, "this was obviously a trap. Though if I had to guess, I'd say it wasn't put here by Alvarado's men."

"Why do you say that?"

"Because," Tommy answered for his friend, "see the decorative carvings around the spikes?" He pointed his flashlight at one of the nearest cones. "Those aren't Spanish. They're Mayan."

Tommy stepped away from the grizzly scene and joined his friend.

Sean was standing off to the side of the circle of deadly spikes where the floor was tiled with large, smooth stones similar to those he'd seen in so many city streets. He put his beam on the far wall in what he thought was the direction of the mound above and lowered it until the broad circle of light hit something out of the ordinary at the base where it met the floor.

"What is that?" Tommy asked.

His question drew the attention of everyone else in the group, and they all turned their lights in the same direction.

"Looks like a pile of rocks," Sean said. He moved slowly toward it, minding every step in case there were other traps in place. If the people who built this temple—if that's what it was—had taken the time to put in one trap, they'd have installed more.

As Sean drew near, he could see what happened. "They blocked this corridor," he said.

"Is it a way out or a way in?" Lilian asked.

"Let's move these rocks and see."

The men with lanterns set them on the ground around the pile of stones to light the area while others began removing the rocks one by one. Some were heavier and required two pairs of hands to get them out of the way. The group formed a line on two sides and passed the rocks from one to another to keep them out of the way.

Pike watched, though the other woman got in line with the rest of the unit and toiled away to clear the passage.

"What does that mean?" Lilian asked, pointing at a dark engraving over the entryway. The image looked like it was half primate, half human, with an enlarged head. The creature was in a sitting position with its knees pulled toward its face.

Tommy glanced up at it and then took the next rock the man to his left handed to him. "That's Yum Cimil," he said. When he noticed the befuddled look on her face, he snorted a laugh to himself. "The Mayan god of death," he explained.

"The Mayans didn't just believe him to be the god of death," Pablo added. "Yum Cimil was a world bringer, a changer of earth and sky. They believed that when the time was right, he would return and cleanse the world of evil and return it to a state of balance. It is as was foretold in the fourth prophecy."

Tommy paused, holding a big rock in his hands, and glanced back at Pablo, then he handed him the stone.

"You don't understand what you're doing here," he went on. "This place is the key to it all. It is the catalyst that will bring about doom for most of humanity. Yum Cimil will return and destroy everything. That's what I've been trying to tell you."

Sean frowned as he passed another rock down the line. He stiffened, stretching his back while he stared at the politician. "Hold on a second. How much of this did you know about?"

Lilian stood like a statue at the end of the two lines, staring at Sean with a lifeless, cold look in her eyes. "You know, I believe your friend here has outlived his usefulness."

She raised her pistol and fired. The loud pop reverberated through the chamber, causing everyone to suddenly cover their ears. Pablo's face contorted in agony for a moment, and then he fell over onto his side.

"No!" Tommy shouted and dropped the rock he was handling.

Sean swung his weapon around and dropped to his knees. His reflexes were quicker than hers, and he squeezed the trigger the second the sights were lined up with her abdomen.

The rifle thundered in the giant room, once more causing everyone there to instantly grab at their ears. The round hit its mark and plowed through Lilian's lower chest and out through her back. The blow knocked her backward, and she fell to the floor in a splattering of blood.

The blonde woman immediately turned to her and got down on one knee to lend aide while the rest of the men went after Sean and Tommy.

Sean knew what they would do the second he took aim at Lilian Pike. He immediately turned to the nearest man to his left as the guy tried to whip his gun around to fire. Sean grabbed the barrel and jerked him forward, smashing his elbow into the man's nose. Blood poured from the broken appendage a second later as the guy grabbed at the wound with both hands.

Tommy saw the mercenary next to him taking aim at Sean and reacted. He swung his weapon around and slammed the butt of his gun into the guy's jaw, knocking him out instantly. The gunman right behind him saw what happened and lunged forward to return the favor. Tommy caught a glimpse of movement out of the corner of his eye and ducked as the guy waved his gun around in a wide, horizontal arc. Then Tommy jammed his muzzle into the man's gut and squeezed the trigger. Bullets tore out of the man's back, flying dangerously at the rest of Pike's men.

Kirk dove out of the way, narrowly dodging the deadly barrage. Two of his other men weren't so lucky. One caught a round in the chest, and the other took one in the groin.

The other three hired gunmen were able to dive clear in the nick of time, rolling to the side as Tommy's gun clicked. He was out of rounds.

Sean let his opponent fall to the ground and charged toward Kirk, who'd rolled to a stop next to one of the lanterns. Kirk raised his weapon as Sean rushed forward, the gun in his hands already leveled at his target. Sean shot first, spraying a volley at Kirk, who once more was forced to roll clear of the bullet storm. One of the rounds missed wildly to the right and struck the lantern closest to where Kirk had been only a moment before. That half of the room suddenly plunged into darkness.

One of Kirk's men on the other side of the temple entrance saw what was about to happen. Sean was moving in for the kill shot while their leader tried to recover. The guy saw the second lantern at his feet, reached over, and switched it off.

Suddenly, the entire temple antechamber was thrown into a deep black with only a dim light coming in from the hole above and the residual glow of flashlights that had been placed on the ground during their earlier work.

Kirk fired his weapon three times at Sean's silhouette, but the rounds sparked off the far wall and ricocheted dangerously for several seconds before dying somewhere in the room.

Sean hit the floor as the enemy's weapon blazed. He slid out of the light and into the shadows to level the playing field. If he couldn't see Kirk, there was no reason he should stay in plain sight either.

On the other side of the room, Tommy crouched low, doing his best to stay hidden in the dark. Pike's remaining three men huddled in a group, still visible in the flashlight corona. One of them hurried over to three of the lights and picked them up, switched them off, then returned to the others.

The room sank deeper into blackness. Even the light coming in from the jungle above dimmed as the sun ran farther toward the horizon, far from the view of everyone in the underground chamber.

The other two guys in the huddle removed their sidearms from their holsters and aimed at the remaining flashlights they deemed too far away. One shot after the other obliterated the last of the lights until the only ones left were the three they held in their hands. It was nearly impossible to see anything, which was exactly what they wanted.

"Kirk!" one of the men shouted. "You okay?"

Kirk didn't respond. He wasn't about to give away his position. Wyatt could be anywhere. To say anything could be a fatal mistake.

The voice spoke up again from a different position in the chamber. "Kirk?"

A sudden sound of fabric swishing echoed through the room. Someone was moving. Who was it? One of his men, or was it Wyatt or Schultz? It was impossible to know.

One of the other three flipped the switch on his flashlight on and then off again, giving a strobe effect to the place. The other two had spread out to cover more ground in their search. A minute later, he did it again from a new spot.

Sean and Tommy were on opposite sides of the room, but they both had the same thought. The guy was sweeping the area, staying on the move to make finding him more difficult. If he happened upon either Tommy or Sean and shone that light in their face, it would be momentarily blinding and would mean certain death.

The gunman flashed the light once more. This time, Sean made a note of his position relative to the last place he'd flipped the switch. He was moving in a clear pattern around the base of the wall, probably to close in the center gradually like a boa constrictor. Another blink of light showed Sean the other two men were doing the same thing, but in the opposite direction, slowly working their way into the center of the room.

Tommy was tucked behind one of the big spikes. He knew there was only one chance to gain an edge. When the gunman flashed his light on and off again, Tommy took off at a dead sprint toward the temple entrance. There were still some stones in the way, but the opening was 90 percent clear.

The hunters heard the footsteps and switched on their flashlights. Their beams were aimed haphazardly all over the room, but there was enough light to see Tommy making a mad dash for the door.

The gunmen leveled their weapons to shoot, but Kirk yelled out at them.

"Hold your fire, you idiots! You'll kill us all!"

Sean heard the man's voice come from a position not far to his left. After crawling to the relative safety of the back corner of the room, he'd crouched with his weapon ready in case someone tried anything stupid.

He hadn't expected the someone to be Tommy.

Sean lined up one of the gunmen in his sights and picked him off with one shot. The guy fell backward with a hole at the base of his neck. The light clanked on the floor and stopped, pointing straight at Sean. The other two men and Kirk immediately turned their attention to where the shot had come from. They aimed their guns from the hip, but there was nothing but a wall.

Kirk looked back toward the temple entrance, but Tommy was gone, too.

"You two!" Kirk shouted. "Go after him! I'll handle Wyatt!"

The men shut off their lights, and the world turned black again. Sean crouched behind one of the spikes near the impaled body of the man who fell through the hole. He couldn't see the last two of Pike's mercenaries feeling their way along the wall toward the entrance, though he figured that's what they were doing.

"It's just you and me now, Sean," Kirk said, emboldened by the dark. "Mano a mano." The chamber went silent again for a moment before Kirk spoke again from somewhere else. "I have to admit, I'm impressed. You and your friend killed some of my best men. Unfortunate, but they can be replaced. That's the nature of the beast, isn't it?"

Sean turned his weapon toward the sound of the voice but saw nothing. His nostrils filled with the familiar scent of burned powder as it lingered in an unmoving cloud throughout the area.

"I've always wondered what it would be like to fight one of you white-collar guys. Your kind didn't get forged in the crucible of war like me and the others. Sure, you went through some government training and whatnot, but nothing trains you like the battlefield."

He was egging Sean on, trying to get a reaction that would give away his position. In doing so, Kirk continued to let Sean know where he was for a moment before shifting quickly to another part of the room to throw him off.

"Why don't you come out and play with me, Sean? Enough of this hide and seek."

Kirk felt a warm muzzle press against the base of his skull and froze.

"You want to play, Kirk? I'll play with you."

"Very good, Wyatt. Cute trick. Although I have to say I'm disappointed. I was hoping we could do this like men."

"What is going on here?" Sean asked, pressing the gun deeper into Kirk's neck. "What was Pike really after?"

A wicked laugh escaped Kirk's mouth. "You're a smart guy, Wyatt. You know all about this ancient mumbo jumbo. What do you think it's about? Huh?"

"Pike sent us here to find a source of power. She said she wanted it for green energy to share with the world."

"And you were stupid enough to believe it."

Sean pulled the man's head back harder against the gun's muzzle. Kirk grunted from the pain, but he didn't give in.

"You'd better start talking, and you'd better start right now," Sean said.

"Or what? You'll splatter my brains all over this wall? That's not going to stop it, Wyatt. Nothing can stop it now. You and your friend brought us here. The world is going to crumble, and you'll have a front row seat."

Sean's head swirled. World crumble? Led them here? What was he talking about? It didn't take long for the epiphany to hit. The murders in Washington, the mission to find this place, Pike's crusade against those she thought responsible for the death of her son and subsequently, her husband—all of it was one big plot for revenge. That's why she was so quick to shoot Pablo. She didn't need him. She only needed Sean and Tommy. Alone, Pike couldn't have found this place. She'd used them, playing them like a a couple of naive rookies until they brought her right to the doorstep of the lost temple.

"It's a cataclysm machine," Pike's voice suddenly pierced the darkness from the other side of the room.

Sean's eyes narrowed as he peered into the soaking blackness. *That's impossible,* he thought.

"Yum Cimil is the bringer of death and the cleanser of the earth." The other two gunmen turned on their flashlights, and Pike came into view in the doorway, standing amid the last remnants of stones. She stood behind Tommy, holding her pistol to the back of his head.

Chapter 38

CHIAPAS

"I'm surprised you two didn't figure it out before now," she went on. "All the signs were there. Luckily, I was betting on you both being too trusting to think I'd send you into the jungle to find something so sinister."

"The dead congressman?" Sean asked.

"Just the tip of the iceberg," she answered. "I had two more executed after him. Their oil took my family from me. It took my life, everything I'd worked so hard to build. They stole everything from me. So yes, I had them killed. Seems fair enough."

"Cold-blooded murder is never fair," Sean said.

She rolled her shoulders. "Oh, get off your high horse, Sean. I didn't walk into a monastery and gun down a bunch of priests. They were bad people. The world is better off without them...well, what's left of the world will be, anyway."

"So, that's it? You think whatever is down here is going to destroy the world, including yourself. If Lilian can't be happy, no one can?"

"Oh no, Sean. You're thinking too narrow. You see, I intend to cleanse the world of its filth, of the problems that have wreaked havoc on humanity. Greed, deception, hate—they're all deeply rooted in every culture across the planet. It's time to dig those roots out and start anew. Of course, I'll keep a few people safe from the destruction. I wouldn't let them perish after all they've done to help me." She motioned to Kirk and the others. "I've taken precautions. I own a thousand acres of mountain property in Colorado. I call it the ark. While the rest of the earth suffers through the apocalypse, we'll be safe in an underground bunker in the Rocky Mountains."

Kirk shifted a little, and Sean had to grip him tighter to remind him he was still at gunpoint.

"If you really believe this place is capable of that, then you surely know we'll all die, too."

"That might have been a problem before." She let the words linger to make him wonder.

Before? Before what? He gazed across the room and saw her step out from behind Tommy while still keeping the weapon pointed at the back of his head. A new light, pale orange with a hint of yellow glowed from her chest.

She had the Zerzura medallion. The relic had saved Sean's life once before. Now, apparently, it had saved Pike's.

"Don't bother asking how I came by this," she said, as if reading his thoughts. "Let's just say that your security system in Atlanta wasn't that difficult to crack."

Sean felt something brush against his skull and then sink deeper into his skin. He winced both from pain and from irritation with himself.

"Put the weapon down," the blonde woman said from behind.

"Do as she says, Sean. I don't want to kill you. Not yet, at least. However, if you don't comply, I'll be more than happy to eliminate your friend here."

"Don't do it, Sean!" Tommy shouted. "She's bluffing!"

"I assure you I am not," Lilian said. "You're a smart guy. Put the weapon down, and I don't spray your friend's face all over this room."

Sean cursed himself for not sensing the blonde woman sneaking up from behind. Had he been paying closer attention, perhaps he would have heard her movements. Instead, he'd been caught up in the conversation with Pike.

He pulled back on the gun, removing it from the back of Kirk's head. His grip loosened, and Kirk stepped forward, taking a deep breath as he moved away.

Sean lowered the weapon and placed it on the ground, then stood up straight with his hands by his shoulders.

Kirk spun around and punched him in the gut. Sean doubled over, grabbing his abs in an effort to ease the sudden throbbing pain. Kirk reared his left hand back and was about to smack Sean across the face when Pike stopped him.

"That's enough," she said. "Bring him."

The blonde shoved Sean forward, nearly causing him to bump into Kirk. He sidestepped the mercenary and regained his balance, struggling forward with his stomach still sore from Kirk's punch.

Kirk fell in line behind the two until they reached the other side of the room where Pike still stood with Tommy held hostage.

"That's better," she said. "You know, I had my doubts about this little trinket," she said, holding up the amulet. "Now, though, I can see how wrong I was to question its power."

Her shirt was covered in blood, but no more seeped from the wound. Sean didn't have to see to know what happened. He'd experienced it himself when taking a bullet to the chest. The amulet healed him. Now it was being used by a maniacal woman bent on destroying humanity.

Pike turned to the other two henchmen and motioned to the tunnel beyond the doorway. "Lead the way, gentlemen. We have work to do."

The group made their way into the dark passage. The walls were bored smooth just like those in the huge antechamber. There was a strange smell in the air, like a mixture of sulfur and something burning, but Sean couldn't place it.

"How is it we always find ourselves in spots like this?" Sean asked his friend, who trudged through the passage a few feet ahead.

"I was just wondering the same thing," Tommy answered. "Maybe we're not that good at our jobs."

"Don't be so hard on yourself. You're very good at what you do. It's my fault we're in this mess."

"Shut up, both of you," Lilian ordered. "You'll both have plenty of time to figure out your issues when you're dead."

Sean bit his lip to hold back the smart-aleck comment he wanted to make. There was no point. They were in a bind again without any foreseeable way out.

The passage made a series of sharp right-hand turns, working its way down farther into the crust until the group came to a place where a stone frame was cut into the rock. More Mayan symbols were carved into the header.

"Another door," Lilian said. The two men in the lead had stopped short, suspicious of passing through. "What do those symbols mean?" she asked.

"Why don't you build a time machine, go back to college, and major in ancient Mayan languages?" Tommy said.

He winced, knowing what was coming next. He wasn't disappointed. Kirk drove the butt of his gun into Tommy's lower back, dropping him to the ground in agonizing pain.

A second later, Kirk grabbed the back of Tommy's shirt and hauled him to his feet, albeit unsteadily.

"How many times do you have to piss blood before you're gonna learn to keep your trap shut, Schultzie?" Sean asked.

"Hopefully, no more." Tommy wobbled and braced himself on the wall with his right hand to keep his balance. He looked up at the header where the two gunmen were shining their beams. The engravings were on both of the stone studs as well.

"Well?" Lilian urged.

"Give me a break, lady. Jeez. There are three rows of symbols here. It's not like they're in an easy-to-read language. It's going to take a minute."

"I would suggest you don't try to stall, Mr. Schultz. No one can save you now. No one is coming to your rescue."

"No one ever does," Tommy said, inching forward to get a better look at the engravings.

His eyes passed over the symbols one after the other, carefully taking mental notes as he translated the ancient script in his mind. It took several minutes to go over all the lines, and he did it twice just to make sure the translation was correct.

"It's about the fourth prophecy," he said when he was finished. "Pablo was right. This is a giant death machine."

"What does it say exactly?" Lilian demanded. "How do we activate it?"

Tommy didn't say anything.

Lilian turned to the blonde. "Erika."

Erika raised her weapon and pressed it to the back of Tommy's skull.

"I'll ask you again," Lilian said. "How do you activate the machine?"

Tommy chuckled. "Do you not see how ridiculous putting a gun to my head over this really is? You're planning on killing all of us anyway. What's the difference if I die from a bullet or from some ancient doomsday device?"

Lilian's eyes twitched with anger.

"Very well." She raised her weapon and pointed it at Sean's knee. "Yes, you two are going to die. However, there's still plenty of time for you to suffer. I'll start with your friend's knee, then maybe shoot him in the top of the foot. Then the other knee, knock out an elbow after that. There are so many directions I could take it. So, you can die for a cause and in such a manner that won't put you in a tremendous amount of pain. Or I can make it hurt for a very, very long time."

"Don't do it, Schultzie. Let her figure it out for herself."

A blow to the lower back from Kirk dropped Sean to his knees. He coughed violently, and his body heaved violently for nearly a minute before the fit subsided.

Sean began to say something, but another weak cough escaped his lips as he started to stand up again. Kirk put his hand on the back of Sean's neck, forcing him down again. He pointed his gun at the top of Sean's head.

"We can do this all night, gentlemen. And if you prefer, we can make you suffer for days."

"There's a sequence," Tommy blurted. "It's very precise. There are four keystones you have to activate. According to the engraving, by turning those in the correct order, it will start the...the...whatever doomsday device this thing is. From what I can tell, it appears to cause a chain reaction with most of the volcanoes in the region."

Sean's head sagged. He appreciated his friend doing his best to keep their suffering at a minimum, but at the same time, he wished Pike and the others could be kept in the dark.

"Volcanoes?" Lilian asked with a hint of suspicion in her voice.

Tommy gave a reluctant nod. "Thousands of years ago, an ice age covered most of the continents. In North America, there is a distinct line where the continental glacier progress halted—where the rich, black soil turns to red clay. Many experts agree that multiple volcanoes erupting at the same time was the primary cause of the last ice age. Most of the sky would have been blocked out by volcanic ash, keeping away precious sunlight and causing the planet's temperature to drop significantly."

"Yes," Lilian said. It sounded like she was enjoying Tommy's tale a little too much. "Only this time, billions of useless people will die as a result and we can begin again."

Sean wanted to lunge at her, take her weapon, and shoot her in the face with it. She'd played him and Tommy masterfully, a fact that only further inflamed his anger. He resisted, albeit with a great deal of effort. It wasn't the first time he'd been in situations like this. In a strange way, he'd almost become comfortable with them.

"You played us like a cheap piano," Sean said. "You used us to get here. Can't believe I actually felt sorry for you when all this was just a way for you to get some kind of twisted closure on your family tragedy."

Lilian's nostrils flared in the glow of the lantern and flashlights. "This is the natural order of things, Sean. Life comes and goes. Look around you. How many lives have you taken? How many people have you killed in the name of justice, honor, America? You take the lives of wicked people. I'm simply going to do it on a much larger scale. I will wipe evil off the face of the earth."

"And billions of innocent people will die in the process. I guess that doesn't matter, though, as long as you kill the small percentage of bad people. Right?"

She snickered. "Innocent? There is no such thing. No one is innocent. Not even me. The difference is I have a plan, direction, a way to give this world a new start, a chance to do things right." She turned to Tommy. "Now, lead the way. The time is at hand."

Sean and Tommy exchanged a concerned glance. Sean was ready to make his move right then and there. Normally, Tommy would have been, too. What did they have to lose? Tommy, however, had other plans.

"If we're gonna go, we might as well go big," he said.

Sean caught something in his tone. He'd heard it before through the years. To Sean, it meant his friend had something up his sleeve.

Chapter 39

CHIAPAS

"Lead the way," Tommy said to the two mercenaries.

The men looked at Kirk, who in turn gave a questioning glance to Pike. She nodded, and the two stepped cautiously through the doorway.

The second their feet touched the floor on the other side of the threshold, the earth began to shake. A thunderous rumble resonated from deep below. Dust broke loose from the ceiling and drifted to the floor.

The two men looked back at Kirk and Pike, wondering what was happening.

"Keep going," Lilian ordered.

Reluctantly, the men pushed ahead. The tunnel steepened, and everyone in the group had to lean back as they walked, pressing their palms to the wall to keep their balance.

The air seemed to grow hotter with every step and filled with a bitter, acrid smell like sulfur. The rumbling ceased as the group continued downward, casting them into an uneasy silence.

After walking for 150 feet or so, the left-hand wall cut sharply in the other direction and gave way to a dramatic drop-off. One of the men in the lead pointed his light down into the abyss. A crevice about forty feet wide dropped hundreds more feet to the bottom where a narrow river of bright orange flowed through the pitch blackness.

Sean risked a look over the edge for a nanosecond before taking a wary step back toward the safety of the right-hand wall. He leaned his shoulder into the stone as Tommy stole a quick glance down into the ravine.

"Hot lava," he said.

"Is there another kind of lava?" Sean asked with a tremor in his voice.

Tommy knew his friend was cracking the joke to play off his fear of heights. The drop to the hot river of liquid magma below was the stuff of Sean's nightmares. As far as Tommy knew, it was his friend's one true weakness.

"Keep going," Pike ordered. "I don't want to be here all night."

The group proceeded down into the depths until the ramp leveled off and curved around to the right. The temperatures had to be pushing over 100 degrees Fahrenheit. The air was thick and difficult to breathe, full of the fumes coming off the lava river.

After marching around the bend, the path widened slightly and passed through another stone doorway. The room on the other side was cast in a pale orange glow. The hot, orange river below disappeared into a hole that must have come out in the chamber on the other side.

More Mayan symbols adorned the doorposts and header. Pike looked at Tommy for answers.

"It's more stuff about the fourth prophecy," he said. "And another warning about Yum Cimil. It says that whoever passes through this door may only taste eternal life after they die and are reborn. Then it goes on to reiterate the four keystones and all that."

"Very well," Lilian said, motioning with her pistol for the group to keep going. "We have a date with destiny. I'd rather not keep it waiting."

The men walked through the doorway and into the next room. The earth shook again, and the rumbling they heard before returned, although considerably louder than the first time.

The artificial light from the lantern and flashlights illuminated a massive box-shaped chamber with ceilings over sixty feet high. In the center, spaced about ten feet apart, were four stone pillars standing five feet tall. Each had an image carved into the side. The images matched on all four sides of the pillars, but each column was different. On top of the four plinths were rounded rocks that looked like primitive dials.

"The keystones," Tommy muttered. "This is it."

Kirk walked over to one of the pillars and motioned for his men to keep an eye on Wyatt and Schultz. The two underlings did as instructed and took a step back behind the two captives. Kirk reached out his hand to touch one of the dials.

"I wouldn't do that if I was you," Tommy warned.

Kirk turned his head and scowled with a look of irritation. "Why not? You said these were the keystones that activate the machine."

"They are," Tommy said. "But if you turn them in the wrong order, it won't work."

"I'm okay with experimenting."

"That's fine...if you want to kill us all and break the thing."

Tommy stared at Kirk with a smug look on his face.

"Step aside and let Schultz handle it," Lilian said, "Only he knows the correct sequence." She pointed her pistol at Sean's head. "If you try anything stupid, though, I will kill your friend."

"I assumed as much."

"Don't do it, Schultzie," Sean said.

Pike swung the side of her weapon into Sean's temple. The weapon struck hard and sent a dizzying pain through his face and head.

Tommy swallowed hard, fighting off the urge to help his friend. Sean touched the fresh wound with his fingers and checked for blood. There was none, but that didn't stop the new pain from pulsing through him.

Tommy reluctantly stepped up to the pillar closest to him and examined the image. Then he moved to the next, and so on until he'd inspected each one. He returned to one on the far right that had an image of a jaguar engraved into it and placed his hand on the dial.

"You're sure that's the first one?" Lilian asked.

"I'm sure," Tommy said with a nod.

He took a deep breath and tried to twist the stone dial. Nothing happened. The thing wouldn't budge. He frowned and realized it was going to take a little more effort than just a one-handed twist of the wrist. With both hands on the dial, he leaned into it, grunting as he wrenched the knob to the left. The thing resisted but gave way under Tommy's strength. As it turned, a low grinding sound came from the pillar and the floor beneath until the dial would move no more.

Next, he stepped over to a pillar with a bird carved into the side and repeated the process. This time, the sound of stones grinding came from the walls around them.

Pike's men turned their heads to see where the noise was coming from and realized that panels on the walls were sliding open, revealing what appeared to be vents. Troughs protruded several feet above the floor.

Tommy moved to the third column. He rechecked the symbol on the side to confirm it was the right one. "The serpent," he said and then started turning the dial as he had the others.

This time, the floor trembled beneath them. Little bits of debris fell from the ceiling. A pebble landed on Tommy's shoulder and startled him, but he stayed focused on the task at hand: one more dial to turn.

He stepped slowly over to the final plinth and stared at the symbol on the side. It was a human head, but not just any head. He recognized it from before. It was the head of Yum Cimil, the god of death. Tommy looked over at his friend with regret in his eyes. Guilt washed over him. Sean could see it on his friend's face, the sadness of killing so many people.

Sean couldn't let it happen. If he was fast enough, he could take the gun from one of the men behind him and turn the tables. It would be risky, but given the circumstances and the prospects of facing certain death anyway, it was probably a risk worth taking.

Mind made up, he was about to make his move when he caught a subtle twitch from Tommy's right eye. No one else noticed the gesture.

Tommy placed both hands on the dial. The tension in the room reached the boiling point. Everyone leaned in closer to see what would happen.

Tommy turned the knob as hard as he could until it would go no farther. Then he stepped back and waited.

He looked up at the ceiling and around at the walls. The others did the same, wondering what was going on.

Suddenly, a deafening thud rocked the chamber. Pike clutched the amulet dangling from her neck, probably as a reflex. The floor beneath their feet began to vibrate. Another loud boom came from outside the entrance to the temple door. A moment later, a ten-foot-wide section of the floor closest to the wall shook violently and then crumbled from view. One of the men watching Sean was standing too close to the perimeter when the giant stone tiles began collapsing. His heels hung over the edge for seconds that seemed like minutes. He flailed his arms around, desperately trying to regain his balance before toppling backward and down into the fiery abyss.

The temperature in the room skyrocketed. Pike spun around, watching the drama play out.

"This is it!" she said with triumph in her voice. "We are at the epicenter of a new beginning for mankind!"

The floor beneath her buckled and she fell forward onto her face. Kirk and Erika rushed to her aide, momentarily forgetting their prisoners. The second guy guarding Sean was now all alone and doing his best to keep clear of the ledge that dropped down into a flowing river of magma. While he was momentarily safe, he had a terrifying epiphany; the floor was sinking.

Sean dropped to one knee and spun around, sweeping his foot in a wide arc until it struck the mercenary's heel. The man tripped and nearly lost his balance, but he forced his weight forward and stumbled away from the deadly opening. He turned his weapon toward Sean, who was only a few feet away to the left, but it was already too late. Sean sprang at the man and kicked the rifle to the side, then jabbed him in the nose. The guy tried to fight back, but Sean jumped high into the air and kicked out both legs, driving his feet into the man's chest. He landed with a thud on the hard surface but managed to watch the gunman stagger backward and disappear from view, falling into the lava below.

The odds were improving; however, the fight was far from over.

Kirk spun around and saw his last two men were no longer there. He whipped his weapon around and opened fire. The thunderous shots sounded like a cannon in the confined space.

Sean saw the enemy's move and took off, running in a circle around Kirk's position. Kirk swiveled the weapon in an arc, spraying a deadly barrage of bullets at his target, but the reckless shooting spree had immediate repercussions.

Rounds ricocheted off the walls with bright sparks flashing everywhere. One bullet zipped by Kirk, narrowly missing his head by mere inches. He took his finger off the trigger and tossed the weapon aside. His ears rang from the loud gunfire, but he didn't care. Sean Wyatt was going to die.

He pulled out his big tactical knife and charged at Sean to cut him off in his path.

Sean saw Kirk's intent and changed his angle, running directly at Kirk. They rushed toward each other like two freight trains plowing down the rails at full speed in a deadly game of chicken. Kirk held the blade menacingly in his hand, ready to tear Sean to shreds.

Kirk made his move first. He swung the knife in a blinding flash, ripping through the air with the tip just a few inches from Sean's chest. Sean anticipated the attack and hit the deck, sliding like a baseball player under the sharp knife. The second he stopped, he sprang up and drove his fist into Kirk's abdomen. The killer doubled over, but he recovered instantly and jabbed backward with his elbow, crunching it into Sean's jaw.

Behind the two men, Tommy lowered his shoulder and barged into Erika, knocking her to the ground and sending her weapon clattering across the floor to the precipice. Tommy pressed the attack and swung his foot at her ribs. Erika was stunned but she was also well trained, and her experience in hand-to-hand combat was extensive. She caught Tommy's boot with both hands, absorbed the momentum, and then twisted it hard to the outside. His knee torqued in a painful motion a split second before he flipped over in the air, tumbling sideways to the floor.

Erika took the offensive and rolled to her feet. She stepped quickly toward Tommy and snapped her shoe at his face, aiming for the temple to end the fight in one crippling blow. The ground shook again, causing Erika to lose her balance just enough that the kick went high, right over Tommy's face. He took advantage and rolled toward her other foot, grabbing her by the ankle and yanking it hard toward him.

She lost her footing as the shoe on the ground went airborne. Erika crashed to the floor, knee first. The bone shattered on the hard surface, sending immediate and agonizing pain through her leg. Tommy pushed himself up and stood over the blonde woman.

"Normally, I wouldn't hit a woman. In your case, I think I'll make an exception."

He raised his fist and punched hard at her right cheek. Despite the agonizing pain from her destroyed kneecap, she managed to raise a hand and deflect the blow. With her other hand, she drove her fist into Tommy's groin, dropping him to his knees amid a fresh swirl of throbbing nausea.

In the middle of the four pillars, Lilian Pike stood up from the ground and braced herself on one of the plinths with both hands as the floor shifted unsteadily below, gradually sinking into the fiery river. She saw the fight raging between Sean and Kirk. She looked to the left and saw Tommy and Erika duking it out as well. Then her eyes shifted to the smoke wafting up around them. The searing heat raked across her skin. The temperature spiked with every second. Lilian panicked as she realized that the if she didn't escape, the lava would consume her.

She ran to the far edge of the platform and looked down. She looked across the expanse at the wall leading up to the passageway, desperate to find somewhere she could jump to.

Across the room, Kirk swung the knife to the left, then the right, and back again. The blade caught Sean's wrist on one go-around, opening a fresh cut on his skin and sending a stinging pain through his arm. He jumped back and grabbed the wound instinctively before having to dodge further attacks. He didn't immediately realize it, but he was being backed toward the precipice and he was rapidly running out of real estate.

Inch by inch, Sean kept shuffling backward as his opponent continued the attack. The knife clipped Sean's shirt on another pass, ripping through the fabric and barely missing his stomach. Kirk wasn't getting tired, and there was no sign of him letting up anytime soon.

Sean felt the heat growing stronger from beyond the edge and risked a quick peek to the side. He realized the danger, and with the next swing from Kirk, Sean put up both forearms and struck the opponent's wrists, ceasing the deadly motion. Kirk wasn't finished. He altered his position, pointing the tip of the blade at Sean's neck. Then he put his free hand on top of the other and pushed. The knife started moving toward the base of Sean's neck despite his best effort to leverage every ounce of strength he could against the attack.

Kirk leaned into the knife handle, using every bit of his weight to outmuscle Sean's resistance. Searing heat from below washed over the two men, causing sweat to pour from their skin. Humans couldn't last long in this cauldron, but that was the least of Sean's worries at the moment as Kirk's superior strength and size forced Sean to his knees.

The sharp knife point was mere inches from Sean's throat. His muscles burned from the losing battle. He tried to rock forward to get a little momentum against the larger man, but it was no use. Every motion ahead produced an equal motion backward, which brought the blade a millimeter closer to ending his life.

"I always knew you agents were soft," Kirk spat through clenched teeth. "Pretty boys in your white-collar jobs." He grunted and pushed harder.

Sean could feel the metal tip graze his skin. He pushed back one last time, using every ounce of strength he could muster. The blade retreated a half inch.

"The thing about us, Kirk, is we have to find ways to win without always using brute force."

Kirk's eyes narrowed, and he let up for a brief moment. Sean knew what the guy was doing. He could see it in his eyes. There was a look of fierce determination, of knowing what was about to happen. Kirk raised the blade another inch only to get more muscle behind the next thrust. As he drove the knife down with all his weight behind it, Sean shifted his body. He let Kirk's weight collapse down onto him and then grabbed the bigger man's wrists and tugged.

Kirk knew Sean's plan the second he started going over. Sean rocked back hard onto his shoulders, kicking his legs up like a human rocking chair. Kirk's eyes went wide as he tumbled over his opponent. His back hit the floor first and jarred the knife loose. The momentum was too great, and he rolled over the edge. Sean stood up and pushed his fear of heights aside for a moment as he stared down at the enemy clinging with white knuckles to the ledge. His fingers slipped, and he kept shifting his weight in a desperate attempt to get a better grip. His feet slipped on the rock wall as he tried to get a foothold that wasn't there.

Sean stared into Kirk's eyes. A million smart-aleck one-liners ran through his head, but he didn't say anything. He didn't have to.

Kirk didn't ask for help. He didn't beg for mercy. First, his right hand lost its hold. Putting all his weight on the left hand fingers was too much. It only took two seconds for the second hand to come free. The man didn't yell as he fell into the bubbling inferno below. He wouldn't give Sean the pleasure. All he did was grimace as he plummeted downward.

The second his feet hit the magma, he screamed in agony, but the pain didn't last long. A moment later, Kirk was consumed by fiery death.

Chapter 40

CHIAPAS

Erika struggled to her feet, keeping her wounded leg extended out to the side. She swung a hammer fist at Tommy's face and smashed it into his left cheek. His head snapped to the side and recovered only to receive another blow. She raised her hand again and swung hard, but this time Tommy put up his forearm and blocked it. Both fighters winced from the bones striking each other. Tommy, however, had a little more muscle between the two of them and forced her back with a heavy push.

She renewed the attack, but he sprang from his crouched position, fighting off the nauseating pain in his groin. She jabbed. He deflected. She swung hard with the other fist, and Tommy grabbed her wrist and pulled her close while raising his boot high off the ground. Then he stomped hard at her wounded knee, driving the heel of his foot into the side. The follow-through caused a loud popping sound, and her joint bent at an unnatural, clearly excruciating angle.

Erika screamed and dropped to the floor again, clutching her knee with both hands. Her face contorted in wretched pain.

Tommy loomed over her for a moment before bending down and grabbing her by the ponytail. He yanked her head back, tilting it up to the ceiling. Then he raised his hand high, palm up, ready to smash the side of it into her nose to drive it into her brain.

"Stop!" Lilian yelled from a dozen or so feet away.

Tommy's head snapped to the side, and he saw Pike standing amid the pillars with a pistol pointed at him.

"Let her go," she ordered.

Tommy hesitated for a second. Then he saw the streams of lava oozing out of the vents in the rocks above. The slight slope toward the center of the floor caused the melted rock. Soon, the entire platform would be covered in molten lava.

The scientist in him wondered how the magma was being pushed out of the vents, but there was no time to question such things.

He let go of Erika's ponytail, and the woman fell prostrate on the ground.

"What did you do?" Lilian yelled.

Tommy offered a smug grin. "You were in such a hurry that you didn't even bother to wonder what would happen if I did the sequence out of order."

Her face scrunched in confused anger.

"What?"

"The prophecy. The directions to activate the machine. Did you think all of that was just the correct way to do it? By using the wrong sequence, I basically killed the doomsday device, along with all of us."

Her eyes raged hotter than the lava creeping closer and closer toward them. "You fool! Fix it! Do it now!"

Tommy shook his head slowly. "I can't. It's done. Once it's started, there's no going back. No redo. It's over, Lilian."

"It's never over," she said, clutching the amulet with one hand and the pistol with the other. "I can't die! But you two can!"

"Pretty sure that thing doesn't work when you're consumed by hot liquid magma," Sean said from her right.

She spun to the side and pointed the gun at him, then Tommy, then back again, trying to decide whom to shoot first.

"They killed my family!" she roared. "Do you have any idea what that feels like? To lose everything? Everyone you love? This world needs to be washed away! Can't you see that?"

"The world does have too much evil in it, Lilian," Sean said. "That doesn't mean we kill everyone to make it right again. There's a better way."

She shook her head, and a crazed look filled her eyes. He'd seen it before, and he knew what was coming. It was too dark to see her finger tense on the trigger, but he knew that's what was happening. The muzzle would fire. The bullet would hit him. And this time, there would be no miraculous salvation.

"Goodbye, Mr. Wyatt."

A low pop came from outside the temple. A pink mist exploded out of her back. Sean saw the hole in her chest and frowned. Where had the shot come from?

Her body wavered for a second before she toppled over onto her side.

Sean and Tommy simultaneously spun around toward the temple entrance.

Standing on the other side of the wide gap was Collin O'Rourke, holding a rifle in one hand. Leaning against the wall next to him was Pablo, grimacing in pain but alive.

Tommy hurried over to the ledge next to his friend and looked across at the other two.

"You're going to have to jump!" Collin yelled. A burst of sulfury smoke rolled up through the chasm between them.

Sean shook his head. "We'll never make it!"

Pablo grinned despite the pain from his bullet wound. "That's why we brought this."

He produced a black rope from behind his feet and tossed it over the ravine. The bulk of the rope landed beneath Sean and Tommy's. They glanced at each other with a question in their eyes.

"You know I'm not going first," Sean said. "Fear of heights."

Tommy sighed and shook his head. "You're such a drama queen."

He grabbed the rope and held it tight. He started to step back to get a running start and then realized something.

"Hey, what is this anchored to?"

"We're holding it!" Collin said. "Hurry!"

A huge chunk of ceiling broke free and fell between the four men, narrowly missing the rope. The men watched the huge rock drop into the lava below, sending sparks soaring into the air in a bright flash of yellow and orange.

"Come on!" Pablo urged.

Tommy took one step back and then surged forward, rushing toward the ledge. When his toes hit the lip, he jumped as hard as he could and flew across the chasm. His feet hit the opposite wall, and he dropped a yard or two before the rope went taut. The men above pulled hard, grimacing as they hauled Tommy up the side of the cliff. Tommy kept his grip as tight as he could as he walked his way along the vertical climb until he finally reached the top.

Once he was safely on the landing, Collin took the rope and tossed it back to the other side for Sean. He picked it up, pulled it tight, and ran toward the edge. He leaped as hard. His body flew across the span, crashing into the side with more force than planned. His shoulder took the brunt of the blow and sent a dull pain through his body. He gripped the rope tight, though, and started walking his way up the side of the precipice.

The scorching heat from below washed over him unlike anything he'd ever felt before. Part of him hoped the rope wouldn't catch fire or melt. He wasn't sure which would happen first.

The other three men pulled hard, tugging him up the side until he was nearly to the ledge. Suddenly, gunfire popped from inside the temple.

Pike was standing between the flowing streams of lava, shooting her weapon wildly at the four men.

Rounds sailed by, pinging off the rock in the tunnel and on the ledge. Tommy and the others instinctively ducked for cover and momentarily let the rope slip. He was the first to correct the mistake and grabbed it before Sean dropped any farther. The other two renewed their efforts and pulled hard on the rope.

Pike fired the last of her rounds, desperately hoping to hit something from that range. As luck would have it, she did hit something. The bullet tore through the rope just as Sean was about to reach the ledge.

He felt gravity suddenly winning the battle. He let go of the rope and fired his hands out toward the cliff's edge. His fingers dragged on the smooth rock surface, unable to find a grip.

A split second before he ran out of rock to hold, he felt a pair of strong hands wrap around his wrists. Sean looked up and saw Tommy holding him. Collin wrapped his arms around Tommy's waist and leaned back as hard as he could.

Sean ran his feet up the side of the precipice as fast as he could and a moment later felt solid ground underfoot. He dove forward into the tunnel to get as far away from the dangerous ledge as possible, rolling to a stop against the wall.

The other men looked down at him for a moment before Collin offered him a hand.

"Lucky for you we showed up when we did, huh?" Collin asked.

Sean nodded. "Indeed."

"Guys," Tommy said, "this place is going to implode, so maybe we can do our thank-yous and all that later?"

"Good call."

Tommy and Sean grabbed Pablo, who was still bleeding from the bullet wound just below his collarbone. They dragged him upward, following Collin through the corridor toward the surface.

Back in the temple, Lilian Pike watched from the ledge as the men disappeared into the passageway. Behind her, Erika screamed as the lava began to pool around her and eat away at her flesh.

Pike clutched the amulet in both hands. She could feel the heat swelling behind her, but she didn't dare look back.

"I am immortal," she said to herself. "I cannot die."

The lava inched its way closer to her heels. The back of her shoes suddenly caught fire as the material touched the liquid magma. She yelled as her skin burned.

"I am immortal!" she shouted. "I am immortal!"

The lava seeped around her, engulfing her feet first. A moment later, the bones, muscle, tendons, and everything else holding her up were consumed, and she toppled over into the searing liquid.

Chapter 41

CHIAPAS

Sean, Tommy, and Collin sat by the fire, staring with exhaustion into the flames. They made sure they were a safe distance from the fire pit, having had enough heat to last a lifetime.

Pablo was resting on a cot in one of Jack's tents. Jack didn't have a doctor, per se, but one of the men knew how to patch up a bullet wound and declared that the patient would survive.

"What are you doing here?" Sean asked after a long silence. He looked over at Collin, who offered a devilish grin.

"A mutual friend sent me."

"Emily sent you to help us?"

Collin chuckled. "No. She sent me to find Pike and bring her in. Hope I don't catch too much heat for that."

"Could you pick a different pun to use?" Tommy asked. "I think we've had enough heat for one night."

Collin nodded. "Flak, then. I hope I don't catch too much flak."

"I doubt you will. I'll vouch for you. And besides, we got the person behind all this, though I have to say I was a bit surprised."

"Hell hath no fury," Tommy said. "Pike was a woman scorned. I guess when you go through a loss like she experienced, it changes you."

His words lingered in the air for a moment.

"Shame we lost the amulet," Sean said.

Tommy nodded. "We never got to fully understand how it works. That thing could have been the cure to all the world's diseases if we'd had it a little longer."

"If I may," Collin said, "I don't think we were meant to live forever like this."

The other two frowned. "What do you mean, like this?" Sean asked.

"We're sinners. We hurt and kill each other in any number of sick ways. The last thing the universe needs is our species to keep doing that forever. That's in the Bible, you know."

Tommy and Sean glanced at each other.

"Genesis," Tommy said. "When the Elohim said they had to take the tree from the garden lest mankind would live forever in sin."

"Exactly. Glad to see you two know your scriptures."

"We've flipped through them a few times."

Tommy and Sean smirked.

Collin didn't really understand the joke, but he returned their grins with one of his own.

"So, what's next for you two? Off on another adventure? Maybe a treasure hunt somewhere in the world? If I were you, though, I'd steer clear of anywhere with seismic activity."

"That's a good idea," Sean said.

"I don't know what's up next," Tommy said. "That's one aspect of this job that makes it so interesting. We never know what's coming."

"I know one thing," Sean said. "I'd rather us skip out on any future privately offered projects. You were right. Working for someone else is murder."

Tommy snorted a laugh. "I told you so."

Jack approached from the mess hall with a few plates of food. He passed the dishes around to the men and then crossed his arms, looking down at them.

"You guys sure you don't need a lift out of here?" Jack said. "I could have one of my men drive you."

"No, we're good. Collin's going to take us out of here."

Jack nodded. "Your friend Pablo is going to be fine. I think he's going to join up with my merry band."

Sean looked a little surprised. "Really? I didn't think this sort of thing was his cup of tea."

Jack cocked his head to the side. "I guess you made an impression."

Sean nodded. "I guess so."

The men ate their food while they discussed the plan to get back to civilization. When they were done, they set their plates on the ground and looked up into the night sky. Billions of stars sparkled in the velvety blue blanket above.

"I wonder what the girls are doing right now." Tommy said, breaking the silence.

Sean chuckled to himself. "You know, I almost forgot all about them the last day or so."

"Me, too," Tommy confessed. "I mean, is that a bad thing?"

"I don't think so. We needed some guy time."

"Yeah, but maybe next time we have guy time without all the lava."

Sean laughed. "That would be nice." He saw a shooting star fly across the sky through the hole in the forest canopy. "I'm sure the girls will tell us all about their shopping adventures when we get back."

"Adriana would kick your butt for saying that."

Sean laughed. "Yeah, you're probably right."

THANK YOU

I do this at the back of all my books, but my appreciation is always sincere. I just wanted to take a moment to say thank you for choosing to spend your time reading my work. I put one of these little notes at the end of all my books because I know that you could have spent your money and time on something else, but you chose this book.

I am honored and hope you enjoyed it.

Please swing by one of your favorite online retailers and leave an honest review. Those reviews help authors because they let other readers know if the book is something they might enjoy. Plus, reviews help readers decide on what to read next. It's a win-win.

So thank you once more for reading me. I appreciate it and look forward to entertaining you again.

Ernest

AUTHOR'S NOTES

Lots of people, myself included, love to find out what was real versus what was imaginary in stories like this. In fact, I get emails all the time from readers who thank me for the notes at the end of the story —and even a few complaints about stories where my notes were omitted. (Insert apologetic laugh here).

So, here are the notes about this story to help give you a better picture about what was real and what was made up.

The Fourth Prophecy

The fourth Mayan prophecy is very real, although the meaning and accuracy of it is left to interpretation or imagination. Many people know about the Mayan prophecy pertaining to the end of the world in 2012, which we all know didn't happen. However, the other five prophecies don't get a great deal of attention, so I thought it would be interesting to delve into one of them.

Specifically, the fourth prophecy talks about a cleansing of the world through some kind of mass destruction. While it is ultimately a doomsday prediction, it's also one that gives a bizarre sense of hope.

Locations

While Washington is obviously a real place, I changed the names and descriptions of certain places to fit the story. One of the action scenes takes place on a street like several I visited in Georgetown. The murder scene by the river was a location I passed after my friends and I took a wrong turn and went all the way across a bridge before we found a place to turn around. Maybe it wasn't a wrong turn since I was able to use it in this story. Ha!

Every location as far as the cities, countries, and jungles are very real. Tulum is a pretty little town on the coast that is home to many expats from a variety of countries. Same goes for the other villages and cities I mentioned.

Other locations were a figment of my imagination. An example of this is Devil's Falls. While you might not find that place in Mexico exactly where I put it, there are many rivers and waterways that lead to falls similar to that one.

The jungles in the story can be extremely dangerous places. While the wildlife can be beautiful, the rain forests host a number of creatures that could harm humans in a variety of ways. On top of that, the raging drug war in Mexico makes the area a violent and perilous place to be.

The cartels are renowned for their disregard for human life and look to make an example of anyone who crosses them.

While they generally don't venture into the resorts along the Mexican coasts, one wouldn't have to go far to see some of the trouble they can cause.

The temple that is featured in the story is based on what many believe to be an actual place where a Mayan temple previously existed, though no one has been able to confirm or deny. Part of the problem of getting a closer look at the location is due to the many dangers mentioned previously. As a result, many questions remain about how broad the Mayan empire's reach truly was and what they may have accomplished.

It's always fascinating to think about the possibility of ancient ruins being hidden in a jungle somewhere. What secrets could such structures hold? What might we learn about their history and about our own?

That is why I write these kinds of stories. Because even though our world is small, there is so much left to discover.

OTHER BOOKS BY ERNEST DEMPSEY

The Secret of the Stones
  The Cleric's Vault
  The Last Chamber
  The Grecian Manifesto
  The Norse Directive
  Game of Shadows
  The Jerusalem Creed
  The Samurai Cipher
  The Cairo Vendetta
  The Uluru Code
  The Excalibur Key
  The Denali Deception
  The Sahara Legacy

War of Thieves Box Set
  (An Adriana Villa Adventure)

DEDICATION

For my mom. Without her I'd never be able to share these stories with the world.

ACKNOWLEDGMENTS

None of my stories would be possible without the great input I get from incredible readers all over the globe. My advance reader group is such an incredibly unselfish and supportive team. I couldn't do any of this without them.

My editors, Anne Storer and Jason Whited, must also be thanked for their amazing work and guidance in crafting these stories. They make everything so much better for the reader.

Last but not least, I need to give a big thank you to Elena at LI Graphics for the incredible cover art she always delivers, along with beautiful social media artwork.

Oh, and thanks to my stylist, Monica, for always being such a good sounding board while cutting my hair.

Published in the United States of America by Enclave Publishing.

❀ Created with Vellum

20189764R00194

Printed in Great Britain
by Amazon